THE WOLF CHRONICLES

Promise of the Wolves

Dorothy Hearst

Simon & Schuster
New York London Toronto Sydney

Simon & Schuster
1230 Avenue of the Americas
New York, NY 10020

This book is a work of fiction. Names, characters, places, and incidents either are products of the author's imagination or are used fictitiously. Any resemblance to actual events or locales or persons, living or dead, is entirely coincidental.

First Simon & Schuster hardcover edition June 2008

For information about special discounts for bulk purchases, please contact Simon & Schuster Special Sales at 1-800-456-6798 or business@simonandschuster.com.

Designed by Jaime Putorti

Manufactured in the United States of America

10 9 8 7 6 5 4 3 2 1

ISBN-13: 978-1-4165-6998-5
ISBN-10: 1-4165-6998-7

Dedicated to

my family and friends

and to

Happy, the best dog that ever was,

and

Emmi, the best (and shiniest) dog that there is now

PART ONE

THE PACK

Prologue

40,000 YEARS AGO

It got cold. It got so cold, the legends say, that rabbits hid underground for months at a time, the elk took to living in caves, and birds fell from the sky as their wings froze in midflight. It got so cold that the air crystallized in front of the Wide Valley wolves as they hunted. Each breath seared their lungs and even their thick undercoats did not protect them. Wolves are made for winter, but this was a winter beyond all wolves. The sun stayed always on the far side of the Earth, and the moon, which before had been a vibrant beacon, chilled to black dimness.

The raven king said it was the winter to end the world. That it would last three full years and that it was sent to punish those who ignored the will of the Ancients. All Lydda knew was that she was hungry, and that her pack could not hunt.

Lydda wandered away from her family, not bothering to sniff for whatever voles or hares she might find along the way.

Tachiim, her leaderwolf, had told the pack that the hunt was off, that the elk that ran the Wide Valley were too scarce, and the pack too weak to catch the few that remained. Now they merely waited for the colder chill of death to replace the chill in the air. Lydda would not wait. She had walked away from her packmates, and especially away from the pups with their bones clearly visible through their fur and their hungry eyes. It was the duty of every wolf in the pack—even a youngwolf like Lydda—to provide for the pups, and if Lydda could not do so, she was not worthy to be called wolf.

Even the light outer layer of her fur weighed her down as she forced her way through the deep drifts of snow. Ravens flew above her head, and she longed for wings to carry her to the hunting plain. Lydda was looking for the largest, fiercest elk she could find, and she would challenge it, fighting it to the death. Weak as she was, she knew it would be her death.

Lydda reached the crest of the snow-covered hill that overlooked the hunting plain and dropped to her belly, breathing hard. Suddenly she stood, her pale brown fur bristling. She smelled a human, and she knew that she must keep her distance, for it was forbidden by ancient laws for wolves and humans to come together. Then she had to laugh at herself. What did she have to fear? It was death she was seeking. Maybe the human would help her on her way.

She was disappointed when she found him, his back against a rock, weeping. He was, like she, barely grown. He looked about as threatening as a fox pup. He was thin and hungry like the rest of the creatures in the valley, and the long, deadly stick his people carried lay harmlessly at his side. The human raised his eyes as she came near and Lydda saw fear, then acceptance, then welcome come to them.

"Have you come for me, wolf?" he asked. "Take me, then. I cannot bring food to my hungry brothers and sisters for I am too weak to hunt the fleet elk. I cannot return empty-handed to my family yet again. Take me."

Lydda looked into the human's eyes and saw her own despair reflected in them. He wanted to feed his people's pups just as she did. The warmth of his flesh drew her and she found herself stepping slowly to him. He threw his sharpened stick far from his side and opened his arms, baring his neck and his belly to Lydda so that, if she wanted to, she could easily tear the life from him. Instead, she stood perfectly still, watching the human. She had not looked long at a human before. She had been warned against doing so.

"Any wolf consorting with humans will be exiled from the pack," Tachiim had said when she and her littermates were pups. "They are equal to us as hunters and see us as prey. You will be drawn to them by a force as powerful as the hunt. Stay away or you are wolf no longer."

Lydda looked at the young human and she felt the pull Tachiim had mentioned, as she would feel the pull of one of the pups in the pack, or of a wolf who could be her mate. Confusion shook her as she might shake a rabbit she had caught. Her mind warned her to run away, but her heart felt as if it would leave her chest to get to him. She imagined herself lying beside him, chasing the cold from her bones. She shook herself, and stepped back, but found she could not break the hold of his eyes. A cold gust of wind pushed her from behind and she took one step toward the boy. He had dropped his arms, but raised them again, tentatively.

She stepped into his open arms, and stretched her body across his legs, placing her furred head against his chest. The boy wore many layers of prey skin in an attempt to keep the cold away from his lightly furred body, but still she felt the warmth of him. After a moment of surprise he closed his arms around her. She did not let her gaze leave his face.

For a thousand heartbeats they lay together, the wolf's heart slowing to match the boy's and the boy's quickening to match the wolf's. Lydda felt the strength rising within her, and the human boy must have felt it as well, for they both rose as if one and turned to the hunting fields.

Together they crossed the plain toward the prey and, without speaking, selected a buck. The elk shook his head nervously when they came near, revealing his vulnerability. Moving like the sunlight, Lydda ran behind the elk, fatigue lifting from her legs. She ran the elk and ran him, confusing and tiring him. Then, in a burst of speed, she drove him toward the waiting boy. The boy's sharpened stick flew, sinking deep into the elk's chest and, as the beast stumbled, Lydda tore the life from his belly.

As Lydda ripped into the flesh of the elk, dizzy from the smell and taste of food at last, something heavy knocked her aside. The boy had shoved in to take his share. Growling, she reasserted her place and the two of them ripped at the carcass. Before she was too full to move, Lydda remembered her duty, and began to tear at the beast's haunch to bring some of it home to her hungry family. By the time she had worked it loose, the human had cut through the other haunch with a sharp stone and was tearing away at more of the prey. She took the heavy leg in her mouth, glad she was not far from home. Given strength by the new meat in her belly, she set off for her pack.

She was so caught up in her full belly and the taste of good, fresh meat, that she forgot for a moment about the human. But she turned as she reached the edge of the forest and looked to him. He had stopped as well, the heavy leg of the elk slung over his thin shoulders and an elk rib dragging from one hand. He raised his other arm to her. She dropped the haunch, and dipped her head in acknowledgment.

Her packmates smelled the good meat even before she reached the sheltered clearing. When Lydda approached them, the adult wolves looked in disbelief at the meat she carried. Gently, she set it down.

It was little meat for so many wolves, but it was meat, and that meant hope. It was the first real meal the pack had eaten in well over half a moon. Once the pack realized the meat was real and not a death dream, they crowded around Lydda, forgetting their weakness in their joyful greeting. Lydda stepped aside, bowing to Tachiim, offering him the meat. He touched her gently with his nose and signaled to the pack to share the meat. Then, along with the other wolves still fit enough to run, he set off along Lydda's trail to find her kill.

Lydda turned to the pups, who were mewling at the smell of the fresh meat. She bent her head down to them and, as one weakly nudged the corner of her mouth, regurgitated her food for them. Though her starved body craved the meat that she gave up for the pups, their joy in feeding was worth it. The pups of the Wide Valley pack would not starve again.

Lydda leapt after Tachiim and the others to share in what was left of the kill. So excited was she by her successful hunt, so pleased to provide for her pack, and so giddy from her encounter with the human boy, that she did not notice the new and growing trickle of warmth in the air, so slight it could be mistaken for a dream.

Lydda and her boy rested against the rock where they had met, in a patch of warm dirt newly revealed by the melting of the snow. For one full cycle of the moon, the wolves of Lydda's pack had hunted with the humans. For one cycle of the moon they shared the humans' meat and played with their young, and ran with them in the light of the dusk and of the dawn. Lydda spent every moment she could with her human, for in him she felt as if she had found something she did not know she had lost.

They sat together against their rock, and Lydda curled herself against the boy's strong legs as he ran his fingers through her fur. Sun shone upon them and Earth reached up blades of grass to greet them. Moon waited jealously for her turn to see them again. And Sky—Sky spread all around them, watching.

For the Ancients had been waiting. Waiting and hoping. They did not really want to end the lives of creatures.

1

14,000 YEARS AGO

The legends say that when the blood of the Wide Valley wolves mingles with the blood of the wolves outside the valley, the wolf who bears that blood will stand forever between two worlds. It is said that such a wolf holds the power to destroy not only her pack, but all of wolfkind. That's the real reason Ruuqo came to kill my brother, my sisters, and me in the faint light of the early morning four weeks after we were born.

Wolves hate killing pups. It's considered unnatural and repulsive, and most wolves would rather chew off their own paws than hurt a pup. But my mother never should have whelped us. She was not a senior wolf, and therefore had no right to have pups. But that could have been forgiven. Much worse than that, she had broken one of the most important rules of the Wide Valley, the rules that protect our bloodlines. Ruuqo was only doing his duty.

He had already given Rissa a bellyful of pups, as was proper

for the senior male and female of the pack. Unless given permission by the leaderwolves, no other wolf may mate, for extra pups can be difficult to feed unless it is a very good year. The year I was born was a time of conflict in our valley, and prey was growing scarce. We shared the Wide Valley with four other packs of wolves and with several tribes of humans. While most of the other wolves respected the boundaries of our territories, the humans did not—they drove us from our own kills whenever they got the chance. So the Swift River pack did not have food to spare the season I was born. Even so, I don't think my mother truly believed that Ruuqo would hurt us. She must have hoped he wouldn't notice our Outsider blood, that he wouldn't smell it on us.

Just before dawn two days before Ruuqo came to end our lives, my brother, Triell, and I climbed eagerly up the incline of soft, cool dirt that led from our den to the world outside. Dim light filtered into the deep hollow of the den, and yips and growls from the wolves outside echoed off the walls of our home. The scents and sounds of the world above intrigued us, and anytime we weren't eating or sleeping, we were trying to sneak outside.

"Wait," our mother had told us, blocking our way, "there are things you must know first."

"We just want to see what's out there," Triell wheedled. I caught the mischievous glint in his eye, and we tried to dash past her.

"Listen." Our mother placed a large paw over us, pressing us to the ground. "Every pup must pass inspection to be allowed into the pack. If you do not pass, you do not live. You must listen to what I teach you." Her voice, usually soft and comforting, held a worried tone I'd never heard before. "When you meet Ruuqo and Rissa, the leaderwolves, you must show them you are healthy and strong. You must prove that you are worthy to be part of the Swift River pack. And you must show them respect and honor." She released us, gave us one more worried look, and bent to wash my sisters, who had followed us up to the mouth of the den. Triell and I retreated to a corner of the warm den to plan what we would do to become part of the pack. I don't think it occurred to me that we could fail.

Two days later, when at last we emerged from the den, we saw Rissa's five pups already stumbling around the clearing. Two weeks older than we, they were ready to be presented to the pack and given their names. Rissa stood slightly back, watching, as Ruuqo looked over the pups. Our mother hurried us to join them, though our weak legs made us stagger.

Mother stopped as she looked around the small, dusty clearing. "Rissa is letting Ruuqo make the choice to accept pups or not," she said, her muzzle pulled tight with anxiety. "Bow to him. You must show him respect and win his favor. The more you please him, the better your chances at survival." Her voice grew harsh. "Listen, pups. You must please him, and you will live."

The world outside the den was a jumble of unfamiliar and intriguing smells. The scent of the pack was the most powerful and exciting. All around us, wolves had gathered to watch the pup welcoming. At least six different wolf-scents mingled with the smell of leaves and tree and earth, confusing our noses and making us sneeze. The warm, sweet air beckoned, drawing us out and away from the safety of our mother's side. She followed, whining softly.

Ruuqo looked at our mother and then looked away, his gray face unreadable. His own pups, all of whom were bigger and fatter than we, yipped and trembled around him, licking his lowered muzzle and rolling on their backs to offer up soft bellies. One by one he sniffed them, turned them just a little this way and that, carefully checking for disease or weakness. After a moment, he accepted all but one of them into the pack by taking each small muzzle gently in his mouth.

"Welcome pups," he said. "You are part of the Swift River pack, and each wolf of the pack will protect you and will feed you. Welcome Borlla. Welcome Unnan. Welcome Reel. Welcome Marra. You are our future. You are Swift River wolves." He ignored one small, raggedy pup, leaving him to the side and refusing him a name. Once a pup is named, every wolf in the pack is pledged to protect him, so the leaderwolves do not name a pup they think might die soon. Rissa crawled back into her den and brought out one limp form, a tiny pup that had not survived to greet the pack. She buried it quickly at the edge of the clearing.

The pack howled a welcome to its newest members. Each wolf bounded up to the pups in turn to welcome them to the pack, tails wagging and ears pricked in delight. Then they began to play, chasing one another and rolling in dirt and leaves, yipping in excitement. I saw them dance with joy, a joy inspired by pups no different from us. I nudged Triell's cheek.

"There's nothing to be afraid of," I said to him. "You just have to show that you're strong and respectful." Triell's tail wagged gently as he watched the pup welcoming. I looked at his lively eyes and small, strong neck and knew we were just as healthy and worthy as Ruuqo and Rissa's pups. My mother had worried for nothing. Soon it would be our turn to win Ruuqo's approval. Our turn to be given our names, and granted our places in the Swift River pack.

Ruuqo lowered his eyes as he approached us. He was the largest wolf in the pack, broad across the chest and taller by an ear than any other Swift River wolf. The muscles under his gray fur moved commandingly as he left his own pups with the rest of the pack and stalked over to where we stood. He hesitated. Then he bent over us and opened his great jaws. Our mother stepped in front of us, blocking him.

"Brother," she begged, for she and Rissa had been littermates, and had joined the Swift River pack together, "you must let them live."

"They bear the blood of Outsiders, Neesa. They will take meat from my children. The pack cannot support extra pups." His voice was so cold and angry that I began to tremble. Next to me I heard Triell whimper.

"That's a lie," our mother said as she raised her head to look up at him, amber eyes unwavering. She was much smaller than Ruuqo. "We've managed before when prey was scarce. You're just afraid of anything different. You are too much of a coward to lead the Swift River pack. Only a coward kills pups."

Ruuqo growled and slammed into her, pinning her to the ground.

"You think I like killing pups?" he demanded. "With pups of my own standing not two wolflengths away? Your pups are not just 'something different.' They smell of Outsider blood. I did not bring them into this world, Neesa. I did not break the covenant. That is your responsibility." He took her neck in his teeth and bit down until she yelped, then he stepped off her.

Mother scrambled to her feet when Ruuqo released her, and backed away from him, leaving us to face his deadly jaws. We all ran back and clustered around her. "But they are named!" she said.

My mother had given us names at birth, in defiance of wolf custom. *"If you have names,"* she told us, *"you are pack. He will not kill you then."* She named my three sisters after the plants surrounding our den, and named my brother Triell for the dark of a moonless night. He was the only black wolf in her litter and his eyes shone like stars from his dark face. She named me Kaala, daughter of the Moon, because of the white crescent on the gray fur of my chest.

Triell and I stood trembling beside our mother. My sisters cringed on her other side. We had believed our mother when she told us we could find our places in the pack. I had laughed at her worries. We believed we needed only to act like wolves worthy of pack to be accepted. Now we understood that we might not even be granted a chance at life.

"They are named, brother," she said again.

"Not by me," Ruuqo said. "They are not legitimate and they are not pack. Stand aside."

"I will not," she said.

A large female wolf, almost as big as Ruuqo and scarred along her face and muzzle, leapt upon my mother, forcing her aside. Ruuqo joined the large female, forcing our mother away from us.

"*Pup killer!* You are not my brother," she snarled at him. "You're not fit to be wolf."

Even I could tell my mother's words hurt Ruuqo, and he growled and chased her back to the mouth of our den, leaving us alone on a rise on the warm side of the clearing. The large female guarded her. Then Ruuqo turned to us. Rissa stepped forward, leaving her pups crying and trying to follow behind her. She stood beside Ruuqo.

"Lifemate," she said, "this duty is as much mine as yours. I should have kept closer watch on my sister. I will do what must be done." Her voice was deep and rich and her white fur shone in the early light. She smelled of strength and confidence.

Ruuqo licked her muzzle and rested his head briefly against her white neck, as if gathering courage from her. Then he shouldered her gently aside, moving her away from us. The rest of the pack stood around the clearing, some of them whining, some merely watching, all keeping a distance from Ruuqo, who now stood towering above us. Even now, I sometimes look at him and see him standing over me, ready to grab me by the neck and shake me until I stopped moving. That is what he did to all three of my sisters and then to Triell, my brother, my favorite.

Ázzuen says I can't possibly remember what really happened that day since I was only four weeks old, but I do. I remember. Ruuqo took my sisters, one by one, in his jaws and shook the life out of them. Then he picked up Triell. My brother was lying beside me, pressed up against me, and then he was not. The warmth of his flesh and fur was suddenly gone from my side, and he yelped as Ruuqo lifted him far off the ground. Triell's eyes held mine and, forgetting my terror, I struggled to stand on my back legs to reach him. My weakness betrayed me and I fell to the ground as Ruuqo's sharp teeth closed on Triell's small, soft body. He grasped my brother in those teeth and crushed his small form, until the bright light of Triell's eyes flickered out, and his body sagged and then was still. I couldn't believe he was dead, that he wouldn't lift his head again to look at me. Ruuqo dropped him beside the limp bodies of my sisters. And then he turned to me. My mother had crept back from the mouth of the den. Now she crawled forward on her belly, her ears flat against her head and her tail invisible beneath her, begging Ruuqo to stop. He ignored her.

"He does what he must do, Neesa," an old, gentle wolf said to her. "The pups bear Outsider blood. He does what any good leaderwolf must do to protect his pack. You shouldn't make it harder for him."

I stood, looking up at Ruuqo's massive height. Cringing and pleading had done my brother and sisters no good. When Triell's body left Ruuqo's jaws and landed on the earth with the softest of thumps, my trembling turned to fury. Triell and I had slept and fed as one. Together we had dreamed of winning our places in the pack. Now he was dead. I bared my teeth and copied the growl I'd heard in Ruuqo's voice. Ruuqo was so startled he stepped back and shook himself before coming for me again. Anger swept away my fear, and I leapt for his throat. My weak legs took me only to his chest, and he easily cast me aside. But Ruuqo looked as though he'd stared the Deathwolf himself in the face. He stood still, watching me for a long moment as I snarled with as much fury as I could summon.

"I'm sorry, littlewolf," he said softly, "but, you see, I must do what's right for the pack. I must do my duty," and he bent his head and opened his jaws to crush me. The other wolves of the pack cried out in distress, trembling and pressing against one another. Dawn was turning to day, and the bright light of the morning stung my eyes as I looked up at my death.

"I think this one wants to live, Ruuqo."

Ruuqo froze, his jaws still open, his pale yellow eyes wide and startled. Then, to my amazement, his deadly jaws closed, and he raised his head, flattened his ears, and stepped back to greet the newcomer.

When I followed his gaze, I saw a wolf larger than any wolf could be. His chest was level with Ruuqo's muzzle, and his neck, which seemed to me to be nearly as high up as the beams of sunlight now filtering into the clearing, was thick and strong. His voice rumbled with amusement. He had strange green eyes, unlike the amber eyes of the adult wolves of my pack, or the blue eyes of the pups. After a moment, another huge wolf with the same green eyes and a darker, shaggier coat stalked up to stand beside him.

All the wolves in my mother's pack hurried from the edges of the clearing to greet these strange and frightening creatures. They approached respectfully, lowering ears and tails, and dropping to their bellies to offer the larger wolves the greatest respect.

"They are the Greatwolves," my mother whispered. She had crept close to me when the large wolves entered our clearing. "Jandru and Frandra. Two of the only ones left in the Wide Valley. They speak directly to the Ancients, and we all answer to them."

The Greatwolves graciously accepted the greetings of the smaller wolves.

"Lordwolves, welcome." Ruuqo spoke respectfully with his head down. "I do what I have to do. I did not authorize this litter and I must care for my pack."

"Second litters often are allowed to live." Jandru bent his head to nuzzle Triell's still form. "As you well know, Ruuqo. It was only four years ago that you and your littermates were spared. A long time for you, perhaps, but not for me."

"That was a time of plenty, Lordwolf."

"One pup does not eat so very much. I would have her live."

Ruuqo did not speak for a moment, unwilling to risk Jandru's anger.

"There is more, Lordwolf," Rissa said, stepping forward.

"The pup is of Outsider blood. We cannot break the rules of the valley."

"Of Outsider blood?" There was no longer any trace of laughter in Jandru's voice. He glared at Ruuqo. "Why didn't you tell me that?"

Ruuqo lowered his head even farther. "I didn't want you to think I had so little control of my pack."

Jandru watched him a long time without speaking and then turned to my mother, speaking to her in real anger. "What were you thinking, risking the safety of your pack?"

Frandra, the female Greatwolf, spoke for the first time. She stood even taller than her mate, and her voice was strong and sure. Her eyes shone from her dark fur. She spoke so loudly and startled me so much that I leapt back, falling on my backside.

"Easy for you to say, Jandru, when you can breed wherever and whenever you please without consequence. She did not conceive alone." Jandru looked abashed and lowered his ears just the slightest bit. Frandra watched him for a moment and turned her great head to my mother. "But why did you allow them to live long enough to call themselves wolf? You must have known they could not live. You should have killed them when you bore them."

"I wanted them to be pack. I thought they would be important." My mother's voice was soft and frightened. "I dreamed they would save wolfkind. In some dreams, they stopped the prey from leaving the valley. In other dreams, they drove the humans away. Always they saved us. See how fearless she is?"

I stood again, and tried to still the trembling in my legs, to look like a wolf worthy of pack.

"Lordwolves, my sister has always wished to have a greater role in the pack," Rissa said. "Sometimes her dreams have led us to good hunting, but she's always wanted pups."

"It doesn't matter," Jandru said abruptly. "The pup's of Outsider blood and cannot live. Do what you must, Ruuqo."

Jandru turned away, almost stepping on me, so I growled at him, too. "I am sorry, Smallteeth," he said. "I would save you, but cannot go against the covenant. May you return to the Wide Valley again."

I felt the unfairness of it like the cold, damp wind that seeped sometimes into my mother's den. How could a creature be so great and not be able to do what he wished? I began to look again around the clearing, searching for a place to hide. I turned to run. Frandra stepped over me, placing her own body between me and Ruuqo's sharp teeth.

She growled.

"I will not let you kill this pup," she said. "So what if it is not what we usually do! Things are changing, Lifemate, and we must change with them. The humans are taking more prey than ever before, and each day they grow more out of control. The Balance has already been upset and we can wait no longer to take action. We must change and change now." The Greatwolf looked down at me. "If she's of the blood, so be it. Letting this fierce one live may have consequences, but it may also be our hope. The will to live is too strong to ignore. We must listen to the messages the Ancients send to us."

"Frandra," Jandru began.

"Have you lost use of your nose *and* ears, Jandru?" she snapped. "You know we are almost out of time. And we are failing."

"I won't take the risk," he said. "We did not give permission for this exception and we cannot go against the Greatwolf council. That is my decision."

"The decision is not yours alone." Frandra met his eyes steadily. "Do you want to fight me? Come, fight me if you will."

Jandru stood still as death for the briefest moment. Frandra spoke again.

"Look at her chest, Lifemate," she whispered softly, urgently, so that only Jandru, my mother, and I could hear her. "She bears the mark of the moon, the mark of the Balance. The council is rigid, and they do not always see what is before them. What if she is the one? Maybe the Ancients have chosen this one for us."

"I have named her Kaala, daughter of the Moon," my mother said.

Jandru looked at me a long time. He flipped me over onto my back to better see the moon shape on my chest. As he held me there with a paw nearly as big as my body, I tried to think of something, anything, I could do to convince him I deserved to live. But I could only stare into his strange eyes as he decided my fate. Finally, he stepped away from me and bowed to Frandra.

"Give her the chance," he said to Ruuqo. "If it's a mistake, the Greatwolves will bear the burden."

"But Lordwolves," Ruuqo began.

"You are not to kill this pup, smallwolf." Frandra towered over him. "The Greatwolves make the rules of the valley, and we may grant exceptions as we so choose. We have good reason for sparing this pup."

When Ruuqo tried to speak again, the Greatwolf growled and, placing both her front legs on his back, forced him to the ground. When she released him, he scrambled to his feet and bent his head in submission, but resentment burned in his eyes. Frandra ignored his anger.

"Good fortune, Kaala Smallteeth." Frandra opened her great jaws in a smile as she shouldered Jandru aside and trotted into the woods. "I will certainly see you again." Jandru followed behind her.

As the Greatwolves left the clearing, my mother whispered urgently to me. "Listen, Kaala. Listen carefully. Ruuqo will not let me stay with the pack. I am certain of it. But you must stay, and you must live. You must do whatever you have to do to survive, and become part of the pack. Then, when you are grown and accepted into the pack you must come find me. There are things you must know about your father and about me. Do you promise me that?"

Her eyes held mine and I couldn't refuse her.

"I promise," I whispered. "But I want to go with you."

"No," she said. She pressed the soft fur of her muzzle to my face. I inhaled her scent. "You must stay and become part of the pack. Do not come for me until then. You have promised."

I wanted to ask her why. I wanted to ask her how I would find her, but I didn't get the chance. As soon as the Greatwolves were out of hearing range, Ruuqo turned on my mother and bit her savagely on the neck, drawing blood and making her yelp. He knocked her to the ground and as she fell, she shoved me out of the way with her hip. I stumbled backward, landing on my back. I staggered to my feet.

"You have brought chaos to your pack, my children, and me," Ruuqo snarled, "and forced the Swift River pack into conflict with the Balance."

Wolves do not normally hurt each other when they fight,

since most wolves know their place in the pack and avoid conflict. But Ruuqo could not take out his frustration on me, and he certainly could not fight the Greatwolves. So he turned instead on my mother. She tried to fight back, but when Minn, a yearling male, and Werrna, the big, scar-faced female, attacked her, too, she whimpered and scrambled to the edge of the clearing. When she tried to come back to the rest of the pack, they attacked again, driving her away. I wanted to run back to my mother, to help her, but my courage had deserted me and I could only watch in terror.

Rissa took the closest pup, Reel, in her mouth and ran back into her den.

"Let me stay long enough to wean her, brother," my mother said desperately. "Then I will leave."

"You'll leave now," he said. "You are no longer pack." He chased her to the edge of the clearing and each time she tried to come back, he and the other two wolves attacked her again. At last, bleeding and whimpering, she darted into the forest, her three attackers chasing her away.

When he returned, Ruuqo gave a commanding bark, and he and all the rest of the adult wolves except Rissa quit the clearing. They had only a few hours before the hot sun would make hunting impossible and Ruuqo had a pack to feed.

I wanted to follow my mother into the woods, but I was exhausted in body and soul and sank to the hard ground, cold even in the warmth of the morning sun.

Two of Rissa's largest pups, the ones named Unnan and Borlla, swaggered to where I sat and looked me up and down. Borlla, the bigger of the two, poked me painfully in the ribs with her muzzle.

"Doesn't look like it'll live long," she said to Unnan.

"Looks like bear food to me," he said.

"Hey, Bear Food," Borlla said. "Better stay away from our milk."

"Or we'll finish what Ruuqo started." Unnan's mean little eyes swept over me.

The two pups trotted toward the entrance of the den into which Rissa had disappeared earlier. On their way, Borlla swatted the smallest pup of the litter, the raggedy male who had not been given a name, and Unnan growled at Marra, another smallpup, and tumbled her into the dirt. Satisfied, they lifted their tails high and strutted into the den. After a moment Marra got up and followed, but the smallest pup stayed crouched where he had fallen.

I stayed alone in the clearing, waiting for my mother all that day, even as the sun grew hot and oppressive. I thought if I just waited long enough she would return for me, take me with her in her exile.

My mother did not return for the rest of the long day, or into the night, though I waited until the pack returned for their afternoon slumber and left again for the evening hunt, until the terrifying sounds of unknown creatures made me fear for my life once again. Still she did not come back. I was alive, but I was alone, frightened, and despised by the pack that was supposed to care for me.

2

I would not return to my mother's den, for it smelled of my dead littermates and meant only loneliness. But I did smell milk and warm bodies, and heard the unmistakable sounds of suckling. Hunger pierced the numbness that kept me huddled in the dirt. A part of me wondered how I could think about food when my mother was gone forever, but I couldn't see the point of standing up against Ruuqo only to die of hunger mere wolf-lengths from Rissa's warm milk. I didn't know if she would feed me, but I was her sister's pup and shared her blood. I had to try. I hadn't forgotten Borlla's and Unnan's threats, but the pull of hunger was stronger than my fear. I turned my back on the bodies of my littermates and crept toward the good smells and sounds coming from Rissa's den. I stopped when I saw the raggedy pup hunched miserably at the edge of the den.

"You'll starve if you just stay out here." He looked up at me when I spoke, but didn't answer. He had a cut over his right eye where Borlla had swatted him, and his matted dark gray coat made him look even smaller than he was. But he had bright, sil-

very eyes. It was those unusual eyes, so like Triell's, that stopped me and kept me from ignoring him on my way to my meal.

"Littlewolf," I said, using the endearment our mother used for us, "if you let them bully you, you'll always be a curl-tail." Most packs have a curl-tail, a wolf who is picked on, one who doesn't get as much to eat and is kept at the fringes of the pack. But I didn't think the smallpup would even live to be a curl-tail if he didn't get some food and the safety of the den soon.

He wrapped his scraggly tail around his legs and looked back down at the equally scraggly grass growing in the dirt. His scowl hid his brilliant eyes. "That's easy for you to say, with the Greatwolves on your side. They all want me to die. That's why they didn't give me a name."

Impatient, I turned from him. I didn't have time for a pup who didn't even want to live. My brother, Triell, would've given anything to have this chance at life. He wouldn't have whined and trembled in fear had he survived. A pack had no place for such a wolf. I poked my nose in the den and Rissa spoke.

"Come, pups," she said. "Come drink and rest."

My heart lifted and I began to climb into the den. And then I stopped and looked again at the smallpup. The memory of being alone and unwanted nagged at me. I couldn't leave him to starve. I backed out of the den and, without wasting any more words, shoved him from behind, toppling him into the den. He rolled forward with a surprised yelp and I crawled in after him.

Rissa's den was larger than my mother's had been, its solid dirt walls held steady by the roots of the great oak that dominated the den site, but was still small enough to feel safe. The four pups fed hungrily at Rissa's belly. As the small-pup and I crept closer, Unnan rolled one eye toward us and growled. The smallpup standing next to me trembled and backed away.

I was heartsore from the loss of my littermates and my mother, and angry at the way the entire pack had treated me. My body grew hot and tight and I felt the fur on my back rising up and when I saw Unnan and fat Borlla feeding so contentedly, keeping everything for their greedy selves, I shoved Unnan away, making room for myself and the smallpup. I didn't stop to think about the consequences of making an enemy of Unnan. I was just mad. When the smallpup hesitated, I grabbed the soft fur at the top of his neck and dragged him to a feeding place.

"Eat," I told him.

Unnan harried me as I tried to feed, and Borlla growled, but I ignored them, reaching for Rissa's rich, life-giving milk. The smallpup nestled between me and Marra, the kindest of Rissa's pups. Full and warm, we all fell asleep against Rissa's strong body.

The next morning Unnan and Borlla tried to get rid of me for good. Rissa, weary of her long confinement, left us with the pack's two yearling wolves and bounded off beside Ruuqo to join the predawn hunt. Yearling wolves are often pupwatchers when adults are away. Minn, who had helped chase my mother away, was a bully and not particularly interested in watching us, but he was afraid of his sister, Yllin, and she took her responsibility seriously. They played roughly with us, and I loved how they growled and pretended to fight us. When they tired of allowing us to pounce on them and bite their tails, they watched us from a shady spot as we continued to wrestle with one another. When they slipped into their naps, I played with Marra and the smallpup. He was almost as small as I, even though he was two full weeks older, and he did not have the physical strength of a survivor wolf. But I looked more closely at his sparkling eyes and saw that he no longer had the hopeless, weary look that a pup-to-die would have. He was alert and lively, even with too little food in his belly, and in spite of the harassment of Borlla and Unnan. Surprised and pleased by this change in him, I pounced on him and he yipped joyfully as we rolled in the dirt.

Because he was dark-coated as Triell had been, and not much bigger than my lost brother, I felt I had known the smallpup for longer than a day. Amidst our scuffling, I nosed him gently on the cheek. Delighted, he poked his cold nose into my face hard enough to knock me over. I landed with an undignified thump, sending up a cloud of dust. At first he looked startled and apologetic, but then he pounced on top of me, and we wrestled happily. With a yip, Marra joined the game. The three other pups ignored us at first. Borlla was fat, pale-coated, and smelled of the milk she took first of all of us. Her fur was not the bright, pure white of Rissa's coat, but a duller, dingy shade. Unnan was a dirty gray-brown and had a thin muzzle and tiny eyes that made him look more weasel than wolf. Reel, though larger than Marra and the smallpup, was smaller than Borlla and Unnan, and he struggled to keep up with the big pups as they fought each other in a rougher game. I played and wrestled with Marra and the smallpup until finally, too tired to continue, I sat to rest by a prickly berry bush as Marra chased the smallpup under the oak tree. I closed my eyes, lulled by the rising sun and the happy exhaustion of playing with the other pups.

Moments before my assailants attacked, I heard them and leapt to my feet. Unnan, Reel, and Borlla all pounced on me at once, knocking me flat on my back. I was unprepared for the attack and they quickly pinned me down and began to bite. To Yllin and Minn, watching sleepily from the shade, it might have looked like play. But the pups were not playing. Their teeth bit into me and they tried to crush the air from my chest.

"Ruuqo was too weak to finish killing you, but we'll finish," Unnan growled.

"There's no room for you in our pack," Borlla whispered as she tried to bite through my neck.

Reel was silent as he tried to rip at my belly.

I growled and bit and snarled and fought against them as best I could, but there were three of them and only one of me, and I knew that even if they did not kill me they could injure me severely enough to make me too weak to survive.

Just as my strength was giving out, something knocked Unnan and Borlla off me. I bit Reel on the shoulder and scrambled to my feet. The smallpup had come to my aid and had so surprised his two littermates that they had fallen awkwardly onto the hard ground. Now Unnan had him pressed to the ground as Borlla prepared to rip at his throat. I leapt over Borlla, landing on Unnan, rolling him off the smallpup and biting into his ugly fur. He tasted like dirt. Borlla abandoned her attack on the smallpup and came to help Unnan. Together they pinned me to the ground.

"Your father was a hyena," Borlla sneered, standing over me, "and your mother a traitor and a weakling."

"That's why she left you," Unnan added, baring his teeth.

Both pups growled and snarled, expecting me to be afraid of their larger size and greater strength. But I had been angry already when they ganged up on the smallpup. Their insults about my mother only made me angrier now.

How dare they? A voice in my head was so loud I could not

hear the sounds of the clearing. The stench of blood in my nose blocked all the scents of oak and spruce and wolf. *Kill them. They are not fit to be wolf.* For the second time, fury took me like the wind takes a leaf, and I threw off both pups. I would have killed them both, I know I would, but Reel had the smallpup trapped and I had to help him. When I tumbled Reel off him, the smallpup stood beside me, and together we faced the three of them, snarling. I heard Marra running to get help from the pupwatchers. I smelled hatred in Unnan and Borlla, and fear in Reel. I saw the smallpup looking at me out of the corner of his eye, with something like awe on his face. My back left leg bled from a deep gash I had not noticed in the fight, and I felt it weakening beneath me. The smallpup held his right forepaw up as if it hurt him.

I looked over the heads of our adversaries to see Yllin racing back across the clearing followed by an angry Ruuqo. The other pups followed my gaze and Borlla, Unnan, and Reel spun around to face Ruuqo, dropping to their bellies. The pack had returned early from an unsuccessful hunt. As they drew close I heard Yllin speaking softly.

"I'm sorry, leaderwolf," she said, ears low. "They were playing, and then the big pups attacked. The smallpups fought only to defend themselves." She paused, and dared to speak again, which I thought was very brave, since Ruuqo might be angry at her for letting the fight get out of hand. "They fought well."

Ruuqo raised his ears at her but did not discipline her. I could tell he liked Yllin. He let her get away with more than another young wolf might. His eyes swept over us.

"No wolf deeply injures or kills a packmate without cause," he said. "If you cannot learn that, you cannot be pack. All Swift River wolves know the difference between challenge fights and a fight to kill." He turned to a cowering Reel. "What is the difference, pup?"

Reel looked around at Borlla and Unnan for assistance and Ruuqo swatted him.

"I did not ask your littermates, I asked you. Well?"

Reel said nothing, just rolled over on his back and whined.

"Yllin," Ruuqo said, "please explain the difference."

Yllin's ears and tail lifted. "Challenge fighting is the fighting a wolf must do to win his or her place in the pack, or the fighting a leaderwolf must do to discipline pack members, to keep order. And you hurt your opponent only as much as you must," she said. "In a fight to kill, you are trying to hurt or kill your opponent. You only fight to kill when you have no other choice."

Ruuqo whuffed in approval. "All wolves must know how to fight or they will have no place in the pack," he continued. "But only leaderwolves may kill or tell others to kill a pack member. And we of the Swift River pack will not kill another wolf unless we are being threatened by a rival pack or if pack lives are at stake."

Ruuqo struck Borlla when she tried to rise. Unnan and Reel had more sense and stayed low. Then he turned to the smallpup and me. We lowered ourselves to the ground and awaited his blow. He nosed the smallpup gently. He did not even look at me.

"There is more to being wolf," he said, "than the strength to win a fight, or the speed to catch prey." He spoke loudly enough for the whole pack to hear, but his words were clearly directed to the pups he had disciplined. "Size and strength and speed are all part of what makes a wolf worthy of pack. But courage and honor are just as important. The interests of the pack come first, and every wolf must serve the pack." He spoke directly to Borlla,

Unnan, and Reel. "Wolves who cannot learn that are not welcome in the Swift River pack."

I know it wasn't kind, but I have to admit I took pleasure in the trembling and whining of Borlla and Reel, and especially of Unnan, who had lowered himself so far to the ground I thought he might disappear into the earth. But what Ruuqo did next surprised me. Usually, when a pup is not given a name, he waits as long as three moons to be accepted into the pack and then is almost certain to be low ranking. Ruuqo turned to the smallpup, and spoke softly.

"You have shown courage, honor, and strength of spirit, all qualities of a true wolf. And I welcome you into the Swift River pack." He took the smallpup's muzzle in his jaws.

Rissa eagerly stepped forward, tail high, her white fur shining in the sun, and spoke before Ruuqo could continue.

"We name you Ázzuen, a warrior's name, the name of my father," she said. "Carry your name well and do honor to the Swift River pack."

And just like that, the smallpup became pack. It had happened so quickly I couldn't untangle my happiness for him from my jealousy—my mother had given me a name, but no one would call me by it. I had fought more fiercely than Ázzuen, but Ruuqo had snubbed me, would not acknowledge *my* courage. For just a moment, I'm ashamed to say, I wanted to take Ázzuen by his neck fur and shake him. But as he walked back to the den, his little tail whipped proudly back and forth so temptingly I couldn't resist it. I felt the meanness in me dry up and I snuck up behind him, leapt, and playfully nipped his tail. He turned in surprise, and I grinned at him and ran into Rissa's den. With a bark louder than should have come from so small a pup, he leapt after me, into the milk-smelling earth. I could never bring Triell back, but in Ázzuen I had once again found a brother.

⌑

Ruuqo would not defy the Greatwolves and kill me outright, but he would not accept my name and did not make it easy for me to survive. The first time we pups fed outside the den, he stood glowering in front of Rissa, stepping aside to let the other pups pass by to reach their food, but growling and snarling when I tried to do so. It took all of my courage to wriggle past him to get my meal. Every time he saw me, he growled. Though they dared not try to kill me again, Unnan and Borlla followed Ruuqo's lead, attacking me whenever they got the chance.

Three nights after the Greatwolves intervened to save my life, Ruuqo howled to assemble the pack, to tell them to prepare to journey the next morning.

"*Ruuqo!*" Rissa raised her head angrily from where she rested by the den. "None of the pups are old enough for the journey."

"What journey?" Reel asked Borlla.

"The journey to our summer home," answered Yllin, the young female who had spoken up for us after the fight. She stood beside us by the large oak that shaded the den site.

"It's our best gathering place, where you can be safe while we hunt and bring back food for you. The den site is too small and too warm to stay in all summer."

"Is it far?" I asked.

"For a pup, it's far. Most packs have summer gathering places near their den sites, but our old den site was flooded last winter so we must travel farther." She frowned. "Last year Ruuqo waited until we were eight weeks old to move us. I can't imagine what he's thinking."

Rissa narrowed her eyes, watching Ruuqo as he paced the clearing.

"You want to get back at the Greatwolves," she accused. "You want the pup to die." None of us had to ask which pup she meant. She rose and walked to him, placing her nose to his cheek. "The decision has been made for you, Lifemate. You cannot defy Jandru and Frandra."

"No," he said, "I cannot. But I cannot anger the Ancients, either. You know the wolves of the Wide Valley must keep their blood pure, or risk the consequences. If we allow her to live, the Ancients could send drought, or a freeze that kills all the prey, or a plague. It's happened before. The legends tell us so." He shook his head in frustration. "And where will Frandra and Jandru be if the other Greatwolves see her and do not like what she is? Or other packs in the valley? Greatwolves do not live with the same consequences we do, and yet they can force us to take action that could be our ruin. I won't let my pack suffer."

Werrna, the scarred female who was Ruuqo and Rissa's secondwolf, spoke up. "The Stone Peak wolves killed the Wet Woods pack—while a pair of Greatwolves watched—because they allowed a mixed-blood litter to live. And it's not as if we can hide it," she said, looking at me. "She bears the mark of the unlucky. She could bring death to our pack."

Rissa ignored Werrna. "Then we will carry the smaller pups, if they cannot make it across the plain."

"No pup is carried. Any pup that cannot make the journey is not fit to be a Swift River wolf," Ruuqo replied. "If the Wolf of the Moon means *her* to live, so be it. But I will allow only strong wolves in my pack."

"I will not let you endanger my pups for your pride!" Rissa snapped.

"It is not my pride, Rissa, it is our survival. And we journey when the sun rises." Ruuqo almost never used his leader voice with Rissa, almost never bullied her. But when he did he made it clear that he considered himself top wolf. Rissa was several pounds lighter than he, and weak from giving milk to us pups. If she challenged him, she would lose.

His voice softened. "We have known since we were young that we must honor the covenant, Rissa. And we have both made sacrifices to it before." I had not heard sadness in his voice before, and wondered what caused it.

Rissa stared at him for a long time and then stalked away. His ears and tail drooping, Ruuqo watched her go.

⊡

Early the next morning, the pack set out. Rissa refused to take part in the leave-taking ceremony and stood aloof as the rest of the pack gathered around Ruuqo, each touching him and crying out for a good journey. I watched, fascinated, as the adult wolves wove around Ruuqo, touching their noses to his face and neck. He in turn placed his head on shoulders and necks, and licked outstretched faces.

"Won't you join us, Rissa?" he asked. "A good ceremony means a good journey."

"Good planning means a good journey," she snapped. "I will not celebrate this leave-taking."

Ruuqo said no more to her, but lifted his voice in a great howl. One by one the other wolves joined him, singing to the sky. And the journey began.

We walked away from the den site and the old oak, and scrambled up the rise that protected the den. Our clearing was at the very edge of a small stand of trees that sheltered us, and beyond the trees stretched a vast plain. It sloped gently uphill, and I could not see the end of it.

I remember little of the first part of that journey. At four weeks old, I was only two weeks younger than Rissa's pups, but it made a difference. My legs were that much shorter, my lungs that much weaker, my eyes just a little less able to focus. The wound in my leg had not yet healed and it hurt to put all my weight on it. I could see that Ázzuen's front paw was still hurting him, too. We were all terrified of being left behind, and did not even try to sort out the new sounds and smells. But Ázzuen, Marra, and I were the smallest and it was harder for us than for the other pups. Soon we fell behind the others. After we walked for what seemed like hours, we saw the wolves ahead of us stop in the shade of a large boulder. We hurried to catch up, and collapsed in a heap of fatigue. Even Borlla and Unnan were panting with effort and were too tired to harass me. We were allowed to rest for only a few moments before the adult wolves pushed and prodded us to our feet and we began the journey again. I had less time to rest than the others since I had reached the boulder last of all, and my legs shook as I stood. As we reached the crest of the long slope, we could see across the great plain to a distant stand of trees.

Rissa gave a great howl. "Your new home lies on the other side, pups. Once you make it to the woods and to Fallen Tree Gathering Place, you will be safe. You will have passed your first test as wolf."

The rest of the pack joined her in the howl. "Keep to the journey. Call on your strength."

We walked forever across that great plain, cringing against the openness of the sky. We were so used to trees above us, and the sights and sounds of this great flat land overwhelmed us. After what seemed like a lifetime of walking, I looked up at the sun overhead to see the day half over, and I could not believe we would reach the other side before dark. Ruuqo and Rissa led the way, with the rest of the pack following, the adult wolves surrounding the pups. Rissa, the yearling wolves, and the old-wolf, Trevegg, kept coming back to check on stragglers, and one of them always walked beside us. Marra, two weeks older than I and better fed than Ázzuen, managed to keep up, but soon the gap between the core pack and the stragglers grew, leaving Ázzuen and me behind.

Ruuqo barked for the adults with us to catch up. Trevegg turned back to me and lifted me gently in his jaws. From far ahead, Ruuqo gave another sharp bark.

"Every pup must walk the journey. They will arrive on their own feet, or they are not fit to be wolf."

Trevegg hesitated, but put me gently down.

"Keep walking, littlewolf. If you do not give up, you will find us. Keep the strength. You are part of the Balance."

When Trevegg set me down, I could not lift myself up again, but sat in despair as the rest of the pack moved away. Ázzuen sat beside me, whimpering.

Then Yllin, the strong-minded yearling female, broke away from the pack again and ran back to me. Her strong legs closed the distance between me and the rest of the pack in a matter of moments and I despaired of my tired legs ever being strong enough to carry me far enough and quickly enough. Yllin had a sharp tongue and little patience for weakness and I was certain she had come to mock me. But when she stopped, ignoring Ruuqo's angry warning, there was mischief in her amber eyes.

"Come, little sister," she said. "I plan to be leaderwolf of Swift River someday, and will need a secondwolf. Do not disappoint me." She bent to speak so softly only I could hear.

"It's the way of the wolf. This is the first of three tests you must pass. If you pass all three—the crossing, the first hunt, and the first winter—Ruuqo has to give you *romma*, the mark of pack acceptance, and every wolf you meet will know you are a Swift River wolf and that you are worthy of pack." She paused. "Sometimes a leaderwolf will help a weaker pup through the tests. All of us love pups and want them to live. We'd sooner give up hunting and live on grass than hurt a pup. But if leaderwolves want to test a pup's strength they may challenge her. If a pup is strong enough to survive such trials, she is strong enough to be pack. If not, there's more food for the others."

Then, before Ruuqo could come back for her and punish her for her defiance, Yllin pelted back to join the rest of the pack, tail low, and I could see her asking Ruuqo's pardon.

The pack moved farther and farther away, until I could barely see their dark shapes on the open plain. But Trevegg's kindness and Yllin's cheerful defiance heartened me, and I got to my feet and began to take one painful step after another. Ázzuen followed. But after an hour, my breath came in gasps and I no longer looked up so often to see where the rest of the pack was. The gash in my leg began bleeding again and burned with every step. Ázzuen began to fall behind me and I slowed my pace even more, allowing him to catch up.

We walked. We walked until my paws felt bruised and each breath took so much effort I wished again and again I did not need the air. I could no longer see my pack and their scent grew fainter and fainter until I could no longer trust the trail I followed.

The sky darkened.

Grown wolves travel at night, avoiding the heat of day, but a pup is prey and any pack that values its pups does not take them out in the open after dark until they are old enough to fend for themselves.

"Bear food," Unnan had whispered to me before we left that morning. I was listening to Ruuqo and Rissa argue about the journey and had not heard him come up behind me.

"You'll be bear food before tomorrow morning. Or a mother long-fang will get you for a snack for her cubs."

I had stalked away from him with as much dignity as I could scrape up, but now as Ázzuen and I stood alone out in the open, Unnan's words haunted me.

And yet we kept walking. I was angry and hurt that the pack did not care if I lived or died, but I had nowhere else to go and they were the only family I had. So I walked on until my legs gave out beneath me and my tired nose could no longer distinguish the scent of my pack from the other scents on the plain. As a cloudy dusk crept over the sky, I sank down on the ground and waited for death to come. Ázzuen crumpled beside me.

Sleep came, and dreams. Dreams of bears and sharp teeth. But as I fell deeper into sleep, I saw a face, the kindly face of a young shewolf. She was no wolf I knew, for only my pack was familiar to me. She smelled of juniper and an unfamiliar warm-acrid scent. And, like me, she had a white moon shape on her chest, like no other wolf in the pack had. I wondered if she might be a vision of my mother from a younger, happier time.

The dreamwolf laughed. "No, little Smallteeth, though I am one of your many mothers from a time longer ago than you can imagine." I felt a warmth suffusing me, easing the aches in my body. "You are not meant to die today, sisterwolf. You promised your mother you would survive and become pack. You must live and carry on my work. You have much to do." And her kind face grew suddenly sad, and then angry. "You will suffer for it," she said. Her sadness and anger left as quickly as they had come. "But you will also find great joy. Stand now, my sister. Walk, my daughter. Your way will always be a difficult one and you must learn now to persevere when you think you cannot. Walk, Kaala Smallteeth. Take your friend and find your home."

Dazed, I struggled to my feet, ignoring the pain in my sore leg. I poked Ázzuen awake and, ignoring his groans, bullied him to his feet. When he fell to the ground again, I bit him.

"Get up," I hissed, my throat too dry and tired to speak loudly. "I'm going now and you're coming. I won't let you die here."

"They gave me a name and they still don't care if I live or die," he whispered miserably. "They just left me here."

Impatience with Ázzuen's self-pity rose in me and I bit him again, much harder this time.

"Stop feeling sorry for yourself," I said, ignoring his yelp of pain. "You saved my life when the other pups tried to kill me, so you have to come with me now. Show them you belong in the pack. Do you want Unnan and Borlla to be right about you? To be able to say you're too weak to be pack?"

Ázzuen stood shakily and thought for a moment. "I don't care about Borlla and Unnan. You cared if I got milk or not. I'll go where you go, Kaala." He looked at me with simple trust as if

I were a grown wolf, and his belief in me gave me strength. Ázzuen trusted me to get him home, and so I would.

The pain in my feet and in my chest seemed distant from me, and the dreamwolf's scent guided me as the pack-scent had before. I did not even know if it would lead me where my pack had gone, but I could no longer distinguish the scents of my family, so I followed it. I looked up and saw the great light of the moon, completely round and so bright that my way was not dark. It did not give warmth as did the sun, but its light heartened me, and I walked with determination. I could see, out of the corner of my eye, the shape of the young dreamwolf guiding me on. If I tried to look directly at her, she disappeared, and I got the sense that she was laughing at me. When my legs tired, I would remember Ázzuen plodding trustfully beside me and keep on going.

And, then, when I thought I could walk no more, the night became darker and the ground beneath my paws cooler. Trees rose above my head, dimming the light of the moon. I had crossed the great plain. The dreamwolf faded with the moonlight and everything in my body hurt. Being alone in the forest didn't seem much better than being alone on the plain, and my weary nose could not pick up the scent of my pack. At last I caught a familiar scent.

"I waited for you." Yllin stood tall at the edge of the wood. "I knew you'd find your way here, little sister. And welcome to you, smallpup." She grinned at Ázzuen. I was too tired to do anything but gratefully touch my nose to her lowered muzzle. We found the pack-scent and walked the last hour to the gathering place and fell into a heap of exhaustion.

Ruuqo didn't even greet us. He just looked over at Rissa, who gazed at him with a challenge in her eyes.

"She can stay," he said, "until her winter coat comes in. But I make no promises that I will make her pack."

I didn't know what he meant, but Yllin had spoken of something similar. I didn't have the energy left to figure it out. And after a moment I didn't care, for Rissa, and then the rest of the pack, came to me and licked me in greeting, and called me by my name.

3

The place that was to be our home as we grew strong and learned the ways of the pack was a wide, shady clearing an hour's walk, for a pup, from the forest edge. It was surrounded by the same spruce trees and juniper bushes as our den site, and smelled like safety. A small hill at the north side of the clearing gave a good view into the forest. I learned later that Ruuqo always chose places with lookout spots—hillocks, or rocks, or stumps of fallen trees—to better protect the pack. Two sturdy oaks stood sentinel at the west entrance to the clearing, and a fallen spruce ran nearly from one end to the other. There was springy moss to lie in and soft dirt to play in, and the tall trees would give us shade in the hot summer afternoons to come. I could hear a spring full of good water burbling nearby. It was worth the long, terrifying walk and the sore leg.

Ázzuen, Marra, and I stood together at the roots of the fallen spruce, looking in wonder at this good place. Borlla and Unnan huddled together by a large boulder, whispering and looking at us. Reel poked his nose between them, trying to hear what they

were saying. I knew they were planning some harm for us. But before they could make trouble, old Trevegg trotted across the clearing, bringing them over to where we stood. I resisted the temptation to knock Borlla ears over tail when she stepped hard on Ázzuen's injured paw, making him yelp.

"Listen, pups," Trevegg said before Ázzuen or I could retaliate, "this is Fallen Tree Gathering Place, one of the five gathering places, or homesites, in our territories. You must learn it and remember it."

Trevegg was the oldest wolf in the pack, and Ruuqo's uncle. He had the same dark-rimmed eyes as Ruuqo, but Ruuqo's eyes always seemed anxious while Trevegg's were open and kind. The fur around his muzzle and eyes was faded to a lighter shade than the rest of his coat, giving him a gentle, welcoming appearance. He opened his mouth to breathe in the scents of our new home.

"Gathering places are where we come to plan hunts, and to develop strategies to defend our territories. They are where wolves who have wandered from the pack can return, and where pups can grow strong while the pack hunts. Wolves must wander to eat, but good, safe, and healthy gathering places make a pack strong." He gazed across the clearing. "Never forget a gathering place, for you never know when you may need it again."

I lifted my face to the wind, tasting the acorn-tinted scent of Fallen Tree. I memorized the rippling of the breeze in the bushes and buried my nose in the dirt that smelled of my pack.

"Watch, pups!" Yllin called from halfway across the clearing. She dropped onto one shoulder and rolled onto her back, turning to and fro in the dirt and grunting happily. She and her brother, Minn, were just a year old, Rissa and Ruuqo's pups from the year before. Although they were nearly as large as the grown wolves, and considered almost full members of the pack, they were not really grown up. We watched her curiously.

"When you leave part of yourself on the earth," Trevegg explained as Yllin continued to roll gleefully in the dirt, "on a bush or a tree, or on the body of an animal whose spirit has returned to the moon, you speak to the Balance." Trevegg seemed younger when he taught us, years of hunting and fighting lifting from his face. "The Balance is what holds the world together. The Ancients—Sun, Moon, Earth, and Grandmother Sky—who rule the lives of all creatures, created the Balance so that no one creature might grow too strong and cause problems for all others. You will learn more of the Ancients," he said sternly as Ázzuen opened his mouth to interrupt with a question, "if you survive your first winter. Know now that they are more powerful than any creature. And know that we must obey their rules, and the rules of the Balance. Every creature," he continued, "every plant, every breath of air is part of the Balance. With everything we do, we must remember to respect the world we have been granted. So even as we take things—water from the river, meat from a successful hunt—we leave part of ourselves as well, to show our gratitude for what the Ancients have given us."

One by one, we dropped onto one shoulder and rolled in a spot where weeks before a rabbit had died. A pungent fox had long since carried him away, but the scent of what had been life remained. We coated ourselves with the scent, adding our own essences to the spot and claiming Fallen Tree Gathering Place as our home. I knew then what I had not known before: Ruuqo could decide whether or not I was a member of the Swift River pack, but no one could take from me that I was wolf, and part of the Balance. I noticed Unnan watching me, a conniving look on his weaselly face. *I'm here,* I thought, *and you can't do a thing about it.* I raised my head and took in more of my new home.

All at once, after the effort of marking my scent and exploring the gathering place, a wave of exhaustion overcame me, and I could barely stand on my feet. I spied a soft patch of moss under the shade of the big boulder. Feeling as if I walked barely ahead of sleep, I made wearily for this good resting spot. Before I got halfway there, Borlla and Unnan blocked my way in a quick and hostile scuffle of dust. Borlla narrowed her eyes.

"You aren't going to our rock, are you?"

My fur bristled and I envisioned taking a piece out of her neck. She opened her mouth and panted, waiting for me to attack. Ázzuen's voice pierced my fury.

"Kaala, over here." He and Marra had found a shady spot in the shelter of the fallen spruce. I shook off my anger—I wanted sleep more than I wanted to teach Borlla a lesson. I trotted over to my friends, turning up my nose at Borlla and Unnan, and lifting up my tail to show them my backside. The ground under the tree was wonderfully soft and moist, and just the right amount of sun kept the patch from getting too cold. Gratefully, I sank into the welcoming earth and nuzzled the soft fur of Ázzuen's neck. Marra rested her head on Ázzuen's back and fell asleep almost immediately. But Ázzuen looked at me for a long time.

"Thank you," he said at last. "I don't think I would have made the journey if you hadn't helped me."

"We helped each other," I said, embarrassed.

"No," he said, shaking his dark gray head and making Marra turn in her sleep. "You're the strong one."

I wanted so much to tell him that I wasn't so strong, to tell him about the spiritwolf who had come to me on the plain and lent me her strength. Our journey across the plain and our fights with the other pups had forged a bond between Ázzuen and me, and I was tired of being alone in the pack. But I didn't tell him. The last thing I needed was to be seen as any more different than I already was. I just gave Ázzuen a quick touch on his face, and allowed myself to sleep.

A sharp pain in my ear awoke me. As I tried to stand, the pain got worse. Someone was tearing my ear off. Shaking my head and wondering what in the name of the moon was after me now, I tried to back away, but could not free myself. Ázzuen snored beside me, oblivious to this new threat. I couldn't see Marra, but could smell that she was nearby. I twisted onto my back, trying to see my foe, but only succeeded in increasing the pain in my ear.

I twisted farther, until I thought my head would come off my neck, and looked into a pair of beady brown eyes set in a sleek, small head. I saw long, black feathers, and smelled leaves and wind. A large, black, glossy-coated bird had me in its grasp, pinching my ear in its sharp beak. It made a soft gurgling sound in its throat, and looked extremely pleased with itself. It saw me watching it and tugged harder on my ear. I whimpered. The bird released my ear and looked at me with shiny eyes. Then it gave an earsplitting shriek.

Tasty babywolf.
It awakens just in time.
Oops. No meal for me.

The bird's strange way of speaking confused me, and I stared dumbly at it. It stared back, waiting to see what I would do. I looked around the clearing for help from the rest of the pack. I saw Minn and Yllin chasing and being chased by more of the black birds while the older wolves watched. I didn't understand why they didn't help. Was this another test? I wanted to cry and curl up in a little ball, but I was wary of that sharp beak. The bird did not attack again at first, but regarded me, head cocked to one side. I wearily stumbled to my feet and growled at it. Even to my own ears, my growl sounded half-hearted. Marra was awake and standing stock-still beside me, watching the bird. I shoved Ázzuen with my hip to get his attention. He slowly opened his eyes and looked at the large bird. His eyes widened and his mouth dropped open. He yelped and scooted behind me. The bird gave a cry of laughter and flapped its wings, sending twigs and dirt over us and making us cough.

Hide now, babywolf.
Maybe raven won't catch you.
At least not this time.

I looked again for help from my pack. The clearing was in chaos. The senior wolves had finally joined the fray but, to my surprise, did not seem to be taking the fight seriously. Birds swooped down on wolves, trying to grab their tails, their ears, their rumps, anything they could get in their beaks. The wolves snapped at the air, trying to get a mouthful of bird. But they were not snarling in anger or hurting the birds. They yipped excitedly and waved their tails.

"They're having fun," Marra said slowly. "They're playing with the stupid birds."

At first I thought she was crazy but, as I watched Ruuqo flip head over paws in pursuit of a bird, I realized she was right. I tried to count the birds in the clearing, but they moved so quickly it was hard to tell how many there were. I guessed there might be twelve of them. One especially large bird, bigger than Yllin's head, landed atop her neck, and flew away again before she could snap at it. It flapped just above her head, laughing at her.

My attacker had been watching, but suddenly whipped its head around to seize my other ear. It pulled hard.

"Let go of me, bird!" I squealed.

Let go, oh let go.
The littlewolf is so scared.
Crybaby wolfling.

It let go of my ear and, as I shook my head in relief, made a grab for my nose. I yelped, pulling away and tumbling into Azzuen.

"Stupid bird," I said under my breath. "I should bite you in half."

It looked at me and laughed, then took flight with a whooshing of wings as both Minn and Yllin pounced on it from behind.

"Come on, Rainsong," Yllin said. "Leave the pups be. Or are you afraid of a grown wolf?" She turned to Minn. "I think she's afraid of grown wolves," Yllin said, eyes dancing. I was impressed that she spoke so boldly. But then again, she was a lot bigger than the stupid bird.

"Who's a grown wolf?" Rainsong said, dropping her strange way of speaking. "I remember when you were a mewling, puke-eating pup." She flew over Yllin's head and Yllin leapt high in the air, twisting her body in an amazing acrobatic leap. I thought for sure she would snatch the bird from the air. But Rainsong was too quick. She gave a yell of laughter as she flew up and away. Marra, who was the most adventurous of us, took an experimental swipe at the bird, but she was too small to reach her.

"Yllin, why do they attack us?" Ázzuen's voice shook with fear and fatigue. "I thought we would be safe here." He glared at the birds. "Why don't we just kill them?"

Keeping an eye on Rainsong, Yllin snorted. "They aren't attacking us, stupid. Haven't you learned the difference between fight and play? If you can't even play, how're you going to hunt?"

"Be nice, Yllin. You were a pup once, too," Rissa said, trotting over to us.

She shook a raven from her back, its black feathers a startling contrast to her white coat. Her eyes were bright as she turned to growl at the same raven, who was trying in vain to catch hold of her fast-moving tail. Rissa was thin, still, from birthing and feeding pups, but her energy was high and I felt my own tail begin to wag in response to her good spirits. Yllin gave an unapologetic snort and chased after two ravens. "I was never that much of a curl-tail," she said.

"She was, you know," Rissa said, looking fondly after her daughter.

When Borlla, Unnan, and Reel saw that Rissa was paying attention to us, they pelted over from their boulder. Two ravens, in close pursuit, stopped short as the pups tumbled into Rissa and hid behind her. With mocking cries, the birds flew to join the rest of their friends.

"Listen, pups," Rissa said, giving gentle bites to get our attention. "There are creatures that are not wolf and are not prey or rival." We must have looked confused, for she thought a moment and began again. "In the world, there is wolf, and there is not-wolf. Most important among wolf, there is pack. The good of the pack outweighs the good of any one wolf. Pack is more important than life, more important than the hunt." She let that sink in, and then went on. "After pack, there are wolves that are not pack, some of which are our enemies, some our friends. Among not-wolf, there is prey, which we kill. Any prey may be killed as long as you follow the rules of the hunt."

"How do you know if something is prey?" Ázzuen asked. I'd noticed that he was always the one to ask a question, and to figure things out more quickly than the rest of us.

"You'll know," said Yllin, who had returned, panting, to join us. "If it runs, you chase it!"

"It is somewhat more complicated than that," Rissa said, opening her jaws in a smile. "You will learn more when you are old enough to join the hunt. Listen!" she said, swatting Unnan lightly as he crouched to pounce on Marra's tail. "In addition to prey, there are rivals, some of which are more dangerous than others. Foxes, dholes, and many of the hunter birds must be dealt with, and kept from stealing prey, but are not much of a threat to a grown wolf. Dholes hunt like we do in a pack, but are smaller than we are, and rarely challenge us. Bears, longfangs, rock lions, and even hyenas can kill a grown wolf and are true danger. And then there are the other creatures, all of whom are part of the Balance, but who play no great part in the life of a wolf."

I thought of all the creatures I'd already seen, and how many more there were that I had not yet met, the insects and small animals of the woods, the owls I had so feared. It seemed like too much for my mind to hold. I did my best to understand it all, and to remember what Rissa was telling us.

"Then," she said, watching two ravens sneak up on Ruuqo, "there are creatures that are almost-wolf. They are the creatures closest to us in the Balance and are granted many of the privileges of wolf. Ravens are such creatures. They help us find food and improve the hunt." She shook herself again, dislodging Rainsong, who had landed on her back, and was swaying in time with her words.

It was a lot to think about. I noticed Unnan and Borlla squirming impatiently, as Ázzuen sat still, trying to puzzle it all out.

"It's not that difficult, pups," Yllin said, poking Ázzuen in the ribs with her nose. "We join them in games, and they lead us to good hunting."

"Take my word for it, pups," Rissa said with a laugh. "Raven play is good practice for hunting. And it is never too early to prepare for the hunt." She trotted to the center of the clearing where Minn, Ruuqo, and Trevegg were waging war with several ravens. Unnan, Borlla, Marra, and Reel ran after her, but Ázzuen looked after them skeptically.

"This is playing?" he said, too softly for anyone but me to hear. He sighed. "Come on, Kaala. We'd better go play."

He sounded so like a little oldwolf that I had to laugh as he trudged to join the rest of the pack.

Tentatively, I snuck up behind a smallish raven who stood apart from the others. I felt the thrill of the hunt pounding in my chest and I narrowed my field of vision to focus on his feathery back and tail. I was sure he couldn't see me as I crept up behind him. I would have him for sure. I bunched up my legs behind me, ignoring the pain in my sore leg, and leapt. The little raven spun around and flew above me, flapping his wings in my face.

Clumsy wolf can't jump.
Tlitoo is too fast for you.
Raven always wins.

Exasperated, I sat on the ground and glared at the bird as he regarded me. He blinked several times, and opened his beak again as if to speak. I was as surprised as he was when Minn almost caught him from behind. Feathers ruffled, Tlitoo retreated to the protection of the larger ravens. But he kept watching me with an intense and very unnerving stare.

At some signal I did not see, wolves and ravens ceased their play. The largest, glossiest raven settled beside Ruuqo on the boulder that Borlla and Unnan had earlier claimed.

"So, Sleekwing," Ruuqo said, speaking to the raven as an equal, "what have you seen of prey in the valley? The Great Plain is empty of elk."

"The prey still leaves the valley, but there is some good hunting. The elkryn remain." It seemed the ravens could speak normally when they wished. Sleekwing was an elegant bird, standing tall and proud. The other ravens were silent as he spoke. Now that everyone had stopped flying around, I could see that there were only seven ravens, not twelve as I had thought before, and that most of them were almost as small as Tlitoo.

Sleekwing continued. "Stone Peak wolves and humans are taking whatever they can, but there is prey left for clever wolves. The horses are still plenty. The elkryn feisty."

"Just what we need," Minn said. "Feisty elkryn."

"Ah," said Sleekwing. "Last year's pup." More sober than Rainsong, he was still not above teasing Minn. "Feisty prey makes you work harder, keeps you from getting fat and slow."

He eyed Minn slyly. "The aurochs are tasty. A long-fang killed one for us just last week and it was splendid. Do you want to catch one, Minn-ling?"

Trevegg had told us of aurochs. He said that one of them could feed a pack for weeks, but that they are large and dangerous. One of their males could be the weight of twenty wolves.

Minn's pride was wounded.

"I can hunt aurochs!" He appealed to Ruuqo. "Why don't we hunt aurochs? That would show the Stone Peaks who runs the valley."

"We do not hunt aurochs when we can find other prey," Ruuqo said patiently. "Let the Greatwolves have them and the broken ribs that go with them. It's bad enough we must hunt the elkryn." He looked at the raven. "Leave him be, Sleekwing."

"What's the fun in that?" Sleekwing looked as petulant as a scolded pup. "Since when are wolves so serious? 'Mustn't hurt the littlewolf's feelings or he won't hunt well. O poor little wolf.'" He cawed as Minn leapt to grab him.

Slow wolf, dawdle wolf.
Won't ever catch the auroch.
Poor hungry wolfling.

"Sleekwing," Ruuqo said warningly.

Minn-ling scared to hunt.
Wants to eat raven instead.
Sad. Raven too smart.

Ruuqo growled, and not entirely in play. He leapt at Sleekwing, who retreated to the fallen tree. Rainsong flew to his side.

"You lack a sense of humor, Ruuqo," Sleekwing said, preening his ruffled feathers.

"No wonder you look like an oldwolf before your time," Rainsong added. "No offense to you, handsome Trevegg." She blinked her eyes at old Trevegg, who grinned at her.

"Maybe pretty Rissa will find another mate," Sleekwing said, raising his wings as if to fly at Ruuqo.

"I said *enough,* Sleekwing," Ruuqo snapped. "Now, unless you want to live on bugs and berries this season, tell me where the prey runs."

Sleekwing shook himself and settled back with an injured sigh. Out of the corner of my eye, I saw the small raven, Tlitoo, creeping up to stand just beside Sleekwing. The leader bird must have seen him, but did not chase him away.

"The humans and Stone Peaks drive prey from the Great Plain." I was surprised to hear him suddenly so serious. Ázzuen pushed in beside me to better hear what the raven said. "Neither Stone Peak pack nor humans will share with us. And something is wrong." He glared at Ruuqo as he started to interrupt him. "*More* wrong, wolf, and no, I do not know what it is. But there is something wrong with the prey. Something wrong in the air. We are concerned." He shook himself, and the mischief returned to his eyes. "But the Tall Grass plains are crowded, the antelope and horses are plenty, and the elkryn roam the territory. They will return to the plain. With our help you will find good hunting."

"What are the humans? Who are the Stone Peaks?" Marra asked impatiently from beside me.

"Be quiet," Ázzuen whispered. "I want to hear."

"The Tall Grass plain is too near Stone Peak territory," Ruuqo said, ignoring us. "It is contested. And it's too close to the humans' current homesite."

"If that is where the prey is, that is where we go," Rissa said decisively. "I'm tired of the Stone Peaks taking over our lands bit by bit. It's time we took what's ours."

"I will keep that in mind," Sleekwing said, with a gleam in his eye. "Come, let us plan for the coming hunts. I am bored with eating moles and voles. They have too many bones." He looked longingly at us pups as if he would like to swoop down upon us again, but gave a sharp sigh and flew to Rissa at the lookout rock.

Ruuqo, Trevegg, and two ravens joined them. They huddled, whispering together by the boulder. I tried to hear what they were saying, but they spoke too quietly. The rest of the wolves stretched and rested, preparing for the coming night's hunt as the ravens hopped lazily about the clearing. I sat, watching the activity around me.

Something pulled sharply at my tail. I swallowed a yelp. I didn't want to be called a babywolf. I turned to see the small raven, Tlitoo, watching me.

"Hello, babywolf. Come with me." His voice was lighter and crisper than that of the larger ravens. He walked to the edge of the clearing, stopping where the tall oaks stood. He turned to wait for me.

Nursing my bitten tail, I looked him over. "I'm not allowed to leave the gathering place," I said suspiciously. He probably had brothers and sisters waiting to pounce on me on the other side of the trees. He gave a croak.

Babywolf, whinewolf.
Whimpers, scared of own shadow.
Weevilwolf no fun.

I just looked at him until he flew back to me. He brought his beak close to my ear, and I stiffened, fearful of another bite. "The

Bigwolves say to come, Kaala Smallteeth." He flew off before I could answer, alighting on a high branch of the taller oak.

Wondering at my folly, I followed, checking behind me to make sure no one would see me leave the clearing. I stopped just outside the oak tree entrance, in a rocky patch of grass. Tlitoo flew down to meet me.

"The Bigwolves told me about you," he said. "You are not a true wolf."

"I am so!" I said, stung. "I made it across the Great Plain. I am named. I am Swift River." I ignored the voice in my head that reminded me that Ruuqo had not really accepted me, that I was still an outsider.

Tlitoo turned his head side to side. "All I know is that the Bigwolves say you are more and less than wolf, and that I am to watch over you. I am more and less than raven, too," he said proudly. "I am named for our ancestor, who spoke to the Ancients on behalf of all creatures. I bear his mark," he said, raising a wing to show me a white crescent on its underside. "I am born to either save or destroy my clan. As are you."

"Do you want to tell me why you made me come with you? I'm risking a lot of trouble by being here."

Tlitoo quorked quietly. "If you are forever worrying about getting in trouble, we will never get anything done."

"And what is it we are supposed to get done, if you know so much?"

He quorked again, blinking his eyes at me.

"Babywolf," he said impatiently, "the Bigwolves told me to come to you. They told me to tell you to look for them and that you are to be careful not to get in trouble with your pack. They told me that I am to watch over you and you are to watch over me. That is all."

His annoyance amused me. I had the feeling the Greatwolves had not told him as much as he would have liked. I wanted to find out more from him. I wanted to know what the Greatwolves had really said, but I didn't get the chance to ask. When Rissa called angrily to me, he took flight, and I pelted back to the clearing.

"Don't wander off," Rissa said as I slunk back into the gathering place. "Do you want to be a bear's meal? You don't know enough to be in the forest on your own." I saw Unnan and Borlla smirking behind her and knew they'd told her I had left. "I know you are glad to be with the pack, Kaala, but do not forget you still have much to learn." She licked me once and trotted off to rejoin Ruuqo and the ravens in their discussions. I looked off into the forest and saw a flicker of black and heard a rustling of leaves. I knew that somewhere in the bushes, a pair of beady brown eyes was watching me.

4

The warm weather grew hot and the days long. As our bodies strengthened, we did not need so much rest and we began to keep the hours of wolf. We slept in the hot afternoons and played, learned, and ate in the cool dawn and dusk and in the moonlit night. We learned that the moon was not always the same, but rather changed each day in a constant and comforting cycle that helped us track time and seasons. Trevegg told us that by the time the moon grew round and bright five more times, we would be ready to hunt with the pack. We practiced, hunting the voles that ventured into our homesite, and learned more of play from Tlitoo and the other young ravens of Sleekwing's family. Twice the moon was a bright, full circle, making me shiver in memory of our long walk across the plain.

I tasted my first meat at that gathering place, when Rissa would no longer feed us her rich milk, and the pack brought us back meat in their bellies. We were mystified at first, when Trevegg lowered his face to us. We smelled meat, but couldn't figure out where the scent was coming from. Then Ázzuen nar-

rowed his clever eyes and poked his nose in the corner of Trevegg's faded muzzle. The oldwolf heaved twice, and good meat came from his mouth to the ground below. Once we all got the idea, we nudged the rest of the wolves and they gave us fresh, soft meat.

We grew strong and restless, itching to explore the world beyond Fallen Tree. We pestered our elders tirelessly, urging them to let us go with them as they hunted or explored the territories, but they would not take us more than a half hour's journey from home. Finally, three moons after we arrived at Fallen Tree, we got our chance.

Sleekwing and Rainsong had flown lazily into the gathering place just after the break of dawn. Though we prefer to hunt at night, ravens are mostly day creatures, and we are happy to follow them to prey in the daytime. Sleekwing landed atop Ruuqo's head as the wolf surveyed the clearing. Irritably, he snapped at the bird.

"Ungrateful wolf!" Sleekwing said indignantly. "If you do not want the news I bring, I will go to the Vole Eater pack. They will welcome me."

Ruuqo yawned. "Vole Eaters never bring you anything better than a half-grown deer. If you start sharing prey with them, it will be a lean year for you."

"I can always eat little pups if I get hungry," Sleekwing retorted, and abruptly swooped at me and Ázzuen. We were ready for him. I dove to the right, Ázzuen to the left. Sleekwing pulled up short, and barely avoided crashing into the ground.

"You are going to have to be faster than that to catch a Swift River pup," Rissa said. "What news do you have for us, Sleekwing?"

Sleekwing preened his feathers. "Since you ask, Rissa," he

said, glaring at Ruuqo, "there is a mare on the Tall Grass plain, freshly killed, and just one small bear eating it."

Rissa opened her jaws, showing her teeth. "Then I think we should relieve the bear of its meal. How did a slow-bear catch a horse, anyway?"

"It was lame," Rainsong answered, "and half dead already. But the bear acts as if she was the only one on the plain that could kill it. She is not a fast bear, nor a strong one. Brave wolves could take the prey from her." Her eyes gleamed in challenge.

"I thought we were supposed to catch prey ourselves!" Ázzuen said, startled.

"Meat is meat, wolfling," Minn said. "If a stupid bear kills something for us, we are happy to take the meat. Bears steal our prey often enough."

"The greedy bear will not share with us," Sleekwing croaked. "She takes the whole horse for herself and threatens us if we come near. You will share with your raven friends, will you not?"

"If you get us to the horse before the bear has eaten it all, we will share." Rissa gave another sharp-toothed grin. "Will you show us the way, clever Sleekwing?"

"It is far for pups," Sleekwing said, looking us over. "Wolf puppies grow up so very slowly. Do you think the babywolves will make it to the Tall Grass plains?"

I pricked up my ears. Did this mean we were at last allowed to see real prey? I could hear Ázzuen's heart speed up, and Marra's breath come in quick pants.

"My pups are strong," Rissa said serenely, refusing to rise to Sleekwing's taunt. "They are Swift River wolves." I pulled myself up tall. I was concerned about another long journey, but wasn't about to show anyone my fear. And we were not so small. Our heads came almost to the hips of the adults of the pack. Ázzuen yipped in excitement. Unnan rolled his eyes at us and nudged Borlla, making fun of Ázzuen. But he could not keep his own tail from waving in anticipation of our adventure.

Yllin and Minn caught the excitement of the hunt to come. Yllin playfully took Minn's muzzle in her jaws, and he pawed her to the ground. She ran from him and leapt over a mossy boulder, splashing him with muddy water as she landed in a puddle. Grinning, she rolled on her back, inviting him to pounce on her. When he leapt at her, Yllin twisted her body around, tackling him, and climbed atop the boulder, shaking muddy water from her coat onto his upturned face.

As the youngwolves played, Rissa prepared the pack for the hunt, going from wolf to wolf to strengthen the bonds of pack. If a hunt is to succeed, Trevegg had told us, the pack must work as one. Every wolf must be able to smell her packmates' intentions and anticipate her packmates' thoughts. Each wolf must know that if she drives prey to a pack member, that wolf will be ready. So before every hunt, the hunt leader will make sure that every wolf is focused on the good of the pack and the success of the hunt. This coming together is important before journeys and before making decisions that affect that pack. But it is never more important than before a hunt.

Rissa placed her head on Trevegg's shoulder and then nosed Werrna's dark muzzle. Werrna was Ruuqo and Rissa's second in command, a stiff and stolid wolf. The scars on her face were a result of battles fought when she was young. She was a strong warrior, and planned all of Swift River's battles. Her dark gray face and black-tipped ears seemed always stiff and she was the only wolf who rarely played with us pups. I couldn't figure her out. She returned Rissa's caress awkwardly, then sat to watch as the other wolves played. Snorting at her, Rissa trotted over to Ruuqo and placed her front paws on his back. I thought he might be angry with her, but he opened his jaws in a grin and rolled onto his back, wrestling her as if they were no more than pups. Minn and Yllin ran to join the other wolves, pressing their bodies low to the ground so the older wolves would include them. Even Borlla and Unnan joined in, as did Marra and Ázzuen. I sat watching, feeling a little left out.

With a dusty sneeze, Ruuqo got to his feet. Immediately the pack ceased their play and watched him intently. Rissa sat back on her haunches and opened her throat, letting forth a great howl. Ruuqo walked over to her, sat down, and howled with her. One by one, the adult wolves answered, and their voices filled the gathering place. Each howl held a different tone, but they came together in the sound of the Swift River pack. In their howls, I heard the call to the hunt.

"Come pups," Rissa said. "This is your hunt, too."

Our voices were not as strong as the adults', but we joined in song just the same. The vibrations from the howls sent our blood racing. The hearts of the pack began to beat as one, and our breathing fell into rhythm with theirs. I saw fierceness and focus come into the eyes of every wolf in the pack, and felt my own eyes glaze and then focus more sharply than before. The inside of my head rang with the howls and I began to see the world differently. I no longer smelled the varied scents of the gathering place, or heard the rustlings around me. I heard only Rissa's call and smelled the scent of my pack as wolves began to bolt from the clearing. All my senses were focused on following the pack to our next meal. With a nudge from Trevegg, we followed the adult wolves out of the clearing and into the woods.

I was surprised at how strong I had become. In the weeks at Fallen Tree, I had grown as big as Marra, and bigger than Ázzuen and Reel, and my play with the ravens had made me wiry and sturdy. Instead of lagging behind the other pups, I raced Unnan and Borlla for the lead. The woods thinned as we ran, sparse birch trees replacing the denser spruces and pines of our gathering place. It was a perfect morning, not yet too hot to run, and the sweet smell of late summer flowers made me giddy. It was all I could do not to stop and smell every new flower and bush, but the pack ran at a steady trot, and all of us pups kept pace. None of us wanted to be sent back to the gathering place in disgrace.

Then, all at once, a sharp, pungent smell overwhelmed me, and I stopped short, almost falling face-first in the dirt. The other pups had stopped as well. First Borlla, then Unnan plunged into the bush from which the scent came. A moment later the rest of us followed, intoxicated by the rich scent. Ázzuen was the last one in. I heard a scrabbling sound, and turned to see him being dragged out by his tail, a look of surprise on his face. Werrna's scarred face, wrinkled in annoyance, poked back into the bush, and she grabbed Marra by the scruff, pulling her out, too. Ruuqo's voice brought the rest of us scrambling.

"Pups!" he bellowed. "Do not leave the pack. Do not stop a hunt! Come out now, or you can live on sticks and leaves."

"Never let pups near dream sage," Werrna growled, disgusted.

"Last pup out is the last to eat!" Yllin called.

Reel, who was closest to the edge of the bush, darted out. I would've been next out, but Borlla and Unnan blocked my exit. Then they shoved me deep into the bush before scrambling out.

It took me several moments to disentangle myself from the thick branches and fragrant leaves. Then, once I was freed, I was disoriented, and scrabbled in the wrong direction twice before catching pack-scent coming from behind me. Sneezing and shaking dirt from my fur, I pushed my way out of the bush to find the pack waiting impatiently for me. Borlla and Unnan were smirking.

"Pup, if you cannot keep up, you must not need to eat. You'd best not fall behind again." Ruuqo glared at me. I smarted at the unfairness of it. He was not nearly as harsh with the other pups. Without another look at me, Ruuqo led the pack off again.

Keep up, I thought. *I'll do more than keep up.*

My legs felt strong and sure as I crouched down and leapt, sailing over a surprised Azzuen. Then I ran. I felt as if my legs could take me anywhere I wanted to go. Yllin whuffed in encouragement as I raced past the others. To my surprise, Marra was the only pup to keep up with me. Though she was considerably smaller than Borlla and Unnan, her legs were long and strong, her bones light. She ran with an easy lope beside me. I was panting hard, but she was not. I had the feeling she could pass me up if she wanted to. Gasping for breath, I grinned at her.

"Let's show those curl-tails," I said to her, and increased my speed, overtaking Borlla and gaining on Werrna's gray behind. I knew the adults could run faster if they wanted to—our heads still came only to their hips, after all—but I didn't care. We ran, faster than we ever had before. The scents of the forest whipped into my nose, the dry summer dirt lifting in a dust storm under my paws. I stumbled briefly, rolling over in a somersault, and Marra circled around me as I got to my feet. I was faintly aware of Ázzuen trying to keep up with us, his breath rasping in his throat. I knew I should wait for him, that it would be the kind thing to do, but I was having too much fun.

I was so excited at being out of the clearing, at being strong and fast, and at the overwhelming scents and sounds all around me, that I did not catch the aroma of meat or the pungent scent of unknown creature at the edge of the woods. Rissa put her head down sharply to stop my headlong run. Marra smacked into me from behind.

"It's good to be fleet, pups," Rissa said, laughing quietly, "but not without control. You do not want to run into *that*." The woods had ended abruptly, and a sharp slope led to a dry, grassy field. Late summer wildflowers dotted the tall grass, most of which had turned a golden brown. The adult wolves had halted at the edge of the trees. Rissa pointed her muzzle toward the plain, where a huge brown beast ripped at a horse carcass. The pungent scent came from it, mingled with the overpowering aroma of meat. Far across the field, stout horses grazed watchfully.

"How can they just stand there when one of their family is being eaten?" Marra asked. She was not even breathing hard from our run. Ázzuen stumbled up to us, gasping, and looked at me reproachfully.

"The horses are not like us," Minn answered contemptuously. "They are prey and do not mourn the same way we do. Their herds are large and not close, like wolf families. Death does not grieve them much."

"I am not so sure, Minn," old Trevegg said. "How can we know what they feel? I have seen a dam stand over her fallen colt for two full days, keeping us away from a meal. And I once heard of an elkryn who refused to eat after his mother was killed, and died in the spot where she lay." His voice was thoughtful. "We must kill if we are to live, but do not make light of the life we take. We must thank the moon for each creature we are given, and to do so must respect the creatures that we kill. Each one is part of the Balance."

Minn bowed his head in acknowledgment before his restless eyes returned to the plain. An impatient growl rose in his throat.

"Quiet!" Ruuqo and Rissa hissed together.

"You must learn to be restrained, Minn, or you will never lead a hunt," Rissa chided. Minn lowered his ears in apology.

"Pups," Ruuqo ordered, "stay hidden. Do not follow until we tell you it is safe, or I will chew your ears off and stick them to your behinds with pine sap. Minn, Yllin," he said to the yearlings, "do not lose your heads. I know you think you are grown wolves, but follow Werrna's orders."

"It's not a very big bear," Minn muttered. When Ruuqo glared at him, he lowered his head again. "I'll follow, leaderwolf," he said meekly. Yllin just narrowed her eyes, watching the bear intently.

The bear looked big enough to me. She hunched over the dead horse, but when she stood to look uneasily over the plain, she stood nearly as tall as four wolves. I couldn't believe Ruuqo and Rissa were thinking of challenging her.

Rissa led the attack. She lowered herself to the ground and crept forward to the very edge of the trees, followed by the rest of the adults. "Werrna," she whispered to the secondwolf, "take Minn and Yllin and go around behind the clumsy bear. Wait for my signal and then join the fight. Remember, we are one wolf short."

My mother's the missing wolf. A wave of sadness overwhelmed me. The other pups took family for granted. They had their mother and father. Rissa took care of me as her own, but Ruuqo did not, and I had no one that was really mine. I wondered how long it would be before I was able to look for my mother. How could I possibly find her? I didn't even know where to start. I swallowed a whine of sorrow and frustration. I looked out at the bear and my packmates surrounding her. This was going to be my first time taking part in a packhunt, and my mother should be there with me.

I thought I hid my feelings well, but Ázzuen licked the side of my face, and I turned to see his eyes full of sympathy.

"Yllin says your mother was the fastest wolf in the pack," he said awkwardly. "She gave you her quickness."

My heart hurt in my chest, and I knew that if I spoke, my voice would tremble. I did not want to show Ázzuen my weakness and I could not think of any way to thank him for his sympathy, so I just lowered my face to my paws and watched the attack.

Werrna took the youngwolves along the outer edge of the trees, reappearing on the plain, a good thirty wolflengths on the bear's right side. They ran quickly past the bear far enough away to keep her from feeling threatened. She looked up, decided they were not a danger, and returned to her feast. Werrna stopped just beyond the bear, to its right, and said something to Yllin. Yllin sank to the earth in a patch of heather as Trevegg and Minn ran on. They circled the bear, stopping directly behind her, and Minn lowered himself to the ground as Werrna continued in a circle, stopping on a small hill at the bear's left flank. They had surrounded the bear on three sides, and she hadn't seen a thing. Rissa and the rest of us closed the circle, completing the trap.

"Are you sure six wolves are enough?" Trevegg asked. "I am not as fleet as I once was." He looked down, ashamed.

"You are our wisdom and our strength, fatherwolf," Rissa said, licking Trevegg's cheek. "How many bears have you fought in your time? If anyone knows how to trick a bear, it is you. Your grandniece and grandnephew are fleet and strong. The pack is powerful. And," she said, grinning toothily, "as Minn said, it is not a very large bear."

An impatient screech made us all jump.

"Are you going to wait until the sun burns a hole in the prairie?" Sleekwing shouted. We had not heard or smelled him come up behind us to land in the branches above. "There will be no horse left by the time you are done yapping."

Yap, yap, yapping, yap
Wolves yap while mangy bear eats.
Worms! Raven still hungry.

He leapt in the air with a loud caw, followed by Tlitoo and half a flock of ravens.

"So much for having the advantage of surprise," Ruuqo sighed, as the bear looked up at the loud birds.

"Well, then, no reason to wait until the moon rises," Rissa said. She made a soft, low sound, almost like a moan, deep in her throat. Werrna's gruff voice answered her from across the field. In that instant Minn charged the bear from behind. At the same time Yllin ran at the bear from its right side, and Werrna left her hillock and sprinted toward the bear.

The bear stood on her hind legs. Her paws were almost as big as a wolf's head, her teeth huge. When she saw three wolves running at her through the grass, she turned and roared in arrogant rage. I did not need to understand her language to know she was saying that no puny wolves were going to take her meal. Yllin, Minn, and Werrna darted in and out, just beyond the bear's deadly paws. Then all three wolves leapt at once and, while the bear was distracted by the attack, Rissa, Ruuqo, and Trevegg charged down the hill. For all his concern, Trevegg kept pace with the younger wolves, and the three of them leapt at the same time, sending the bear stumbling back in confusion. The wolves were no longer silent, and growled fiercely at the bear.

Next to me, Ázzuen yipped in fear. The bear was so angry, so ferocious, I could not believe our packmates would escape unscathed. But they darted in and out quickly and with great agility, turning this way and that. Above their heads, ravens shouted encouragement. I understood raven play better now. It had seemed a little like a waste of energy for adult wolves, but now I realized that wolves must keep their skills sharp if they are to fight bears. Yllin's graceful turns and Minn's leaps were just a variation of their games with Sleekwing and his family. I also understood why a weak wolf hurts the pack. If any one wolf did not do his or her share, the bear could easily kill or injure a packmate.

Foxes and hyenas, who had been hoping for scraps left by the bear, watched intently. A lone eagle flew overhead, only to be chased away by Sleekwing's clan. Ruthlessly the wolves attacked the bear, driving her away. She came back again, hoping to reclaim her kill, but six determined wolves were too much for her. I saw now that she was a young bear, not much older than Yllin or Minn, and she could not best a pack of clever wolves. Roaring her rage, she lumbered off across to the far side of the plain, over a small rise and out of sight. Werrna's team ran after her to make sure she would not return, while Rissa, Trevegg, and Ruuqo guarded the carcass, keeping the foxes and hyenas away.

Werrna and the young wolves came trotting back, tails and ears high. Growling fiercely at the foxes and greedy hyenas, they approached the kill. The pack danced around Ruuqo and Rissa, celebrating their success. Ruuqo settled on his belly to take the first bite of horse, and the rest of the pack arranged themselves around him, feeding on every part of the prey.

"Pups, come!" Rissa shouted.

We pelted down the hill to the horse carcass. As we neared it, Werrna called a warning.

"Watch your backs," she said gruffly, pointing her now bloody muzzle at the scavengers. "If the scroungers can't have our horse, they'd just as soon have a pup. Wait until the adults have fed, and then join in."

Keeping their eyes on the foxes, hyenas, and the lone eagle, the pack tore at the carcass. We pups waited as instructed. After the adults fed for what seemed like forever, we crept closer. We all hesitated. My mouth watered and my belly ached, but I was a little intimidated by the ferocity with which the pack was eating. Sleekwing and his flock ate beside them, unconcerned with the jaws and teeth tearing at the horse, but I feared the adults might bite us if we drew near. The bear had not had a chance to eat much of the horse, and the pack feasted. After what seemed like an eternity, Rissa called to us again.

"What are you waiting for, pups? You must get your own meat now. You are too old for us to bring you food in our bellies."

We crept toward the dead prey, stopping every few paces to check with Ruuqo and Rissa, who were feeding at the horse's middle, to make sure we would not get in trouble for approaching. We whined and begged, making ourselves small, ensuring the adults knew we came only at their sufferance. Minn and Yllin were at the front end of the horse, Trevegg and Werrna at the rear. As we approached, Minn and Yllin growled at us. Rissa growled back.

"Let the pups feed," she ordered. "You have had enough." Minn and Yllin, as the least senior of the adults, reluctantly stepped aside, still growling at us. Meekly, we took their place. I was a little hurt that Yllin had growled at me, but soon the fresh meat distracted me from any other thoughts.

I tore at the body of the mare. After the first bite, I couldn't stop myself from gorging. The taste of fresh meat consumed me, almost choked me. Determined to get as much of the meat as possible, I bit and growled and snarled at the other pups. My blood pounded in my veins and my heart felt as if it would burst through my chest. Suddenly I understood why Yllin had growled at us. Unnan tried to push me out of the way, but I bit him on the muzzle. He yelped and rolled away. When Marra accidentally bumped me, I growled at her, too, and she backed away from the prey. I even snarled at the head raven, Sleekwing, who responded by pecking me hard on the head. I winced in pain, but kept eating.

I was still tearing at the good meat when Minn's rumbling growl gave me scant warning as he swatted me from my meal. Yllin and Werrna pushed Borlla and Unnan away. We whined and tried to return to our meal, but the adult wolves chased us off, leaving us to watch them eat. It was then that I noticed that Ázzuen, Marra, and Reel had already been shoved aside. I dimly remembered biting all of them as they tried to feed. I felt a little sorry for them, but couldn't help thinking that if they didn't want to fight for their meal, they could just wait until I was done. I dropped to the ground and watched the adults. Borlla and Reel sat next to each other, and Unnan settled sleepily beside them. Tiredly, I got up and walked over to rest my head on Ázzuen's soft back, but he stalked away from me, settling down with Marra.

Yllin, who had been shoved away from the kill by Werrna, walked over to me, her belly thick with meat.

"It is good to be strong, little sister," she said, "but don't become a bully." She looked contemptuously at Borlla and Unnan, and snorted. "A leaderwolf must fight for what's hers, but must also look out for her pack, and use her strength carefully. A leaderwolf can't let anger and greed overcome her."

Yllin's argument would have been more convincing if she had not growled so ferociously at me earlier, and if she did not immediately trot over to the carcass, bite Minn on the leg, and take his place. But I saw what she meant when Marra shied away from me, and when Ázzuen, who had been so kind to me earlier in the day, turned up his little nose and refused to sleep beside me. Even Tlitoo just hovered above me. I looked up to see what he was doing, and he dropped a large pebble on my back.

"Greedy babywolf," he said, and flew away.

Shame washed over me. I should've known better. It was not long ago that I was the weakest wolf in the pack. I did not want to be a bully like Borlla and Unnan. I would have to remember to keep my temper in check, or I would be alone. I wanted to make it up to Ázzuen and Marra, but the meat weighed heavily in my belly and I couldn't keep my eyes open long enough to think of what to do.

A cool breeze awoke me and I looked up to see the adult wolves napping around us. It was the sleeping time, the hot part of the day that was no good for hunting or running. The rich smell of meat floated on the breeze, and my mouth watered. Werrna and Rissa slept next to the prey, guarding it. Several ravens hopped on what was left of the horse, eating as the wolves rested. They would also, I realized, give warning if any scroungers moved in. But they might not raise the alarm if I came near. Low on my belly, I crept back to the kill. I was as silent as I could be. I slipped between Werrna and Rissa, but just when I got a chewy piece of ligament in my mouth, Rissa lifted her head, growling as she came fully awake. When she saw it was only me, she relaxed, but nonetheless pushed me away from the kill.

"Enough, pup," she said. "No more for you now." She smiled. "You will burst if you eat more, and then we will have to pick the pieces up off the plain." She rested her head in her paws and closed her eyes.

I walked back to the other pups. I was bored with waiting for the rest of the pack to wake up, and I looked restlessly about the plain. I thought of waking Ázzuen, but didn't know if he was still mad at me. It was too hot to play, and the moon shape on my chest ached and itched in a way it never had before.

It was because of this aching that I was the one who saw the strange creatures first. There were two of them, and they watched us from across the plain, where the grasses ended and a new stand of trees began. The wind blew toward them, and none of us had picked up their scent. They stood on two legs, like the bear when it challenged us, but they were not as tall and were much more slender. Their forelegs hung straight down, and in them they held long sticks. I could not tell if they had only a little fur, or if some of their fur was very short. The wind changed, and I could smell them. Like the horses on the field, their skin was damp and gave off a strong, wet scent. It was an odd, juniper-acrid odor that I found familiar. Startled, I gave a warning bark.

The other wolves looked up at me annoyed. Then they caught the odd scent and saw what I was looking at.

The adult wolves rose at once, growling and surrounding the kill. The ravens took to the air, screeching. The strange creatures lowered their sticks to point them at us, and I saw that the ends of the sticks were sharp, like very large thorns. The creatures took several steps forward. They were still at least forty wolflengths away, but I had no idea how fast they could run. A long-fang could cover that distance in a breath.

Ruuqo growled deep in his throat and the fur on his back rose menacingly, making him look twice his normal size. He pulled his lips all the way back, showing every one of his forty-two sharp teeth. All around him the wolves of the Swift River pack growled and showed their fierceness. The two long-limbed creatures began to walk backward, sharpened sticks lowered, until they disappeared into the woods. The pack remained, growling and protecting the kill, for several moments.

"Werrna," Ruuqo said to his sharp-eared secondwolf, "are they gone?"

"They walk toward the river, leaderwolf," Werrna answered, dark-tipped ears straining forward. "We are safe for now." The ache in the crescent on my chest eased. I realized it had grown as the creatures moved nearer to us.

Ruuqo relaxed just a little. The other wolves settled down again, this time all of them staying at the kill. Rissa remained standing, a few wolflengths away, looking after the strange creatures. She stood tense, fur raised, tail still stiff behind her. Ruuqo noticed she had not yet joined the rest of the pack.

"Lifemate?" he said.

She was silent for a moment.

"I do not like this," she said. "I do not like it at all." She looked at us, then spoke to Ruuqo. "When the moon rises," she said, "we cross the river. It is time for the pups to learn about the humans."

5

The pack fell silent. I was aware of every sound around us—the ravens squabbling over bits of meat, small prey rustling in the bushes, even the fleas jumping on old Trevegg's fur. Ruuqo stared at Rissa.

"The humans," he said. "You want to take them to see the humans. When they are barely four moons old? I thought you were cautious with your pups, Rissa."

"I am cautious," she snapped, stalking up to him. "That is why I want to take them now. You had no problem marching them across the Great Plain, Ruuqo, for no other reason than to soothe your pride. This is my decision to make!"

Ruuqo stumbled back. If I hadn't been so shocked myself, I might have laughed at his astonishment. Upon seeing Rissa angry, I realized that anyone who thought Ruuqo was the only leader of the Swift River pack would have to think again. Sleekwing and Rainsong looked up from the kill, cocked their heads to listen for a moment, then fluffed their wings and returned to their feast.

"Humans," Ázzuen said softly, tasting the word. "They are not like other creatures. Are they prey or rival?" His brow wrinkled in confusion.

"Since when do the humans come to the Tall Grass plains in the summer?" Rissa demanded. "They should be at the mountain's edge this time of year, or at the salamander lake. Not here, not now. They no longer stay within their territory. They go wherever they want, whenever they want. Do you want the pups to come upon them on their own, with no preparation? In another moon they will be taking journeys by themselves. They must know before then."

Ruuqo growled, as if to make up for his earlier cowering. Rissa narrowed her eyes and pulled back her lips. She was no longer weak from bearing pups, and was nearly Ruuqo's weight. Her white fur was sleek and healthy, her shoulders broad and strong. It was clear she would not back down. The two leaders of the Swift River pack stood, glaring at each other. Around them the rest of the pack grew restless. No one likes dissent between the leaderwolves; it calls into question the strength of the pack. Trevegg walked up to Ruuqo and whispered something in his ear, but Ruuqo pushed him away. Minn whined anxiously, his thin frame trembling. My own stomach clenched in apprehension. What would happen if Ruuqo and Rissa truly fought? Beside me, I could feel Ázzuen shaking and could hear Marra's sharp breaths. Only Yllin and Werrna seemed interested as well as concerned. Yllin's eyes went from Rissa to Ruuqo and back again. I could almost hear her thoughts as she watched them, learning everything she could about being a leaderwolf. Werrna growled very softly in her throat as she observed the battle with a calm and calculated eye. Any show of weakness by either leaderwolf could mean the possibility of advancement for an ambitious wolf. I didn't think I'd like Werrna as a pack leader.

"I think only of the pack, Rissa." Ruuqo did not give ground, nor did he press Rissa into a spot where she would have to fight him. "The Stone Peak pack is strong and you must enter their territory to watch the humans," he said reasonably. "We cannot afford to lose pups this season. Come winter, we will need all the hunters we can get. Prey is not what it once was."

Anger surged in my chest. Ruuqo hadn't cared if Ázzuen and I died crossing the plain. I'd heard him telling Werrna that every pack loses pups, so what did a couple of weaklings matter? Now he pretended to care about our safety. I owed Ruuqo my loyalty, but I did not like him much. I stifled a growl.

But Rissa's voice softened as she, at least, saw concern in Ruuqo's reasoning.

"Yes, prey is not what it was," she said. "Prey is not what it was because the humans take it all. It will soon be time for our winter travels, Lifemate, and we will surely see them then. The pups must know, and they must know now."

"I don't like it," Ruuqo said, but the fur settled along his back. "If we are careful we can just ignore them until winter."

"Like Hiiln ignored them?" she asked.

Ruuqo winced. I had heard the adults whisper of Hiiln. He was a wolf who had left the pack before we were born.

"You can't ignore a long-fang at the kill, Lifemate," Rissa said. "You know as well as I do that this must be done. We will wait until moonrise. The humans are as blind as baby birds in the nighttime. It will be safe enough."

Ruuqo's shoulders drooped a little, but he dipped his head in acknowledgment.

"Minn and Trevegg will stay here with me to guard our meat. You will take Yllin and Werrna with you." Yllin and Werrna were strong fighters. Maybe Ruuqo did care what happened to us. Or at least he cared what happened to Rissa. Rissa placed her chin gently on Ruuqo's neck, and all around me I felt the pack relax. The ravens, who had seemed busy with their feast, gave pleased burbles. Then Sleekwing opened his beak and gave a warning squawk.

The strange tingling in my chest returned, and I knew the humans were coming back. Before I could give warning, Werrna's ears shot up.

"They return. And there are more of them." A rumble started deep in her chest. "They are coming to take our prey!"

We all turned to Ruuqo.

"How many are there?" he asked Werrna.

"Seven," Sleekwing answered from the kill, raising his wings. "All adults, all male." He gave a rasping sigh. "Better take what meat we can now. Before there's nothing left but bloody grass."

"You could come with us to the humans," Rissa said to the raven, amused.

"If you were not afraid to see them in the daytime we would," Rainsong answered. "*We* are not afraid of them. *We* go whenever we wish."

"The humans throw things at us," Tlitoo confided, landing beside me and Ázzuen. "But they leave good things to eat at the edge of their homesite. There is plenty to take if they don't see you." He blinked at us. "I will take you there if your pack will not. I know the way."

"May we fight them this time, leaderwolf?" Werrna's eyes were hard and eager.

I waited for Ruuqo to give the command to fight, hoping he would include us pups this time. I felt a thrill of excitement. I could understand why the adults would not let us fight the bear; one swipe from one of her paws and we would be dead. But surely they would let us join in battle with the weak-looking humans. They did not have the powerful limbs of the bear. They were not very big.

"They are so noisy!" Marra whispered as the humans crashed toward the Tall Grass plain. We could hear them well, though they were still far off. "Are they stupid or just careless? We aren't allowed to make that much noise."

"Maybe they have reason not to worry," Ázzuen said, his bright eyes intent. "They didn't seem afraid of us before, just cautious. They are different, that's for certain."

"They're rivals, idiot," Unnan said. "You're just too stupid to know it."

Ázzuen was untroubled by Unnan. "No," he said. "It's something more. Can't you sense it?"

Unnan rolled his eyes and turned away, but Marra nodded slowly. I wanted to tell them how I had felt, how the crescent on my chest warmed as the human creatures drew near, but I was afraid to do so. If anyone could help me understand it, clever Ázzuen could, but I would not take the chance of the others hearing. But the warm feeling in my chest grew, and I imagined myself leaping through the air to knock over one of the creatures. Ázzuen would be at my side, and together we would triumph over one of them. I would not kill it, though. I would spare its life and perhaps befriend it. It was a strange thought, but I could see myself running with one of them, racing through trees and meadows. I shook my head. One did not run with prey or rivals. You hunted them, fought them. I turned again to Ruuqo.

"Retreat, wolves," he said. "Take what you can from the kill and withdraw to the woods."

Yllin, Werrna, and Trevegg immediately began tearing meat from the horse. I couldn't believe Ruuqo wanted to run. A sharp bite from Minn made me yelp.

"What in the name of the moon are you waiting for?" he said. I noticed for the first time how much his thin face resembled Unnan's weaselly one. They had matching personalities, too. "Do what you're told."

Still baffled, I started toward the kill. Yllin had managed to tear off one of the horse's front legs, including most of the shoulder and some ribs, and was struggling to drag it to the trees. Ázzuen and I ran to help her as Trevegg hustled the rest of the pups up the slope and into the woods. Each grasped a small piece of horse. "Hurry up!" Trevegg said. "The humans are moving quickly today."

"Why don't we fight them?" I asked Yllin as I grabbed hold of the horse's shoulder. Ázzuen grabbed the leg farther down and yanked. Tlitoo hopped up to balance on the piece we carried, picking at the shoulder as we struggled with it.

"Because Ruuqo is afraid of the humans," Yllin said, pausing for breath. She looked over her shoulder to make sure no one was near enough to hear her, and lowered her voice. "His brother, Hiiln, was banished for spending too much time with humans, which is how Ruuqo became leaderwolf. And Rissa was to be Hiiln's mate, not Ruuqo's. That's why he's so uncertain of his power. He thinks he's second best. Even his name means 'second son.' His father named him that when he and Hiiln were only four weeks old."

Rissa trotted by with a large chunk of meat in her jaws. She whuffed at us in approval as she saw the size of our prize.

"Hurry up," Yllin said, taking the shoulder in her mouth again, and giving it a great yank, which nearly sent Tlitoo into the dirt. He flapped his wings to regain his balance and glared at Yllin reproachfully.

"You are as clumsy as a lame auroch," he grumbled.

Grinning at him, I clamped my jaws around the horse shoulder and pulled hard. Together, Ázzuen, Yllin, and I dragged it into the trees, closer to where the rest of the pack was already hiding. The size of the meat we carried slowed us down. We stopped again, panting with effort. Tlitoo looked at us in disgust and flew off, back in the direction of the kill. Yllin watched him go.

"We're supposed to stay away from the humans anyway," she said. "It's wolf law. But Ruuqo takes it too far. You aren't allowed to kill them or hurt them unless they threaten you. And you can't spend time with them. But you are allowed to steal from them, and protect your kills, as long as you don't harm them unnecessarily. And as long as your leaderwolf gives you permission. You're not supposed to starve to death to avoid fighting with them. If I were leaderwolf, I would fight them."

"But you are not leaderwolf, Yllin, not yet." Yllin cringed at the sound of Trevegg's voice, but the oldwolf was amused. "You know as well as I do that we are forbidden to have unnecessary contact with the humans. It is a leaderwolf's task to enforce that rule. Now, let's bury this meat, before even the humans' useless noses find it."

"Yes, elderwolf," Yllin said meekly, but she didn't lower her ears.

Trevegg took note of her less than submissive agreement and snorted. "You will be a bad influence on the pups. Come on, youngwolf. You still have something to learn from us oldsters." He took the whole leg—shoulder, ribs, and all—and pulled it into the woods himself, leaving the three of us to watch in admiration. As if she had not been rebuked at all, Yllin bounded after him.

We did not get to watch as the human creatures stole our prey. We hid in the bushes like rabbits. The humans were as loud as ravens, as if they didn't care if every bear and long-fang in the Wide Valley heard them. We buried the meat at the fringes of the forest in a place that Rissa told us was Wood's Edge, a small gathering place we used when hunting the Tall Grass plains.

When the meat was hidden, Rissa gathered us pups around her. Trevegg sat beside her, still panting a little from the heat. One by one the wolves of the pack joined us, settling into the softest, coolest spots they could find. Only Ruuqo stood apart, looking back toward the kill where we could still hear the humans taking our prey. Rissa waited until we all were watching her, and then she spoke.

"The Wide Valley is not like other places," Rissa began, "and we are not like other wolves. We are chosen to fulfill a great task, and sworn to follow certain rules. So you must listen to what I say now, more carefully than you have ever listened before."

Rissa didn't look at me when she spoke of the rules, but I could feel the eyes of the rest of the pack upon me. No one had forgotten what Ruuqo and the Greatwolves had said about my birth going against the rules of the Wide Valley. Ázzuen pressed against me, but I found I wasn't afraid. At last I might learn why I was different, why Ruuqo hated me. I leaned forward as far as I could, intent on catching every word.

"Tonight we will take you to see the humans who share our valley," Rissa continued. "They are more dangerous than the bear, more dangerous than hunter-birds when you were small. You are forbidden to have anything to do with them. If you see them when you're without leaderwolves, walk away, even if you are feeding on the best prey you've ever killed. If leaderwolves tell you to, you may steal from them or compete with them for prey, living or dead."

I heard Yllin grumble softly at this, still peeved that Ruuqo had not let us fight the humans for the horse. Rissa ignored her.

"Any wolf who otherwise consorts with the humans," the leaderwolf said, "will be exiled—not only from the pack, but from the Wide Valley itself."

I looked around me. From our hiding place in the woods I could see neither the mountains nor the hills that bordered our home. But the valley was vast. I couldn't imagine leaving it.

"Most important of all," Rissa said, "you must never kill a human, unless you are defending your life or your pack. If you kill a human without cause, you and your entire pack will be killed. The Greatwolves will destroy every wolf who shares your blood."

That got our attention. We all stopped fidgeting and looking around Wood's Edge and stared at Rissa.

"It is time," Rissa said, "for you to learn of the covenant of the Wide Valley."

She paused for a moment, and looked over to Ruqo as if

she expected him to argue with her again. He met her eyes coolly.

"If you are taking them to the humans when they're still mud-brained pups," he snarled, "then you may as well tell them of the legends."

He stalked several wolflengths away, found a patch of damp earth by a rotting log, and lay down, turning his back to us.

"Very well," Rissa said, refusing to respond to his anger. "There was a time when humans and wolves fought, and all of wolfkind nearly came to an end." She paused. "You remember what you've learned of the Ancients?" she asked us.

"Sun, Moon, Earth, and Sky," Ázzuen answered quickly, repeating what Trevegg had told us many moons before. "They created creatures and the Balance, and we have to follow their rules. But Trevegg wouldn't tell us anything else," he said.

Rissa whuffed a laugh at the exasperation in Ázzuen's voice. He hated not knowing things. "That is correct," she said. "And you will learn more when you need to. What you need to know now is that our ancestors promised the Ancients that this valley would be a place of peace. That is what the covenant is about. It is why we must keep the promise, and why the fate of all wolfkind rests upon our backs."

Her voice took on the cadence of story, of legend passed down from one generation of wolf to another.

"The promise was made long ago," she said, "when wolves had just become wolf and when humans were not yet human, when a wolf named Indru met a human at the northern edge of a great desert. Both were very hungry, and both were leading their packs in search of food."

"This was a time," Trevegg added, "when humans were not so different from all other creatures." The oldwolf lay down with a contented sigh. "They were cleverer than some, and less clever than others, better at survival than some, and not as good as others. There were fewer of them than there are now, and they were covered with fur like a normal creature, not half naked like they are now."

Borlla snorted, and Trevegg opened his mouth in a grin before continuing.

"Even then they stood tall on their hind legs, and even then they had some use of tools, though not nearly as many as they have now."

"What are tools?" Ázzuen asked before I could.

"You have seen ravens strip twigs and use them to dig grubs out from the inside of trees?" Trevegg asked. "It is like that. That twig is a tool and the humans are better at using them than any other creature. It's one of the gifts given to the humans by the Ancients, as we are given fleetness of foot and the cleverness of the hunt."

"Their tools weren't anything like they are now, though," Yllin asserted, interrupting the oldwolf. "The human-to-be that Indru met only had a stick for digging and a sharpened rock for cutting. They were the same tools his ancestors and their ancestors before them had used. He hadn't thought to put the rock on the end of a stick or to sharpen the stick to throw at prey."

Yllin looked suddenly abashed when she realized she had taken over telling the story, but continued when Rissa nodded to her.

"Humans were scroungers then," the youngwolf said, "living mostly by eating others' prey, and by catching what small prey they could on their own."

"They're just scroungers?" Unnan demanded. "Why do we have to worry about them, then?"

"Be quiet, pup!" Ruuqo ordered from beside his log. Ázzuen startled beside me, and Marra gave a small yip. I'd thought Ruuqo was sleeping but clearly he was listening to everything. Unnan flattened his ears and Ruuqo watched him for a moment before turning away from us again.

"They were scroungers then," Trevegg said, glaring at Unnan. "They are not now."

I muffled a grunt of pleasure at Unnan's embarrassment, and settled onto my haunches.

"It was a harsh time," Rissa continued as if Yllin had never been interrupted, "and food was scarce. The humans-to-be were losing their fight to survive. Indru's pack was struggling, too, and he had led them far in search of food. Although they fared better than the humans, he could not allow good prey to walk away. And by all that is wolf, the weak creatures standing before his pack should have been prey."

I remembered how I'd felt when I saw the humans across the Tall Grass plain. How I'd been torn between wanting to fight them and wanting to run with them. I could imagine myself standing next to Indru, watching the humans. And before I knew what I was doing, I spoke.

"But he didn't see them as prey," I whispered, and then gasped when I realized what I had said. I lowered my ears before anyone could reprimand me.

Rissa pulled her lips back just a little, and then sighed. When she spoke again, her voice was very soft.

"He did not see them as prey. He looked into the eyes of the human and saw something he thought he recognized, something he might see in the eyes of a wolf."

Ruuqo growled quietly from beside his log, and raised his head.

"Against all logic and sense," Rissa continued, "Indru did not tell his pack to hunt the humans. Instead, he invited the tall-standing creatures to join his pack in play. And when the sun rose in the sky and it got too warm to run, they lay down together, and they slept, side by side."

Rissa half closed her eyes. "When they awoke," she said, "they awoke changed. Indru saw that the humans were not so different from wolves. When he looked more closely, he saw how sickly the humans really were—how close to death they were. And Indru did not want them to die. He wanted to be with them, to run with them as he would run with his pack. He could no more leave them to die than he could leave one of his pups hungry when his own belly was filled with meat. He decided to teach the humans some things to help them to survive. Some say that when the wolf and the human lay down together, their souls intertwined, and even when they stood and moved apart, each kept a piece of the other's soul."

"That is not part of the traditional story!" Ruuqo snapped, standing suddenly and making us all jump. He stalked over to us. "That's not the legend as it's meant to be told."

"It's what I heard as a pup," Rissa countered. "Just because you don't believe it doesn't mean it's untrue."

Ruuqo growled deep in his throat. He paced back to the rotting log and turned restlessly in a circle. I waited for him to lie down again. Instead, he strode back to Rissa and sat next to her, poised on his haunches as if ready to pounce. Rissa gave a soft, annoyed growl of her own before continuing.

"The wolves taught the humans how to work together to bring down prey so that they no longer needed to rely on others to catch their food," she said. "They taught the humans to set up gathering places where they could come together to rest and plan."

"These were the secrets of the wolf clans," Ruuqo interrupted, "and Indru should have known better than to share them with the humans-to-be. Each creature has secrets—skills given to them by the Ancients—and all are forbidden to share them. For the Ancients knew that if one creature learned too much, it could grow too powerful and upset the Balance. Indru was so blinded by his feelings for the human-creatures that he ignored the law of the Ancients, and continued to teach the humans things they should not have known. Before long, the humans were changed."

He stopped speaking and stalked back to his log. When it became clear he would not start again, Rissa took up the story.

"They were greatly changed. Because they hunted as a pack, they had more food to eat, and they grew stronger. In their new gathering places they came together, and found that many minds were better than one. They learned new ways to seek food, and better ways to shelter themselves. One cold night, when they wearied of shivering and of hiding from the beasts that hunted them, they learned to control fire."

I'd seen fire when it sometimes ate through the trees and bushes of the forest. It seemed impossible that any creature could rule it, and I couldn't help but wonder what such a creature would be like. Rissa's voice interrupted my thoughts. I shook myself and crept in a little closer to her.

"When the humans learned to control fire," she said, "they no longer needed their thick fur, and it fell away from their bodies like leaves off a tree. They learned new ways to use their tools and ways to make tools that their ancestors would never have imagined. They found new ways of killing and fighting. They grew arrogant and proud. 'We are different,' they said. 'We are better than other creatures. See how no other creature makes fire? See how no other creature makes tools of rock and of wood.'"

The sound of flapping wings made all of us look up. Sleekwing landed in front of Rissa and Trevegg, his beak still bloody from his meal. My stomach rumbled at the thought of that good meat, just out of reach.

What wolf and human
Share is pride. To humble both
Is the ravens' task.

He pulled Rissa's ear and flapped his wings in Trevegg's face. When the oldwolf grinned and snapped his jaws at the raven, Sleekwing took flight, alighting on a branch just above us, where Rainsong waited for him. I wondered how long the ravens had been listening and why they cared to listen to our legend. Rissa watched them warily for a moment, and then spoke again.

"The humans decided that all other creatures should serve them," she said. "The wolves refused, and humans and wolves fought. The humans, in their anger, began to kill every creature that would not submit to them. Then they set fire to the very forest they lived in."

I shuddered. Trevegg had told me that fire had burned two of our best gathering places three years ago. I couldn't imagine deliberately causing such destruction.

"That was what caught the attention of the Ancients," Trevegg said. "And when the Ancients saw what the humans had learned from the wolves, and saw what the humans were doing, they knew that these creatures would threaten the Balance. That they would keep killing and keep destroying everything and every creature around them. And the Ancients would not allow such things to come to pass. So Sky announced to the wolves and humans of the world that the time had come for them to die."

"When Indru heard this," Rissa said, "he howled in sorrow and despair. He scaled the highest mountain he could find, and called out to the Ancients, to beg for the life of wolf and humankind. At first, they didn't hear him."

Rissa raised her head to look at Sleekwing and Rainsong in the tree above her. They both raised their wings, and Sleekwing spoke.

"Then, Tlitookilakin, the raven king, who had been watching the wolves and humans, flew all the way up to Sun and jabbed the Ancient with his sharp beak. Sun looked down and saw Indru, and called the other Ancients—Moon, Earth, and Grandmother Sky—to listen. Tlitookilakin flew to Indru's side, for he did not want his ravens to starve for the foolishness of the wolves."

The raven turned his head side to side and then settled back on his branch. Trevegg raised his muzzle to the wind, and then lowered it, and spoke to us again.

"Ears humbly lowered and tail tucked politely between his legs," he said, "Indru stood before the Ancients. He spoke to them, showing as much courage as any wolf has ever had.

"'Do not punish all wolves and humans,' Indru begged, 'for it was the fault of me and my pack that this happened. Do not end our lives. There are so many things we have yet to learn, so many things still to discover.'

"Sky sent a warm breeze through Indru's fur. 'All creatures have their time to live and their time to die,' she said gently to the wolf. 'It is time for you to make way for what comes next. It is the way it has always happened, and the way it must always be.'

"Indru looked at Sky in despair, not sure of what to do next. The raven king poked Indru hard in the rump, and the wolf spoke again.

"'Our time is not yet done,' he pleaded. 'We have just begun to explore this lovely world we live on.'

"Earth rumbled in response to the compliment, making the mountain shake. Then Indru sat back and howled a song so sweet and mournful that even Sky trembled, and Moon and Earth held perfectly still for the first time in their long lives.

"The Ancients watched Indru with great curiosity. No other creature had stood before them and so courageously and so calmly argued its cause. The Ancients had lived a long, long time, and had grown tired of one another's company. They were lonely—as lonely as a wolf without a pack. In the howl of the wolf, they saw the possibility of companions to end their loneliness. They spoke together while Indru and Tlitookilakin waited, shivering on the mountaintop. Finally, after what seemed to Indru like a lifetime, Sky spoke.

"'We will grant you this request,' Sky said, and Indru's heart began to beat once more.

"'But you must make us a promise—a promise that your children and your children's children must keep.'

"'I will promise anything,' Indru said.

"Sky rumbled in approval. She had expected no less.

"'Since humans now think they are better than all others,' she told Indru, 'they will become stupid with their own power. They will set fires larger than you can imagine. They will fight and they will kill, and they will not care if they destroy anything and everything that is not like them. Left alone, they will destroy the Balance itself, and then we will have no choice but to end the lives not just of wolf and humankind, but of the entire world.'"

Trevegg paused and looked at us. "You remember what I told you of the Balance, when you were smallpups?" the oldwolf asked. "That it is what holds the world together and that every creature, every plant, every breath of air is part of? Well, Sky—who is the leader of all the Ancients—feared that if the Balance were to be destroyed, the Ancients themselves might die. So she took a great risk in trusting Indru. But she was lonely, and wanted the wolves to succeed."

The oldwolf stretched once again and closed his eyes, as if better to see Indru on his mountaintop.

"'We will send challenges to the humans, great storms and droughts and fiery death from both the mountains and from above,' Sky said to the wolf. 'This will keep the humans from growing too strong and arrogant. They will struggle, and their struggles will keep them too busy to cause us trouble. But this you must promise us, wolf. You must not help them again. You and your kind must stay forever away from them. You must shun their company.'

"Indru would've given Sky his nose and his teeth if it had been asked of him, but he did not want to make this promise. He could not imagine staying forever apart from the human creatures. It would be as bad, he thought, as leaving packmates to die. He turned his face away from Sky and from Sun, and did not answer.

"Earth trembled beneath his feet. 'It is the only way,' the Ancient said.

"'If you do not renounce them,' Sun beat down hard upon Indru's head, 'they will learn more from you; they will grow too strong even for us to control. You will fight them and they will fight you.'

"'It's the price you must pay,' Moon cried loudly to be heard from the far side of Earth.

"But it was only when Tlitookilakin poked Indru so hard on his head that the wolf could not hold back a cry of pain, that Indru gave his answer. He bowed his head then, and promised Sky that the wolves would forever spurn the company of humans."

Trevegg paused, and for the briefest of moments, the old-wolf's eyes met mine.

"For years upon years," he said, looking away, "the wolves did their best to keep Indru's promise. But try as they might, they could not stay forever away from the humans."

"They didn't realize how difficult it would be," Rissa said, picking up the story when the oldwolf paused. "Neither the wolves nor the Ancients understood the strength of the pull between the humans and the wolves. Whether it was because wolves and humans shared a soul," she looked to Ruuqo, daring him to challenge her, "or because they had spent too much time together, it was impossible for Indru's children to keep distant from the humans. Time and time again they came together, and each time Sky grew angrier and pulled them apart. Then, many years later, long after the time of Indru, a youngwolf—not so much older than you pups are now—hunted with the humans, and taught her pack to do the same. In doing so, she caused a great war. That's when the covenant of the Wide Valley was born."

"The Ancients had warned the wolves that if they failed to keep the promise, all wolf- and humankind would die," Trevegg said. "So when the wolf Lydda hunted with the humans, Sky sent a winter three years long to end the lives of humans and of wolves. But then, when all seemed to be lost, giant wolves appeared, wolves who said they were sent to be our guardians. These were the first Greatwolves, and some say that they walked down from the sky on the rays of the sun, and that they are part of the Ancients themselves."

"The Greatwolves came to give us one last chance. They came to watch over wolfkind and to ensure that wolves never again forgot Indru's promise," Rissa said. "And since the Greatwolves knew they could not stay forever upon the Earth, they sought out wolves who would someday take their place as guardians of wolfkind, wolves who would watch over all others to make sure wolves and humans did not come together again. They searched across the world for wolves that might have the strength to fulfill this task, and brought those wolves here to the Wide Valley. Then the Greatwolves closed off the valley, choosing which wolves might bear pups and which might not and allowing in the valley only those wolves who would swear to the Ancients to obey the rules of the covenant."

"That we would keep away from the humans as much as possible," Trevegg said.

"That we would never kill a human unprovoked," Yllin added.

"And that we would protect our bloodlines and mate only with wolves inside the valley," Rissa finished. "These three rules would be passed down to every wolf born in the valley, and any who did not obey would be killed or sent far away. Any pack that did not enforce the rules would be wiped out. Since then, the Greatwolves have spoken for the Ancients and have been the guardians of the wolves and of the promise. But one day, when they return to the sky, we will take their place. We must prove ourselves worthy. We must be ready when that day comes, or wolfkind will be no more."

Unnan was the first of us to speak.

"Why is it so important that we don't mate with wolves outside the valley?" he asked, looking pointedly at me. "Why is it so wrong to let a mixed-blood wolf live?"

Trevegg narrowed his eyes at Unnan, but answered. "Mixed-bloods can be dangerous," he said. "Some of them are too drawn to the humans. Others cannot help but kill them. Either way, the covenant is broken and we fail in our task. Other mixed-bloods are neither one thing nor the other, and go mad. No one knows how they will behave."

"So having a mixed-blood in the pack puts us in danger?" Borlla asked with false innocence. I restrained myself from trying to rip her ears off. Marra, pretending to scratch a flea, dug her claws into Borlla's hip. Borlla growled and leapt on her. Before the rest of us could join the fight, Trevegg grabbed Borlla by the neck fur and pulled her away.

"Enough!" the oldwolf said. "At times, we do mix our blood. The Greatwolves sometimes bring in wolves from

outside the valley. Otherwise our bloodlines would grow weak."

"You end up with wolves with three ears and two noses," Yllin said, playfully swatting Unnan. He fell over onto his side and glared at her.

"We permit mixed-bloods when the Greatwolves allow it," Rissa said, "as they did with Kaala."

"The Greatwolves could be wrong, though, couldn't they?" Borlla persisted. "She could still be dangerous."

"That is not for you to say, pup," Trevegg said.

Ruuqo raised his head once again to look at me. Rissa walked over to stand beside me and licked the top of my head.

"We will discuss it no more," she said. "It is the will of the Greatwolves and it is done. You must remember what I have told you of the humans and the covenant. Sleep now, and be ready to run in a few hours' time."

Then, as if nothing unusual were happening, the pack settled down to sleep away the rest of the hot part of the day. Ázzuen and Marra lay down as close to me as was comfortable in the afternoon sun, and I was grateful for their support. But my heart was racing. It wasn't just that Ruuqo didn't want me in the Swift River pack. It was much more than that. I could be dangerous for everything in the valley. I desperately wanted to know more about the humans and what it was about them that made them so important. I wanted to ask Trevegg or Yllin more questions while the other pups slept. But the late afternoon heat made me drowsy, and before I knew it, I had joined my pack in sleep.

⧈

Rissa woke us two hours after moonrise. I rolled happily in the cool evening air, in a much better mood than when I'd fallen asleep. I was a pup of the Swift River pack, and nothing Borlla or Unnan could say would change that. Our leave-taking ceremony was quick and quiet, with only the softest yips and calls. The humans were gone from the kill—only a memory of their scent remained—but we weren't about to take any chances. Rissa said that our howls disturbed them, even from afar.

We left Wood's Edge and crossed the Tall Grass plains at a run, quickly entering the woods on the other side, all of us pups doing our best to keep up with the adults. Ruuqo had warned us against disobeying before we left.

"Any pup who does not follow orders will be sent back alone. You must not stray from the path Rissa sets you. Any pup who cannot obey must stay here." His tone allowed no disagreement. We had all promised to obey.

The woods on the far side of the Tall Grass plains were heavily scented with trees and bushes I did not know, but we did not stop to investigate the new scents. Both the field and woods smelled strongly of humans, and the acrid scent made me dizzy. It was easy to follow, even after several hours, and we moved quickly in the moonlight. It was a bright, nearly full moon, and it lit the world with the crisp contrasts of night, making everything clear and sharp. The leaves were outlined in moonglow, the earth rich with shades of light, and we could see much farther than in the blurring daylight. This was the hunting time, and it was easy to track the broken alder branches and displaced dirt the humans had carelessly left behind. The human-scent was so strong we could have tracked them on a moonless night, but I didn't mind the extra help of the bright moon illuminating the nighttime world.

We heard the river before we saw it. It sounded like a strong wind blowing through a hundred thickly leaved trees. It smelled of water, of course, but also of damp earth and decaying wood, of woods fed by the richness of the river and of small, fat animals—mouthfuls of lizard and mouse. I began to pant in excitement as we neared this river that divided our territory from the humans. I wondered how different the land across the water would be.

The river was larger than I'd expected, and faster moving. The slope down to the river was a gentle one, but the bank across the way rose steeply. I hesitated at the water's edge. So did the rest of the pups.

"It's just water, pups," Rissa said, checking the area for any danger, and then lowering her head to drink.

Her loud lapping made me realize how thirsty I was. We had not had water since our meal. The water was delicious. It tasted of leaves and fish and faraway places.

"I wonder where it ends," Marra said, gazing downstream.

"I'm more concerned about getting to the other side," Ázzuen said, looking worriedly across the river. Unnan snickered, and Ázzuen's tail drooped slightly.

"Come, pups," Rissa said, cheerfully. She strode into the river, and then looked back at us. "You must be comfortable in moving water. Some prey swim across rivers, and you must be able to swim after it. You do not want your meal floating away from you." She grinned. Rissa was able to wade most of the way across, swimming only when she reached the very middle of the river. We pups would have to swim much of the way. She climbed out easily on the other side, shook herself off, and looked back at us. Werrna waded in, stopping just where the river deepened.

The water moved like the wind. I liked swimming, and had paddled happily enough in the pond by our home, but I'd never tried anything like this. I stuck one paw in the water, getting up the nerve to cross.

Something hit me hard from behind, and I fell, smacking hard into the river. I swallowed a mouthful of water and mud, and scrambled back up the bank, coughing and shaking water from my fur and eyes and catching Borlla smirking on the shore behind me. Without thinking, forgetting Ruuqo's warning, I leapt at Borlla, knocking her into the mud. She could have drowned me and she certainly made me look ridiculous. I wasn't going to let her get away with it.

"Pups!" Werrna thundered, wading back across the river, as Yllin put her head down to stop Unnan and Ázzuen from joining what looked to be a good fight. "Is this how you behave? You are not babywolves anymore. You are supposed to be responsible enough to go on a journey without being watched constantly. Do I need to send you back to Ruuqo?"

Reluctantly, I let Borlla up. Her eyes glittered in anger, and I could tell she wanted to fight me. But she would wait for another time. She was no more likely to give up the chance to see the humans than I was. We both bowed our heads to Werrna and dropped to our bellies. Borlla dug her left paw into my ribs. I resisted the urge to bite her neck. Werrna watched us closely. Apparently satisfied that we were done fighting, she waded back into the river as if the swift current were no more to her than a light breeze. She stood stolidly in the water, wet fur pressed flat to her body, eyes glowing in the moonlight.

"Don't wait all night," she grumbled as we hesitated. "The moon will be beyond the mountains before you have the courage to get your paws wet."

Across the river, Rissa paced back and forth.

"Come *on,*" Yllin said when none of us waded in. "The river is slow this time of year. Just wait until after the rains when it flows as quickly as I run."

I took a deep breath and stepped into the water. Borlla shouldered me aside.

"Some wolves are afraid of everything," she said, "and some are not." She walked confidently into the river and began to wade, and then swim across. Unnan followed, pausing to kick water in Ázzuen's face. They weren't graceful when they swam, legs paddling almost frantically beneath them, heads stretching above the water, but they were strong swimmers.

"I don't think I can do it." Ázzuen's voice was so soft, I had to strain to hear him. He sat huddled beside Yllin. I should have gone to him, but Unnan and Borlla were almost to where Werrna stood in the middle of the river.

Marra poked her nose in my side.

"Race you across," she said, and dove into the water.

"Come on," I shouted to Ázzuen, and jumped in. I didn't look back to see if he followed. I couldn't keep up with Marra, but made it across the river much more easily than I expected. The current carried us downstream, since we could not swim as strongly as Rissa, and she trotted along the bank to join us.

"Nicely done, pups," she said in approval, and then turned her gaze across the river. Only then did I look back to see Ázzuen and Reel on the far side of the river, staring nervously at the moving water. Yllin nipped at their rumps. The water carried her voice to where we stood.

"Do I have to bring you across?" she mocked. "What will Ruuqo think when we tell him you were so afraid?"

Come on, Ázzuen, I thought impatiently. If he let them see his fear he'd never be part of the pack. Hesitantly he, and then Reel, waded in. Ázzuen swam awkwardly and slowly. Three-quarters of the way across, he grew tired and began to sink. I called to him.

"Keep swimming! If stupid Unnan can make it, so can you!"

My voice seemed to give Ázzuen a fresh burst of energy, and he made it the rest of the way across, and climbed out of the water, shaking the river from his fur. I was proud of him, pleased that it was my encouragement that helped him cross—and a little bit ashamed that I hadn't waited for him.

"I knew you could do it."

"Yes," he said. "Now I just have to make it back across." He touched my cheek with his nose.

I turned to Borlla, expecting to see her mocking us for our affection for each other, but her eyes were on the river. Reel was struggling. He didn't seem to understand how to swim, and stopped moving his legs halfway across. He quickly began to sink. Rissa gave a sharp bark. Yllin and Werrna both waded over to Reel, but the current bore him downstream.

Borlla leapt into the water, swam strongly to Reel, and grabbed him by the scruff. She kept both of their heads above water until Yllin reached them and dragged Reel across to safety. Rissa checked him all over, making sure he was not injured, and licked him all over, as if she could wash the danger from him. Borlla made her own way back to the riverbank, and lay, panting, in the mud. Reel walked shyly up to her and licked her face in thanks. I expected her to make fun of him for being weak, but she placed her chin gently on his neck. I felt a surge of jealousy. I had not thought to comfort Ázzuen. I turned to see him watching me carefully, but before I could say anything, Rissa spoke.

"You have done well by your pack," she said to Borlla. The

approval in her voice infuriated me. "You," she said to Reel, stern with him now that she knew he was safe, "must grow stronger." She touched her nose to his head once more, and shook the last of the water from her fur.

"That was the least dangerous part of this night, pups," she said. "Follow me, and make no noise. We will not stop again until we reach the human gathering place."

Running one by one, so no passing wolf could guess how many of us there were, we set off into the thick woods, and toward the deepening smell of humans.

⊡

The woods thinned and we reached the bottom of a small, dry hill covered with tall summer grasses and spiny bushes. The scent of humans was overpowering. Rissa called a halt and gathered us around.

Rissa's voice took on a warning edge. "From just over this hill we will be able to see the human gathering place. Do not go near them. Do not leave the side of an adult."

My heart beat quickly in excitement. Solemnly and silently, as we had seen our elders stalk the bear, we crept to the top of the hill. We could not quite see the humans, but we could smell and hear them. Rissa stopped again and we waited beside her. Yllin and Werrna kept watch—over us and over anything that might notice us. Ázzuen, sitting beside me, began to shake a little. I turned to lick him on the face, and gently took his muzzle in my mouth, as Rissa had done to us pups when we were younger and afraid of something. I could hear his heartbeat slow as I comforted him. Marra, who had been so brave by the river, came up to me then, and whined very softly. I took her muzzle in my mouth next, and she sighed in relief. I looked over to the other pups, and saw Borlla doing the same with Reel. She looked at me defiantly.

At a nod from Rissa, we dropped to our bellies and crept forward, hidden by the tall, dry grass. Rissa had said the humans were night-blind, but still I was glad for the cover that the grass and prickly bushes gave us. Ázzuen, and then Marra, gave little yips of excitement and fear, until a glare from Rissa and a few sharp nips from Yllin quieted them. Finally, we crawled over the crest of the hill, and looked into the human homesite. At last we could see them, as well as smell and hear them.

There were several packfuls of the two-legged creatures. Like bears before the strike, they lumbered around a clearing six times the size of our gathering place. Their long bodies were smooth like a lizard's or a snake's, but were dappled with patches of sleek fur. Around their shoulders and haunches many of them wore pelts of dead prey. They smelled of salt and meat and soft, damp earth, of prey skins and river water. But their own scents were overpowered by the acrid odor that made them so easy to find, even from a great distance. It was fire-scent, I realized abruptly, fire-scent mixed with an unfamiliar burning rock smell. The fire was contained by circles of stones. There was something strange about the scent, something I couldn't identify.

The humans were clustered in groups the size of small packs, adults and young together. Their young scrambled around the clearing, yipping and squealing. They ranged in size from the size of a month-old pup to nearly the size of a grown wolf. The smaller ones stumbled awkwardly around the clearing, so much like wolf pups that I felt my tail begin to wag. Most of the adults were larger than grown wolves, the males bigger and more densely furred than the females. Suddenly I felt lonely. As lonely as I had when my mother left.

"No wonder they are taking all the prey in the valley!" Werrna's voice was harsh with shock. "There have never been so many of them before. They used to honor pack size!"

"They are worse than the Stone Peaks," Rissa agreed. "They are no longer satisfied with taking food from within their own territories. I think they would walk into our very gathering places without thinking they were doing anything wrong."

I was stunned. No wolf would ever enter another's territory without knowing she was courting danger. You do so only if you must and then you are very, very careful. And prepared to fight.

"If their packs get too large, they should send some away, as we do," Borlla said. Her lip curled in contempt. "They are more like a herd of prey than a pack."

"They are hunters," Rissa said. "Never forget that. They are hunters who do not respect the rules of hunt or territory. That is why you must know of them so soon, pups. When I was young, we could fulfill the covenant simply by ignoring them. We stayed out of their way and they out of ours. Now they are everywhere, so you must always be aware of them."

We watched as a human female nestled in the arms of a male. A small child clung to another female's neck as she walked about the clearing. I felt a whine rise up in my throat and quickly swallowed it. It didn't seem right that we couldn't be with the humans, but after everything Trevegg had said about my mixed blood, I wasn't going to ask anything about it.

I saw Ázzuen watching me. "But why can't we be with them even a little?" he asked. "I understand why we can't spend a lot of time with them or help them, but why can't we at least go near them?" I wanted to pounce on him in thanks but just gave him a grateful look.

"Once we begin to spend time with them," Rissa answered, "we don't want to stop. We want to help them and teach them things, as Indru did. At least," she said, averting her eyes, "that is what I was told when I was a pup. And also," she paused as if deciding whether to tell us more, "there is something in the souls of the wolves and humans that cannot live side by side. Most humans fear the wildness that is wolf, because it is something they can't control. When we spend too much time with them, we either give up our wildness to please them, or we refuse to do so, which makes the humans angry. Or *we* get angry and try to kill them, and then the Greatwolves have to slay an entire pack. That's why our ancestors promised that wolves of the Wide Valley would completely avoid contact with humans. Except, of course," she said, a gleam coming into her eyes, "to steal from them when we can!"

Ázzuen's face had grown thoughtful. "Then, why," he said, "didn't the Ancients kill wolves when the youngwolf hunted with the humans—in the legends? Wolves broke Indru's promise. If it's that dangerous to be with them, why did the Ancients give us another chance?"

"You should be glad they did," Werrna rumbled, glaring at Ázzuen. "And it's not your place to question the legends."

"But staying away from them doesn't really work, does it?" Ázzuen insisted, standing suddenly. "If the humans are taking what's not theirs and not respecting territories. And Sleekwing said they're driving prey from the valley!"

"Get down, pup!" Rissa snarled. "And keep quiet!"

Ázzuen sat down hard, taken aback by Rissa's ferocity. He opened his mouth to protest, and Rissa growled at him.

"You were told not to question the legends. Now be quiet or you can go back across the river by yourself."

Chastened, Ázzuen lowered himself all the way to his belly. I touched my nose to his face, feeling a little guilty that his first question, anyway, had been on my behalf. Then I turned my attention back to the humans.

They did not look dangerous. A small girl curled up at the feet of a male and female pair who seemed to be her parents. She smelled like freshly fallen rain.

Yllin watched two young males scuffling like yearling wolves. "You'll want to go to them," she said softly. "You'll want to touch them, and be near to them, to interact with the humans as you would with each other. But it is your duty as wolf to resist. Duty to pack and the covenant comes before your own desires."

Rissa dipped her head in approval.

"Won't they smell us?" Reel asked, backing away a little.

"Their noses are as useless as wings on an auroch," Werrna sneered. "You could stand right behind one and fart and it wouldn't smell you."

"Well, I wouldn't quite say that," Rissa said, laughing in spite of herself, "but their noses are much weaker than ours, and they cannot smell us at this distance."

I thought about that. How could a creature go through life without being able to smell rivals and prey? My own nose was still busily sorting out the scents of their home, worrying over that strange fire-scent. I realized at last what it was. Meat and fire together. Burnt meat. The smell was somehow shocking and wrong, and at the same time irresistible. It drew me in as much as the creatures themselves did. It made me hungry. Hungry for the meat, but also hungry deep within my body for something else.

"How do they live?" I asked, to shake the hunger from me. "How do they hunt if they can't smell?"

"They live and hunt as we do," Rissa said. "Their eyes function quite well in the daylight, and they work as a pack. But instead of teeth and claws, they make their tools to kill with. Sharpsticks—a kind of long thorn—and a second stick that they use to throw the first one. They can kill prey from far away. They are fine hunters," she said a little wistfully.

We settled into silence as we all watched the human home. I understood now why there was such a strong rule against being with them. They were like us in a strange way, even more so than the ravens. They made sounds that sounded like language, and their body language was as clear as any wolf's. Their young crouched and played much like we did. I could tell that a tall, well-muscled male was leader of the group. He smelled of power, and skinny, rangy youngsters tried to win his approval. I couldn't imagine how he kept order of such a large pack, but I was enthralled.

The air around me grew suddenly warm, and I felt another wolf beside me. Her smell was familiar, but she was not of my pack. I was surprised that a strange wolf would join us without greeting Rissa, and without being investigated by my packmates. I turned my head, and saw a young shewolf, about Yllin's age, looking with longing at the humans. I did not want to disturb her, but she looked so sad that I nudged her with my nose.

The strange wolf turned her head, and when I saw the white crescent of fur on her chest, I knew why she was so familiar. She was the wolf who had come to me when I was desperate on the Great Plain, the wolf I thought I had made up out of my exhaustion and despair. She looked ordinary enough. She was a smallish wolf, light brown and a little thin. But her scent was the one I had followed across the plain to my pack, the scent that had saved my life and Ázzuen's. And suddenly I realized that the acrid part of her scent was similar to the fire-rock-meat scent of the human camp. The strange wolf smelled of humans.

"You have grown well, little Smallteeth," she said, touching her nose to the white crescent on my chest. "You will not be a pup much longer. Tell me, how are things with the Swift River pack?"

The wolf's human-scent continued to confuse me. "Are you part of the human pack?" I asked her.

"Not quite," she answered. She took another longing look at the human homesite and yet another at Rissa and the pups. I couldn't believe that my packmates neither greeted nor challenged the newcomer.

"What is your pack, then?" I asked.

"Why, I am Swift River, little one. That and more. Your pack is my pack."

Now I was truly puzzled. I'd heard that some of last year's pups, Yllin and Minn's littermates, had left the pack seeking mates, and might return for the winter travels. But surely such a returning wolf would greet Rissa immediately. I wanted to ask her more about herself, but didn't, realizing that if she had left the pack in disgrace, she might not want to talk about it. Still, if that were the case, I wondered, why did Rissa let her lie next to us?

I was staring at the strange wolf in confusion, and she laughed at me.

"You are supposed to be watching the humans, little one, not me. Watch them. You, more than any other wolf of the Wide Valley, must know them."

"Why?" I asked, surprised.

"I started a journey that you must complete, daughter-wolf."

A deep and distant howl startled us both. The young wolf pricked up her ears.

"I must leave now, sisterwolf. Take care of my packmates." She looked again at the humans. "All of my packmates." She touched her nose to the crescent on my chest once again, and slipped away into the forest. I shivered a little as the air around me cooled.

I stood, meaning to follow the strange wolf. The moon shape on my chest was still warm from her touch, and I wanted to ask her what she meant about taking care of her packmates. Then something began to draw me toward the human camp, so strongly I could not resist. I took a step down the hill.

"Lie down!" Werrna snarled. My legs shook and my head whirled. My chest began to burn like the very fires the humans kept, and I felt as if an invisible vine had wrapped itself around my heart, and now pulled me over to the human homesite. Everything in the human gathering place was sharper, clearer. Their words no longer seemed like meaningless gabble, but were instead as clear as the words of a wolf. I watched a human child nuzzle in her parent's arms, and wanted those arms around me. I wanted the firemeat in my mouth, the warmth of the fire on my fur. The pull I had felt before was increased tenfold, and I could not fight it.

I took another step, and then a third, and then scrambled quickly down the hill. Suddenly, a hard shoulder and chest slammed into me, crushing me. I could not hold back a yelp as Werrna jumped on me, pinning me to the ground.

"Be quiet, idiot pup," Werrna hissed. "Do you want every creature in the forest to know we are here?"

Still I tried to get to the humans, scrabbling my legs under Werrna's strong body. It hurt when she stopped me. The ache in my chest had lessened as I moved to the humans, and it intensified when I could not go to them. I kept fighting Werrna. My desire to reach the humans was greater than my fear of trouble or pain. Finally, she bit me hard on the shoulder, and the hold the human-scent had on me loosened. I remembered that I was wolf, and Swift River. I allowed myself to be dragged up the hill to where Rissa was waiting angrily. Ázzuen and Marra watched me, eyes wide. Even Unnan and Borlla were too surprised to speak.

"What in the name of the moon were you thinking?" Rissa demanded. "How dare you go to the humans after everything you've been told?"

I couldn't find an answer. I couldn't tell her about a wolf that may or may not be real. I couldn't tell her how drawn I felt to the humans, how I felt I was one of them. Rissa would think I was crazy, or that I would follow the humans and have to be banished from the pack. Just thinking about the humans made me feel I was falling off a cliff, tumbling uncontrollably. I hung my head.

"Answer me! Or I'll send you back across the river to the plain by yourself." I'd never seen Rissa so angry with one of us pups. I looked at her in alarm. "Tell me why you disobeyed me!" she demanded.

"I'm sorry," I said in a whisper. "I felt something pulling me to them."

Werrna and Rissa exchanged concerned looks and I heard Borlla mutter something about mixed-bloods under her breath. Ázzuen watched me anxiously. I could tell he wanted to come to me, but did not dare. I was grateful for his caring, but annoyed at his fearfulness. I didn't look at Yllin, didn't want to see the disappointment in her eyes.

"What do you mean?" Rissa asked. "Pulled how?"

"Like I was on fire," I whispered, "like the only way to stop burning was to go to them. I'm sorry." I didn't tell her about the strange wolf. I couldn't.

"Blood will tell," Werrna said, looking me up and down. "Only four moons old and already, it's happening."

"Oh, be quiet, Werrna," Rissa said. "It's nothing but an overly imaginative pup. Plenty of pups try to go to the humans when they first see them. It means nothing." But she looked at me with concern, and poked the white crescent on my chest with her nose.

"It means nothing—yet," Werrna said. "Are you going to tell Ruuqo?"

"No," Rissa answered. She raised her head and met Werrna's gaze. "And neither are you."

Werrna hesitated for a moment, then lowered her ears. "If you like," she said, and turned away to chew at a patch of fur on her leg.

Borlla strutted up to Rissa. "I felt them pull me, too, but I didn't try to go to them," she said, her voice filled with spite.

Unnan dipped his head in agreement. "None of the rest of us went. Just Kaala."

"Quiet, both of you," Rissa ordered. "And you will not mention this again. Do you hear me? Kaala, you will wait at the bottom of the hill. *Away* from the humans. The rest of us are going to take back some of what the humans stole."

"Ruuqo won't like that," Werrna said.

"Ruuqo does not make all the decisions for this pack," Rissa retorted. "If we cannot keep the humans from stealing our prey, we will take what they carelessly leave at the edges of their gathering place." Her eyes swept over Werrna. "You can stay here with the smallpups."

Werrna opened her mouth to argue, but the expression on Rissa's face stopped her.

"Yes, leaderwolf," she said. "Move, pups!" She bullied Ázzuen and Reel to one side.

"Go," Rissa ordered when I hesitated. "You do not have the self-control to be part of this."

If Werrna was not going to argue with Rissa, I certainly wasn't going to. Trying to ignore the ache in my chest, I turned away from my packmates and away from the humans that drew me so.

7

I trudged down to the bottom of the hill, trying to ignore the ache in my chest. I looked up at the half-moon and wanted to howl my frustration. But Rissa had already chided me once for lack of control. Dejectedly, I kept walking, feeling every grain of dirt in the pads of my feet, whimpering a little to myself. I stopped when I heard soft footsteps padding quickly behind me.

"I'll come with you," Ázzuen said, running to catch up. His little face was filled with concern. I was more grateful than I wanted to admit. It was bad enough being sent away, separated from the humans. To be alone was even worse. Ázzuen and I reached the bottom of the hill, and sat, watching the moon through the trees.

"Won't Werrna notice you've left?" I asked.

Ázzuen grinned. "She's too mad at being left behind to care if I wander a few wolflengths away. One of the advantages of being a smallpup is that the adults couldn't care less if you

wander off. They figure you're going to starve before winter's end anyway."

"That's not true!" I said, alarmed that Ázzuen thought so little of himself and his place in the pack. "They cared about whether or not you made it across the river."

"They don't want us to die," he said, "but they aren't counting on me or Reel making it through winter."

"I'll make sure you make it through winter," I said, then felt terrible. I didn't mean to imply he was weak.

Ázzuen was silent for a moment, thinking about what I'd said. But when he spoke again it was of the humans.

"Why *did* you go to them? After everything Trevegg and Rissa told us about the covenant? We all felt a pull to them. But you could have been kicked out of the pack. Or worse." He was not accusatory, just curious.

"For me it was different, Ázzuen. At first it was just a pull, like you said. But then it changed. I couldn't *not* go to them. Just like Rissa said about Indru. When I think about it, I know it's wrong, but that doesn't change anything. If I didn't know Rissa and Werrna would stop me, I'd go right now."

Ázzuen regarded me. His face was filling out a little, I noticed. In spite of his claims to being a smallpup, he was growing stronger.

"Next time you want to go," he said, "tell me. And I'll sit on you."

I laughed, and the ache in my chest eased a little. I almost jumped out of my fur when I heard a whooshing of wings above me. Tlitoo landed in front of me, and immediately began preening his wings.

"You aren't very smart," he said. He looked up from his grooming and pulled a small twig from his wing. He threw it at me.

"The Bigwolves cannot help you if you get yourself kicked out of your pack, babywolf. You are going to need to learn self-control. The humans make the mark on my wing burn, but I have learned to ignore it. You don't have to act on everything you feel, you know."

"What are you doing here in the dark?" I asked grumpily. Ravens do not usually like the night. "Why aren't you with your family?"

"I am old enough now to be on my own, unlike a babywolf," he said. "I can fly where and when I choose. And someone has to keep you from whining all night." Tlitoo peered at me through the darkness, blinking rapidly. "The Bigwolves will be displeased."

The last thing I needed was someone else criticizing me.

"If they care so much, where are they?" I snapped. I wanted to see them now more than ever. I wanted to ask them who my father was and if I really did have Outsider blood. I needed to know if I was dangerous to my pack. I needed to know if there was something wrong with me.

Tlitoo gave a low honk and flared his leg feathers.

"The Bigwolves come when they please, babywolf," he said. "They have more important things to worry about than your hurt feelings. Dimwolf."

"Watch what you say, raven," Ázzuen said, coming to stand beside me. I was surprised at his protectiveness.

Tlitoo cocked his head. "It is good to have friends," he said. "Make sure you keep them. It will be good to not be alone."

"Are you finished?" I said, annoyed. I was tired of him coming to me with mysterious messages and word of the Greatwolves, and never giving any real information.

"Listen to me!" Tlitoo's sudden seriousness unnerved me.

Ázzuen pressed himself against me, giving comfort, not seeking it. "Don't get yourself exiled when you are still too young to feed yourself. You must not show your difference so much. Do not stand out so much. Do you think you can do that? Think a little?"

I could find no answer. I leaned against Ázzuen and looked at Tlitoo.

His voice softened a little. "You knew you were different. Why do you think the Bigwolves saved your life?" He gently drew his beak through the fur on my head, humming softly. "I do not like the Grumblewolves' secrets, either, wolflet, but I do not pluck out my feathers over it. You have other things to worry about right now."

I was surprised at his affection. I opened my mouth to thank him, but he turned and flipped his tail feathers at me.

Wolflet mopes too much;
Moping wolflet bores raven.
Yanking tail will help.

He raised his wings as if to fly at me. To my surprise Ázzuen pounced, making Tlitoo hop aside, gurgling cheerfully.

"Ha," Tlitoo said. "Good. A wolf that is not so worming serious." He fell silent, cocking his head, as if listening for something.

Ázzuen looked back and forth at us. "Strangest raven I've ever met," he said, half laughing. "And why is he here at night?" He bent low to whisper to me. "I think we should not believe everything he says, Kaala."

I felt affection for Ázzuen well up in me. He had his little oldwolf expression on again, and I wondered if he would ever grow into his personality, if he would have the chance to. He and Reel were definitely the weakest wolves in the pack. If they both lived, one of them was destined to be the curl-tail. It wouldn't be Ázzuen if I had anything to do about it.

But Tlitoo had more questions to answer. I narrowed my eyes as I looked at him.

"Now listen," I said, as reasonably as I could.

"You'd better get moving, babywolves," Tlitoo said suddenly, interrupting me. He peered at me for a moment. "And try not to stand out like a sore beak." With a laughing caw that filled the night, Tlitoo took flight.

I heard a crashing in the bushes behind us. My packmates came pelting down the hill, most carrying meat in their jaws. Shouts from the human camp followed them. Yllin had a gleam in her eye, and a large slab of meat, firemeat, in her jaws.

"She didn't get *that* from the edges of the gathering place!" Ázzuen said.

"They went *into* the homesite!" I said, envy filling me. I'd gotten in trouble for just going near it. The scent of burnt meat made my mouth water, but there was not time to stop to eat anything.

"Run!" Rissa woofed through the hunk of meat she held in her mouth, a grin softening the urgency of the command. No longer bothering to be quiet, we dashed through the woods. We ran through the bright, cooling night, sprinting back toward our territory with stolen meat in our jaws. As Ázzuen and I ran, behind the others, I could swear I saw the shadow of a young shewolf running silently beside us.

⧈

The humans did not chase us far. Their slow, loping gait made it impossible for them to keep up with us, and since they could not smell or hear well, we didn't have to worry about them tracking us. Once we'd outrun the range of their throwing sticks we were safe from them. Even so, we kept on running. The woods smelled of Stone Peak wolves, and the human shouts behind us sounded very angry. I couldn't help laughing at their futile attempts to catch us. We ran like the wind, the excitement of the chase beating in our chests.

Marra, Borlla, and Unnan each carried small pieces of stolen food, their tails whipping in pride. I had to run meatless with Ázzuen and Reel, the smallpups, even though I was as strong as anyone. Unnan let a scrap of meat drop and I gulped it down, not even breaking my stride. Marra caught me at it. I grinned at her. She rolled the eye nearest to me, and put on a burst of speed, stretching her long legs to catch up with Rissa.

"Show-off," I laughed, gasping a little.

At last we slowed to an easier, quieter trot, running one by one in the moonlight. The scent of the Stone Peak pack faded as we neared the border of our territory, and I felt all of my packmates relax. I could tell from Reel's and Ázzuen's wheezing that they were glad to slow down.

I expected Rissa to take us back to the place where we had earlier crossed the river. Instead she took us along a well-trodden path, made by deer on their way to drink, and then along the muddy riverbank, far upstream from our earlier crossing. I didn't understand why we were taking such a long route back home. We journeyed nearly an hour before Rissa stopped us at a river crossing, and we would still have to backtrack along the other side of the river to return to the Tall Grass plain. It made no sense. Then I saw a fallen alder bridging the expanse of water. I looked in surprise at the slender tree as Rissa led the way across it. Werrna helped Reel across, and Unnan and Borlla followed.

"Why did they make us swim the river if this is here?" I asked Marra.

Yllin answered. "Every wolf must swim if she is to hunt," she said. We three were the last to cross, Yllin watching to make sure Ázzuen made it safely. "And it's a long way to the Tree Crossing. Energy wasted is energy we don't have for the hunt."

She looked across the river to where Rissa waited on the far side. "I don't think Rissa realized the smallpups would have so much trouble swimming. They weren't in any real danger—Werrna and I would've reached them—but we can't watch for weakpups *and* carry meat across." She narrowed her eyes in amusement. "Besides, last time we tried to swim across with meat, Minn let a whole leg bone float away. So we often use the Tree Crossing when we return from the human homesite."

"How often do we steal from the humans?" Marra asked, surprised.

Yllin grinned. "Often enough that we need to be able to cross the river when we wish. Come on." She picked up her piece of meat and trotted easily across the river to join the others.

It still didn't make sense.

"Ázzuen and Reel could've drowned," I said to Marra. After everything Rissa had said about protecting us, I didn't understand why she would take that chance. I shook my head to clear it, and looked after Yllin.

"They were testing us again," Marra said, following my gaze. She had managed to steal a ripe-smelling deer rib that still had some meat on it, and she had set it down as we waited for the others to cross. The light of first dawn was touching the sky, and my eyes began to shift to take in the brighter, blurry light of the sun.

"They didn't want Ázzuen or Reel to drown," she said, "but they wanted to see which of us are strongest. Just like they wanted to see who stole the best meat." She grinned. "You should've seen Yllin. She ran in when the humans' backs were turned and stole meat right from their fire. That's why we had to run away so quickly. Rissa pretended to be angry, but you could tell she was impressed."

Rissa was impressed with Yllin for stealing good meat, I thought, and impressed with Borlla for helping Reel across the river. And to make things worse, I was in trouble for not being strong enough to resist the humans. I sighed. Then I looked again at Borlla and saw that she, too, had firemeat.

"Why did Borlla get to go into the human gathering place?" I asked, indignant.

"She didn't," Marra said, stretching her long, lean back. "Yllin dropped a piece of firemeat and Borlla picked it up. But to hear Borlla tell it, stealing cooked meat was all her idea."

Rissa called to us. "What are you waiting for, lazypups?"

I followed Marra as she picked up her deer rib and trotted over to join the others. Rissa looked over all the stolen meat.

"You deserve to eat some now, Swift River wolves," she said, stopping just past the crossing. She nosed through the meat, saving much of it to take back to Ruuqo and the others. My mouth watered. I noticed she kept all the firemeat aside for us.

"Ruuqo won't eat it anyway," she said, noting Werrna's disapproving expression. "He says fire food is not real food." She shook her head, making her ears flap. "So we will save him the trouble of tasting it."

We all dove for the firemeat, but Werrna roughly pushed me out of the way.

"None for you. You are too fond of the humans already."

I whined indignantly, and tried to slither past her to the meat, but then Rissa and even Yllin pushed me away. Reel and Ázzuen were also shoved aside. They both lowered their tails. But I was angry. I was not a weakpup. I took two steps toward the meat, but Werrna's cold, angry gaze stopped me. I almost growled at her, but I remembered Tlitoo's warning about not doing stupid things. I shoved my anger down and watched as my packmates gobbled the firemeat. Finally, when only one piece remained, Rissa gave the call to move out.

She had only taken a few steps when she stopped. Her fur bristled and a deep growl rose from her throat. She set down the meat she carried and planted her feet far apart. Werrna, who had taken up a guarding position at the back of our line, ran past all of us to stand beside her.

"Stone Peaks," she snarled, "on our side of the river."

I looked up to see that two large wolves, a male and a female, had stepped out onto our path. I couldn't help staring at the male. I had thought Werrna's face was scarred, but this wolf had more scar than face. The left side of his mouth was torn half away and his left eye was nearly completely closed by the flap of skin that fell down over it. He smelled wrong, too. Sour and decayed, like sickness. He smelled like he should not even have been able to stand on his feet, much less be as strong and powerful as he appeared to be. But there was no doubt he was a strong wolf, a leaderwolf. Both wolves were larger even than Ruuqo and heavily muscled. They did not seem concerned to be facing three rival wolves.

"Torell, Ceela," Rissa acknowledged the two wolves. She

stood stiff-legged and stiff-tailed, her white fur standing straight up on her back.

Werrna and Yllin flanked her, their tails held a little lower than Rissa's but just as rigid.

"This is not the first time you have trespassed on Swift River lands." Rissa's voice was mild, but fury seemed to rise from her like mist.

"Rissa," Torell, the male wolf, said with the barest dip of his head. "Werrna." He did not acknowledge Yllin or any of us pups. "I do not think you should be so quick to accuse. You have been in our territory this night."

"In shared territory, Torell. You know that there is free passage to the humans' homesite. We needed to show our pups what they are. All packs acknowledge this."

"I never agreed," he said, his voice as mild as Rissa's. "The decision about my territory was made without my consent. But I will let it pass, in spite of the fact that you have taken meat from my lands."

"You'd better," Werrna snorted, "since we outnumber you."

Torell ignored her. "These are your pups for the year?"

"All of the ones that lived through their first moon," Rissa said proudly.

"How many of yours live?" Yllin asked, raising her tail a little higher. "Last year it was only two, wasn't it? And they both left the valley."

"Quiet," Rissa ordered.

Ceela lifted one side of her lip, speaking for the first time. She was slightly smaller than Torell, and had a yellow-brown pelt. "Perhaps you will teach this year's litter better manners. Though I see some that I don't expect to last through the winter." Her eyes rested on Reel and Ázzuen.

"No need for you to worry about that," Rissa said. "Pups, this is Ceela and this is Torell, leaders of the Stone Peak pack. There is no need for you to greet them."

"As if any of us would move," Ázzuen whispered.

"You will leave Swift River lands, now," Rissa said, stepping slightly aside. "We will allow you to pass without injury."

Ceela gave what in any other wolf would be considered a smile. From her, it seemed more of a snarl.

"We will go for now. But hear this, Rissa. Our territories are compromised. The humans take our prey. Already the longfangs in our territory are dying. We will not let our pack suffer because we had the bad luck to have the humans on our side of the river." Ceela's eyes swept over us. "The Swift River lands are among the richest in the valley. We will have our share of prey."

Rissa growled again. This time Werrna and Yllin joined her. We could feel the ground shake under our paws.

"I think it's time for you to go," Werrna said.

Torell met Ceela's eyes and gave the slightest of nods. The two of them began to walk past us. The path was narrow and they had to pass close by or else they would have to walk through the woods, which would make it hard for them to move quickly if we attacked.

Torell let his gaze linger over us pups as he walked by. When he saw me, he stopped.

"What is this?" he hissed, staring at me. "She bears the mark of the cursed, and smells of Outsider wolf."

"Move," Yllin said, coming to stand beside me. But I could not.

"I have told you before that the affairs of Swift River are none of yours," Rissa snapped. Werrna spun to face Ceela, trapping the Stone Peak wolves between herself and Yllin on one side and Rissa on the other.

"We don't like repeating ourselves," she said. "Will you leave our territory freely, or will we need to escort you?"

Torell narrowed his eyes.

"We will leave for now," he said. But his eyes lingered on me, and only when Werrna and Rissa began to move toward him did he and Ceela step onto the crossing tree. They ran easily across it and stared at us from the other side.

"Come, pups," Rissa said. "They will not come into our territory again tonight."

She picked up the piece of firemeat she had let drop and allowed her fur to rest again along her back. Soon we began moving again, more quickly this time. I couldn't stop shaking. Something about Torell's gaze, the hatred in his voice, chilled me. But there had been too much strangeness for one night, and I pushed it from my mind. I had enough to worry about if anyone told Ruuqo I'd tried to go to the humans. I could worry about Torell and the Stone Peaks later.

8

By the time we reached the Tall Grass field, the sun was up well over the eastern mountains. We were all tired from the night's adventures. The rest of the pack waited for us at Wood's Edge, gnawing lazily at the pieces of leftover horse we'd managed to save. Rissa told Ruuqo of our confrontation with the Stone Peaks. He listened carefully and licked her muzzle, speaking quietly to her. He didn't seem concerned. Conflict between packs was as common as rain, and this one had not ended in a fight. Ruuqo was pleased with the extra meat, and if he was upset that Rissa had allowed Yllin and the others to venture into the human gathering place, he said nothing about it. He ignored the firemeat scent he must have been able to smell on the breath of the wolves that were lucky enough to get some of it. Rissa slipped the piece she had saved to Trevegg. The old-wolf rumbled his thanks, devouring the meat in one gulp.

To my relief, Rissa did not tell Ruuqo that I had tried to go to the humans, and she had ordered the others not to tell him. Still, every time Borlla or Unnan went near Ruuqo, my stomach

clenched in fear. If he thought my father was an Outsider wolf, and if he was looking for reasons to get rid of me, my attempt to go to the humans would give him the excuse he needed. But they said nothing. Rissa did tell him that Borlla had helped Reel across the river and that she had successfully stolen meat.

"You have done well, youngwolf," Ruuqo said. "You will do good things for Swift River pack."

It was the first time he had called any of us anything other than "pup." A youngwolf was a wolf who had made the transition from pup, who is completely dependent upon others, to a contributing member of the pack. Borlla almost burst out of her fur with pride. Ruuqo praised Unnan, too, and Marra, which I shouldn't have minded, but I couldn't help myself. But Borlla got the most praise, both for her skill in meat-stealing, and her courage at the river. Yllin, Trevegg, and even gruff Werrna made a big fuss over her.

When Borlla caught me watching her, she strutted over to where I stood and breathed in my face, sending the crisp, sweet scent of burnt meat over my nose. Then she turned and raised her tail at me. I felt fury rising up in me, but I just walked away. Then I heard the whoosh of wings from above, and a cry of disgust from Borlla. I looked back to see her jumping up to try to catch Tlitoo as he hovered just above her head. A large splotch of bird dung had hit her on top of her head, splattering her face and eyes. Tlitoo kept dipping down within range and then flying above her head, cackling as she tried to catch him.

Pup looks better now.
Dirty fur is nice and white,
Thanks to raven's help.

Yllin was the first to start laughing, followed by Minn and the rest of the pack.

"You'd better learn to move faster than that, Borlla," Rissa said, snorting dust from her nose as she dipped her head to the ground. Trevegg laughed so hard he rolled to the ground, legs waving in the air. Ruuqo joined in, pouncing on the oldwolf as he rolled in the dirt. Yllin tumbled Borlla onto her back, and when Borlla growled at her, she laughed all the harder.

"That will teach you to be so proud, pup!" she said, snorting. She let Borlla up, and then dove out of the way as Tlitoo let loose another stream of droppings. He missed both wolves. Disappointed, the raven flew over Borlla again, and she ran for cover under Rissa's belly. Rissa collapsed in laughter as Tlitoo, apparently at the end of his supply, flew to a nearby rock.

Borlla's face was tight with anger, but she couldn't challenge Rissa or any of the other adults. Ears down and shoulders hunched, she stalked off into the trees. Feeling much better, I helped bury the rest of the stolen meat near the pieces of horse we had hidden earlier. I took a small piece of old horse in my mouth, thinking that if I couldn't have the firemeat, I at least could have that scrap. But Werrna knocked me over and took it from me.

"You did not earn that food, pup," she said.

I appealed to Rissa, but she turned her face away from mine. Now it was my turn to stalk away, growling softly to myself as Ruuqo gave the order to rest until the cooling time. The adults settled in the shade, and Rissa lifted her head.

"Pups," she said, "you may explore nearby if you do not wish to sleep. But do not go far."

I walked away from the others. I did not like that my status in the pack was so low. I should be as important to the pack as

Borlla or Unnan. Hadn't I been holding my own, getting more meat than any of the others at the horse carcass, and swimming as strongly as anyone? I was afraid the pack would hold it against me that I had tried to go to the humans. I walked until I reached the edge of the Tall Grass plain. Ázzuen followed behind me. Then Borlla emerged from the woods. She'd managed to clean much of the bird dung from her head, and sniffed at the edge of the trees, several wolflengths to my left, keeping a wary eye out for Tlitoo. Unnan and Reel cautiously joined her. Marra poked at tangy berry bushes near where we'd buried the stolen meat, and chewed at their sticky leaves. I nosed an empty gopher hole, and pawed the loose earth, looking for something interesting. Then I heard Borlla's voice, pitched to carry.

"You know they won't be able to hunt when the time comes," she said to Unnan. Ruuqo raised his head, woken from his nap by Borlla's voice.

It annoyed me that she was so obviously trying to prejudice Ruuqo against us, to make him think of us as weak hunters.

"She could at least be a bit more subtle," Ázzuen grumbled.

"They couldn't even cross the river, or steal food," Borlla continued. "How are they going to hunt anything?"

Reel winced. I thought it was pretty mean of her since she was supposed to be watching out for the smaller pup. Ruuqo gave Borlla, and then me and Ázzuen, a long look before stretching out in the soft-sage and falling back asleep.

But Borlla had given me an idea. I smelled living horse nearby. After tracking the scent for several wolflengths, I spotted the tall, heavy-bodied shapes of horses feeding on the dry grass of the open plain.

"We'll see who's a hunter," I said, mostly to myself.

"What are you going to do?" Ázzuen said, alarmed.

I settled down on my haunches and watched the herd. Before long, we would be expected to hunt with the pack. If I were the first pup to touch live prey, Borlla's words would be made meaningless. And maybe no one would care that my father might have been an Outsider wolf. Maybe, I thought, I could even catch a prey myself. My heart beat fast as I realized what I was going to do. Looking over my shoulder at Ázzuen, I set off toward the herd, stopping after a few paces. Ázzuen followed reluctantly. I caught Marra's eye, and she left her exploration of the berry bushes to join us.

"You know we aren't supposed to wander so far away," she said, eyeing the horses. She didn't sound particularly concerned. She was just letting me know how insane she thought I was.

"I know," I said, "but I want to see them up close, don't you?"

"Of course I do," she said with a grin. "Just don't get caught. I am not so fond of trouble as you are. You take too many risks."

I snorted. Marra was the most likely of us to take chances. I took a few more steps to the horses and then broke into a fast walk-run. Ázzuen and Marra followed.

We were halfway to the horses when I heard a sound behind me. Borlla, Unnan, and Reel ran to catch up to us. Anticipating a fight, the three of us turned to face them. But they did not attack. Instead, they ran past us. I knew then that they were planning to get to the horses first and get all the credit for the idea. Ruuqo and Rissa would once again praise Borlla and ignore me.

Determined not to let Borlla and Unnan reach the horses first, I raced after them. I passed Reel easily and caught up with Unnan and Borlla when they stopped a good ten wolflengths from the horses. Marra was right behind me, and a determined, panting Ázzuen brought up the rear. I leaned close to Borlla's dirty white ear.

"I'll bet you're afraid to go right up to a horse. I bet you don't really have the courage to be a hunter. This prey isn't lying on the ground, waiting for you to pick it up."

Borlla didn't answer, but looked at me and then at the herd. She turned her nose up and away. I heard Ázzuen snicker behind me. Borlla took a step forward to the prey, but stopped when Reel whined and pressed into her with his shoulder. He looked at her beseechingly, and whispered to her. Her eyes softened, and she nosed him gently. Once more I felt a stab of jealousy at their closeness.

"Thought so," I said. I should have just left it at that, but I wanted to make sure that Unnan and Borlla—and especially Ruuqo—knew I belonged in the pack. Before long our winter coats would grow in; we pups would need to sort out our positions in the pack before then.

"Come on," I said to Ázzuen and Marra. On shaking legs, I walked a few steps closer to the horses. They looked a lot bigger close up, and a lot more dangerous than the one the bear had already killed. They smelled of prey—an aroma of sweat and warm flesh. Their breath was scented with chewed grass and dirt. I looked back to see both Marra and Ázzuen watching me nervously. I didn't want to do this alone. I gave them a pleading look and, after a moment, they followed me. I wasn't the only one who knew this could determine the status of us pups from now on. Still, I was grateful that they backed me up.

As I knew they would, Borlla and Unnan moved, too, eager to be the first ones to the prey. Reel, after a brief hesitation, followed along. I felt a little sorry for him. He wasn't a bully like

Unnan and Borlla. On his own, he seemed to be a decent wolf. But I didn't have time to think about him. When I heard Borlla and Unnan coming up behind me, I broke into a run, racing them to get to the horses first.

And then we were among the sturdy beasts, inhaling the scent of their flesh and the grassy smell of their dung. Their breath was warm—I hadn't expected that—and they began to breathe more shallowly as we darted around their legs. From a distance I heard Ruuqo's warning bark, but ignored it. I didn't have the patience to wait to hear what he was saying. I felt the hunter heart beat within me as I moved among the horses.

"They're just dumb prey!" I shouted giddily to Ázzuen. "No wolf need be afraid of dumb prey!" I laughed. My heart beat with excitement. The blood quickened in my veins. My nostrils flared to take in every drop of scent and my ears lifted to capture every sound. I'd had no idea that this was what the hunt would be like. This was nothing like stalking mice or tracking rabbits. I had never felt so alive, so eager. The dim-witted horses just stood there like rocks. They were meant to be killed, meant to be prey. I understood now that we were the cleverest hunters because we were meant to take the stupid and the slow.

It was then that I remembered that we were supposed to be finding the sick ones, the slow ones. I could not. I could not concentrate on anything but the smell, the feel, the sound of prey around me. I grew light-headed and my stomach turned flips. My head felt distant from my body, and I breathed hard. What was this frenzy? The others were captured by it, too. We grew bold and restless, chasing one another between the horses' legs. A thrill rushed through me as I imagined myself leading a hunt and biting into the soft flesh of a horse's belly.

Suddenly the temper of the herd shifted. The horse nearest

Reel lowered its head and blew out air with an angry snort. It stamped its feet, shook its head, and reared up on its back legs. The horse beside it screamed in anger and lunged toward Marra, snapping its teeth together. She dodged out of its way with a frightened squeal. All around us, horses stamped and reared and began to run, their hooves striking at our heads. I turned and looked for a way to run, but seeing nothing but moving legs, and crashing hooves, I crouched low in fear. I looked up to see a mass of horses rushing around us, faster than any creature should be able to move.

"*Run!*" Trevegg shouted. "Run or you will be crushed!" Through the throng of horses, I saw the adults racing toward us. Trevegg's voice cut through my terror, and I was able to get my legs to stand and support me. Struggling to stay on my feet, I bent to shove Ázzuen out of his terrified stupor. He looked at me in confusion, still crouched low.

"Stand up!" I yelled. "Get out of the way!"

I could smell Ázzuen's fear and confusion. We were surrounded by pounding feet and swirling dust. Now that the first wave of terror had washed over me, I felt all of my senses sharpen. I pushed the fear to a distant corner of my mind.

"We have to avoid their feet until the adults get to us," I shouted to make myself heard. "We have to keep moving." A snatch of memory from one of our hunting lessons came back to me.

"If you are much smaller than your prey," Rissa had said, "there is no point in trying to use your weight to knock the prey over. You will end up fallen in the dirt. You must use your wits, for wits are what make us good hunters. Run in and run out. Use strategy, not force."

I saw Borlla standing, glaring at a horse and growling, trying to protect Reel, who crouched behind her. Brave, I thought, but stupid. They were too far away for me to reach. Marra was already moving, dodging agilely among the horses, her face fierce with concentration. Ázzuen stood motionless beside me, staring up at the horses in fear. Unnan crouched low, a wolflength away. I shoved Ázzuen hard, pushing him out of the way of moving hooves. Each time he stopped, I shoved him again. The adult wolves reached us then, growling at the horses to keep them away from us. Werrna jumped straight at a horse that was about to crush Unnan, knocking the surprised beast off balance. Even in my fearful state I was impressed by her courage. Ruuqo and Rissa were trying to gather the other wolves in a circle around us, between us and the horses. Marra dove into the circle, and watched, panting, from the relative safety of the protection of the larger wolves. My stumblings had brought me close to Unnan, and I shoved him toward the adults. Yllin grabbed him and dumped him in the middle of the circle. I picked Ázzuen up by his scruff and all but threw him in the direction of the adults, pulling a muscle in my neck so hard it made me yelp, before a horse's head swung at me, knocking me back. I dodged and ran, then dodged again. Borlla, too, stood outside the protective circle, still growling frantically at the horses as Reel crouched low, whimpering a little.

"Move!" I yelled again. "Keep moving!"

She glared at me, and looked up at a large horse. I dove for her, pushed her out of the way, and then rolled away as a huge hoof came down toward my head. I heard a wolf scream, a terrible yowl of terror and pain, through a cloud of dust.

Then, as quickly as it began, the horse frenzy was over. Yllin and Werrna chased off the horses, who retreated to the far side of the field. Rissa ran from pup to pup, making sure we were safe. I crouched, dazed, and frantically returned her caress when she bent to lick my head. She repeated the gesture with Ázzuen, who climbed shakily to his feet; with Unnan, who had a cut over his left eye; and with Marra, who stood, staring at the retreating horses. Then, tail drooping and an anxious whine in her voice, Rissa nosed a pale lump that smelled like Reel, but somehow different. Her whine deepened, and Ruuqo and Trevegg walked slowly to join her. They pushed and prodded Reel, but he did not move. His head was covered with blood, his body oddly flattened.

"Get up, Reel," Borlla said, a little impatiently, nudging his still form.

Rissa gently pushed Borlla aside and sat back on her haunches, releasing a long and mournful howl. Ruuqo, Trevegg, and Minn added their voices to hers. Yllin and Werrna, trotting back from chasing off the horses, stopped, and stood very still, then added their songs of sorrow. I felt my throat open and a deep howl I did not recognize as my own sounded from my throat.

I looked in disbelief at the small, dirt-covered form on the trampled grass. My head hurt and my chest felt heavy. My stomach pulled in on itself, and I thought I would vomit up the little bit of meat I had eaten. Just moments before, I'd been running with Reel to the horses. Now he was just fur and flesh. Yllin and Werrna had reached the rest of the pack and we all stood around Reel, the hot afternoon sun beating down on our backs, making me feel even sicker.

I don't know how long we stood there, waiting, hoping Reel's life would come back to him, but he was gone. I hadn't liked Reel that much, hadn't thought that much about him at all, really, but he was as much a littermate as I was ever going to have. He was pack. And his fate could easily have been mine. I had dared him to run to the horses. I wanted to lie down on the plain and bury myself in the dirt. Rissa howled again, longer and deeper, and the pack joined her in singing farewell to Reel. All except Borlla, who just stood and stared in disbelief at his body, the fur on his lifeless flesh now rippling gently in a breeze.

With one last look at Reel, Rissa led the pack away from the Tall Grass plain. Borlla would not go.

"You can't just leave him here! You can't just leave him for the long-fangs and hyenas!" she cried.

"It is our way, littlewolf," old Trevegg said, his eyes creased in sympathy. "He has returned to the Balance. He will become part of the earth, as we all will someday. He will feed the grass that will feed the prey that will feed our pack. It is the way."

"I won't leave him," Borlla said stubbornly. None of us had ever spoken back to an adult wolf in this way.

"You must," Trevegg said. "You are wolf and Swift River and you must follow your pack." When Borlla didn't move, Trevegg shoved her away, less roughly than he might have normally, and forced her to follow the pack.

We walked slowly back to the edge of the wood. Borlla and Unnan kept hanging back, staring at Reel's body, until Trevegg or Werrna would go back to gently push them along.

At last Werrna took Borlla, half grown as she was, in her strong jaws. Borlla struggled at first, but then the fight went out of her, and she hung limp in Werrna's jaws, her legs dragging on the ground. We were quiet as we plodded toward home, except for Borlla's quiet whimpering. We had walked just a few wolflengths when Unnan ran to me, knocking me over and standing on my chest, his narrow face contorted in anger.

"You killed him," he spat. "That horse should've killed you instead." There was hatred in his voice. "You're the one who should be dead."

I hardly had the heart to fight back. Unnan was saying nothing I hadn't said to myself. I rolled Unnan off me, then limped away. I did not want to return his attack. But when he grabbed me by the neck, choking me, I bit him hard enough to make him cry out.

Ruuqo called a halt, and the pack gathered around Unnan and me. Werrna set Borlla down.

"What are you talking about, Unnan?" Ruuqo asked.

"*She* made us go," Unnan said. "We were just sleeping and she made us go. It's her fault Reel is dead."

My heart sank in my chest and I could barely breathe. Ruuqo looked at me, waiting for an answer, but I could find none. Marra spoke up for me.

"It was Kaala's idea," she said, "but we all wanted to go."

"No one made you go, Unnan," Ázzuen said. "You could've stayed behind. Reel could have, too. We all wanted to see the horses," he said to the leaderwolves. "And Kaala saved Unnan and me when we couldn't get out of the way. She knew what to do when we didn't." I looked at him gratefully.

"What do you have to say for yourself, pup?" Ruuqo asked.

The trees and bushes seemed to close in on me, making it harder to breathe. The ground was hard against my chest as I dropped onto my belly. I wanted to make excuses, to blame Unnan and Borlla for goading me, to blame the horses for running. But I saw Ázzuen and Marra watching me. They had had the courage to defend me. I couldn't turn coward.

"It was my fault," I said, unable to keep a quaver from my voice. "It was my idea to see the horses up close. I didn't know they would do that—that they could run like that." I cringed down as low as I could. "I didn't mean for anyone to get hurt."

"At least you do not hide your fault. I do not keep liars in my pack. Why did you lead the others to the horses?"

I was glad that I had not tried to blame someone else. I stayed as low to the ground as I could, ears as far back against my head as I could force them.

"I wanted to see if I could hunt." My answer seemed inadequate. "I wanted to be the first one to touch prey."

"Pride means death for a wolf," Ruuqo said. "And it was pride and foolishness that led you to approach prey without respecting it, without knowing enough about the hunt."

My throat tightened as I awaited Ruuqo's judgment.

I was so tense my eyes hurt, and I could feel the veins pounding behind them. Ruuqo had been waiting for an excuse to get rid of me since I was born. I was sure he would send me away. But he looked around the pack, his eyes coming to rest on Rissa. She approached him, followed by the rest of the adults in the pack. They pressed themselves against him, moving around him, talking quietly.

"It is true," Rissa said, pressing her head to Ruuqo's neck, "that Kaala caused the pups to go to the horses, but pups are curious. They will try to hunt before they are ready. They would not be wolf if they did not test prey. It is not Kaala's fault the horses were agitated today. And she had the courage and the wit to help the others when the horses ran. If not for her, we might have lost three or four pups, rather than one."

"I have never seen so young a pup do such a thing, protect the others in such a way," Trevegg said, "and I have seen eight seasons of pups."

Yllin lowered herself to the ground before she spoke. Yearling wolves did not often participate in such discussions. "I could not have done so when I was a pup," she said, "and I was bigger than Kaala."

To my surprise, Werrna rumbled in agreement. She had never taken my side before.

"She caused the death of another pup!" Minn protested, then lowered his ears when Rissa glared at him.

Ruuqo twitched his ears. He took the muzzle of each wolf in his mouth, and then walked away, his brow creased in thought. I realized that I had forgotten to breathe and drew a deep gasp of air into my lungs. The energy of the pack reminded me of when the adults came together to decide what to hunt. A leader-wolf makes decisions, but if no one agrees with him, his authority is weakened. I could almost see Ruuqo's mind working, testing the pack's wishes and his own. He looked at me with dislike, and I shivered.

Trevegg walked over to him. "No wolf is a pack unto himself, Ruuqo," the oldwolf said softly. "The pack wishes her to stay. You know that. If you go so hard against the wishes of so many, against the will of the pack, you may lose them. They may seek another leader." He looked out of the corner of his eyes at Werrna's scarred face.

"Do you think I am a fool," Ruuqo snapped, brushing Trevegg aside, "to anger my pack because of my feelings toward this pup? A strong wolf is a strong wolf, even if she does not hold my favor."

Ruuqo turned to face the pack, then caught Rissa's clear, direct gaze. "You are right. If Kaala had not acted as she did, we would have lost more pups. Such spirit is needed in the pack." Ruuqo spoke to Rissa, but his words were for the pack.

I looked at him in amazement. I couldn't have been more

surprised if he had stood up on two legs and held a sharpened stick like a human. He looked over the pack.

"It is the way of things. We will all learn from this. And we will watch this pup carefully," he said, giving me a look that made my insides turn to mud. "If she shows more unstable behavior, we will have to reconsider whether or not she stays in the pack."

Unnan's whole body shook with fury. "But she went to see the hu—"

Werrna's large paw came down on him as Rissa swung her head around angrily.

"Silence, pup!" Werrna hissed. "You've been given a command by your leaderwolf. Follow it!" Unnan looked at her resentfully, but said nothing more. It was my turn to shake, but this time in relief, not anger.

It all happened so fast I was stunned. Finally, I remembered myself and crawled to Ruuqo to thank him. He must have been able to sense my astonishment, for he snorted as I licked his muzzle in thanks.

"What are you so surprised about, pup?" he asked.

I could think of nothing to say but the truth, and I could not refuse to answer. "I thought you wanted me gone!" I blurted.

"And you think me so stupid and selfish as to place my own wishes before those of my pack?"

I could find no answer to that and just stared at him.

"I am watching you, pup. You are a threat to my pack and I have not forgotten that. Do not make more mistakes," Ruuqo said, so softly only I could hear. He turned to the rest of the pack. "We will not stay at Wood's Edge today. We return to Fallen Tree."

He trotted purposefully along the path, back toward our gathering place. Borlla walked on her own feet this time, stopping every few steps to look back toward the spot where Reel had died. I could not bear to do so. I kept my head low and, trying not to think about my role in Reel's death and my tenuous position in the pack, I followed my family toward home.

9

Pups die. It's as natural as hunting prey or running in the moonlight. Our pack was unusual in that so many of us had survived for so long. Still, I couldn't help but feel guilty about Reel's death. If I hadn't been trying to prove myself, if I had not dared the others to go to see the horses, he might not have died. I could not get the sight of his small, still form out of my mind. And then there was what was happening to Borlla.

She had taken Reel's death the hardest of any of us. She had grown silent and solemn, and had eaten little in the half-moon since the stampede. It had been a time full of rain. The gathering place was slick with mud, and all of us were short-tempered. Werrna bit me two different times when I walked where she wanted to be, and even Yllin growled when we pups came near. But no one snapped at Borlla, or bit her.

She seemed unable to believe that Reel was gone; whenever the adults were not watching her carefully she returned to the Tall Grass fields to look for him. I thought Ruuqo and Rissa

might be angry with her for leaving so often without permission, but they were not. Each time she left, they sent a wolf to retrieve her, and Trevegg, Werrna, or Minn would return with her. Sometimes they had to drag her back, which couldn't have been easy, nearly grown as she was.

"He is not there anymore, littlewolf," Trevegg said gently, after he had dragged her back a third time. It was true. Ázzuen and I had followed Borlla back the first day she returned to the Tall Grass field. Reel's body was gone. Though his scent remained strong, mingled with it was the scent of hyena. It didn't take much imagination to figure out what had happened. The scroungers had carried him off somewhere, no doubt fearing our return. The thought that one of us could so easily become a meal haunted me. Borlla refused to believe it.

I thought she would hate me, would look at me in resentment as Unnan did, but when I looked in her eyes I saw only bewilderment and sorrow. I would have preferred anger. I watched her as she sat in the rain, waiting patiently for her chance to slip away again, and guilt weighed me down more than my rain-soaked fur. When I tried to eat some of the old deer meat that Werrna had dug up from one of our hiding places, I could not choke it down. I watched Borlla, hoping to see some change in her. The rain was warm but I shivered and placed my head in my paws.

"It is time for you to stop moping, pup," Trevegg said sternly, slogging over to me. "The strong survive and the weak do not. We are all sorry for Reel's death, but prey does not jump into our jaws just because we are sad. You don't see Rissa sitting around feeling sorry for herself. She knows that the hunt must continue. The day we stop chasing prey is the day we are no longer wolf."

"I know that," I said, blinking against the rain, which seemed to be coming up from the ground and into my eyes. "I know he might not have lived anyway. But I still feel bad."

"I am glad to hear that," the oldwolf said, chewing caked mud off his shoulder. "You would not be a good member of the pack if you did not. But now you must stop brooding. Would Reel have lived through the winter if you had not gone to the horses? Maybe. Would Unnan and Ázzuen have died if you had not thought and acted quickly? Almost certainly."

Trevegg's voice softened a little. "Some pups do not live through winter's end. That's the way it must be if wolves are to remain strong. Did you know the Vole Eater pack can only keep one or two of their pups alive each year, since they are too small to catch large prey? And the Stone Peak wolves won't even let their smaller pups near food. They let them starve without even giving them a chance to prove themselves. Rissa is known throughout the valley for keeping most of her pups alive. If the Ancients take one of our pups, we must be grateful that so many do stay with us."

"Where are they all? Rissa's other pups from last year, and from before that?" Ázzuen asked, trotting over to us. He had been watching me for days, but had seemed afraid to come near. I remembered that I had growled at him when he had first tried to comfort me.

"Most leave the valley," Trevegg answered. "There is not room here for many packs, and the rules of the valley are not for everyone." He shook the rain from his fur.

"So now you must decide, pup. Do you stay with us, or do you follow Reel? None of us can make that decision for you." He licked the top of my head and went to speak to Borlla. She turned her face away, then stood shakily and walked off into the woods. Trevegg's shoulders drooped a little, then he shook himself and trudged over to speak to Unnan.

Suddenly I heard a splash and a growl from behind me. Yllin had pushed Minn into a muddy puddle. The two youngwolves began to fight, rolling in the mud and biting harder than necessary. Rissa broke up the fight and separated them.

"I hate summer storms," she said, glaring after the two youngwolves. "I look forward to the winter snows, when the running is better and so are everyone's tempers. Pups," she said, "you are now old enough to explore on your own. Stay within a half hour's run of Fallen Tree and come the moment we call you."

I was surprised. They had been watching us all carefully since the stampede, keeping us within sight.

"Aren't they just a bit young, Rissa?" Trevegg said, laughing at her. "Usually you wait another half-moon before sending pups out on their own." He butted her affectionately.

"I want some peace in this gathering place so we can have a decent hunt!" Rissa said. She narrowed her eyes at Werrna, who was deep in conversation with Ruuqo. "Go on, pups. You may stay here and nap or you may explore."

"We weren't the ones making trouble," Marra said, squelching over to me and Ázzuen, then sitting down to lick mud off a front paw. "But I don't mind exploring. Maybe we can find some small prey."

Ázzuen's ears pricked up. The last hunt had been unsuccessful and we were all a little hungry. The adults had brought us some food from their hiding places, but not a lot.

"Let's go, then!" Ázzuen said.

I laughed, and, feeling better than I had since Reel's death, followed Ázzuen and Marra into the woods.

Ázzuen was the one who found the mouse homesite. It was just a rocky, grassy patch exactly half an hour's run from Fallen Tree. The rain had flooded the mouse homes, forcing them into the open. After less than an hour, we got good at catching them, but just as quickly they figured out that it wasn't safe near that homesite anymore. The mice ran into a hole we hadn't seen before, and we lost their scent. Pleased with ourselves, but still a little hungry since mice are not that filling, we settled down to sleep. That's when the young spiritwolf found me again.

I had not forgotten her. I had thought about her often since she spoke to me at the human gathering place. But I didn't know how to find out more about her. I was afraid to ask even Trevegg or Rissa, lest they think I was crazy and not fit to be pack. Wolves don't appear out of thin air. When I wasn't thinking about Reel, I looked for her behind trees and in the shadows, but it was in my dreams that she came to me again.

Ázzuen and Marra slept soundly, tired from mouse hunting, but my sleep was restless. Each time my mind would try to take me to dreams of running with the pack or hunting with Ázzuen and Marra, the young wolf's face would appear before me. Then she would turn as if to run and wait for me to follow. But sleep kept me in one place, and I just tossed and scrabbled on the wet ground. Finally, she gave a bark, loud enough to startle me from my dreams.

I awoke, leaping to my feet, and waking Ázzuen and Marra

from their own dreams. I saw a flash of tail disappearing into the forest, and caught just a whiff of the juniper-acrid scent I remembered so well. I shook off my sleep and a layer of rain, and followed the scent into the forest. Marra grunted and settled back into her nap, but Ázzuen followed me.

"Where are we going?" He was sleepy and a little cranky.

I ignored him and kept running. He could follow me or not as he chose. The scent grew stronger as we ran deep into the woods. It took us to a dense part of the forest, a place we were not supposed to go without the adults. Not only had Rissa told us to stay a half hour's run from Fallen Tree, we also had to stay at least a half hour's walk from the edges of our territory in case a rival pack was roaming. Before long, Ázzuen and I reached a scent marker that Ruuqo and Rissa had left specifically to warn us pups not to go too far. I stopped, knowing we shouldn't go any farther. When a strong wind carrying the juniper-acrid scent whipped around me, pelting me with painfully sharp rain, I crossed the scent marker. After I did so, the rain let up a bit. Ázzuen, too, stopped for a moment, and then followed, shaking his head a little. We had only walked a few more steps when we came upon a path the humans used to cross through the thick woods and where the young spiritwolf's scent mingled with the human-and-fire scent.

I stopped again, confused, and looked around. I knew from the sounds of rushing water and the wet leaf and mud smell that we were near the river. But it was a different part of the river, far downstream from the crossing we'd swum and even farther from the Tree Crossing. We were, I realized a little guiltily, much too close to the human homesite. If one crept through the woods a bit farther and jumped straight over the river, it would be a quick run to their gathering place. I didn't need Ázzuen's frightened whine to remind me we were in danger of breaking the most important of rules.

"Let's get out of here," I said.

Then I heard the cry coming from the river. It was not the sound of one of our kind in trouble, but it was definitely a creature in need. Somehow I knew it was not prey, and I felt drawn to the sounds of distress, and took a few more steps in the direction of the river. I should have turned tail and left. I didn't need any trouble with Ruuqo watching me so carefully, and with Reel's death on everyone's mind. Apparently Ázzuen had the same thought.

"Kaala, we should leave," he said urgently. "Whatever it is, it's not our concern."

I knew he was right. I began to back away, down the human trail and away from the river and the frightened cries coming from it. Then, suddenly, a forceful gust of juniper-acrid wind pushed me forward, through the trees and back toward the river. With a surprised yip, Ázzuen followed.

The woods ended at a steep, treacherous drop to the river. "No wonder we don't cross here," I muttered to myself. Then I saw it. In the rushing water, clinging to a rock, was a human child. I recognized it for what it was, for we had seen ones like it playing and shouting at the human gathering place. The child was struggling in the fast-moving water, for the days of rain had swelled and quickened the river. It was just barely keeping its head above water, crying out whenever it could.

It sounded so much like a wolf in distress, so much like the death cries of my brother and sisters, that I had to help it. After

I had gotten in so much trouble for trying to go to the humans, I had promised myself I would pretend they did not exist. Every time I thought of them, the mark on my chest ached, and I was determined not to get in any more trouble with Ruuqo. But I couldn't ignore that desperate, helpless cry. I watched the child for a moment as it struggled for life, then I began to pick my way down the steep slope.

Ázzuen nipped at my flank, trying to keep me from going, but I ignored him. I ran down the bank, sliding down the last few wolflengths and landing hard beside the water, hurting my hip. Caked with mud, I splashed ungracefully into the water. The river was deep enough that I had to start swimming right away, and I swam hard to the child. Its dark eyes met mine as it lost its hold on its rock and began to slip underwater. I swam closer. It grabbed frantically at my fur and wrapped its thin forelegs around my neck, pulling me under the water. Water ran up into my nose and into my throat. I struggled back up to the surface. As soon as I caught a breath, the child's forelegs pulled at me. I was sure that I would be dragged all the way under by its weight, and was afraid that I would not be able to fight my way to shore. But the child clung to me so desperately that I could not have freed myself if I wanted to. It suddenly seemed to understand what I was trying to do and began to kick its legs, helping me stay afloat. Its long, dark pelt fell into my eyes and nose, and I grabbed the soft fur in my mouth to help me pull the child in the right direction. Its fur tasted different than the fur of a wolf. It didn't have a warm-body taste, but was more like the fur a wolf leaves behind on a tree or bush. Summoning all of my strength, I swam. I reached the far edge of the river and dragged the child onto a narrow, flat stretch of bank. Shaking myself hard, I got the child to release its grip, and it slid to the ground. It began to squall again, as soon as it caught its breath. But as I stood over it, it stopped. I heard a splash from across the river as Ázzuen jumped in and swam across to join me. It surprised me that he so easily swam the river since he'd had so much trouble just a half-moon before, but I kept my gaze on the human.

It was a girl child, half grown, one of those we had seen romping like pups in the human homesite. She stared at me fearfully for a moment. There are many creatures that will kill and eat a human child if they can, and there was no way for the girl to know a wolf would not. I lowered my ears a bit, so as to appear less threatening and, after a moment, the fear fled the girl child's eyes. Then she reached out her forelegs. Arms, Yllin had told us they were called.

"Kaala!" Ázzuen's voice was urgent. "Let's go!" He sniffed the air anxiously. "With all the noise she's made, someone will come soon."

Yes, I thought, some bear or rock lion will come and take her. Or some scrounger too lazy to hunt real prey. I didn't want her to be prey. But I could not stay and risk exile. After watching the child a bit longer, watching her large, dark eyes and soft, dark skin, I touched my nose to her cheek and started toward the river. She tried to stand but collapsed back into the mud and began weeping again. The human's fur was not thick enough to warm her well and the water had been cold, even in the summer rain. The bank on this side of the river was almost as steep and slippery as the bank on our side. The rain showed no sign of letting up and the girl was shivering. She would die if I left her there. Even if she didn't become prey, she would freeze and the scroungers would have her anyway. Her eyes had looked at me with such trust. I felt something stirring within me. The crescent on my chest grew warm, but this time the feeling was not uncomfortable at all.

Before I could change my mind, I turned my back on the river. I took the girl's shoulder gently in my jaws, careful not to bite down hard enough to hurt her. But she squealed in fright at the feel of my teeth and began to thrash. Concerned that I would hurt her as she threw herself about in my jaws, I let her go. I thought for a moment. How could I carry her without hurting or scaring her? She had no scruff, and surely it would hurt her if I dragged her by her long head fur. Then I remembered the way she had clung to me as I swam in the river, and remembered the way I had seen human children grabbing their adults by the neck and hanging from them as the adults walked.

I lowered myself to the ground and pressed up against the child. After just a moment's hesitation, she threw her forelegs around my neck and her rear legs over my back. I tried to stumble to my feet, but staggered under the girl's weight. It had been easier to carry her in the water. Ázzuen watched in confusion.

"What under the moon are you doing?"

"Help me carry her!" Ázzuen could act like a curl-tail when he was frightened or confused, and I didn't have time to argue.

"How?" he asked.

"I don't know," I said, frustrated. "Think of something."

The girl had slipped off my back when I sagged to the ground, but kept her forelegs tight around my neck. Ázzuen thought for a moment and then lay down next to me, scooping the girl's rear legs so that they hung onto his back and then onto the ground beside him. The weight on my own back eased, and we both stood. The girl lay across both of our backs, her long legs dragging on the ground beside Ázzuen.

"You really think this will work?" I gasped.

"Do you have a better idea?" he replied.

I couldn't argue with that. Both Ázzuen and I shook with anxiety as well as with the weight of the child. If I had known what I was starting, I wouldn't have asked for his help, but I just wanted help up the slippery bank.

I was sure no wolf had ever carried a burden in such a way, but need creates wisdom and we needed to move the girl quickly and quietly. Her front paws were long and curved, and grasped with surprising strength. Her limbs looked weak and spindly, but were not. I could feel her warm breath on my neck and her heart beating against my back. We climbed the bank and began to run. We ran slowly and awkwardly, side by side, and Ázzuen began to laugh. "We must look ridiculous," he said.

We were also breaking another pack rule. It is unwise to run side by side in enemy territory, and by crossing the river we entered Stone Peak domain. It's better to run one by one to hide your numbers. But it was too late to worry about that now, and so we kept running. Ázzuen and I both remembered the way to the humans' gathering place, even though we came at it from a different direction this time. The scent of humans grew strong, and I knew we were not far from them. But I felt the girl shivering and, concerned, I stopped to set her down. Her lips were pale and her face paler. She shook hard. I licked her skin. It was cold and damp.

I curled my body around the girl child, ignoring Ázzuen's anxious whining. The two of us together could have warmed the girl better, but I didn't want him to help. I had found her. She was mine. Ázzuen would have left her in the river to drown, left her to be prey for some creature. I felt her heartbeat again, strong and sure, and her long forelegs went around me as far as they could reach. Her rich scent filled me. I had not realized before how sweet their scent was, like firemeat mixed with flowers and fragrant leaves. Because we were supposed to stay away from them, I had not had the chance to distinguish one human-scent from another. Now, inhaling the girl's unique scent, I came to know her as I did my packmates.

I couldn't keep her very warm with my fur still wet and the rain coming down, and Ázzuen was edging toward home. So I tried to take her on my back again—this time without Ázzuen's help. But the child's back legs dragged heavily on the ground and I couldn't take even two steps without collapsing. I wasn't strong enough to carry her on my own. Then, as she had in the river, she began to help me. She stood on her own, and pressed heavily on my back. We staggered toward the human gathering place, the girl gripping my fur and stumbling beside me. Ázzuen hesitated and then followed behind me.

"You can go back, you know," I said. For some reason I didn't want him with me now.

"Someone has to keep you out of trouble," he said, his voice almost steady.

I heard a rustling above us and smelled wet raven. I looked suspiciously up and to the left, where the smell came from. Tlitoo was trying to hide himself in some branches.

"Just what I need," I gasped, "more help." Tlitoo stopped trying to hide, cackled, and flew ahead of me toward the human gathering place.

"To keep you *in* trouble," he said over his wing as he flew into the mist.

Ázzuen and I neared the human homesite, and I began to look for a safe place to leave the girl. I didn't want to let her go. I wanted to take her back with me. Even though I had started to gain acceptance from some wolves in the pack, I was still an outsider. I wouldn't feel that way if I brought the human child with me. I wanted to take her back to Fallen Tree and keep her with us as we roamed the winter territories. But the rules of the Wide Valley were clear. I shouldn't even have pulled the girl from the river, and if Ruuqo found out I had, it could give him the excuse he needed to get rid of me. Still, I thought, perhaps I could hide her somewhere and keep her near.

A sharp pull on my ear brought me to my senses. "Leave her, wolflet," Tlitoo said. "You still have the winter to get through." He cocked his head. "Uh-oh," he said.

Ázzuen, who had been trailing a little way behind me, caught up.

"The Greatwolves are nearby," he said.

I had been so wrapped up in the girl that I hadn't noticed the scent of the Greatwolves. I hadn't seen them since the day they saved my life and I was surprised at how easily I recognized their scent. My heart pounded. What would they do if they found us here? I was grateful to Ázzuen, both for noticing the Greatwolves and for staying by my side. I called on the last of my strength and helped the girl to the very edge of the human gathering place. I wanted badly to venture farther into their home, to see what it was like up close, but I had broken enough rules for one day, and I wanted to avoid a confrontation with the Greatwolves. So I helped the girl sit on the ground and placed my paw on her chest. She clambered to her feet and returned the gesture. I nudged her gently, reinforcing the command to leave with a soft bark.

"Thank you, wolf," she said. And then she was gone, stumbling toward the warmth of her fires. I looked after her. Ázzuen looked at her and then at me.

"She spoke!" he said. "And I understood her. I thought we might not be able to."

I dipped my head. There are some creatures whose language is so strange you can't understand it at all. I was glad the humans were not such creatures.

"They're not that different from us," I said. "They are not Other."

"Less talk, more running," Tlitoo advised, shaking his wing feathers free of water.

"For once, I agree with him," Ázzuen said. "Let's go."

"Oops." Tlitoo cocked his head left and right. "Too late."

I heard breaking twigs and squelching mud, and Frandra and Jandru stepped out through the buckthorn bushes and blocked our path.

"What are you doing in the company of humans?" Frandra demanded. The Greatwolf was clearly angry. "Don't you know you could be exiled for this? Do you think I saved your life just so you could throw it away?"

I tried to speak but only a frightened whuff of air came out.

"We rescued a human child," Ázzuen managed.

"I know what you did," Frandra growled. "Do you think there is anything in these territories I don't know about? You," she said to me, "were saved for a reason, and you," she turned to Ázzuen, "should be helping her, not encouraging bad behavior."

Frandra's arrogance made me mad. Long-hidden anger was

slowly replacing my fear of her. It was the anger that had helped me fight off three pups when I was very small. It was the anger Tlitoo and Yllin had warned me against. But it felt good. It felt better than being afraid.

"If you know everything that happens in the valley," I said slowly, doing my best to speak calmly, "why did you let Ruuqo kill my littermates? Why did you let him send my mother away?" *Why didn't you tell me about the humans?* I wanted to ask.

Ázzuen looked at me in shock. Tlitoo pulled my tail so hard I almost fell over. I ignored them both. I didn't care if the Greatwolves really were descendants of the Ancients themselves. When I held the human girl close to me I had felt whole for the first time since my mother left. Now I felt the girl's absence like a bite wound, deep in my flesh, and I missed my mother more than I had since the day she left. Seeing the Greatwolves again after they had all but abandoned me made me feel the loss afresh. No one else in my pack had to feel that way. The Greatwolves knew something about who I was and why I felt the way I did about the human girl. I wanted answers from them.

Frandra looked at me coldly and pulled her lips back in a snarl. "Do not challenge me, wolf," she said, and took a step forward and bared her sharp teeth. Wet wings flapped above us and Tlitoo landed directly on her head. She turned to snap at him, and he leapt to her rump. When she turned to try to grab him in her jaws he leapt up and tweaked her ear, then flew to a low branch nearby.

The bigger they are
The slower Grumpwolves will be.
Wolf big, brain little.

To my surprise, Tlitoo's voice wobbled a little. Frandra swung her head away from me, growled at Tlitoo, and stepped toward him. He gave a shaky caw and flew off. We heard a muffled sound to our right, and turned to find Jandru laughing.

"Don't try to fight a battle against the ravens, Lifemate," he said. "You will always lose." He poked her playfully in the ribs. "As for the pup, what did you expect, Frandra? You're just unhappy things aren't going by your plan."

Frandra looked for a moment as if she was going to strike out at Jandru, but then ducked her head and gave her whuffling laugh, her anger leaving as quickly as it had come. Mine still burned within me. But my senses had returned and Frandra's fury had scared me. I would not challenge her again. At least not until I was a lot bigger.

"Maybe so, but this complicates things. And I can't help these two with their packmates." She swept her eyes over to us.

"You must listen. Your path is not an easy one, Kaala Smallteeth," she said. "You must resist the temptations of the humans. You must become pack and gain the mark of romma from Ruuqo. If you do not, no wolf will follow you, and you will never be accepted as a full member of any pack. You have learned of this already?"

"I think so," Ázzuen answered quickly. I think he was afraid of what I would say if I spoke. "We've already passed the first test, when we made it to our gathering place from the den. Now we have to participate in our first hunt, and travel the winter with the pack. After we do that, Ruuqo grants us the mark of the Swift River pack. I don't know what happens if we don't receive romma. And I am not sure what the mark is," he concluded.

"It is a scent mark that can be given only by a leaderwolf,"

Jandru said, "and you must bear that mark or you will not be able to be a part of a pack, and you will wander alone. Or you must start your own pack, which will be doubly difficult if you do not bear the romma mark."

"We need you to be accepted by your pack, youngwolf," Frandra said. "We need you to stay out of trouble. And you absolutely must stay away from the humans."

Jandru lowered his shaggy head to mine. "Even we cannot control all that happens, littlewolf. We do what we can, but that is not much. You must gain acceptance in your pack. You must shun the humans and hide your difference. If you can do this," he said, "if you can earn the mark of romma, we will help you find your mother when you are grown. I promise you."

I swallowed hard. I didn't know if I should trust him. But he certainly knew more than I did.

"We will not be in the territories much over the next moons," Frandra said, not waiting for me to agree. "Try to stay out of trouble when we are gone." And with that, she and Jandru stalked back into the woods. I looked after them. Now my anger was mixed with confusion and frustration. They had left me more upset than when they had first come. I took a step to follow them. I wanted to know more. I wanted to ask them if I was a danger to my pack, and if I was one of the mixed-blood wolves that Trevegg said could be crazy.

"Kaala, we have to get back," Ázzuen said.

"They will tell you no more, wolf," Tlitoo added, returning from his rock. "I can follow them," he suggested. "Try to listen if they say anything else about you." He pulled the fur on my paw gently.

I sighed. Ázzuen and Tlitoo were both right, but I still

wanted to follow the Greatwolves. But I had gotten Ázzuen into this and I owed it to him to get him home. And the Greatwolves were right, too—I had to make it through the winter.

"Come on," I said wearily. "Let's go home."

◘

As soon as we walked into the gathering place, Werrna raised up her nose.

"You smell of humans!" she said. "Where have you been?"

Ruuqo and Rissa heard Werrna's question and walked over to us. I groaned to myself. How could I have forgotten to cover the human-scent? I had been too upset by my encounter with the Greatwolves to think of it. What excuse could I possibly give them? My brain was exhausted.

"We slipped in the mud and fell in the river, leaderwolves," Ázzuen said, smoothly. "By the time we climbed out, we were near the human site. We came back as quickly as we could."

Impressed with Ázzuen's quick thinking, I looked at him out of the corner of my eye. His face was full of innocence. Ruuqo gave us a long look. I wasn't sure he believed us.

"Do not stray so far," he said at last. "And be more careful from now on. The river can be dangerous in the rains." Ruuqo peered into my eyes suspiciously. I was sure I smelled more strongly of humans than Ázzuen did. Fortunately, the rain and mud must have disguised some of the girl's distinct scent.

"Nice thinking," I said to Ázzuen when we were alone.

His ears pricked up at the compliment and he opened his mouth in a happy grin.

"We were lucky," he said.

"You were smart," I replied, touching my nose to his cheek.

Marra trotted into the gathering place, and Ázzuen ran to meet her. I stayed where I was, watching as Rissa and Ruuqo spoke quietly. As Ázzuen whispered to Marra, I chewed on a piece of the girl's fur I had managed to hold in my mouth. It tasted like family.

PART TWO

THE HUMANS

Prologue

40,000 YEARS AGO

Lydda and her pack hunted with the humans. They ate well and grew strong. No other pack brought down more prey, and no other pack had such fat and healthy pups. Even old Olaan, the pack's elder, his belly stretched tight with meat, had to admit that hunting with the humans had its advantages.

Then, the wolves and humans brought down a mammoth. And everything changed.

It was the most successful hunt yet. Grumbling over the melting snow and disappearing ice, the mammoths were trekking to colder places. One mammoth limped, just a little, and every hunter within scent or hearing range knew it. Lydda's pack had run all the way from their gathering place when they smelled the injured beast. There were stories of wolf packs that had killed mammoths, though Lydda wasn't sure she believed them. Even an injured mammoth was clever, dangerous prey, especially because their herdmates often helped them.

This mammoth was alone. Three long-fangs and a pack of dholes already stalked it, while a lone bear watched and waited. Lydda's pack might have challenged one long-fang or a small pack of dholes, but could not fight off so many rivals without risking injury. Disappointed, Lydda and her pack prepared to leave the plain.

Then Lydda heard a familiar shout and turned to see the tall, lean figure of the human boy.

The humans must have brought their entire pack, Lydda thought in amazement. She had not seen their pups before, in their many sizes. The small humans threw rocks with ferocity and frightening accuracy, scaring off the rival hunters. Then the larger humans chased the long-fangs and dholes away with their sharpsticks.

Lydda's boy caught her eye. He raised his arm to her and she dipped her head. She sprinted to the mammoth and her pack followed. The hunt began. The mammoth was already weakened, thanks to the long-fangs and the dholes. Even so, Lydda did not think a pack of wolves could have killed it on their own. They ran with the human pack, trapping the mammoth. Every time it turned to run in another direction, a human with a sharpstick or a wolf with teeth would stop it. It took a long, long time but at last its thick hide was punctured and its haunches bled. It fell with a sound like thunder, and Lydda looked in awe at what they had done. With the help of the humans, she thought, they could hunt anything.

Usually, a wolf will tear into prey as soon as it falls, or even before. But Lydda's pack stopped, and celebrated with their humans, leaping with joy at the capture of this prey that would feed them so well.

When strong-looking humans bent with sharpened stones

to tear open the mammoth, old Olaan moved forward, a little indignantly.

"Wait," Tachiim commanded.

Grumbling a little, Olaan obeyed the leaderwolf. The humans worked hard, cutting through the mammoth's thick hide. It seemed to take forever for them to pull out the good organ meat and cut strips of rich belly.

"Now!" Tachiim barked, and Lydda's packmates dashed in, seizing the richest meat. It took three of them just to drag away the liver. The humans shouted in anger, but ravens swooped down upon them and the wolves laughed, making off with the best of the meat. Lydda was a little embarrassed by the rudeness of her pack, but she couldn't help but grin. She looked up to share the joke with her boy. He was not laughing. He hung his head as an older male—the pack leader, Lydda thought—shouted at him, waving his arms and pointing toward Lydda and her pack. For the first time in many moons, Lydda felt cold. This time, though, the chill was not in the air, but in her heart.

◘

"You shouldn't have taken so much meat!" the young man said, troubled, as they sat at their rock the next day. "My father said that you wolves are more trouble than you're worth."

"Without us there would have been no mammoth," Lydda said angrily. "We could have left you to fight the long-fangs for it."

The human's brow wrinkled in confusion. Before, when they first hunted together, she had been able to speak to him as she spoke to a member of her pack. But lately, he had been having trouble understanding her. "It's all right," he said at last. "I'll tell them you won't do it again."

⊡

Four nights later, Kinnin, one of the pack's youngwolves, walked into the gathering place, a large welt on his head and a hurt look in his eyes.

"I was taking my share of the deer AraNa and I had killed together," he said, speaking of the human female he hunted with. "And her mate took it from me. All of it. When I tried to take back my share, he hit me with his stick. I almost bit him, but it would have upset AraNa. I do not know if I will hunt with her again."

"I think we should no longer hunt with humans," old Olaan said.

Kinnin nodded. "From now on, a wolf who hunts with humans is a traitor."

"They provide us with more meat than we have ever had," Tachiim protested. "We will live well with their help. We just need to teach them we won't be submissive to them. Next time we share a hunt, we will show them that we are not their curl-tails," the leaderwolf said.

"They had better not try to take food from me," Olaan said, "or I will show them what wolves are."

The next time the humans tried to take a whole prey, the wolves protested. A fat reindeer lay on the ground. Plenty to share. The humans tried to chase the wolves away.

"We will give you some when we are ready," one of them said.

"It's our deer," snarled another, "and you may have what we don't need."

"You will do as we say," said a third, "and if we choose, we will feed you."

They bent with their sharpened stones to cut away at the reindeer.

It was not Olaan who attacked first, nor Kinnin. It was Nolla, Kinnin's littermate. What she did was not unusual for a wolf. Every wolf knows that if another pack member tries to push you away from prey, you must assert your place. Otherwise you will always be last to feed. Nolla was young, and still had much to prove. She leapt at one of the humans. She did not bite him, or even push him hard. She just shoved him aside and bent to tear into the reindeer.

The human lifted up his sharpened stick and buried it deep in Nolla's back. The youngwolf gasped and choked, and then she died.

The wolves and humans stood silently for a moment staring. Then the rest of the humans raised their sharpsticks. Kinnin bared his teeth and leapt at the man who had killed Nolla. He tore out his throat. Then the wolves ran.

⧈

For a quarter of the moon's cycle, it was quiet between the humans and the wolves. Then all three surviving wolves of the Dust Hill pack were found dead, killed by sharpsticks. The next night four humans were killed by wolves while they slept. No wolf admitted to killing them, but Olaan and Kinnin returned home with bloody muzzles and no prey.

And so the war began.

⧈

Throughout the valley, humans slew wolves and wolves slew humans. The humans who had been with the wolves had learned much about hunting and killing. They were especially good at killing wolves. Then the war spread like fire as wolf began to battle wolf and human fought human.

"My people fight among themselves," the boy cried to Lydda when she stole away to meet him at their sunning rock. "Those who wish to destroy wolves and all other hunters are trying to take over my tribe. They kill humans who speak up for the wolves. My father and brother are among them. I fear they will tear my tribe apart."

"Mine, too," said Lydda, although she knew the boy no longer understood her. Just that morning, Olaan had challenged Tachiim about whether or not the pack should slaughter a human tribe.

The boy stood holding his sharpstick tightly, banging it against his thigh. For a horrible moment, Lydda feared he might use it against her, and the thought of attacking him darted through her mind. She tossed her head back and forth, to shake away the image. The boy held out his hand.

"We have to do something," he said, tears in his voice.

Lydda pressed up against him. High above her head, she heard the raucous caw of a raven. That's when she looked up. And that's when she saw, striding across the grass, two of the largest wolves she'd ever seen.

10

14,000 YEARS AGO

I could not stop thinking about the human child. I was so preoccupied with thoughts of her that I did not notice at first when Trevegg walked slowly into the clearing, his eyes creased with concern. Minn followed a few steps behind, looking perplexed, and a little frightened.

"I can't find her, leaderwolf," Trevegg said to Rissa, who looked up sleepily from a nap beside the fallen spruce. The rain had stopped at last, and three days of sun had dried out all but the soggiest parts of the gathering place. All of us were looking forward to a rest in the sun before the evening hunt.

The oldwolf shook his head. "I followed her trail to Wood's Edge and then partway out onto the field, and then her scent just disappeared. I don't understand it."

"Perhaps she stopped to rest and has not yet woken?" Rissa said, rising, all signs of sleep gone.

"Borlla's missing," Marra said, bounding up to me. She had

run to meet Trevegg and Minn as they returned from the Tall Grass plain. Ázzuen trotted over from the watch rock, ears cocked to listen.

"She's always missing," I said, feeling a little guilty. I had all but forgotten about Borlla in my fascination with the human child.

"But this time they can't find her. At all. And Trevegg is upset. Listen." She nodded toward the oldwolf.

"Her scent just vanishes, Rissa," Trevegg was saying. I had never seen him frightened or at a loss, but he seemed to be both.

Ruuqo, Werrna, and Yllin hurried over from across the clearing.

"It's not possible," Werrna said, almost angrily. "Even if she was taken by a hunter, there would be a smell of it. I'm sorry, Rissa," she said to the leaderwolf, who growled at the mention of a hunter. "She keeps wandering off on her own, too distracted to be aware of danger and too weak from hunger to run or fight. It was only a matter of time before something got her."

"I am not so old," Trevegg snapped, "that I wouldn't know if something had taken her! She's just gone."

"Her scent was there and then it wasn't," Minn said, sounding spooked. "Trevegg's right. There's no smell of a recent hunter. Her trail just vanishes."

"It's not possible," Werrna repeated stubbornly.

I was shocked to realize that Werrna was afraid, too. I didn't think she was afraid of anything.

"If the Ancients are angry with us," Ruuqo interrupted Werrna, with a glare, "we must determine why."

"We will make sure first," Rissa said, her voice barely a whisper. "I trust you, elderwolf, but we must be certain."

"I would feel better if others looked for her, too," Trevegg admitted.

Rissa touched her nose to his cheek and, without a word, without our usual leaving ceremonies, led the pack out of the gathering place.

"Why are they acting so strangely?" Ázzuen asked Yllin as we ran along the deerpath, gasping a little to keep up. "She's gone missing lots of times before."

Yllin paused a moment by a starflower bush to let us catch up. She glanced up the path to make sure the others were not in earshot.

"It is normal," she said, "for wolves to die—to be carried off by hunters, or to be injured by prey, or to grow ill. All wolves die. But it's unnatural for a wolf to disappear. It's bad luck. The worst luck. The legends tell us that the Ancients send such luck when wolves break the rules of the covenant. Two generations ago three Stone Peaks disappeared when their leaderwolf accidentally injured a human."

Ázzuen and I looked guiltily at each other. Surely, I thought, pulling a human from the river wasn't as bad as hurting one.

"And I've heard," Yllin said, her eyes resting on the mark on my chest, "that Tree Line once lost a wolf when they allowed a mixed-blood litter to live."

I blinked at her. Why had no one told me this?

"There's something else you should know, Kaala," she said, speaking quickly. "Rissa and Trevegg didn't tell you pups everything when they told you of the legends. It's not just that mixed-bloods might be crazy, or that they might act inappropriately around humans. They're considered bad luck for the pack. And," she said, lowering her voice, "wolves with moon markings can be either good or bad luck for a pack, and you never know which until they are grown."

Ruuqo's angry bark interrupted her. "Don't fall behind, wolves!" he shouted. "We will not wait for you!"

"We aren't supposed to talk about it," she whispered. "But it's not fair for you not to know."

"We won't tell anyone you told us," I promised.

She dipped her head and sprinted off to join the others. We pelted after her. My mind worked furiously. "What am I supposed to do if the pack thinks I'm unlucky?" I gasped to Ázzuen, but he was running too hard to answer.

Borlla's scent was clear at first. She'd followed the path we had taken the first time we went to the horse plain, and had been back and forth along it every time she went in search of Reel. The most recent scent was from early morning, before the dew had dried, which meant she had probably passed this way shortly before sunrise. We followed her scent through Wood's Edge Gathering Place to the place where the trees ended and the plain began, and about eight wolflengths onto the plain. Then, just as Trevegg said, her scent disappeared. To my relief the horses were also gone.

"Stay out of the way, pups," Rissa ordered.

Werrna was the best tracker among us, and so she led the search. She lowered her scar-covered nose all the way to the ground and walked in a tight circle, starting where Borlla's scent vanished. When she was satisfied that she had sniffed every stone, every bit of earth and blade of grass, she turned her back on the first circle and paced out another one in the opposite direction. Ruuqo and Rissa followed her, tracing out circles that overlapped with hers. Yllin and Minn carried out a similar search close to the place where Reel's body had lain.

"They want to make sure they don't miss the slightest drop of scent," Trevegg said wearily, always teaching us, even in the midst of his anxiety and fatigue. "Werrna sets the first circles, Rissa walks within them, and Ruuqo walks within hers. The rest of us will stay away so as not to confuse the scent."

It took them all of the hot afternoon and part of the cooler night to look. Trevegg and the others joined the search, which expanded to encompass the entire plain. They wouldn't let us near the searching place. We were only allowed to search a patch of dry grass far from where the horses had been. I think they mostly sent us there to keep us out of the way, but it was good to have something to do. Marra, Ázzuen, and I did our best to pick up some scent, some clue to where Borlla might have gone, but it seemed hopeless. Unnan stood apart, staring across the plain as Werrna searched the spot where Borlla had last been.

"I'm going to talk to Unnan," I said to Ázzuen and Marra.

"Are you crazy?" Ázzuen asked. "He'll just try to fight you."

"He's alone," I said. "Maybe he doesn't want to be."

I walked cautiously over to him. He must have heard me but did not turn around.

"You can search with us," I said. "It's better than doing nothing."

Unnan turned then and pulled his lips back in a tight snarl.

"Why should I? So you can kill me, too? Is that what you're good at? Causing other pups to die? They should have killed you when you were born. You're nothing but bad luck." He leaned in close to me. "If she is dead, I will find a way to kill you, I promise."

My goodwill deserted me.

"Maybe if you were smarter, your friends wouldn't die," I

snapped. I knew as the words left my mouth that I should shut up. "Maybe there's a reason your friends are the ones who die and disappear. I didn't notice you helping anyone during the stampede."

Unnan yowled and leapt at me. Unlike Borlla, he had not stopped eating after Reel's death and was large and strong. Bigger than I was. But I was mad and my anger made up for my lack of size. I easily threw Unnan from me and pinned him to the ground. Anger clouded my vision, and I bent over his throat.

"Kaala!" Ázzuen shouted to be heard over my growls. He and Marra had rushed over to help me when Unnan attacked, and then to stop me when it looked like I might really hurt him. I came back to myself and stepped off Unnan. I was ashamed. I had meant to comfort him and had only made things worse. And I had let my temper get the better of me again.

"*Ilshik!*" Unnan hissed at me. I cringed at the word. It meant wolf-killer. An ilshik was not fit to be in the company of other wolves and was destined to forever walk alone. I did not turn to face him, but returned to Ázzuen and Marra as we continued to search. Soon we all grew weary and sank tiredly into the grass.

I was almost asleep when Ázzuen's sharp whisper startled me to wakefulness.

"Greatwolves!" he hissed.

Frandra and Jandru strode onto the field. The adults of the pack had moved the search for Borlla to the edge of the field nearest to the humans' territory and were huddled together, speaking in agitated whispers. I wondered what they had found. Ruuqo and Rissa went to greet Frandra and Jandru. I was surprised to see the Greatwolves after they'd said they would not be around, and even more surprised at the anger in Ruuqo's gait as he approached them. I was too far away to hear what he said to the Greatwolves, but Jandru leapt upon him, pinning him to the ground. The Greatwolf spoke a few words and let Ruuqo up. They argued fiercely for several moments. Then Frandra and Jandru stalked away from the plain. I was afraid they had returned to berate me for my contact with the human girl again, but they did not even look in my direction. Ruuqo did, though. He gave me a furious look from across the plain. I stepped back. He gave his command bark and led the pack from the fields.

Ruuqo took us back to Fallen Tree. He would not let any of us discuss Borlla or her disappearance. Nor would Rissa. They would not let Minn travel the territories to look for her. And they wouldn't tell us what they'd found at the far side of the field.

"The hunt continues" is all they would say. "We will discuss this no more."

⊡

I waited until the pack was asleep and then quietly started toward the Tall Grass plain. If the pack believed that bad luck had come, and if they thought I had caused it, I had to find out as much as I could. And I wanted to know why they wouldn't let us pups near the spot where they'd found something. I did not object when Ázzuen followed me.

It had been a long day and night, and I was exhausted by the time we reached the spot where the pack had last searched. Ruuqo had led us away so quickly after the Greatwolves' arrival that I had not had a chance to investigate it. I lowered my nose to the ground.

The scent of our pack was there, of course, as well as those of Frandra and Jandru. And then, fainter than the others, the smell of Borlla. But what stopped me, and made my heart race in my chest, was a scent so faint I almost didn't find it. I checked again to make sure I was not mistaken. It was acrid and meaty. A scent of salt and sweat. The scent of humans. Ázzuen had picked it up, too.

"The Greatwolves told us to stay away from the humans," I said to Ázzuen, "but their scent is here, with the scent of humans. What are they doing?"

"I don't know, Kaala," Ázzuen said, "but I don't think you should try to find out."

"I need to find out, Ázzuen. The Greatwolves saved my life and then disappeared for four moons. Then they come to us twice in a few days. Ruuqo is angry with me again, and Yllin says the pack might think I'm bad luck. Everything seems to come back to the humans. I have to find out why. I have to find out why I am different."

He listened to me, his eyes worried. "Then find the Greatwolves and ask them. But don't go to the humans. I know you are thinking of it." I was a little annoyed that he could read me so easily. He stepped closer to me, his breath warm. "You heard what Yllin said. You can't risk it."

"I know," I said softly, taking some of the pack-Borlla-Greatwolf-human-scented grass in my mouth. "I won't go back. I promise."

⊡

I didn't want to lie to Ázzuen, but I had to know what was really going on. I had to know what the Greatwolves were doing and what it had to do with Borlla's disappearance and my place in the pack. And it all had to do with the humans. Besides, I wanted to see the human girl again.

The name her people gave her was TaLi, though I still thought of her as Girl. I heard one of the females of her pack call her by her name more than once during the time I spent watching them. Their grown females were called "women," and their males "men." In addition to calling their front paws "hands" they called their rear paws "feet," and their fur "hair." Their pack was called a "tribe." They were more active in the daytime than at night, and as the weather cooled they wore the skins of hunters as well as prey. I had not yet seen them wear the skin of a wolf and wondered if they did. The thought made me shudder.

A breeze blew across my ears and through my thickening undercoat. The hot summer days had turned cooler, making my long vigils by the human gathering place more comfortable. I settled more deeply into the soft dirt of the watching hill. Next to me, Tlitoo rustled his wings impatiently.

"How much longer are you just going to watch, wolf?" he demanded. "You have been coming here for a moon and done nothing but watch. Cowardwolf."

I ignored him, straining my nose and ears to find my girl. It always took me a while to sort her scent from the others. It was daylight, and the human homesite was a flurry of activity. Several humans, male and female, scraped prey hides with sharp rocks. Others fastened what seemed like bones to the ends of short, thick wooden sticks. Many of the humans of all ages clustered around fires. I hadn't been sure, at first, why they kept the fires going in the warmth and light of midday, but when I smelled the distinctive burnt-meat smell I understood. They were cooking their prey. Two males held deer meat over the fire at the end of long sticks. My mouth watered. A loud noise startled me and a group of four small males ran through the gathering place wielding sharpened sticks and jabbing them at invisible prey. I wanted to run to join them. I knew play when I saw it.

Tlitoo buried his beak in a pile of leaves, sticks, and fox dung, pretending to look for bugs, and then threw the mess into my face.

"You have learned everything you can by watching, dull-wolf," he said. "It is time to do more than watch. Soon the winter travels will come and you will not be able to sneak away so easily."

I sneezed the dirt out of my nose, and shook a leaf and a clump of fox dung from my ear. Tlitoo was the only one who knew I watched the humans. And that was only because I couldn't escape him. I was able, just barely, to sneak away from Ázzuen and Marra, who had followed me everywhere since the stampede. But losing a raven was like trying to get the stink of skunk from your pelt. It was hardly worth trying.

"You're not the one the Greatwolves will come after," I said. "You aren't the one who will be exiled."

In the moon that had passed since I rescued the human child from the river and since Borlla disappeared, I had been tempted to venture into the human homesite many times. But, although it was impossible for me to stay away from the humans entirely, I hadn't gone completely crazy. I wasn't about to wander into the middle of the human gathering place in the bright sunlight. I had no intention of getting banished from the valley before I was made wolf.

"There is something the Bigwolves are not telling us, wolf-let," Tlitoo rasped. His voice was unusually serious.

I looked at him and saw worry in his eyes.

"They are keeping secrets, and the secrets are about the humans," he said.

"I'll think about going to humans when I have hunted and when I'm accepted as wolf."

Tlitoo gurgled skeptically. He didn't believe Ruuqo would accept me even once I had hunted and taken part in the winter travels. But I didn't want to think about that. If I hunted successfully and traveled the winter, Ruuqo would have to grant me romma, even if he did not want me in the Swift River pack. It was wolf law.

At last I sorted out Girl's scent from those of the other humans. She sat with several females in the shade of a small shelter. In front of her she held a hollow, gourd-shaped half rock. Another, narrower stone fit in her hand and she was using the slimmer stone to crush something in the gourd rock. The smell of yarrow and a plant I did not recognize floated on the air each time she struck the stones against each other. Her face was peaceful and intent and I could hear her making a soft humming noise as she worked. More than anything else, I wanted to go to her. The earth under my belly grew uncomfortably warm and my skin began to itch.

I felt a familiar warmth beside me. I turned, expecting to see the young spiritwolf, but there was no one there. *Wonderful,* I thought. *Now I really am going crazy.* But a powerful juniper-acrid scent seemed to gather in the air and a strong breeze sent it drifting into the human gathering place.

Girl looked up. I knew she couldn't possibly see me, but it seemed to me that she stared right at me as prey does when it knows you crouch nearby. I could not see the expression on her face from where I lay, but her body stretched toward me and she leaned forward. She lifted her head as if sniffing the air. She began to rise.

I stood up. The mark on my chest pulled me, and, try as I might, I could not stop myself from creeping closer to the girl. I stopped smelling the plants around me, stopped hearing Tlitoo's impatient rustling. Even the humans seemed to blend into one scent, their voices into a blur of sound. Only Girl remained distinct. I heard a distant howl—Ruuqo's voice—calling the pack together and shook the sound from my ears. I tensed my legs, and prepared to leap down the hillside.

Tlitoo pecked me sharply on the rump. I swallowed a yelp and glared at him.

"Wake up, wolflet. *Now* is not the time to go. The leaderwolves call you to the hunt."

I heard Rissa's voice mingling with Ruuqo's. I could not ignore their summons. Regaining my breath, I shook myself, and backed away from the humans' clearing.

"Stupidwolf," Tlitoo said, kindly. I thought about biting at his tail feathers but knew he would only fly away.

Released from the power the humans held over me, I ran all the way back to the river, dove in, and swam across. I rolled in the river mud to cover the human scent, waded into the river again, emerged, and shook myself. But before I could start toward home, I heard leaves rustle, and smelled Ázzuen's familiar scent. He poked his head out from the tartberry bushes that lined the riverbank.

"So much for wolves having good ears," Tlitoo chuckled from above me. He had flown to a branch of a willow tree to avoid getting wet when I shook the water from my fur. "Night comes," he said. He gave his raucous raven laugh.

Uh oh, wolf is caught!
Raven might help stupidwolf.
No. It is time to roost.

He paused a moment and opened his beak again.

Now wolf is too late
To find out more. Now wolf knows:
Listen to raven.

With that, Tlitoo flew off and left me to deal with Ázzuen. I thought I had managed to discourage him from following me, but apparently I had been mistaken. I glared at him.

"You've been to see the humans," he accused without even greeting me. "You've been going to see them all along. For a whole moon."

I could smell that Marra, too, was somewhere near. I tried to figure out exactly where. In the bushes to my right, I thought.

"Why can't you mind your own business?" I said to Ázzuen.

"Because you promised not to go. And because you could have told me. You should have told me. We're supposed to be friends."

I felt a little guilty. And surprised. Ázzuen hadn't argued with me before. He usually just did what I told him to do.

"I didn't want to get you in trouble," I said weakly. "And you told me you didn't want me to go." I turned to my right and spoke to the bushes where I figured Marra was hiding. "You may as well come out."

I heard a soft padding to my left and Marra trotted out. She licked my muzzle in greeting and bent to lap from the river.

Ázzuen snorted. "I can take care of myself. And if you are going to go, you should take someone with you."

"She wants to keep the humans to herself," Marra said, when she was done drinking. "You should let us come along," she said to me, "to keep you from doing anything dumb."

"How did you know where I was going?"

"We've been following you," Ázzuen said. "And the raven. He makes a lot of noise."

Marra sat down and regarded me.

"We wanted to know where you kept disappearing to," she said.

"Well *stop* following me." I was grumpy and short-tempered from having to leave the humans. "Can't you find something to do on your own?"

Ázzuen and Marra lowered their tails and ears a little, making me feel guiltier. They had both stood up for me after the stampede. And if it weren't for them, Borlla and Unnan probably would have killed me when I was still a weakpup. I owed them better. I sighed.

"I'll let you know if I go again," I said ungraciously.

Their ears and tails lifted.

"We'd better go watch the adults hunt again," I said, hearing Ruuqo howl once more.

"Maybe they'll let us join this time," Ázzuen said hopefully.

"Maybe the ravens will grow fur and kill aurochs," Marra snorted.

I had to laugh. I touched my nose to Marra's cheek and then to Ázzuen's. The last of my frustration with them lifted and I gave a howl to answer Ruuqo's. Ázzuen and Marra joined in and I led my packmates toward home.

11

The pack caught nothing that night, but a quarter moon later we awoke to the bellowing of the elkryn. It was a strange sound, halfway between the howl of a wolf and the moan of a dying horse, and it pierced the night.

Rissa raised her head and sniffed the air.

"It is time for the pups to join the hunt," she said.

My ears rose, and I could feel my heartbeat quicken. Next to me, Marra yipped in excitement. Rissa had refused to let us join the hunt for so long, I was sure we'd be a year old before we got to chase prey. Ázzuen and the others were six moons old, and I was nearly so, but Rissa had not let us anywhere near large prey since the stampede.

Marra was the first to reach Rissa, and Ázzuen and I were not far behind. We leapt in excitement, imitating the hunt dance we had so often seen the adults perform. Unnan came more slowly and was more reserved in his greeting. Rissa looked at us all. We were nearly as tall as she, and growing strong. She smiled for what seemed like the first time since Reel's death.

"It is time," she said, almost more to herself than to us. "I cannot keep you in the den forever. We will go to the Great Plain to hunt the elkryn."

Ruuqo came over and touched his nose to her cheek.

"They are ready," he said. "And we will watch them carefully." He glowered at us. "The elkryn are dangerous prey," he warned. "We used to hunt their smaller elk cousins, but the humans have driven them from the valley. Elkryn are aggressive and dangerous. You must pay attention." His eyes swept over us to make sure we were listening. He howled once more, and then led us to our first prey. Even his glares could not dampen our excitement, and we tripped over one another leaving the clearing.

We ran through the woods on a soft pelt of newly fallen leaves. I tried as best I could to remember the hunting instructions we had been given over the past moons. But I could not focus. I had been waiting for the first hunt for as long as I could remember. The hunt is what makes us wolf. Long ago the world was divided into hunters and prey, and wolves were made the best hunters of all. Our lungs give us breath and the strength to run long and hard. Our teeth are built from a piece of the wolfstar to be sharp and strong. We have ears made large enough to hear the very thoughts of prey, eyes meant to track its motion as it flees, noses meant to capture each drop of prey-scent, and legs to run across the world. But none of it matters if you have not the skill and courage to hunt. We would have our first chance to demonstrate that courage and skill this night. Proving ourselves in the hunt was one of our most important tests. If we hunted and survived our winter travels, we would be full wolf, and Ruuqo and Rissa would perform the ceremony that would bring out the scent of Swift

River adult within us. From that point on, wherever we traveled, we would be known as Swift River wolves and successful hunters. I knew we were not expected to kill anything in our first hunt, but if I could, if I could show Rissa and Ruuqo that I was a strong hunter, I would be that much closer to being pack, to receiving romma. No one could question my rightness as wolf.

I couldn't believe how quickly we reached the Great Plain. It had seemed an impossible distance before. I placed one paw and then the other on the grass. I had not been there since we had crossed it from our den site so many moons ago. I almost expected it to swallow me up or make me feel as weak and hopeless as I did as a smallpup trying to make my first journey. But it did not. It was rich with Ruuqo and Rissa's scent marks, left to show other wolves that the plain belonged to us. It did not smell so different from the Tall Grass plains and the other hunting grounds around our lands. It was just one more part of our territory. Except that now it was covered with elkryn.

As far as we could see in the clear moonlight we watched their tall, proud shapes. The aroma of their flesh was so strong I could barely smell the grass we stood in or the beetles and ants that crawled past my feet. The heat from their rich skin warmed the night. They were huge—much taller than horses, and well more than the height of two grown wolves. They were powerfully built, with round, blunted muzzles, and their long legs looked like they were made for running. But most amazing—and most frightening—were the giant antlers atop the males' heads. They were broader across than the elkryn were tall. I could only imagine how strong the beasts' necks must be to support those huge antlers. And I didn't want to imagine what those antlers would do to a wolf that got in the way of them.

Just to our left, next to a large, half-moon-shaped boulder, one large male elkryn had gathered what seemed like a hundred females around him. Far across the plain another male had half as many. As far as I could smell, there were clusters of elkryn made up of one male and many females. Other males, young ones, wandered the edges of the groups. As far as our ears could stretch, we could hear the males bellowing in strident, braying tones. I saw that Werrna, Yllin, and Minn had reached the plain before us and were already running among the elkryn. Ruuqo sprinted to join them.

"This is lush elkryn hunting time," Rissa said, leading us out around the perimeter of the herds. We ran along the edges of the plain at an easy pace. It was the hunting run, a relaxed lope that a wolf can keep up for much of the night while seeking prey.

"The elkryn are healthy and strong from summer's good food," Rissa continued, looking back over her shoulder as she ran, "but their minds are on mating, which is good for us."

As if agreeing with her, the male elkryn nearest to us lifted his head and bellowed, telling others for miles around that the females belonged to him. I almost jumped out of my fur. It was one thing to watch these beasts from a distance and another thing entirely to run so near them.

"They gather females they wish to mate with," Trevegg explained, breathing easily in spite of our run. For all he talked about being an oldwolf, he easily kept up with Rissa. "The strongest males are alert at this time of year and are best left alone," he said. "They are unnatural prey and will actually attack hunters. Most large prey will fight back if they must, but male elkryn *like* to fight us. This time of year we hunt the females. They are gathered together and not all can be strong. We can also hunt the young and old males who have worn themselves out trying to steal mates. They are the weakest of all."

"None of them look that worn-out to me," Marra said, a little nervously.

"They look like they might fight back, too," Ázzuen said.

"That is one of the things you must beware of," Rissa said. "Watch the others and see how they test them."

Rissa stopped running and so did we, our flanks heaving, more with excitement and anxiety than fatigue. Ázzuen and Marra pressed themselves against me. I could see that Ruuqo, Werrna, and the youngwolves were running easily among the prey. The elkryn seemed to take no notice.

"It's like the elkryn know we aren't serious about hunting yet," Ázzuen said.

"They do," Rissa answered. "Prey that runs when we are not even hunting hard shows itself as weak. They learn when they are young how to tell when a wolf is ready to hunt."

"Otherwise they'd tire themselves out running all the time," Trevegg added.

Suddenly Yllin turned sharply and ran toward an elkryn, not really charging it, just angling herself slightly in the female's direction. The elkryn raised her head and lifted a foot. Yllin turned just a little bit and ran past the prey, as if that was what she intended all along.

"The elkryn is showing that it would be hard to grab her by the neck," Trevegg said. He snorted. "Yllin should know better. That one is not nearly ready to die." His voice took on an instructive tone. "Prey selection is the most important part of the hunt, pups. If you cannot select prey, you will run yourself to starvation before you catch anything. It doesn't matter how swift your legs or how sharp your teeth, if you do not use your brain you will fail. Our brains are what set us apart, what make us great hunters."

I sighed. We had heard all of this before. Every time the adults took us with them to watch the hunt.

"Listen, pups," Rissa said sharply, but with amusement in her voice. I was not the only one getting impatient. Marra was growling loudly enough to be heard across the plain, and Unnan scuffed his paws in the dirt. "Watching the hunt is one thing. Participating is another. When you are running with the elkryn, you will be so caught up in the hunt that you will chase anything that moves unless you remember to select prey well."

I thought back on the mistakes I'd made when I first tried to hunt the horses. I would not make them again. My ears rose and I stood straighter. I listened for the breath of a young female who ran past us. It was even and unlabored. I tried to catch the eyes of a nearby cluster of elkryn to see if they were weak or strong, and I couldn't help but creep forward a bit on my belly. I stifled a groan as my forelegs ached from so much crouching to watch the humans. One of the female elkryn saw me and looked straight at me. My heart leapt into my throat and stayed there.

Who are you to think I am prey? she seemed to say, pinning me with her haughty gaze. *I have many years of running left, many calves to bear. Do not anger me. I have stomped wolves for less.* I shook a little. She reminded me of the horses right before the stampede.

"That one's not prey, youngwolf," Rissa said with a laugh. "Pay attention. Sometimes you can sniff out worms in them, which make them tired and slow. And the old ones often have a disease that makes their joints stiff. You can smell that and hear it, too."

"And sometimes," Ruuqo said, striding back to join us, "you just watch them. You can tell when prey is ready to die. It hangs its head or startles when you come near it. If it is afraid of you it is because it has reason to be. If it is not afraid of you, it also has reason."

"You can tell by the way that one stands that she's strong," Ázzuen said softly, indicating with a nod of his head the elkryn that had challenged me. "Also, you can see that her pelt is thick and shiny."

"That's correct, youngwolf," Ruuqo said, surprised. "That is what you should look for, pups."

Ruuqo lowered his muzzle to touch Ázzuen's face in approval. I was proud of Ázzuen and glad that Ruuqo saw his smarts for once. I think it was the first time Ruuqo had noticed that Ázzuen was clever. Ázzuen stood and licked Ruuqo in thanks. Then he turned to me. I nosed his face as well, and he thanked me as he had Ruuqo. Marra came to sit beside us. Both their ears and tails were a little lower than mine. Unnan glared at us and lowered his tail a little.

Ruuqo glowered at me. His expression made me fear he would bite me. But he allowed his eyes to sweep over all of us and then back out to the plain where the other wolves were still running among the elkryn. Minn and Yllin caught his eye and ran to join us.

"There is no easy prey," Minn said as he and Yllin flopped down next to us, panting. Werrna still ran determinedly among the elkryn. "We will have to run them." He seemed pleased at the prospect.

"When no prey makes itself easily available, we must test

the elkryn by running after them," Trevegg said, snapping at a fly that landed on his faded gray muzzle. "With a herd this size it is often the best way. It is one of the reasons youngwolves like Yllin and Minn are so important to the pack. They do not know as much strategy as the older wolves"—he glared sternly at the two young wolves who slapped their tails on the ground in response—"but they run quickly and can test many prey without getting tired. That will be your role if you stay with the pack next year."

Ruuqo stood and stretched. "Yllin and Minn will run the elkryn. When they have selected a potential prey, you will join them. You may hunt as a team or one-on-one with an adult wolf. There is value in both ways of hunting, and you will eventually learn them both."

"I will hunt one-on-one," Unnan said quickly. "I am not afraid to hunt on my own."

I hesitated. I would have liked to hunt on my own, but I still felt a little guilty about going to the humans without Ázzuen and Marra. I looked at them. They just looked back at me, saying nothing.

"Well, pups?" Ruuqo asked. "What are you waiting for?"

Ázzuen and Marra were still looking at me expectantly. I waited for them to say something. Marra cocked her head. Ázzuen twitched an ear.

"The three of us will hunt together," I said in a small voice.

Marra dropped her front legs down and wagged her tail. Ázzuen gave a pleased yip. For the second time Ruuqo glared at me, his expression pulled between anger and confusion. Before he could say anything, Trevegg spoke.

"She's the dominant pup, Ruuqo, haven't you noticed?"

He seemed to be taking satisfaction in Ruuqo's discomfort. "She has been since the horse frenzy. The other two follow her."

Ruuqo's growl was so deep in his throat that I felt it in my paws rather than hearing it.

"Very well," he said. "I will take these three. Unnan, go with Trevegg."

Trevegg narrowed his eyes at Ruuqo but obeyed, taking Unnan with him out among the elkryn.

Ruuqo led the three of us forward, so close that we were almost touching the elkryn. My heart pounded in my chest. At last we were hunting. Through the forest of elkryn flesh, I saw Yllin and Minn testing the prey. Minn charged an old, thinnish elkryn, but the elkryn stood her ground. Minn caught Yllin's eye, and the two youngwolves ran together to the middle of the herd as they had before. But this time their attitudes were different. Before, they had seemed almost playful, but now they were serious and their eyes took on the set of a hunter. The herd immediately sensed the difference and shifted restlessly. Without any warning I could see, Yllin and Minn sprinted toward a clump of elkryn. The elkryn ran. Yllin and Minn chased them, scattering them in many directions. They ignored the fastest group and followed a slower one. When that group split in two, they followed the slower of the two groups. They split them and split them again, until there were only two elkryn left running in front of them. One broke to the right, followed by Yllin, and the other ran left, chased by Minn. Minn closed in on his elkryn and out of the corner of my eye I saw my packmates sprinting toward them from every direction. Rissa and Werrna were the first to get there, and then Yllin left off chasing her elkryn to join in. With a gleeful yip, Marra dashed after the elkryn, her legs seeming to blur as she caught up with the older wolves. At the same moment, I saw Trevegg and Unnan running, a bit more slowly, to join the hunt.

"Come on!" I shouted to Ázzuen, and began to run, Ázzuen at my side. Suddenly, Ruuqo stepped in front of me.

Startled, I stopped and looked up at him.

"Where are you going, pup?"

"To hunt," I said, trying to temper my impatience and show him proper respect.

"Not you," he said, "not today."

"Why not?" I asked.

"Do you question a leaderwolf? I do not wish you to hunt today. If you cannot obey me, you are not pack. You will stay here."

Ruuqo ran to join the others. By then the elkryn had made her escape, which was not unusual. Hunts fail ten times out of eleven. But I was stunned.

The pack tested three more elkryn before giving up for the night. Each time I was the only one to sit out of the hunt. Finally, the pack wearied and returned to the edge of the trees.

"Why did you not join the hunt, Kaala?" Rissa asked. "You must join if you are to be wolf."

I was afraid of what Ruuqo would do to me if I said anything to her. She did not wait for an answer, but gave a sigh and lay down to rest. "We will stay on the Great Plain," she said sleepily. "The next hunt will be better."

As the sun rose, the other members of my pack settled into the soft-sage beneath the trees at the edge of the plain and slept. Ázzuen and Marra both tried to sleep beside me, but I chased them off. As soon as I knew everyone was sleeping, I crept away.

Tlitoo was waiting for me, and flew above my head as I began the long walk to the human homesite. The humans were why I was different and why Ruuqo disliked me. They held the secret to who I really was, and whether I was bad luck—and to whether I could ever really be a Swift River wolf. I was done with waiting.

12

Girl sat alone, once again pounding plants into her round rock with the longer, branch-shaped rock. I had no idea how I was going to get to her, but I would not return to my pack until I had. Shame mingled with anger as I remembered that everyone in the pack knew I had not hunted.

After close to an hour, Girl stood and walked to one of her tribe's stone-mud structures. This particular structure had caught my attention because it did not smell as strongly of humans as the others did. It smelled like a den made of plants and forest. It was located at the edge of the homesite, close to where I waited.

I backed out from under the bush that hid me, and, as silently as I could, crept on my belly to the very edge of the gathering place. I remembered what Rissa and Trevegg had said about the humans' eyesight—that they could see quite well by daylight—so I was cautious. I could still smell the route my pack had taken to steal meat two moons before, and I followed it.

"What are you doing, wolf?" Tlitoo asked.

"Going to see her," I said. "Keep quiet."

"At last!" he shrieked. I winced at the noise. "I will help you. They are used to seeing ravens in their home."

"No," I said, alarmed. "Stay here."

But I was too late. Tlitoo launched himself into the middle of the clearing, calling loudly.

Look up, look up, look!
Watch the raven fly over.
No wolf is nearby.

I winced. The humans, who before were intent on their work, looked up, at Tlitoo and at the woods surrounding their home. One of them, an old male, threw a fruit pit at Tlitoo. Another threw a burnt black stone from the fire. Tlitoo dodged both and swooped down, grabbing a piece of cooked meat from a rock on which it was drying. The two who had thrown things at him and one of the others at the fire chased after him, hurling rocks and bits of wood, and anything else they could get their hands on. The two remaining humans sitting by the fire looked after them. Tlitoo screamed happily.

Rocks and sticks won't work.
Best to throw meat instead.
That will hit its mark.

I shook my head. I wanted my entrance into the human site to be *quiet.* But I took the chance while the humans were preoccupied with Tlitoo to dash across the open space and hide behind a small lean-to near the herb-smelling den.

Girl had disappeared into the den and I had lost precious moments while Tlitoo made a fuss. I crept closer to it. To do so, I had to cross through another open part of the human gathering place—there would be no trees or bushes to hide me. Taking a deep breath, I stepped out into the open. Tlitoo chose that moment to dive again, shrieking, for another piece of meat. The humans rose, shouting. I froze in place, thinking myself invisible.

"Idiot, loudmouthed bird," I muttered. I bolted over to the plant-smelling den and hid behind it. It was made of stones stacked up to the height of two grown wolves and topped by mud, river reeds, and large wooden poles, which seemed to hold up a top made of dried grass and more mud. I could smell that Girl was the only one inside. Taking a great chance of being spotted, and hoping Tlitoo would keep his beak shut, I lowered myself to the ground and slowly and carefully crawled around to the opening in the stone and mud where Girl had entered the structure.

The pelts of several antelope, held together in some way I did not understand, hung in front of the opening. Girl had pulled the skins aside when she went in. I stuck my head under the skins and then, making myself as small as I could, crawled the rest of the way inside. The structure was a large rounded shape, about eight wolflengths wide by ten long and arched up like a cave or like a large den made by the roots of a tree. The mud walls were lined with wooden ledges that held more rounded objects. Some of these were actually gourds, dried and hard. Others were made of stone and even of hardened skins. There were also large folded pieces of soft deerskin. Each skin and gourd and rock carried the scent of a different plant of the forest—either its leaf or its root—and there were many scents I did not recognize. I would like to have had time to sort them all out, but Girl's scent was the most powerful of all.

Girl was using her small, clever hands to scoop out bits of

what smelled like the bark of a willow tree, her face intent. I hadn't noticed it before, but her nose was almost flat against her face, her mouth completely pressed in. Her eyes were large in comparison, and her hair fell flat down her back. She did not hear me come in. I stayed close to the opening so I could leave if I wanted to, but not so close that I could be seen by anyone on the outside. Gathering my courage, I gave a very soft bark.

Girl turned, startled, and dropped the folded deerskin she held in her hands. Bits of willow bark fell to the ground. I noticed that the bark was very dry as if it were the middle of summer, even though the rains had come. Girl gasped and stumbled toward the rear of the den. She was frightened. I was a little hurt, though I knew that many hunters killed humans. Bears did, and long-fangs, and a wolf pack could easily do so if we were allowed to. But still, Girl seemed more frightened than she needed to be. I didn't want her to fear me.

I heard a slapping of wings and Tlitoo pushed his way through a gap in the antelope skins and strutted over to stand beside me, cocking his head in curiosity. He walked to Girl's feet and began pecking through the fallen bark. He spit it out.

"It makes my tongue numb," he said in disgust. "It is not good to eat." He glared at Girl reproachfully.

"Shoo," she said, prodding at him with her foot, her eyes still on me.

Tlitoo walked a few paces away and flew up onto one of the shelves, poking his thick beak into one folded skin after another.

"Stop that," I said. "You're not helping."

"I am hungry," he retorted, and kept poking through the skins. "There is every plant in the forest in here. Try to keep her distracted. I will find us some seeds."

Girl picked up a cluster of wheat held together by a reed and brushed it at Tlitoo.

"Get out of here, bird!" she said, stamping her foot. "You are not allowed to eat that."

Glaring at the girl and at me, Tlitoo flew to the opening of the structure and stared beadily at us, making a gurgling noise deep in his throat. Girl made a strange whuffling sound. She reached up to a high shelf and took the top off a stone gourd and took out some millet seeds. She scattered them on the floor for Tlitoo, who quorked happily and snapped them up.

Girl looked again at me, more relaxed than she had been before. The mark on my chest was warm, but not uncomfortably so. Tlitoo ran his beak through the white marking on his left wing. It was cool in the mud rock structure, as good as any den. I could see why the humans built them, why it was worth staying in one place if they had such solid dens as this. It did raise problems, though. When the horses left the plain and the elkryn finished their mating, we would move where the prey moved. I wondered what the humans would do.

I stayed as still as I could. Girl lowered herself to her haunches, respectfully as any wolf would do. She held out her hand to me. We stayed like that for a moment, about two wolf-lengths from each other. When I felt she was no longer afraid, I crept forward no more than the width of two paws. The girl did the same, staying low on her haunches. Bit by bit, we came together, until finally her soft hand reached up to stroke my shoulder. I realized that I had been holding my breath and exhaled, ruffling her hair with my breath. I placed my nose against her hand, and she smiled and gave what sounded like a soft bark, like her earlier whuffling sound, only louder. *Laughter,* I realized, pleased.

I had thought about what to say. I was going to invite her to hunt with me, to take her somewhere apart from the other humans. But I found myself suddenly without words. I just stared at her. Girl's eyes were dark and absorbed light, unlike a wolf's. They were more like a raven's but without the second eyelids. She blinked at me several times. Tlitoo gave a krawk of warning.

I heard footsteps and smelled male human. A loud, rough voice came from just outside the structure. Girl gasped and leapt to her feet. She picked up the folded deerskin, scooped the bark back inside, and dashed from the structure before the male human could come in. My heart beat hard in my chest. I slunk to the back of the structure and pressed up against the stone of the lower wall. I heard her light steps and the heavier angry-sounding ones hurry away from the shelter. I hid in the structure for long moments listening to make sure no one was near. I wanted to stay there and wait for Girl, but I was getting hungry, and I knew it was only a matter of time before another human would come to the structure. It was time to leave.

I poked my nose outside. Tlitoo walked boldly out in front of me.

"There is no one to see you. Come now."

I crawled on my belly out of the structure and then dashed toward the woods. I heard a shout and bolted past two surprised-looking humans. I glared at Tlitoo—realizing that I should have known better than to trust his judgment about what was safe and what was not—and ran into the woods.

I felt exhilarated, just as I had before the hunt. I felt as warm as I did when Marra, Ázzuen, and I lay together. I had no more answers about Ruuqo or Borlla and still had no better way into the pack. But if I'd had wings, I'd have flown with Tlitoo above the tops of the trees.

⊡

The next time we hunted, Ruuqo made it even clearer that he would never let me join. I was the one who found the best prey, the one who fed the pack that night. But still he would not allow me to hunt.

This time, Rissa took us all out, one by one, to lie among the prey. Each of the four of us was at a different place, alone among the elkryn.

"Each of you must select a prey and chase it. That is your task," she had told us. "Don't chase the first elkryn that walks in your shadow. Choose carefully and find one that is real prey. If you choose well, the rest of the pack will join you in the hunt."

Ruuqo was at least twenty wolflengths from me. We were separated by many elkryn and he was talking to Unnan. I hoped he might forget about me. The other adults settled themselves among the herd. I couldn't see them all but I could smell them nearby. Their scents were reassuring and gave me confidence. I knew I could pick good prey.

I started sorting out the different scents of each elkryn. All the ones closest to me smelled healthy and strong. I stood and started walking through the herd. I caught sight of Ázzuen doing the same not far from me. I concentrated. I could smell that some of the strong ones were a little less strong, and some were tired. I sensed that there might be a weaker elkryn in the next cluster over, and made my way to them, trying to seem relaxed so I would not startle them. That was why Yllin and Minn had been so casual in their first foray last time. We wanted the elkryn off their guard.

All of a sudden there was a disturbance to my right, and a clump of elkryn began to run. Unnan had taken off after a perfectly healthy animal. The elkryn and its companions easily evaded him. I sighed in exasperation. He had no reason to chase that group and had made the elkryn wary. But Ruuqo licked him in praise and Unnan raised his tail and ears.

"Tail-licker," Tlitoo commented, landing in front of me. He had a piece of the humans' firemeat in his beak. As soon as he saw me watching him, he threw it in the air, caught it, and swallowed it in a gulp.

"Go away," I said. "You're scaring the elkryn."

"I will wait for you at the river," he said, and flew away.

It seemed like the elkryn had only stopped running for a moment when Unnan took off after the same group. Rissa caught Ruuqo's eye, and Ruuqo spoke softly to Unnan, who lowered his ears a little and lay down again in the grass. This time he stayed put.

The night deepened. A half-moon suffused the plain, making the elkryn glow with light as well as with their own body heat. I was not tired. I felt myself falling into the trance of the hunt. I could stay there all night if I needed to. After close to an hour, I heard a scuffle of dust and then the pounding of elkryn running. Ázzuen had scattered the elkryn, and had selected one that limped a little as she ran. Ruuqo seemed too intent on the hunt to see that I was nearby. The elkryn ran, and you could tell it hurt her to do so. Trevegg and Marra were nearby and they and Ruuqo were the first to get close. The rest of us ran to catch up. It looked like we might succeed in the kill. But the elkryn turned sharply and kicked out, barely missing Trevegg's head. It ran to another cluster of females. We followed, meaning to separate her out again.

Just then we heard a great bellow, and a large bull elkryn stepped out from the cluster. He bellowed again and lowered his head in a challenge. Trevegg, Ruuqo, and Marra, who were closest to him, stopped short. Trevegg stepped in front of Marra, protecting her as the bull elkryn approached. The elkryn lowered his huge antlers and looked at us with half-closed eyes.

"It is Ranor," Yllin said, panting as she stopped beside me. She had been far to the east side of the plain when Ázzuen's elkryn ran and had sprinted all the way over. "He is the strongest elkryn in the valley. He and Ruuqo hate each other."

"But he's prey!" I said. "I know the elkryn will fight if cornered, but why would he risk himself by challenging a wolf?"

"He is a strong elkryn in mating season. He would like nothing more than to prove his strength by killing a wolf. That is why you have to be careful picking prey."

"Then why doesn't Ruuqo back away?" We had been told to retreat from any elkryn that looked dangerous.

"Same reason Ranor challenges him," she answered shortly. "Sometimes a wolf will pick out the toughest prey he can find. It's a way of showing everyone how strong he is."

That was confusing. It was exactly the opposite of what we had been taught. Every time I thought I understood what I needed to know to be wolf, something else would come up.

"It's a part of the hunt they don't like to teach you until you are older," Yllin said, watching intently. "But it's important. They have to prove to each other they are powerful. Ranor has fatally injured wolves before. He likes to kill."

The elkryn, Ranor, spoke. I found that I was able to understand him, much as I had understood the female elkryn that had challenged me. Apparently elkryn, too, spoke in a way we could understand.

You are looking thin, wolf, he said to Ruuqo. *Would you like to try to catch me?*

"I am not going to wear down the pads of my feet so you can prove yourself to your females, Ranor," Ruuqo said condescendingly. "I do not have so much to prove." But Ruuqo's hackles were raised and his body tensed.

"Wolves do not have the luxury of showing off," Rissa added, stepping up to stand beside her mate. "Unlike you, we take our responsibility to our pack seriously. We will have one of your mates before the night is done."

Ranor ignored her, still looking at Ruuqo. Another elkryn, almost as large, strode out to stand beside Ranor.

"Yonor," Yllin whispered. "Ranor's brother."

Torell and the Stone Peaks will challenge us, the new elkryn said. *They are not so fearful as you are, smallwolf. They are wolves, not bunny rabbits.*

Ruuqo's fur bristled. I saw that Werrna was watching him carefully. Yllin's breath beside me grew shallow and sharp. Ruuqo took four steps toward Ranor. The elkryn stepped forward, too, then halted when Ruuqo did not run. Ruuqo lowered his head. Ranor lowered his. They stood that way for several moments.

Another time, then, smallwolf, Ranor said. And walked back among his females. Yonor followed.

Ruuqo shook himself and looked over his pack. When he saw me he narrowed his eyes in dislike.

"Continue the hunt," he said. Ruuqo walked slowly away from Ranor and his females, leading us to a different group of elkryn a five-minute walk away.

Again we spread out among the elkryn. This time Ruuqo was closer to me, once again helping Unnan. I walked among the elkryn, finding none that were prey. Finally, as dawn approached, I smelled an elkryn that seemed somehow different. I couldn't quite tell what it was that made her different, but I drew closer to try to figure out what was wrong with the elkryn. She looked healthy enough. Then I remembered what Rissa had said about how sometimes a prey's joints will smell sore. That was what it was. There was something about the way the elkryn moved that seemed stiff. That, coupled with the wrongness of her scent, made her prey.

I stalked the weak elkryn, moving slowly until I was close behind her. My heart pounded so hard I thought it had moved directly into my ears. I closed my eyes for just a moment and saw myself leaping up, grabbing the elkryn's flank, her neck, pulling her down. My muscles bunched and I ran, putting forth a burst of speed that surprised me. The elkryn stumbled and began to run from me. She was afraid, I could smell it. She knew I was hunter, knew I was wolf. My muscles were as smooth as the river and as powerful as the thunder. I felt like I already had the rich flesh in my mouth. "Prey!" I called out to my packmates. "Prey runs!" Deep in my heart I heard howls. Out of the corner of my eye I saw the shapes of my pack. They had acknowledged my choice and chased my prey. I was a hunter. I ran faster and when it looked like I was within range, I leapt.

Suddenly, something that felt like a tree smashed into me, slamming me to the ground. I looked up into Ruuqo's face. I was strong enough now to struggle to my feet, but he quickly slammed me down again. My back was pinned against the hard ground, and a sharp rock pressed painfully into my hip bone.

"I thought I told you that you were not to hunt."

"But Rissa told us all to," I began. "I found good prey."

"Do not question me." Ruuqo was immovable. "You can wait and watch." I waited. I watched as my packmates brought down my elkryn. My first prey. Unnan took credit for selecting it and Ruuqo did not tell anyone that it was mine. I didn't even try to feed. I didn't want to know if Ruuqo would push me away. I was too angry and too hurt to care whether or not anyone saw me leave. Tail down, I fled.

13

I slowed when I heard Trevegg call my name. I didn't want to, but he was an elderwolf and was always kind to me. I owed him respect. I was surprised to hear him breathing heavily when he caught up with me. He had been fine earlier when we hunted the elkryn, and I had not had the chance to run far before he called out to me.

"You youngwolves run too fast," he complained good-naturedly.

I felt a twinge of sadness as I looked at his whitening face and worn-down teeth. I didn't know what I'd do if he no longer walked with the pack.

"I had to get away," I said. "I couldn't stay there while they ate my elkryn."

"I know," he said gently. "That is why I came after you. It's likely that Ruuqo will not ever allow you to hunt, and you must be ready in case that is so."

"Why?" My anger left me, and hopelessness took its place. "Does he think Borlla's disappearance is my fault? Does he think

I'm bad luck?" I didn't want to betray Yllin's confidence, but I had to know.

"He isn't certain," Trevegg answered, looking surprised. I was grateful that he didn't ask me how I knew about the bad luck. "But he doesn't want to take the chance."

"I don't expect him to let me stay in the pack after winter, but why won't he let me hunt? Why won't he give me a chance to become wolf?"

"If you hunt successfully and live through the winter, he will have no choice but to grant you romma. If he does so and you are bad luck, you will carry the Swift River scent everywhere you bring your bad luck. It will reflect poorly on him and on the pack. He would rather let you go out without the Swift River mark." He sighed. "And more than that, you have grown strong. You are the strongest pup in the pack and Ázzuen and Marra follow you. The others might pressure Ruuqo to let you stay in the pack after the winter travels and he does not want that. It would be better for you if you had less strength."

He touched his nose to my cheek.

"I must return to the pack. You are right to spend some time away. You should think about how you will live your life if I am right."

"Thank you," I said. I waited until I could hear Trevegg was on his way back to the plain, and then set out toward the humans.

I stopped at the watch rock nearest the river. It smelled of a dhole that had been there before me. I leapt atop the rock and covered the dhole's scent with my own. I sat for a moment, thinking about Trevegg's words. How could I become wolf without Ruuqo's approval? I took a deep lungful of air, breathing in the birch trees and sloebushes. I closed my eyes halfway, and listened to a lizard scuttling along the rock, the sparrows arguing behind me, the wind in the trees. Then I caught a familiar scent growing closer and heard a rustling from the direction of the Great Plain. My anger flared again. Ázzuen was following me. I stood tall on the rock, waiting for him, looking down at the bushes from which he would have to emerge. I heard him running quickly, and then heard his footsteps slow as he came upon me, hesitating as he realized I had stopped, then moving forward again more quickly. I stayed standing as the low brush parted and Ázzuen's head, and then the rest of him, emerged. He spoke before I could snap at him.

"I'm coming with you."

"I'm not going anywhere," I retorted.

"You're going to the humans," he said, "and I'm coming with you."

I was furious. The hurt and anger of Ruuqo not letting me hunt surged within me and I snarled at Ázzuen. It wasn't fair that all he had to do to be pack was to muddle along.

"Why don't you go back and feed on the elkryn?" I snapped. "You could use the weight."

I expected him to cringe and lower his ears, to be hurt, and a part of me was ashamed. Ázzuen trusted me and followed me, and it was easy for me to hurt his feelings. But I needed him gone. I was surprised when, instead of cowering at my words, he merely sat back and looked at me.

"The humans are *mine,* Ázzuen." I could hear my voice rising in frustration. "You would've let the human girl drown. Can't you think of anything to do on your own? Leave me alone!"

Ázzuen leapt upon my rock. He wasn't challenging me, but

he wasn't giving in, either. There was a quietness and certainty in him I'd never seen before.

"I'm going with you, Kaala, or you aren't going. One howl from me and Ruuqo will be here to stop you. I saw what Ruuqo did and it wasn't fair. I want to help you. I won't let you go alone."

At first I was too shocked to do anything but stare. Then I felt the burning of anger rising in me, warming me, cleansing me. I leapt for Ázzuen, knocking him off the rock and trying to pin him to the ground. He didn't roll over and give in to me, as I expected. Instead he gave a deep growl and pushed *me* to the ground. For a moment he had me pinned, standing on my chest and looking down at me.

"You're being stupid and stubborn," he said. "You can ask for help, you know."

Furious, I twisted and bit at Ázzuen's face, bucking to throw him off me. I threw him so hard he hit the watch rock and bounced off it. He leapt to his feet immediately. We stood, a wolflength apart, growling at each other, hackles raised, lips drawn back. I was shocked. I looked at Ázzuen, really looked at him. He was no longer a weakpup. He was almost as big as I was, beginning to deepen through the chest like an adult wolf. He had grown strong and confident while I was sneaking off to see the humans. Shame pressed my ears down. I still saw Ázzuen as the small, scraggly pup he had been many moons ago. But he was not. He was a strong and confident young wolf. And he was my friend. I hadn't been in a real dominance fight since my battles with Unnan and Borlla when we were smallpups. It would be different now. Pup fights don't mean much, and the results are not long-lasting. That's not true, though, once you are past six moons old. I didn't want my first true dominance fight to be with Ázzuen. Apparently he felt the same way. When he spoke, his voice was gentle.

"I don't want to fight with you, Kaala. But I won't let you go alone. Besides," and now he grinned, his fur settling along his back, "why should you have them all to yourself?"

Relief smoothed the fur upon my own back. I wasn't ready to lose Ázzuen. The day we would have to sort out our positions in the pack was coming sooner than I'd thought and we would not be the same afterward. I'd always assumed I would be senior to Ázzuen. I had even daydreamed of being a leaderwolf and graciously offering him a position as my secondwolf. I would have to defend him from challenges from stronger wolves, as leaderwolves had done before. A leaderwolf could choose a clever secondwolf even if that wolf was not strong. It never occurred to me that Ázzuen could be a fighter in his own right. As I looked at his bright eyes, sleek coat, and strong shoulders, I was ashamed of how I had thought of him as a pup-forever. I had treated him like a curl-tail and that was wrong.

Ázzuen watched me expectantly.

"If you can keep up," I said, "you can come."

With a loud yip, Ázzuen accepted the challenge. We began to race, running toward the river at top speed. When we reached it, we dove in without stopping and swam quickly across. I made it to the other side just a nose ahead of Ázzuen. We stopped to shake the water from our fur. Ázzuen was looking at me good-naturedly. Then I gave him a gentle shoulder slam and licked the side of his face, as I had seen Rissa do to Ruuqo. That stopped him. Leaving him to stand in confusion, I set off toward the humans. After a moment, he followed. Tlitoo, who must have been watching from the trees, flew above us.

"It is not mating time yet, wolflets," he said.

I winced but Ázzuen grinned at him. Tlitoo cocked his head and looked at me.

"If you are done trying to change what cannot be changed, we have things to do."

I would have answered him, but Ázzuen increased his pace, challenging me. My fatigue and anger forgotten, I put forth a burst of speed racing Ázzuen to the human homesite.

⊡

This time I found Girl right away. During my last visit, I had figured out that the humans separated their gathering place into different areas designed for different tasks. There was a place where they prepared food, a place they worked with skins, a place they made their sharpsticks. Girl was often at a place where things were done with plants. I found her there. This time she was sitting by herself with a pile of river reeds in her lap, deftly bending them together with her agile fingers. Ázzuen's nose twitched as he took in all the scents of the human homesite, and his ears strained forward so much that they seemed like they would fly off his head. Tlitoo looked like he was considering pulling on one of them. I glared at him and he blinked his eyes at me innocently.

At first I had hoped Ázzuen would get bored and leave, but he was just as fascinated by the humans as I was. Suddenly, I was glad to have him there. Glad to have someone other than Tlitoo to share this experience with. I turned and nuzzled Ázzuen's cheek. He looked at me in surprise before returning the caress. Tlitoo gurgled a laugh. I ignored him. My heart was warm and full as I watched the girl.

"Stay here," I told Ázzuen. "You, too," I said, as Tlitoo raised his wings to follow me. He quorked softly but stayed put.

I padded to the edge of the homesite nearest to where Girl sat, and whined softly to get her attention. It was noisy, and her ears were not as good as a wolf's, but she heard me. She looked up from her reeds and saw me. She set down her work, brushed her hands against the skin she wore around her middle, and came to me. I couldn't believe it. When she reached the edge of her home, she looked over her shoulder, then stepped into the trees.

"Hello, Wolf," she said softly. "You came back."

I began to leap to greet her as I would a packmate, but she drew back, afraid of me again. She approached me, then, the way an unknown wolf will approach another, tentatively, carefully. Her nostrils flared and she held her arms folded around her. I looked at her. I had understood her when she spoke; maybe she would understand me.

"Would you like to hunt with me?" I asked. I wasn't really sure if I could hunt anything more than small prey, but maybe she wouldn't mind. She wrinkled up her face and pressed her hand to her head as if it hurt her. I tried again.

"There is a good mouse place across the river. Would you like to come?" Then I remembered she might be frightened of crossing the river after almost drowning. "Or somewhere else if you like."

She just stared at me for a moment, then held her hand out, lightly touching my shoulder.

"What do you want, Wolf?" she asked.

She couldn't understand me. I didn't know why, since I had no trouble making sense of her speech. Each kind of creature has its own language. But most languages are similar enough that, if we open our minds, we can converse with almost any creature. We most easily speak to those who are close to us in some way. Wolves and ravens hunt together and so we communicate with them effortlessly. And we speak to most hunters easily, though some are so inarticulate as to be incomprehensible. When we talk to prey or rivals, we speak wolf and they speak their own language and we understand as well as we need to. So why couldn't Girl understand me? I whined in frustration.

"Are you hungry?" she asked. She reached into a pouch looped on a piece of skin around her waist and pulled out a piece of meat. She gave it to me, and I swallowed it in one gulp. It was cooked meat. Unlike the meat Yllin had stolen, it was dry and chewy, like the meat I had seen Tlitoo with. Old meat, but without the sweet decay taste of meat that had been on a carcass for several days. Once I ate dead frog that had sat in the sun for several days before anyone found it. It had a similar taste. But this meat also tasted of fire. It was the best thing I'd ever eaten. The bushes beside me whined indignantly. I glared at the spot where Ázzuen crouched—I realized he must have followed me from the watching place—and turned back to Girl, my mouth watering from the taste of the firemeat. I wanted more. I wanted to stick my nose in her pouch and get the rest of it, but I remembered my manners. I still had not made myself understood, though she seemed less afraid of me.

I took a great chance and took her wrist in my mouth and tugged gently, looking a question at her. Her eyes widened as my teeth touched her skin, but then she allowed me to pull her farther into the woods.

"Wait," she said. She ran back into the human site and came back carrying a flat piece of folded deerskin over her shoulder and, to my surprise, one of the sharpened sticks the humans carried. Up close I could see that it was not the stick itself that was sharp, but rather a dark stone that was attached to its end. Girl held it confidently, as if she was accustomed to it.

This time when I walked farther into the trees, Girl followed me, placing her warm hand along my back. As soon as we were a few wolflengths away from the gathering place, Ázzuen came cautiously into view.

Girl's hand tightened in my fur and I could hear her swallow rapidly several times. I pulled away from her to greet Ázzuen so I could show her he was a friend.

"Remember she is afraid of us," I told him. "Don't go too close for now."

Ázzuen dipped his head, keeping his eyes on Girl. Tlitoo landed at our feet.

"I remember you," she said to the bird. "You are Wolf's raven friend."

Tlitoo preened himself. Girl relaxed a bit and looked again at Ázzuen.

"We could take her to the mouse place," he said.

I was glad he suggested it. He had found the spot, and we don't share good hunting ground with just anyone. I was grateful he had offered it without my asking. I thought about it. If she was afraid to cross the river, I could help her. I nodded and led the way. I took her toward a wide but slow-moving part of the river. I would have taken her to the Tree Crossing, but I thought it might be too far for her to walk.

"Wait, Wolf," Girl said, when she realized we were heading toward the river. "This way."

Girl tugged on my fur and I allowed her to take the lead. She began to walk downriver, which concerned me, since the current there was stronger. She stopped at a place where the water was shallow but fast moving. I could see why she liked the crossing. The riverbank was flat and wide, and there was no sharp drop down to it, but the water moved so quickly. She stepped out onto a rock in the river. I whined a little in concern. She looked over her shoulder at me.

"I am not always so clumsy as to fall in," she said.

Surprised that she correctly interpreted my concern, I lowered my ears a little in apology. She gave a whuffled laugh and stepped into the river.

"I do this all the time," she said, balancing on one foot on the rock. "My grandmother lives on the other side, so I am used to crossing. She says I should learn to swim but I'm not sure I can."

Girl stepped onto another stone, and then to another, then leapt upon a half-submerged tree trunk. Stepping from rock to rock, some of which I could not see, she made her way across the river. The last rock was a full wolflength from shore, but she leapt the distance easily, landing on the muddy bank. Her manner of crossing made me nervous, but she seemed confident enough. Ázzuen and I followed her across and then we led her to the mouse place.

⌑

Mice can be clever. If you stalk and run, as you do with larger prey, they'll quickly find a place to hide. So you attack from above, as a bird will, so you can surprise them. I made sure Girl was watching, in case she didn't know how to mouse-hunt, then selected a mouse that was crouching in the tall grass, sniffing the air. It knew hunters were nearby, but not which direction we would come from. That's how you can catch mice; they can tell you are near but can't always figure out what to do about it. I crept closer to it. I brought my hind legs all the way up to my forelegs and crouched, tensing my muscles. The mouse held perfectly still, for it knew that if it ran, it might run right into me. I reared up on my back legs, leapt straight up in the air, and landed with the mouse trapped in my front paws. Before it could even struggle, I snapped it up.

I heard an odd sound coming from Girl. At first I thought she was upset, or even hurt, for she was gasping and making hooting noises. I ran to her to see what was wrong and the noises grew louder. I looked at Ázzuen. He was as perplexed as I.

"She is laughing at you, dullwolf," Tlitoo offered. "She finds you amusing."

He was right. But instead of the short and quiet whuffling laugh Girl had given before, this laugh was loud and went on and on. She sat on the ground hooting at me. Annoyed, I went back to hunting mice. Apparently I had a lot more to learn about humans.

Ázzuen and I hunted mice with mixed success. Once, right as I was about to jump on one, Tlitoo swooped in and stole it. He ignored my growl and flew away with the mouse, quorking happily. I kept expecting Girl to join us, but she sat, quietly now, watching. Every once in a while she gave a whuffle of laugh.

"Is she going to hunt or not?" Ázzuen asked.

"I don't know," I replied. "She doesn't seem to want to."

"Then why did she bring the stick?"

We heard a scrabbling sound. A fat rabbit emerged from a patch of sunrose and froze four wolflengths away. We held still, too. A rabbit was a much better meal than a mouse. I noticed out of the corner of my eye that Girl had risen, standing tall with her sharpstick in her hand. We all held perfectly still. Rabbits can be harder prey than mice. They are faster than a wolf over short distances, and you have to be clever to catch one. The first pounce is the most important because that is how you gain your advantage. Ázzuen and I were about the same distance from the rabbit. He blinked at me. He would let me take first leap. I settled on my haunches and prepared to jump. But when I twitched just a little the rabbit began to run. Cursing myself, I shifted my weight to change the direction of my jump. But before I could move, Girl leapt across the grass and, using her long stick to extend her reach, stuck the end of it in the rabbit just as it started to leap toward her. It twitched on the end of the stick and she took its head and twisted, breaking its neck.

I looked at Girl in awe. She was beautiful when she hunted.

"Thanks for the help, Wolf!" she said with the biggest bared-tooth smile I had yet to see her give.

My mouth dropped open as I realized she was right. We had caught the rabbit together. And if we could catch a rabbit, maybe we could catch other things, as well. Maybe, if I could not learn to hunt properly with my pack, I could do so with Girl. I could see it clearly in my mind. I would run after a prey beast and drive it to Girl. Together we would kill it. Then I could show the pack I was a hunter and they would have to make me wolf. I was giddy with excitement and relief. I knew I could make it work. The sound that came from me could only be described as a squeak as I stood on my hind legs and placed my paws on Girl's shoulders, licking her face.

"Stop it, Wolf!" she said, gulping with laughter. "You'll make me drop the rabbit."

"Make her drop the rabbit!" Ázzuen said, laughing, too. "I'm still hungry." He had not taken his eyes off the rabbit since Girl killed it. I dropped back down on my front paws, panting happily. Ázzuen and I looked expectantly at Girl for our share of rabbit.

Instead she reached into the pouch around her waist and pulled out several large strips of the dried antelope meat inside. My ears rose so fast my skull hurt.

"I want to take the rabbit to my grandmother," she said shyly. "She needs fresh meat and can no longer hunt herself."

She gave each of us a large strip of the meat and we sank our teeth into the chewy, fire-tasting stuff, reveling in its flavor and texture. I could catch a rabbit another time. I was more than happy with the firemeat.

"It's the best food in the world," Ázzuen said in awe, sniffing at Girl's pouch.

I expected Girl to eat at least some of the rabbit, but she did not. She really did mean to bring the whole thing to her grandmother. Girl put the rabbit in the folded deerskin she carried over her shoulder. It did not fall out, as I thought it would, but stayed inside. I sniffed at the skin to figure out how she made it do that. She laughed at me.

"That is my rabbit, Wolf. Leave my sack alone. You have had dried meat and quite a few mice."

"I wouldn't steal from you," I said, hurt, momentarily forgetting that she couldn't understand me.

"I would," Tlitoo quorked, scooping up a small piece of firemeat that Ázzuen had let drop. Ázzuen growled at him.

Still hurt, I looked up at Girl. Then I saw her eyes crease as they did when she laughed. She didn't really think I was trying to steal from her. She was playing! I gave a bark of joy and ran behind her. I grabbed the sack, as she called it, in my teeth and pulled, almost toppling her backward. She gasped in surprise, twisted around, and tugged back, laughing. She braced herself and gave a great yank, pulling me forward. Ázzuen yipped in surprise. Tlitoo dove for my tail. I pulled on the sack, hard. I didn't want to hurt her but I wanted that sack. Neither one of us had our full growth, but I had more muscle on me. I pulled strongly, but not too strongly, dragging her forward. Suddenly she hooted like an owl and let go of the sack. I fell forward, just stopping myself from landing on my face. I opened my mouth in surprise and she snatched the sack back, holding it high above her head. Then, still hooting, she ran off, back in the direction of the river.

I leapt after her, Ázzuen close on my tail. Girl took a path that was wide and exposed, which made me a little nervous, but I followed. When we reached the river, she halted suddenly. I stopped quickly to avoid running into her, and Ázzuen stumbled in the mud behind me. Tlitoo soared over our heads, circling back to watch curiously.

When I smelled strange human, I hesitated and then hid in a dense juniper bush. Ázzuen slipped behind a birch tree. Girl gave a cry of joy. She ran headlong and threw herself at a tall, skinny male. He caught her up in his arms.

"I was looking for you!" she said.

"I am glad you found me," he replied, stroking her head fur.

He was as tall as a grown male, but thinner, more like a yearling wolf. His fur was paler than Girl's, but not as light as Rissa's. They greeted each other as a wolf will greet a packmate he has not seen for a long time. And, I realized in surprise, they greeted each other as mates. I would have thought Girl was not old enough. A bubble of jealousy rose in me.

"It was hard for me to get away," she said to the boy. "Father is watching me all the time now." She wrinkled her face. "He doesn't want me going off on my own anymore."

Suddenly the young male held perfectly still and stared at me.

"TaLi," he whispered. "What is that in the bushes?"

She turned to smile at me. "That's Wolf," she said. "Come, Wolf."

Cautiously, I walked out to greet the young male. His eyes widened as he saw me, and he raised the sharpstick he carried just a little. I could tell he acted out of fear, not aggression, and I stopped myself from growling. I tried my best not to startle him. Girl had no such hesitation. She knocked the stick away.

"BreLan! What are you doing? She's my friend."

"You know you're supposed to stay away from them, TaLi. You know what HuLin said." Tlitoo landed near us. The humans took no notice of him. I would never wish to be anything other than wolf, but sometimes I envied the raven, their ability to be unobtrusive.

Girl's shoulders took a stubborn set. "HuLin is an idiot. Not all wolves are dangerous. You can't deny what I am, BreLan."

I was trying to figure out what she meant by that, but Ázzuen chose that moment to creep out from behind his birch. I would have growled at him if I didn't think it would upset the humans more. His timing was terrible.

The boy held perfectly still, and swallowed rapidly several times. Ázzuen opened his mouth, let his tongue loll out, and lowered into a play crouch. The young man's eyes widened in surprise but he let his sharpstick fall. Ázzuen could make himself very appealing when he wanted to. Girl came to stand beside me. The young male—BreLan, Girl had called him—reached out and placed his large hand atop Ázzuen's head.

Ázzuen licked his hand and the boy's mouth opened in the human version of a smile.

"It doesn't seem dangerous," he said, wonder in his voice. He ran his hand down Ázzuen's back. Ázzuen rolled onto his back and offered his belly, as he would to a dominant wolf.

"What are you doing?" I whispered. "He is not a leader-wolf."

"But I have to tell him he is," Ázzuen said, entranced, "so he will not hate me."

"He is right," Tlitoo said. "A wolf must not take a dominant position with a human if he wishes to allay his fear."

I watched, breathless, as Ázzuen won over the human male. It took only moments for the two of them to be sitting on their haunches, stroking each other.

"You can come out now," Tlitoo said.

Marra crept out from the bushes. I shook myself. I had to stop being so wrapped up in humans that I couldn't smell my own packmate. A family of bears could've snuck up on me and I wouldn't even have noticed.

"They are so much like wolf!" Marra said, her voice filled with wonder. "They are not Other."

"No," I said, "they are not. But still they are forbidden to us." I wasn't sure I wanted Marra and Ázzuen to know of my plan to hunt with Girl.

"Yes," she said. "That's the problem, isn't it? But I would like one for myself, anyway. Maybe if we followed them, they would take us to others who like us like they do?"

"I think letting two of them know of us is enough," I said nervously. "Next time, maybe."

"All right," Marra said, disappointed. "Next time."

I looked at her, startled by her acquiescence.

"We must go, TaLi," the boy said at last, pulling himself away from Ázzuen with obvious effort. "We will be missed if we stay away longer, and I want time with you."

Girl nodded.

"Good-bye, Wolf," she said to me.

BreLan wrapped one of his long arms around my girl and pulled her close to him. They walked together along the river. BreLan looked over his shoulder at Ázzuen as they left us. Ázzuen's eyes shone, and Marra watched the humans with hunger in her eyes. I knew they would not let me hunt alone with Girl. I knew they were as captivated as I was. I felt a twinge of jealousy, which startled me. And, as I watched my packmates watching the humans so intently, I began to wonder what sort of trouble I had gotten us into.

14

We quickly mastered the rabbit-hunting technique. Our new way of hunting together worked for turkeys and hedgehogs, and would probably even work on a beaver if we found a place where Girl could stand steady in the river. And if it worked on small prey, it would someday work on large prey. I was sure of it. Girl was too small, I thought, to stop a large prey by herself, but with BreLan's help and ours we would be successful. We had to be, because Trevegg was right—a half-moon had passed, and Ruuqo still would not let me join the hunt. I didn't think he would give me the chance to prove myself before the winter travels. Each time he stopped me, I cared less and less. I was learning how to hunt on my own.

I no longer tried to stop Ázzuen and Marra from coming with me to visit the humans. It was easier to get away with them along, since the pack was used to seeing us together. Wolves our age were expected to explore, and no one thought it strange that we began to range farther from our gathering place. The horses were gone and the reindeer and elkryn had spread

out over the territories, which meant our winter travels would begin soon. Ruuqo and Rissa wanted us to get accustomed to long journeys. Unnan was always trying to spy on us, but it was fairly easy for the three of us to discourage him. Every time I saw him, he seemed to grow angrier and angrier, but it was three against one, and he was afraid of us.

Winter drew near, and with it came the snows. The first time it snowed, we pups were so excited that the adults couldn't get us to do anything practical. We leapt to try to catch the falling flakes and rolled in even the smallest piles of snow. The adults in the pack loved the weather almost as much as we did. Even Ruuqo and Werrna eventually joined us as we played in the cold flurries. Several storms later I was still finding it hard to concentrate on what I was doing when the snow fell.

It was snowing the day we found Girl on our side of the river. Ázzuen, Marra, and I were on our way to the human homesite but we were distracted by the snow, trying to grab the falling flakes in our mouths, and rolling in whatever drifts we could find. We had agreed to cross the river far downstream of where the pack was resting, hoping to track some deer that Werrna had smelled earlier. But I slowed as we neared the river, confused. There was something odd about the trail. Girl's scent was on our side of the water, and it was left recently. I sniffed around the river crossing and back along the section of woods we'd just run through. Then I lost her trail. Ázzuen and Marra, as confused as I was, searched the mud around the river, circling and backtracking to find Girl's scent.

"She visits the old woman she told you about."

Tlitoo's voice came from a pine tree that was still thick with pointed leaves. Unlike the birches and most of the oaks, the pine trees had kept their leaves as winter neared and made good hiding places for a raven. He flew down and cocked his head left and right, clearly pleased with himself.

"I followed her when you were with your pack, playing games with the elkryn. I can show you faster than you can find it with your wet noses. Come, wolflets!"

With a smug gurgle, Tlitoo flew up above us, disappearing into the treetops.

"We can't follow you if we can't see you!" I shouted, frustrated, but Tlitoo was long gone.

I will show you, sisterwolf.

Startled, I turned to find myself nose to muzzle with the young spiritwolf. Ázzuen and Marra still searched the treetops for Tlitoo. They couldn't see, smell, or hear the spiritwolf.

"Who are you?" I asked, sneezing as the juniper acrid scent grew strong around me. I whispered, for I did not want Ázzuen and Marra to think I was crazy. "Why do you come to me?"

Follow me, she said. *There are things I want to show you today.* A mischievous glint lit her eyes. *I am not supposed to be here now, but it will be a few moments before I am missed. There are advantages to being low-ranking in the spirit world.*

The spiritwolf started off at a brisk trot, and I followed.

Sometimes my leaderwolves allow me to come to your world, and other times they do not. Today I have snuck away. Her tone grew defiant. *They can try to stop me, but I will help you if I choose.*

The spiritwolf moved quickly and effortlessly, disturbing neither snow nor leaves, and I had to stretch my legs to keep up with her. I heard a frantic scrabbling behind me as Ázzuen and Marra followed.

"Do you know where you're going?" Ázzuen demanded. "I don't smell anything."

I was panting too hard to answer, but soon Girl's scent grew clear. As I began to trot purposefully in the direction of the scent, the spiritwolf paused.

I will leave you here. I will be nearby as often as I can. She ducked her head. *My biggest mistake*, she said, *was too often doing what I was told. Sometimes those in power are not justified in their beliefs, sisterwolf.* I stopped in surprise.

"What do you mean?" I whispered.

"I've got the scent again now," Marra said, right in my ear, startling me. "How did you keep track of it?"

The spiritwolf dipped her head and disappeared into the bushes.

Marra and Ázzuen were watching me impatiently. I led them onward. Girl was waiting for us where the river met the woods, a thirty minutes' run from the Tall Grass plain.

"I hoped you would come," was all she said by way of greeting. "My grandmother told me to bring you to her."

Tlitoo landed at Girl's feet.

"I told you I would find her for you," he said smugly. He was covered in snow, as if he'd been rolling in it.

Marra made a grab for his tail, forcing him to fly away. I didn't answer, but tried to figure out what was wrong with Girl. She was agitated. She clutched a dead walking-bird by its feet, and was all but twisting its banded legs off. Ázzuen sniffed at the bird hopefully. Marra looked at the bird and then up at Girl.

"If I take it back to my tribe," she said defensively, misinterpreting Marra's look, "they will only take it away from me. And grandmother is not eating enough. She needs the meat."

I realized a little guiltily that I could have brought some of our saved meat to Girl. Next time I would do so. Girl led us farther downriver, to the very edge of our territory. She stopped at a thick slasti bush and placed her hand on its fragrant leaves.

"This is how I know where to turn to get to the path to grandmother's house," she said.

The broad path Girl took us down was as wide and well trodden as a deerpath, but I caught no aroma of deer, just small prey, the occasional fox, and human—a lot of human-scent. Girl's own fragrance was everywhere, and I caught a strong whiff of BreLan. The other human-scent was the strongest, and it smelled a little bit like Girl. But another strong smell surprised me.

"Greatwolves!" Ázzuen exclaimed.

"Their scent is everywhere," Marra said nervously. "And not just Frandra and Jandru—other Greatwolves as well. I didn't know others came to our territory."

"Neither did I," I said.

"More Greatwolves than usual are in the valley," Tlitoo informed us. "I have seen them."

I had no idea what the presence of other Greatwolves meant, but I didn't think it was good. I had not been so confused by smells since the first day we left Fallen Tree Gathering Place. I was so intent on the scents that I did not at first realize it when Girl slowed her pace.

"This is where my grandmother lives," she said, a little shyly.

It took me a moment to figure out what was the human shelter and what was part of the woods. The shelter was not even in a clearing, as were the other human dwellings I'd seen, but seemed to grow out of the forest itself, like a real den. It had the same stone and mud base as the ones in Girl's homesite, and the top was covered with more mud and smaller stones.

There was a large hole in the center from which firesmoke arose. It looked to be a snug den, not as large as the ones where Girl lived, but big enough for several grown wolves.

Girl ducked into the entrance. At first the three of us hung back in the thicker part of the bushes, where no human could see us, but then something drew me forward.

"Wait here," I said to Ázzuen and Marra as I began to creep forward to the shelter.

"But BreLan is in there," Ázzuen protested.

He was right. In addition to Girl's scent and that of the unknown human, BreLan's scent was so strong that I knew he must still be inside.

"Wait anyway," I said firmly. "We have to be careful. I'll let you know when it is safe to go in."

Ázzuen and Marra grumbled a little, but they did what I said, and I stepped toward the shelter. Tlitoo walked back and forth beside me and then flew to the top of the shelter and back again. I did not want to enter a home where a strange human waited, so I sat and waited for Girl to come back. A voice from inside drew me to my feet.

"Bring your friend, TaLi. It is time we were introduced." The voice was rich and deep and very, very old.

Girl poked her head out of the entrance. She looked funny with just her head sticking out, but her expression was serious. She beckoned. I hesitated. It was one thing to bring Ázzuen and Marra to spend time with Girl and BreLan, but something about the old human's shelter seemed like a greater defiance. It was like a place of another world. I knew that going into it would be against every rule of wolf.

My biggest mistake was too often doing what I was told.

I took a deep breath and walked slowly over to Girl. At first I poked just the tip of my nose inside the shelter, exploring the scents within: Girl, BreLan, the old human, and a dried-plant smell similar to the plant structure in Girl's homesite. Fire-scent and smoke. Bearskins. Meat. Next I put the rest of my head inside the shelter, seeing that the smoke from the fire left the structure through a hole in the top of it. The humans might not be able to smell any better than a tree could, but they were clever at making things.

"Come in, Wolf of the Moon," the ancient voice said. "You are welcome in my home."

I crept slowly into the shelter. The old woman sat at the far end. She smelled of stiff joints and tired bones. If she were an elkryn or a deer, she would be prey, I thought, and then was ashamed of myself for having such thoughts about a member of Girl's family. The old woman had no fear of me, and I sensed welcome coming from deep within her. She seemed even smaller than Girl, and she sat amid a pile of bear hides, so that below her hips she seemed to be bear rather than human. In her presence I felt very young, and silly and awkward.

I looked at BreLan. It would be rude to go to him before greeting the old woman, who obviously held the greatest status in the room, but I wanted to acknowledge him. To my surprise, he stood stiffly, holding his sharpstick, as if we had not followed the hunt together. It made me nervous.

Girl placed her hand gently on the old woman's shoulder.

"This is Wolf, grandmother."

The old woman laughed. "You might want to call her something other than that. She bears the mark of the moonwolf, as did the wolf in my dreams."

"I think of her as Silvermoon," Girl said shyly.

"Very well. Do not be afraid, Silvermoon," the old woman

said gently. "Come and say hello to me. I would like to know TaLi's friend."

As nervous as I was, I couldn't refuse so formal a welcome. I walked forward, bowing to the old woman and greeting her by licking her muzzle, acknowledging her status as an elder. I saw BreLan tense as I neared the old woman. Girl glared at him.

"It's not as if you haven't met Wolf before," she hissed. "What's the matter with you?"

"I do not like a hunter, any hunter, so close when the *krianan* cannot get away. I am her guardian." I did not know the word *krianan.* But BreLan said it with reverence, the way we spoke of Greatwolves, and I began to wonder just who this ancient woman was to the humans.

The old woman returned my greeting, placing her hand gently atop my head. I licked her in thanks and stepped away. Then I turned to BreLan. This suspicion would not do. I could hear Ázzuen sniffing at the outside of the shelter, trying to get to BreLan. The last thing I needed was for him to barge in. And I could smell that Marra was right there with him.

"So much for me being dominant to them," I grumbled to no one in particular.

I made myself small and unthreatening, and looked at BreLan with as much kindness as I could muster, but he still stood stiff and angry. Then I dropped to my forelegs, inviting him to play, but when I moved forward he raised his sharpstick.

"BreLan, what is wrong with you?" Girl demanded.

"She's a friend, youngster, and I asked her to come," the old woman said, none too gently. "When I need your protection, I will ask for it."

BreLan lowered his sharpstick, but still stood stiff and anxious. Finally, exasperated, I walked forward, rearing up to shove him in the stomach with my front paws. He stumbled back. Both Girl and the old woman laughed.

"That will show you, boy," the old woman said.

"You need to trust me, BreLan," Girl said. "This is part of who I am."

Outside the old woman's den, Ázzuen's sniffing became more insistent. I hoped no one noticed. I heard another sound from above. Tlitoo was nearly upside down in the roof opening of the shelter, clutching the edges with his feet. I sighed. Just for once I would have liked to not have someone watching everything I did.

"Come to me, young chosen wolf," the old woman said. I walked slowly back to the pile of furs, and lowered myself to my belly so that I met her at her level.

"You have been wondering, I think," the old krianan said to me, "why you are different, why you are drawn to us. My granddaughter is drawn to you as well, you know."

I looked at Girl. She was looking down at her furless feet, which she had covered in prey skins against the cold. *TaLi*, I thought, not just Girl. If she could try to use my name, I could use hers.

"There is a reason you are called. Will you not ask your friends to join us?"

Marra and Ázzuen didn't await my invitation. They must have been sitting right at the entrance. At the old woman's summons, they came quickly into the shelter. Ázzuen gave me a defiant look. They greeted the old woman respectfully. Marra lay by the fire and placed her face in her paws. Ázzuen greeted BreLan, who at last relaxed his guard and lowered his sharpstick so he could stroke Ázzuen's back. He smiled the humans' bared-tooth smile and sat with Ázzuen as if he had never been upset or threatening. Ázzuen sat beside him and placed his head on the boy's feet.

"You are BreLan's friend, I think," the old woman said to Ázzuen. "And you are friend to these two," she said to Marra. "I welcome you both to my home."

The two of them looked at TaLi's grandmother, rapt. Marra stood and stepped deferentially to the old woman, then sat down at her feet. TaLi and I sat a wolflength away, allowing Marra to inhale the old woman's scent. Tlitoo abandoned his perch on the roof and flew down to stand beside the old woman on the pile of bearskins. She took seeds from a skin sack, and gave him some.

The ancient human watched us all, for such a long time that I began to feel uncomfortable.

"It is perhaps too soon to tell you this," she said at last, speaking hesitantly, "but I think I have no choice. I will not live forever, and something must be done, and done soon." She took a deep breath and when she spoke again her voice was strong.

"So hear this, young wolves. It is no accident that you have found my granddaughter and BreLan. Wolves and humans are meant to be together."

I couldn't hold back a whuff of surprise. After everything we'd been told about staying away from humans, about how it was one of our three unbreakable rules, I was shocked to hear the old woman claim with such certainty that the opposite was true.

"Many of my people no longer believe this to be so," she continued, "and I would not be surprised if yours deny it as well. But it is true, and it is more important than you can imagine. If humans do not have contact with wolves, with the keepers of the wild, we forget that we are part of the world around us. It has happened before. And when it happens, humans begin to kill and to destroy, for we do not see that when we harm the world we harm ourselves. The one way—the only way—that humans can be stopped from killing countless other creatures, from devastating our world, is if we remain always in contact with the wolves, for only wolves can bring out in humans the knowledge that we are neither different nor apart. This bond goes back for as long as humans and wolves have lived in these lands."

Ázzuen grunted and Marra stood as if to protest. My head buzzed with confusion. It went against everything we had been told, everything our pack believed. It went against the very reason the Wide Valley wolves lived. *You must stay forever away from them. You must shun their company,* Sky had said to Indru. And when the wolves failed to do so, the Ancients had nearly ended our lives.

I stared at the old woman. I had thought my feelings for TaLi were wrong and unnatural. Now this wise and ancient human was telling us that it was not so, and that so much of what we'd been told about the humans—and about our own history—was untrue. How could I believe her? And yet, more than I had wanted anything for as long as I could remember, I wanted to believe every word.

"Yet it is not as simple as that," the old woman said. "For we cannot be together." She took a deep, labored breath, as if telling us this exhausted her. TaLi left my side and went to sit beside her and the old woman ran her hands through the girl's head fur.

"When wolves and humans come together, appalling things

can happen," the old woman said. "My people have tried to make slaves of yours, and your people have killed our kind. We *must* be together, and yet we cannot be, for every time we have tried, war has come to us. That is the challenge—the paradox—and it is the great test of both wolf and humankind."

I shook my head hard. I didn't understand how it could be that wolves both must be with humans but also must not. I whined a little.

"Wolves lose themselves," Ázzuen said, repeating Rissa's words from so many moons ago. "They are no longer wolf and kill or are killed by humans." His gaze, resting on the old woman, was thoughtful, almost as if something he already knew had been confirmed.

"Yes," the krianan said, ignoring our surprised looks when we realized she had understood Ázzuen, "and many humans cannot see another creature without resenting its freedom and wishing to control it." She reached across TaLi to place her hand on Marra's chest, which was heaving in excitement and anxiety. "For a time, we had found a solution—a way humans and wolves could be together without causing a war. Some of us humans are better able to be with wolves than others. We are not so threatened by the power and wildness within you. We have no wish to control you, and because of that can be open to what you can teach us. The krianan wolves come to us—to those of us who are meant for the wolves—when we are very young. That is how I know of this. Mine came for me when I was younger than TaLi. You know these krianans; they are the wolves who watch over you."

I remembered the scent of Greatwolves that surrounded the old woman's shelter. They must be the krianan wolves she spoke of.

"That would mean we don't have to give up the humans," Marra said, her voice barely a whisper.

"I told you the Grumblewolves were keeping secrets," Tlitoo quorked.

"We meet with the krianan wolves each time the moon is full in ceremonies we call Speakings," the old woman said, "and the krianan wolves remind us we are part of this world. We, in turn, tell our people what we have learned from the wolves. This is the story that has been passed down by our people for generations. Each human krianan teaches the next, as I have been teaching TaLi."

She paused and placed her hand upon TaLi's cheek, and then spoke very softly. "But the Speakings have ceased working as they should, and there are many things the krianan wolves will not tell us. We don't know why this challenge, this paradox, exists. We don't know how it came to be that wolves must be with humans and that humans cannot be with or without wolves. And we do not know why the Speakings are no longer working. The krianan wolves know, but they think we humans are too stupid to understand. But I can see that we are failing. No krianan wolf has come to a human in many years, and I have known of no new ones to be born in my lifetime. Now the last of the krianan wolves grow old, and my people do not want to listen to them, or me, anymore—and I do not know what to do." The ancient voice quavered and TaLi took the old woman's hand in her own. The old woman held out her other hand to me.

"When I heard that you had come to TaLi, Silvermoon, I knew that something was changing. Perhaps you are what will replace the krianan wolves, and you and TaLi will be watchers together."

I wanted to go to her, but I was rooted to the spot. I couldn't just ignore everything my pack and my leaderwolves had told me. Rissa and Trevegg had taught me everything about being wolf—they had never lied to me. And even though the old krianan was TaLi's family, she was a human. She was not pack. A frustrated grunt escaped me.

The old woman held out her hand to me once again, and I went to her. Marra stepped aside to give me room.

"I can see you do not believe me," the old woman said. "Why should you?" She thought for a moment. "You must come to the Speaking, in two nights' time when the moon is full," she said. "TaLi will bring you. Just you, Silvermoon, not your friends. I think hiding the three of you would not be easy." She gave me a tired smile, and I licked her hand to let her know I understood.

"Good," she said. "I will expect you."

The old woman looked at all of us and her smile broadened. "I refuse to believe that hope is gone," she said. "I see you together and I know that something can be done." She gave a deep sigh. "I am tired now, youngsters, and you must leave me. But we will speak again."

Then the old woman closed her eyes and seemed to melt into the bearskins and her breath grew deep with near-sleep. TaLi and BreLan bent to press their lips to the old woman's cheek and crept from the shelter. Ázzuen, Marra, and I each touched our noses to the old woman's hand, and then followed our humans from the shelter, walking as quietly as we could.

⊡

The snow had stopped falling while we were in the krianan's home and the sun warmed the ground. TaLi and BreLan led us a short distance away toward a grassy field.

"Do you believe her?" Marra asked as we followed a few steps behind the humans. "It's completely different from what Rissa and Trevegg told us."

"I don't know what to believe," I said. "I don't know why Rissa and Trevegg would lie. But I don't know why the old woman would, either." I didn't want her to be lying. I wanted it to be right for me to be with TaLi.

"She could just be wrong," Marra ventured. "She didn't know about the promise Indru made, or about the Ancients. Or about the long winter."

"But don't you see?" Ázzuen said excitedly, stopping and turning to face us. The three of us halted, letting the humans get ahead of us. "She has to be right. That's why the legends never really made sense. It doesn't make sense that the only thing we were supposed to do is to stay away from the humans. Why close off a whole valley just for that? Why didn't Sky kill the wolves and humans like she said she would when wolves came together with the humans? And you saw how angry Rissa got when I asked her about it." He was shaking with excitement. "It's never made sense to me and now I know why. The Greatwolves are trying to keep something from us, from all the wolves in the valley. I think the old woman is telling the truth." He looked over his shoulder at BreLan's retreating form. "I know she is."

The three of us stood silent for a moment, thinking of everything the old woman had said and watching our humans walk ahead of us. Thinking about what it would mean if she was right.

"We shouldn't tell the pack about this," Marra said. "Not until we know more."

"No," I agreed, "we shouldn't."

"We'll help you get away from the pack and go to the Speaking," Ázzuen said.

"And you can tell us what you learn," Marra agreed. "Then we can decide what to do."

"Yes," I said, uneasy at drawing Marra and Ázzuen further into what could be trouble. "All right."

TaLi and BreLan had found a patch of grass that was free of snow and not too damp. We slowly walked to join them. TaLi sat and reached out her arms to me. Shaking off as much of my worry as I could, I lay down beside her, suddenly craving her touch.

TaLi immediately rested her head against my back. Ázzuen and BreLan relaxed next to us, and Marra curled up between us. Tlitoo, who had stayed behind with the old woman for a few minutes, soared across the field to land beside me.

"I am going away," he said. "I will be back as soon as I can. You must wait for me."

"Where are you going?" I asked, startled. I had gotten used to having Tlitoo around.

"Away," he said. "Outside the valley. Do not do anything stupid while I am gone."

He raised his wings.

"Wait," I protested.

"Just because you are stuck on the ground does not mean I must be, wolflet," Tlitoo said irritably. "Your lack of wings is not my problem. I must go now."

With that, Tlitoo leapt into the air and flew toward the mountains. Soon he was no more than a speck in the sky and then I saw him no more. I sighed. I knew better than to try to figure out what went on inside that raven brain of his. TaLi leaned harder up against me. I had an itch in my left ribs, but I didn't want to move for fear of disturbing her. I liked having the warmth of her pressed against me, liked feeling her heartbeat and her breath.

"That's why I cross the river, Wolf. Silvermoon," TaLi said, shyly using her new name for me. It was close enough to the true meaning of my name that I liked it.

"I *am* afraid sometimes to cross it," she admitted, "but I must. My grandmother's too old to do so now. And she is the krianan, the spiritual leader of our tribe, and I am to take her place when I am grown." I nosed TaLi in sympathy. Many of us were afraid to cross the river, but a hunter must go where the prey runs. I admired TaLi for overcoming her fear to do what she must.

"I should be living with her now," she confided, "but HuLin, the leader of our tribe, does not want me to go to her. He says she is silly and does not understand how we need to live now. Krianans used to live with our tribes, but the tribe leaders don't like having them around anymore. They say the krianans won't let them hunt enough."

BreLan had risen as TaLi spoke and now paced restlessly, using his sharpstick as a third leg. He rammed the blunt end of it into the earth angrily.

"She threatens HuLin's power," he said. "My father told me that, after the last tribe council."

I remembered that BreLan lived with a different tribe than TaLi, one west of our territories. It was a half day's journey for a human, but he made it whenever he could. He wanted TaLi for his mate. But TaLi had told me that her leader wanted her to be his son's mate. Which is probably why BreLan paced back and forth so. TaLi reached out as he passed by her and pulled him down to rest beside us. Ázzuen lay at the young human's folded legs and BreLan stroked his fur. I could feel the young human's heart slow and calm as he stroked Ázzuen. Now it was Marra's turn to rise and pace, stalking restlessly, jealous of our contact with the humans.

"It's no accident he sent her to live across the river, TaLi," BreLan said. "He doesn't want you learning what she knows. He doesn't want you to meet with the krianan wolves as she does."

"I know that," TaLi said. "But I don't know what to do about it. Old KanLin didn't mind her being in the tribe."

"She was younger then," BreLan said, "less powerful. And KanLin was more confident than HuLin."

"HuLin is our new leader, Silvermoon," TaLi said. "He hates that my grandmother tells him what to do, especially when she tells him he has to stop killing everything he can catch. She told him he had to respect other creatures and he said she was hurting the tribe and sent her to live across the river. He said if she liked spending so much time with the wolves, she should go live with them."

TaLi spoke quickly, barely breathing, as if the words were sprinting out of her.

"What will you do when he forbids you to see her, forbids you to take part in the Speaking?" BreLan asked.

I wanted to ask more about the Speaking, and I whined in frustration with my inability to communicate with the humans.

"I don't know," TaLi said, anxiety filling her voice. "He wants his son to be krianan instead of me." BreLan stiffened at the mention of the leader's son. "I've been lying to him. I say I am going out hunting for herbs or small animal skins. Then I go to see grandmother."

I shifted restlessly, wanting to find a way to ask TaLi questions.

"We are taught that all creatures but humans are either vicious or stupid, Silvermoon," she said. "Animals like you and the bears and the lions are seen as evil. They used to be thought of with respect and admiration. Those who graze on the plain or eat the plants of the forest are seen almost as if they have no life at all. We are told that humans should have power over all, because no other creature has made fire, or tools, or built grand structures. But it didn't used to be this way. As krianan, my grandmother remembers the old traditions. It is her role to make sure we follow the ways of nature, the ways of the world. But now the leaders of our people don't want anyone to tell them not to take what they want."

"And many of our people no longer wish to travel with the seasons," BreLan said, absently running his long fingers through Ázzuen's thickening winter coat. "My uncle asks why they should leave when they have spent so much time building shelters. He says that if the krianans would let them hunt as much as they like, they wouldn't have to move around so much, but could stay in one place longer and build more shelters and grow stronger than any other tribe. Then all the prey in the valley and beyond would belong to us."

That troubled me. I still didn't understand what made humans think they were so different from the rest of us. I wouldn't say we cared much for the life of prey, and I had to agree with BreLan's uncle that it belonged to whoever could catch it. But we knew it had life. We needed dens for our young, but who would want to live all the time in a den? That is why one has fur and the strength to journey.

"Perhaps the humans have to compensate for not having

fur and for their small teeth," Marra said, sounding as confused as I felt. She had finally stopped pacing and lay a few paces from us in a relatively dry patch of dirt.

"The more they have the more they want," Ázzuen said. "But I don't understand why they would not listen to their krianan. Ruuqo doesn't always agree with the Greatwolves, but he still obeys them."

I had no answer for my packmates and no comfort for TaLi, who had buried her face in the fur of my back. I knew that you fight for your position in the pack. I knew that you honor Moon and Sun and the life Earth gives you. I knew that you follow the rules of the hunt and take care of your packmates and defend your territory. But I did not know how to help TaLi. I didn't know what to do about the challenge her grandmother had spoken of. All I was able to do was lean against her and offer whatever comfort I could.

Marra gave a soft growl as a new human-scent blew in on the breeze, and the three of us lifted our heads, tensing for a possible fight.

"What is it, Silvermoon?" TaLi asked, sitting up as she noticed the stiffness of my body.

The human smelled like BreLan, but a little different. He had to be related to him. But after what BreLan had said about the people of his tribe, that didn't mean he was a friend. I stood, as did my packmates. We waited.

A young human male walked across the grass, approaching us. BreLan stood, his hand tense on his sharpstick. Then, while the other human was still far away, he relaxed and raised his hand in a gesture of greeting the humans used.

"It took you long enough to find us," he called.

"Well if you're going to lie in the grass like rabbits, what do you expect?" the other human shouted back.

The young human stopped when he saw me and Ázzuen and Marra standing nearby. But he did not raise his sharpstick.

"These are the wolves?" he asked when he reached us. BreLan must have told him of us. "I doubted you, brother, but it is true. They stand with you." He looked at us in wonder and only a little fear.

"Or we with them," TaLi said with a smile.

"And you hunt with them?"

"Only small things so far," BreLan answered. "But now with three of us, perhaps we can hunt the larger animals," he said eagerly.

I was surprised to hear him echoing my thoughts of hunting large prey. I looked the young human over. He didn't look big enough to hunt much. TaLi noticed my appraisal.

"MikLan is BreLan's younger brother," she told me. "Come meet Silvermoon," she said to the young human.

But MikLan's eyes were on Marra, who was moving slowly toward him as if pulled by the scent of prey. She had watched how Ázzuen and I interacted with our humans and she lowered herself into a submissive posture. She was barely breathing, so intent was she on the boy. He was younger than BreLan, younger even than TaLi, a child still, and he was less suspicious than his brother. A smile split his face and he touched the top of Marra's head. I winced a little, for such a gesture is a sign of dominance among us, but Marra didn't seem to mind. A moment later the two of them were wrestling in the dirt, Marra growling playfully and MikLan panting with laughter.

They stopped playing and rested together. Marra's tail

slapped the ground as she rested her head on MikLan's stretched-out legs. She looked at me smugly. Ázzuen curled up with BreLan next to them. Girl twined her fingers in my fur. All of us seemed worn-out—by our encounter with the old woman and the difficult things she had said. But it was comfortable as we sat together, the six of us, as day began to turn to dusk. And yet I was troubled. For how could I feel both that I had found my home and that my world was ending? That I was whole for the first time, but also being pulled apart? And how were we supposed to solve the paradox the old krianan had spoken of when it was all we could do to be with our pack and sneak away to the humans? It was too much to think about, and I tried to put it out of my mind and drew as much warmth and comfort as I could from the flesh of the human girl.

15

The pack slept in the afternoon sun. Ázzuen and Marra lay close beside Trevegg and Rissa, the lightest sleepers, ready to warn me if either awoke. It was late afternoon, and I had promised to meet TaLi and her grandmother that night for the Speaking. At last I was going to find out more about the Greatwolves and their contact with the humans. Usually it would have been easy for me to slip away, but an antelope herd was passing through the territories, and Rissa wanted to teach us how to track them. She had ordered us to stay in the gathering place until it was time for all of us to leave together.

Wandering about as if I were merely looking for a good place to sleep, I approached the sentinel oaks. I took one last look over my shoulder and stepped out of the gathering place.

"Where do you think you're going?"

Unnan blocked my path. He had only pretended to sleep and had managed to sneak into the woods and wait for me.

"Get out of the way," I growled. I didn't have time to be polite.

Unnan just gave me a sly, nasty look.

"You know I can make you," I said. I had easily won our last fight, and knew I could win another.

"You might be able to." Unnan smirked. "But that would make a lot of noise. You wouldn't get to see your human *streck.*" A streck is the lowest of prey, one that is so easy to kill you do not have to breathe hard to get it.

I looked at him in shock. I didn't want to deny anything. I didn't know how much Unnan knew.

"And Ázzuen and Marra wouldn't get to see theirs, either. Did you think you were smart? You go to see the humans whenever you get the chance, and then lie to the leaderwolves. You hunt and don't bring prey back to the pack."

"If you know so much, why haven't you told Ruuqo and Rissa?" My stomach clenched, but I tried to sound as if I didn't much care.

"Maybe I will, and maybe I won't," he said. "But you aren't going anywhere now."

Before I could stop him, Unnan gave a loud bark. Every wolf in the gathering place woke and glared at us.

"Pups!" Rissa said sharply. "You know you are not to leave the gathering place today. What are you doing?"

"I saw Kaala running off"—Unnan smirked—"and I knew we weren't supposed to. So I stopped her."

"Very well." Rissa seemed more annoyed with Unnan's groveling tone than with my disobedience. "Kaala, this is not the time to wander off. Go sleep by Trevegg and Ázzuen until it is time for the hunt."

"Yes, leaderwolf," I said.

⊡

I greeted Trevegg absently, trying to figure out how I could get away. I did not notice how closely the oldwolf was watching me. He started to speak, but when he noticed Rissa watching us, he laid his head down.

"Sleep, youngster," he said. "We have some matters to discuss later."

I put my head in my paws. I was so tense I was sure that I'd remain wide awake, but I must have been more tired than I thought. As soon as I closed my eyes I was asleep.

⊡

A hand on my back awoke me. My eyes flew open and I looked into TaLi's face. I blinked a few times. And froze in horror. We were only wolflengths away from other members of the pack, and they would be waking soon for the hunt.

I hadn't thought that TaLi would venture into our homesite. I should have anticipated it. And now she had come. I feared what my pack would do if they found her. I wanted to tell her to run, but even the slightest whine could alert the others to her presence. She opened her mouth to speak, and I pressed my nose urgently into her cheek and stood. I saw Trevegg's ear twitch in his sleep. Across the clearing, Minn groaned and turned over. I nudged TaLi with my head, and she gripped my fur tightly. I allowed her to take me in the direction she wanted to go—just so long as it was away. I expected any moment to hear the sounds of my pack behind me. The humans' scent is so strong and so unique that any wolf can pick it up from far away. I couldn't believe no one had found her scent.

Then I realized that even I could not smell the girl, even though she stood right beside me. I sniffed, and sniffed again. She smelled of forest, of a powerful sweet-sap scent in particular, and of many of the plants I recognized from the structure where I'd first greeted her. I wanted to ask TaLi what disguised her scent so well, but we were still too close to Fallen Tree. She pulled softly on my fur, and I let her lead me through the woods. After we were well away from the pack, I stopped, waiting for an explanation. In the meantime, I sniffed at her skin again.

It's *uijin,* Silvermoon," she whispered. "My grandmother makes it from the sap of the highbranch tree, using chokeberries and about twelve different herbs. She hasn't taught me to make it yet—it takes a long time to learn—but she said it would make it so wolves would not smell me." TaLi rubbed her arms and wrinkled her nose. "It's sticky."

I licked her arm, tasting the uijin. I wanted to know more about it. If it could disguise her scent from even me, it could be useful to us in hunting prey. We could sneak up on them and they wouldn't smell us until we were upon them. But there were so many plants in the mixture, and dirt, too. Even, I realized, crushed insects. I didn't think I could duplicate it by rolling in different things. Still, I couldn't stop myself from tasting more of it.

"Stop that, Wolf," TaLi said, a little crossly, pushing my face away. "I still need to cover my scent. It is the night of the Speaking, and grandmother sent me to fetch you. She said it's important."

I realized I had licked part of TaLi's arm almost clean, and nosed her in apology. I looked at the girl in admiration. She had twice the courage I had. I couldn't even sneak away from my pack to meet her, yet she had found her way into our gathering place and dared to walk in the middle of a wolf pack to get me.

"I don't know much about the Speaking, Silvermoon," TaLi

said, walking again. "I'm not really old enough to go, since I'm not yet a woman, but grandmother said we should both be there. I was glad when she told me to bring you."

She sounded lonely. I gently touched the back of her hand with my nose.

TaLi's legs had grown longer in the two moons since I had pulled her from the river, and she moved with an easy lope. Not as swiftly as a wolf, of course, but still, I was surprised at how quickly we were able to move through the forest. We walked in silence until the sky darkened, and then TaLi began to slow. The pack would be waking now, wondering where I was, but I couldn't help that. My human had asked for my help and I would give it to her.

"Wait," TaLi said, and then stopped in her tracks. "I almost forgot."

She took a small gourd from the sack she carried and removed its top. The smell of uijin rose from the gourd. TaLi scooped some of the saplike substance out in her hand and rubbed the sticky stuff into my fur. When she was done, I realized that she had not put any on my feet. She probably didn't know that the scent glands on our feet leave an especially strong trail. I rubbed my forefeet on my muzzle where she had left a lump of uijin and scraped my rear feet on some that had fallen on the ground. I sneezed twice and looked at TaLi. She whuffed a laugh and placed the top back on the gourd, then slid it back into her sack. We began walking again.

After a little less than an hour, TaLi stopped in an undistinguished-looking patch of grass, dirt, and many large boulders. A gap in the trees showed the tall eastern mountains, glowing in the moonlight. It would have made a good gathering place, I thought. TaLi sat and waited, so I sat and waited, too.

Then I smelled them. In spite of what the old woman had told me, I could barely believe my nose. Greatwolves, a lot of them, coming our way. Frandra and Jandru were among them, and many others I didn't recognize. I hadn't realized there were that many Greatwolves in the valley. I whined to TaLi and started to walk away. When she did not follow, I took her wrist in my teeth and pulled gently.

"Are they coming, Silvermoon?" she asked. "We're supposed to hide before they get here."

The girl looked around and found a large rock and tried to guide me behind it. But it was upwind of the direction the Greatwolves were coming from. I didn't want to take the chance that they could smell us in spite of the uijin. I towed TaLi to the downwind side of the field of rocks to find a better hiding place. I spotted two large rocks, side by side. One was broken halfway up, creating a small, flat ledge. In the place where the rocks met was a crack that would fit both of us. I led TaLi to it and leapt upon the ledge. She followed me, clambering up with her strong hands. We squeezed into the crevice between the rocks. I was a little uncomfortable, wedged between the two rocks, with TaLi pressed against me, but I stayed put, breathing slowly to get enough air into my lungs.

The Greatwolves strode into the rock field, not even trying to be quiet. Six pair, including Frandra and Jandru, and one lone, ancient male, gathered in the moonlit patch of grass. They spoke to one another too softly for me to hear, and then each pair walked to a boulder. Jandru and Frandra paused by their boulder and TaLi clutched my fur tightly.

"I notice them watching me sometimes," she said, her voice barely a whisper. "Those two krianan wolves. I recognize them. They're the ones who spend time with my grandmother."

I didn't have time to wonder about what the girl had said before I picked up the scent of humans. They walked solemnly into the patch of grass in ones and twos. I had to struggle not to gasp in outrage. How could Greatwolves and humans be meeting together? I couldn't believe it, even though the old human had said that it was so. The Greatwolves were the ones who were supposed to enforce the rules about staying away from the humans. Frandra and Jandru had threatened me when they found I had rescued TaLi! I would not have believed it if I had not seen it with my own eyes.

The humans greeted the Greatwolves as one wolf greets another. TaLi's grandmother was the oldest human there, though all of the humans had the same bearing, the same smell of strength and wisdom as the old woman. Padding silently beside the humans was the young spiritwolf.

Each human then walked to stand next to a Greatwolf pair, and TaLi's grandmother paused beside Frandra and Jandru. I realized then that the boulders were not scattered randomly in the grass as I had thought, but were arranged in a large circle, so that the Greatwolves and humans formed a ring facing the center of the rock circle.

The young spiritwolf touched the old woman's hand with her nose and trotted through the center of the circle. Neither the wolves nor humans seemed to see her. She walked purposefully to our rock and leapt upon it. After licking me quickly on the top of the head, she settled above us atop the broken rock. I dared not speak to her lest I be overheard. I twisted my head around to look at the spiritwolf and she grinned at me.

Watch and be quiet, Kaala Smallteeth, she said. I still dared not answer her, and turned back to the rock-rimmed patch of grass.

All eyes, wolf and human, were focused on the old krianan. She wore the skin of some creature I did not know, a thick and well-furred pelt. From its folds she drew a blade made not of stone, like the tip of TaLi's sharpstick, but of something lighter and curved. I stifled a gasp. It was the tooth of a long-fang. I shivered. I would not want to get close enough to a long-fang to win its tooth. The fang was attached to the end of a piece of wood from an alder tree. The old krianan raised it high and walked to the center of the rock circle and faced to the east. She seemed to glow in the moonlight, and the long-fang tooth seemed to send a stream of light into the sky.

The old woman's voice was pure and clear as a wolf in its prime calling the pack to hunt. She spoke in a flowing rhythm I had never heard the humans use, and the pitch of her voice rose and fell almost like our howls when we gather for a hunt or ceremony. It sounded a little like the humming noise TaLi sometimes made as we walked, but stronger, more powerful.

I call to Sun,
I invoke your life-giving warmth,
The spirit of flame
Fire and firmness
Light and heat
That give plants and creatures
Strength to reach
To Sky.

It took me a few moments to be able to understand the woman. She spoke in Oldspeak, the most ancient and basic of the languages of the Earth. All of our languages are based on it, and Ruuqo and Rissa had insisted that we learn some of it so we could understand as many creatures as possible. I didn't know the humans knew it, though. I wondered if I could use it to talk to TaLi.

The ancient Greatwolf stepped forward and met the old woman in the center of the circle. He moved slowly as if it hurt him to do so, and faced toward the west. His voice, when he spoke, sounded like dried-out twigs breaking underfoot.

I call to Moon,
Friend of the night
Companion to stars,
Softness hiding true might
Yielding to gain strength
Cool light, guiding vision
To Sky.

"This is what the Speaking is for, Silvermoon," TaLi said, settling herself against me. "I can't understand much of it yet," she said wistfully, "but I will soon."

The old woman spoke again. She spoke of Earth, calling to it as the giver of shelter and of life. I began to understand. The Speaking was a ritual, like our pup-welcoming or hunt ceremonies. It surprised me that they were as important to the humans as they were to us. TaLi leaned over me, resting her weight on my back as the old woman swung her blade to the north.

Then it was again the old Greatwolf's turn.

Sky, blower of wind,
Holder of all that is.
First Father, First Mother

All that is, is yours
Bringing light, darkness
Life and death
To Earth, Sun, and Moon.

The old human lowered her blade and leaned against the ancient Greatwolf's broad back. He pressed up against her, and for just a moment, they seemed as if they were one creature.

"Guardian wolves," the old woman called. "We renew our promise, made to you by our ancestors' ancestors. The promise to keep our people from pride, from destroying, from taking too much and killing too often. We take what we learn from you this night and share it with our people."

The old Greatwolf dipped his head and spoke.

"And we meet your promise with our own, remembering the promise made by our first father, Indru. We promise to keep our people from harming yours. We pledge to act as teachers to your people, and to help you keep the Balance. In the name of Indru, we promise this."

Then each human lay down with a Greatwolf pair. The air was taut with the energy of the Speaking and the moon shone brighter than it should. A faint light seemed to come both from the old woman and the eldest Greatwolf, the one who had spoken. The light grew to encompass all of the Greatwolves and humans. I could almost hear the air thickening and trembling with power.

Come away. It is time for me to go.

I placed my paw firmly on TaLi's chest to let her know she was to stay put. Then I scrambled out of the crevice and, watching carefully lest any of the Greatwolves should notice me, I crawled backward down the far side of the rock. It was steeper on the back side than on the front, and I landed hard on my rear end as I slid down.

Trying to reclaim my dignity, I touched noses with the spiritwolf.

I must go now, she said, *or I'll be missed. But things move more quickly than I expected. I hoped you would have at least a year under your fur before this happened. That you'd be old enough to fend for yourself.*

"What's supposed to happen?"

Quiet, she ordered. *They cannot hear me but they can hear you. You know that wolves must be with humans, and that otherwise humans will destroy too much?*

"That's what the old human told us," I whispered. "She told us that we must be with humans but cannot be, since every time we come together, we fight. But that's not what the legends say!"

Your legends lie, the spiritwolf said. *The human krianan speaks the truth.*

My breath caught somewhere between my throat and my lungs. As much as I wanted it to be right for me to be with TaLi, I hadn't really believed it. I didn't see how everything I'd been taught could be false, how Ruuqo and Rissa and wise Trevegg could be so wrong. Yet even from where I stood with the spiritwolf, I could still hear the Greatwolves speaking with the humans. I couldn't deny my own ears.

I did not know this when my pack ran with the humans. I was like you—I found a human and hunted with him. My pack grew strong on the meat we hunted with the humans. But there was a war—a war between the humans and the wolves. The Guardian wolves said it was my fault—that I had tampered with the humans without knowing what I was doing, and that the Ancients would punish us for the war. They said they knew how to deal with the humans and that the only way I could save my pack was to leave. They sent me from my home. Her voice grew bitter. *For many years their way has worked, and I thought they were right, that I had caused the rift, that I was at fault for the war between humans and the wolves. But now they fail, and I think I was not right to listen to Guardian wolves. That is why I come to you.*

I just looked at her. I couldn't imagine what she expected me to do.

Soon humans and wolves will fight again, and this time there will be no second chances.

"Why would wolves fight?" I whispered. "It's against our rules."

Rules can be broken. Legends can be forgotten. And peace in the valley has always been fragile. The Guardian wolves have kept too much secret from our kind, and secrets are what have led to trouble.

Suddenly angry, I raised my chin to the spiritwolf. Who was she to speak of secrets? All this time I had worried over what I thought were unnatural and dangerous feelings for TaLi. And time and again the spiritwolf had come to me. She'd known about the lies and hadn't told me.

"Why didn't you tell me this before?" I demanded. "Why did you just keep coming to me and then disappearing? Why didn't you just tell me instead?"

She pulled her lips back in a snarl. *You have no idea what it costs me "just to come," as you say. I cannot tell you what is learned in the spirit world. All I can do is show you the way to find out for yourself. You know more than I did. I knew nothing!*

The spiritwolf looked over her shoulder. *I have stayed too long already—and told you too much. You must listen to what the Greatwolves say tonight. You must find out how close humans and wolves are to war, and then you must find a way to stop it.*

"How am I supposed to do that?"

You and your human girl must make it right. You must find the solution I did not. Before the humans and wolves fight. If the humans and wolves battle, then all is lost.

I couldn't believe she expected me to have an answer.

"But how?" I demanded. "How am I supposed to know what to do?"

I must go. You know what I did not. Use that knowledge well!

Before I could ask the spiritwolf any of the questions buzzing in my mind, she was gone, slipping silently into the forest. I wanted to curl up right then and there and sleep, and to forget everything I had heard and seen. But I had left TaLi waiting for me and, if the spiritwolf was right and war was coming to the valley, I needed to hear what else the Greatwolves might say.

Shaking, I climbed back into the rock crevice, and leaned against TaLi. I wished more than ever that I could communicate better with her. I wanted to tell her what the spiritwolf had said. Instead, I pressed close against her and she pulled me to her chest.

The humans and wolves had risen to their feet. We watched as two of the humans helped the old woman climb upon a tall boulder. Steady in spite of her age, she turned to the Greatwolves. She held her arms up, standing silently until every wolf and human in the circle looked at her.

"Most of you know," she said, "that our Speaking is no longer enough. There is discord in the valley. We must know what you have been hearing."

The ancient Greatwolf stepped forward. He did not climb upon a rock, but nonetheless every eye was upon him.

"We have heard this as well," he said, in his voice of dried-out twigs. "With each Speaking it seems to grow worse. We know that some wolves no longer believe the legends. And that many humans wish to destroy all wolves. We understand, NiaLi," he said to the old woman, "that your people no longer respect krianans as they should. That you no longer have the power to influence them."

"It is true, Zorindru." There was an edge to her voice when she addressed the ancient Greatwolf. "We are losing influence. But it is also true that you can no longer control your wolves."

A woman stepped forward. She was much younger than TaLi's grandmother, but considerably older than TaLi. If she were a wolf, she would be the right age to lead a pack—young enough to be strong but old enough to be sure of herself. If she had back fur, it would have been bristling. She spoke angrily.

"NiaLi is right. I'm told that wolves have killed two humans. A young man from Lin tribe and a child from Aln. The people of Aln look to me as their krianan and demand that I bring them the body of the wolf. They wish to retaliate and kill all wolves. So far I have been able to dissuade them. But if you cannot control your wolves, I cannot answer for what my people will do."

"I agree," Zorindru said. "If it is truly a wolf who killed the humans, and not some bear or long-fang, and if the attacks were unprovoked, we will discover who this wolf is and destroy it and its pack."

My heart caught in my throat. To hear that a wolf might actually have killed humans and that the terrible punishment for doing so would be carried out was horrifying. TaLi gripped my fur hard. I wondered how much of the Oldspeak she could understand.

"There is more." The human male who spoke was young, not much older than TaLi, and spoke awkwardly, as if he were not used to Oldspeak. "HaWen is the new leader of the Wen tribe and he has sworn to rid the valley of all wolves. His mate lost the last child she carried in her belly, and he says it is because she saw a wolf when she was out gathering seeds."

TaLi's grandmother nodded. "JiLin also claims that his smallest son broke his leg because he stepped onto a path that wolves had used," she said. "He says we are wrong to pay heed to the needs of the Earth and the sky. He says that the food of the valley, of all the Earth, is meant for humans, and that creatures that take it should be killed. Have others heard such things?"

"Yes," the young male said quickly, then lowered his eyes as the older krianans all looked at him. He swallowed rapidly several times, but continued. "HaWen said the only way our tribes will thrive is if we kill all the wolves, all of the knife-toothed lions."

"It is the same with my tribe," said another female, her voice soft, but clear. She placed a hand on the young male's shoulder. "I have done my best to dissuade the others, but to no avail."

"We have all been doing our best to keep our people from believing such nonsense," TaLi's grandmother said. "But if there is any more talk of wolf attacks against humans, I fear that we will not be able to stop my people from killing all the wolves they see."

There was silence for a few moments. I could feel TaLi's heart beating quickly against my side. My heart raced, too. The spiritwolf had been right. War was coming. And I had no idea what to do about it.

"We hear you," Zorindru said, "and we understand. We will destroy the bloodline of any wolves that attack humans unprovoked. And we will remind those who follow us of their responsibilities. Go in peace," he said, nodding to the humans.

I thought the old woman would say something else. She certainly seemed to expect more from the old Greatwolf, and her shoulders were set in anger. But she merely held her arms out to be helped down from the rock.

"Go in peace, Watcher Wolves."

The old krianan left the rock circle, followed by the other humans.

"I must help grandmother home," TaLi whispered.

Before I could stop her, she scrambled down the rock and into the woods. I started to follow her, but saw Frandra and Jandru looking in my direction. I couldn't take the chance of them seeing me there. I slid down the back of the rock, and started to make my way home, thinking hard about what I had learned, and wondering what in the name of the moon I was supposed to do.

⊡

Trevegg was waiting for me when I returned to the gathering place.

"You missed the antelope hunt," he said. "Ruuqo is displeased."

"I was hunting small prey," I said, not meeting his eyes. "Did you catch anything?"

Ázzuen walked up to stand with me.

"No," Trevegg said. He watched me a long time. When he finally spoke, his voice was soft.

"I have not said anything about your time with the

humans." I jumped and looked up at him. Ázzuen squeaked in surprise.

"When I saw you and your friends going to them, perhaps I should have stopped it right away. But there is something wrong, something we have not been told by the Greatwolves. I hoped that perhaps you might find it. I knew from the moment you faced Ruuqo, ready to fight when you were barely a full moon old, that you would be different."

"I'm not that different," I said. "And I don't want to change things. I just want to be near the humans."

"That is changing things," Trevegg said gently. "You know the legends. Did you know that Ruuqo's brother was sent away for being with the humans?"

"Yes," I admitted.

"Good. My brother was leaderwolf of Swift River then. Hiiln was to be his successor. He and Rissa had chosen each other and I could not think of a better pair to carry on the Swift River line." Sadness crept into his voice. "But when Hiiln refused to stop going to the humans, I knew I had to do my duty by the valley. I advised my brother to send him away, and he did so, though it broke his heart. Looking back, I wonder if I did the right thing. So I have looked away when you have gone to the humans.

"There is a legend told only to leaderwolves," he said slowly. "I was told when it was thought I might lead Swift River. It is why Ruuqo fears you so much, Kaala. I should have told you of it after he would not let you hunt. It's said that a wolf will be born who will shatter the covenant. That wolf will bring an end to wolfkind as we know it. It's said that the wolf will bear the mark of the crescent moon and will cause great disruption that will either save or destroy its pack. Your mother would tell no one who your father was, but if he was one who was drawn to humans, you could be this wolf."

"I'm no legend," I said, barely able to get the words out.

Trevegg gave me a long look. "Perhaps not," he said kindly. "Other wolves are so marked. But now Ruuqo grows suspicious and there is unrest in the valley. You must be careful, Kaala."

I whimpered softly. It was too much to think about.

"This does not have to be resolved today," he said abruptly. "Perhaps it is nothing and you are just another pup who does not follow orders well." He licked the top of my head. "Now go make amends with Ruuqo," he said. "And don't miss any more hunts."

I licked the elderwolf's muzzle in thanks, and went into the gathering place to apologize to Ruuqo.

16

Ázzuen, Marra, and I each carried a piece of deer meat up Wolf Killer Hill. True, our first deer had been old and injured, but its meat was as sweet as any I'd tasted. I had been wrong about MikLan. He was strong for his size, and he had been the one to make the first strike. The humans had special sticks that helped them throw their sharpsticks far, and MikLan was especially good at using them. The six of us brought the deer down so easily I wanted to laugh. And just in time. Most of the elkryn had left the Great Plain and only a few remained at the Tall Grass field. Two days ago Ruuqo had told us that if there were no successful hunts over the next few nights, we would have to begin our winter travels. I spent a lot of time wondering how I would manage to see Girl during the winter. It would be harder to hunt with the humans then, so I was glad we had already succeeded in catching large prey together. And I was glad that hunting with the humans allowed me to forget as much as possible what had happened at the Speaking. Not even Ázzuen had any ideas of what we should do about what I'd learned, and

I could only hope that any trouble would wait until we could figure something out.

Ázzuen, Marra, and I had argued about what to do with our share of the deer. We had buried some, but would still have to explain ourselves to the pack.

"They'll notice it on our breath," Marra said. "It's one thing to smell of rabbits or even hedgehog. We could easily catch those on our own. But not a deer. If they knew we'd caught a deer they'd want to know all about it."

Marra was the best of all of us at understanding pack dynamics. It made sense to listen to her.

"We could say we found it already dead," I suggested.

"It's too fresh," Ázzuen said, "and we smell of the hunt. They'll know we're lying."

Unlike the smell of humans, which was only on the surface of our fur and skin, the large-prey hunt scent was deep within us and could not be washed away or easily disguised.

"Well, what are we supposed to tell them? Do we have to leave it?" I asked, frustrated.

"We can't do that," Marra answered slowly. "They'll know we hunted large prey and wonder why we didn't bring any back to the pack."

"We'll just have to think of something."

Ázzuen sounded confident that he would come up with a solution. I envied him his cleverness. I could almost hear his mind working. Marra and I waited as his ears twitched and he closed his eyes halfway. It wasn't long before his eyes lit up.

An hour later, we carefully made our way up Wolf Killer. It was a relatively small but steep hill that rose up strangely right in the middle of the forest, a twenty-minute run from Fallen Tree. Some said that long ago Wolf Killer Hill had been a great volcano, and that the small jagged hill was all that was left of it. Others said it was made by humans or by the Greatwolves in a time long ago. It got its name because wolves who were not careful would run on it, only to fall off one of its many steep drops onto jagged rocks below. Ázzuen's idea was simple. We'd say we followed a deer to the hill, and chased it off the edge, and that we were only able to reach a little of the meat before it slipped off a cliff. All we had to do was to roll in the dirt near the yew trees that grew only on the top of Wolf Killer. The ancient trees were poisonous, and every wolf knew their distinct scent. There would be no reason for them to question us. We hoped.

"Can't we just leave the meat here?" I mumbled, halfway up the hill. The slope was steep and it was hard to climb while keeping hold of the meat.

"It should smell of the top," Ázzuen panted. "It's not that much farther."

"You both need to run more." Marra grinned around her meat. "You're getting soft."

I stopped to catch my breath and to find a suitable response. That was when I smelled the Stone Peak wolves. Ázzuen and Marra caught the scent at almost the same moment. We heard the mumble of voices, but could not make out the words.

"What are they doing in our territory?" Ázzuen demanded, setting down his meat.

"And more important, where are they?" Marra looked around her.

"They must be on the other side of the hill," Ázzuen said. "Somehow their voices carry over it."

"At least four of them," Marra said, raising her nose to the wind, and then lowering it to the dirt. "I think Torell is one of them. I'm not sure who the others are."

I had also caught Torell's distinctive, sickly scent. Indignation mixed with my fear as I realized the Stone Peak wolves must have been in our lands for at least two days. The hill blocked the flow of the wind so our pack had not yet smelled them.

"We have to tell Ruuqo and Rissa," Ázzuen said doubtfully.

"We can't," Marra said. "The pack will come here to look for them, and then they'll follow our trail back to the humans. We won't have time to disguise the trail."

Marra was right. But our obligation to pack required we tell the leaderwolves about the Stone Peaks.

"We could find out what the Stone Peaks are doing," I suggested. "If they're leaving the territory and aren't going to cause trouble, maybe we wouldn't have to say anything. If they're not, we'd have something more definite to tell Ruuqo and Rissa, and we might have time to disguise our trail."

"Then we'd be bringing valuable information to the pack," Marra said thoughtfully.

"And we could tell Ruuqo and Rissa we heard the Stone Peaks on our way back from Wolf Killer," Ázzuen added. "Someplace they might not be able to find our trail to the humans."

Ázzuen and Marra were both looking at me as if I should make the decision. Oddly, I found myself wishing Tlitoo was around. It had been more than half a moon since I had seen the bird outside the old woman's shelter. I never expected to miss his annoying comments, but at least he never looked at me like he thought I should know what to do.

"We don't want Ruuqo finding out that we're lying," I said, coming to a decision. I had brought Ázzuen and Marra into this. It was my duty to make sure they were not banished from the pack because of me. "We'll find out what the Stone Peaks are doing."

Ázzuen and Marra dipped their heads in agreement. We buried the meat shallowly so that we would be able to find it again easily on our way back.

"Marra, you lead us there; Ázzuen, you listen for trouble," I said. Marra had the best nose among us, and Ázzuen the best ears. Between the two of them, they could track anything. I wanted to make sure we were as careful as possible.

We found the Stone Peak wolves hiding under an overhang just on the far side of the hill. The outcropping provided a good place to rest, and probably helped to hide their scent. If the wind had not changed as we climbed the hill we might never have smelled them. Marra led us downwind of the Stone Peak wolves so they would not smell us, and we had to lie at a sharp angle on bits of broken stone, just above and to the right of their hiding place. The stories of wolves falling off Wolf Killer once again ran through my head, and I dug my paws into the rocks. My heart was beating so fast that I was sure the Stone Peaks would hear it. I twisted my neck a little to see better into their hiding place.

Torell, the fierce, terribly scarred wolf who had challenged us at the Tree Crossing, was there, along with three others—two males and a female. The female was Ceela, Torell's mate. I did not know the other two wolves.

"It's now or never," a lean but strong-looking young male was saying. "Our territory is becoming useless to us. We have no good hunting left, no safe places to rest. If we do not kill them, our bloodline will die out."

"We must be careful," Torell said, his ravaged face grim. "We must be smart. This is not like taking land from Vole Eaters. We are outnumbered. They have strengths we do not."

"Do they mean us?" Ázzuen whispered.

I glared at him, pulling back my lips, warning him to be quiet. I did not dare speak aloud. He lowered his ears in apology.

"I am not afraid of weaklings," the large female said.

"Don't be stupid, Ceela," Torell said. "If we are not careful we will lose everything. We won't get more than one chance. Besides, the Greatwolves will kill us if we are not smart about it. We cannot count on their own conflicts distracting them. We must see if the Tree Line pack and the Wind Lake pack support us. Without them we won't have a chance."

Listening to them wasn't helping me understand what was going on. What did they mean about the Greatwolves' conflict? And why did they want Tree Line and Wind Lake's help? I knew that the Stone Peaks wanted our territory. It had to be us they wanted to attack. I leaned forward to hear better, not noticing the loose rocks at my feet. Several of them clattered down the hill, and the Stone Peaks looked up.

Just then the wind changed, blowing our scent toward them. Torell lifted his nose. With surprising speed, he bounded toward our hiding place. Marra was closest to him, and crouched low to the ground, exploring the scent marks they had left, and she was last to her feet. Before she could rise, Torell had her pinned to the ground. She scrabbled ferociously, then lay still as Torell's weight pressed down upon her.

"The Swift River pack must not care much for their pups, to let them wander the territories like this," he said.

Ázzuen and I had begun to run down the hill, but we could hear the other Stone Peaks coming to help Torell. I turned, and began to run back up the hill, with Ázzuen right behind me. We leapt at Torell, managing to knock him off Marra just as the other Stone Peaks came crashing to the top of the hill. Then we ran.

We skidded down the hill, trying to control our descent as best we could. For an instant I considered stopping for our deer meat, and then thought better of it. We reached the bottom of the hill without injury and pelted toward Wood's Edge, where the horses once had been. We knew our pack was there now, trying for one last pre-winter hunt. It was a relief to run on flat ground. I thought the Stone Peaks would stop pursuing us after a few moments—they were in our territory after all. But they kept coming.

"Why don't they stop?" I gasped.

"Because they don't want us telling Ruuqo what we heard," Marra answered grimly.

I felt my insides grow cold. If Marra was right, then the Stone Peaks would kill us if they caught us. We ran faster than we had ever run, faster even than we had run to surround the deer. Marra led the way, stretching several wolf-lengths ahead. Stone Peaks are large and strong. Their heavy bones make it easier for them to catch large prey, but they are not as fleet as Swift River wolves, and even half-grown pups like us could outrun them over a short distance. And it was our territory. We knew every bush and bramble. One of the Stone Peaks, however, did not fall behind. It was the lean male who had been urging Torell to act. I could smell that he was young, probably not more than two years old. I kept Ázzuen ahead of me. He was a fast runner now, but not as fast as Marra and I, and I didn't want to leave him behind. The woods thickened and the deer trail we ran upon disappeared. It was harder to run fast without the trail, and Ázzuen, Marra, and I were separated by trees, rocks, and bushes. I heard the young male gaining on me as he easily jumped over rocks and limbs.

Moments later, I heard him leap, and he landed on me, catching my back legs and knocking me over. He was nearly half again my weight but I didn't think twice. I bit him hard, where his foreleg met his chest, in a spot where there was tender webbing and not much muscle. He yelped in surprise and pain. I scrambled to my feet. I heard pounding feet around me, but couldn't tell where the Stone Peaks were, or where Ázzuen and Marra ran. I faced the youngwolf, fury burning within me. It felt good to have my anger back.

"This is our territory!" I growled. "You don't belong here."

The youngwolf looked surprised and then laughed. "Why don't you come join us, littlewolf? You are wasted in Swift River. Ruuqo does not appreciate you. Your raven friend told me as much. And I would like a strong female as my mate. I am Pell. Will you remember that?"

Confused, I just stood there and looked at him, even though I heard the crashing of the other wolves around us. Suddenly Ázzuen burst out of the trees and slammed into Pell, snarling. He had come back for me. The attack took Pell by surprise, and Ázzuen was able to throw him off balance.

"Come on, Kaala!" Ázzuen shouted, as he turned to growl at Pell.

I was a little shocked at Ázzuen's ferocity. I could smell Ceela close on Ázzuen's tail and turned to run. We picked up Marra's scent. She was leading Torell and the other Stone Peak wolf in a vigorous chase. We found a shortcut through the trees and caught up to her. She had left the two larger wolves far behind. The three of us ran together to the Tall Grass plains to find our pack.

I put every bit of energy I had into running. We were getting tired, and although they were slower than we were, the Stone Peaks had more endurance. I was glad we did not have much farther to run. I could smell that the pack was spread out along the edges of the woods. Just as we reached the edge of the plain, I almost tripped over Unnan. He was waiting for us. He opened his mouth to speak, but when he saw the Stone Peaks chasing us, he turned and ran. I was too tired to call out a warning to the pack. Even Marra was gasping for air, but she managed a breathless warning bark.

Minn and Yllin were the first to reach us, just as we emerged from the trees. They had been circling a few elkryn who had wandered over from the Great Plain. Perhaps Torell and the others did not bother to smell for the rest of the pack or perhaps they did not care, but they laughed when they saw the two slight youngwolves running toward them. Torell sneered as he and Pell bowled into Yllin and Minn. The youngwolves were outmatched and we leapt to help them. Two breaths later, Ruuqo, Rissa, Werrna, and Trevegg ran to us. Ceela and the fourth Stone Peak wolf reached the plain at the same moment. After a quick scuffle, both packs stood apart. The four Stone Peaks held their ground, but prepared to run, outmatched by six grown Swift River wolves.

Ázzuen, Marra, and I were covered with dirt, twigs, and leaves, and our fur was matted from our encounter with the Stone Peaks, but I had been too concerned about escaping to notice. Ruuqo looked at our disheveled appearance and pulled his lips back in a snarl. It seemed like the late afternoon light actually steamed off his fur. Rissa stood beside him, white fur raised along her back, growling furiously.

"What are you doing in Swift River territory, menacing Swift River pups?" she demanded.

"If you care so much about them, why leave them to run alone?" Ceela snarled.

Ruuqo and Rissa ignored her, awaiting Torell's answer. For a few more moments, the three stood staring at one another. Ceela, Pell, and the fourth Stone Peak stood behind Torell, tensed to fight. Finally, Torell allowed his fur to settle a little. The other three stood guard.

"We would not have hurt them," he said at last. "We have important matters to discuss with you. We were on our way here when we found them spying on us."

"He's lying," Ázzuen whispered, but too softly for anyone but me to hear. Marra looked over at me. I, too, was terrified of the Stone Peaks, but I had to speak up.

"He's lying," I said loudly, lowering my ears as every head swung to me. "They were planning to attack us. And they were in our territory. They want to get Tree Line and Wind Lake to join forces with them against us. We heard them say so."

I shifted uncomfortably as everyone stared at me.

"It's true," Ázzuen said stolidly, standing beside me. "We all heard them."

Marra grunted in agreement, and Ruuqo turned a cold gaze on Torell. I saw Pell trying to catch my eye.

"That's enough reason for us to kill you, Torell," Ruuqo said. "Why should I let you live to attack us when we sleep? We should slay you where you stand."

"You can try, runtwolf," the largest of the Stone Peaks grunted, his brown coat bristling. It occurred to me that he was rather stupid. Which was probably why a wolf of his size wasn't leading a pack.

"Shut up, Arrun," Torell said. "Your pups misunderstood what they heard, Ruuqo. It is not you we plan to kill." He paused. "It is the humans."

The pack fell so silent, I could hear the elkryn chewing on the plain twenty wolflengths away. It was as if Torell had said he was going to pull the wolfstar out of the sky and slay it like prey. I couldn't believe how stupid I'd been. Even after hearing what the Greatwolves and the spiritwolf had said at the Speaking, I had never dreamed wolves would really attack humans. It was like thinking prey would grow fangs and hunt.

Rissa was the first to find her voice. "Have you gone mad, Torell?" she asked very softly. "You know the penalty for killing humans. The Greatwolves will destroy your entire pack, and any wolf who bears your blood. They will wipe out your entire bloodline. Stone Peak will be no more."

"The Greatwolves have grown weak and soft willed," Torell said. "If they know what is really going on in the valley, they don't care. Do you know that the humans have declared war on all of wolfkind, Ruuqo?"

Ruuqo was silent, meeting Rissa's eyes.

"I thought not. You do not even know what is happening in your own lands. The humans on our side of the river kill every wolf they see. They kill every long-fang, every bear, every fox and dhole. Every creature that they think competes with them for the hunt. If we do not kill them, they will kill us."

"I had heard it," Werrna said, speaking for the first time. "But I did not believe it could be true. Are you sure your scouts are not exaggerating, Torell?" She seemed to respect the Stone Peak leaderwolf.

"It is true," he said, acknowledging her with a nod. "I've seen it myself. The humans hate us. All of them."

I saw Ázzuen trying to catch my eye. He wanted me to tell the pack about our humans, who certainly didn't want us dead. But I could not. It would be admitting breaking pack rules. My heart beat so fast I thought it would burst from my chest.

"The Tree Line and Wind Lake packs will join us," Torell said. "Vole Eater may not, but they are not strong enough to matter. You are, Ruuqo. We need you as our allies. You must join us."

"I cannot so lightly break the covenant," Ruuqo said. "You are insane to do so." He paced restlessly. "But if what you say is true, we must do something. I will consult with Tree Line and Wind Lake," he said. "And with my own wolves. And I will let you know what I decide."

"It is no longer your choice, Ruuqo," Ceela said. "All packs in the valley will agree once they know what is happening. You either join with us in this war or you are our enemy. There is nothing in between."

"You cannot make decisions for the whole valley, Ceela," Rissa said. "And you should not threaten us lightly. Torell is right—we make good allies. But you do not want Swift River as your enemy."

Ruuqo took a deep breath. "I will not break the covenant unless I know there is no other way," he said again. "Go from our lands in peace, Torell. But do not trouble my pack again."

Torell's tail still stood stiff and I could tell he was struggling to stifle a growl.

"You have a night to decide, Ruuqo." Torell's ravaged face was grim. "Tomorrow night is moon's wane—the night the humans of the two closest tribes gather together here on the Tall Grass plain. They will have a hunting ceremony where their young prove their worth by challenging elkryn. They will be preoccupied and therefore easy prey. That is when we attack. If you are not with us," he repeated, "we will consider you with them."

With that, Torell nodded to his packmates and the large wolves ran into the woods. Pell stayed back for a moment, trying to catch my attention. I kept my eyes lowered, refusing to meet his. Ázzuen rumbled a low growl. Pell gave a concerned growl-bark, and followed his packmates.

17

"I won't stand by and let any other creature kill wolves!" Werrna burst out as soon as the Stone Peaks were out of earshot. "Covenant or no."

"Quiet," Ruuqo ordered. Then he sighed. "I did not want to make a commitment in front of Torell," he said, "but, no, we can't let humans kill wolves, and I won't let the Stone Peaks do our fighting for us."

I yelped. I couldn't believe the pack would even consider fighting. Ruuqo wouldn't even steal food from the humans.

Trevegg stepped forward. "This fight is wrong," he said. "You know that, Ruuqo."

Ruuqo was not angry with him. "It's wrong," he agreed. "Every choice we have is wrong. But if it's the best of many wrong choices, we must take it. I won't wait for them to come to us."

"Torell likes to hear himself talk," Rissa snorted. "I won't run after him just because he wants us to. We will speak to the leaders of Tree Line and Wind Lake and hear what they know. Then we will decide."

"If there is another way, we'll take it," Ruuqo said. "But the covenant says nothing of sitting by and letting ourselves be slaughtered. I'm not convinced that the Greatwolves have our best interests at heart. I'm not even sure they're watching over us anymore, or that they really will kill us if we defend ourselves. If we must fight, we will fight."

Ruuqo looked to Trevegg and Rissa. "I must have the pack with me on this," he said.

Reluctantly, Trevegg and Rissa nodded their agreement.

"If there is another way, we must take it," Trevegg said. "If that is agreed, then I am with you."

"We will avoid fighting if we can," Rissa added. "But we will fight if we must."

"We can't!" I said before I could stop myself. "We can't fight them."

Every head turned, and as everyone stared at me I lost my words for a moment. I looked to Ázzuen for help. He pressed against me.

"And why can't we?" Ruuqo asked.

A sensible voice in my head told me to be quiet. To find a way to influence the pack without getting myself in trouble. But the humans' hunt ceremony was only a night away, and Torell was determined to fight. I had to stop it. TaLi's tribe would be under attack. She was small, and even though she was skilled with her sharpstick she was no match for a wolf. She would surely die. And my pack would die. The Greatwolves had said so.

"I overheard the Greatwolves," I said. "They meet far away in a stone circle. With humans. They do know what is going on, that wolves and humans might fight. And they will kill any pack that does."

"When did you hear this?" Rissa demanded.

"At the full moon."

"The night you were not here for the antelope hunt," Ruuqo said, his voice dangerously calm. "How did you come to overhear the Greatwolves? How is it that you were there to begin with?"

I paused, trying to think up a good lie. Ázzuen was better at clever stories than I was, and I looked to him. But before he could speak, Unnan stepped forward.

"Because she's been going to the humans," he said. "Since the horse frenzy when she killed Reel. She visits them all the time, and hunts and plays with a human girl. She takes Marra and Ázzuen with her."

Ruuqo's jaw dropped and his eyes narrowed. Rissa gave an anxious whine.

"Unnan, you'd best not be lying to me," Ruuqo warned.

"I'm not," Unnan said. "I've seen her go again and again. I didn't want to tell you because I didn't want Kaala to hurt me." He lowered his ears and tail to make himself look weak and helpless.

Stupid curl-tail, I thought.

"She did try to go to the humans when we first took the pups to watch them," Werrna said. "I would have told you then, but Rissa forbade us."

"You were disposed against the pup, Ruuqo," Rissa said, glaring at Werrna, "and I thought it best you did not know. But now," she turned to me, "you must tell us the truth, Kaala. Have you been to the humans?"

I thought fast. If I said yes, they could banish me. But if I said no, they would never believe me about the Greatwolves and what they had said. Torell would lead a fight against the humans and TaLi would die. And if Ruuqo joined in, my packmates would die, too. I looked at Ázzuen and Marra, at Trevegg and Yllin. I didn't want them to die. I didn't want TaLi or BreLan or his brother to be killed in the fighting. And the spirit-wolf had said we must not fight. I heard Ázzuen's soft whine beside me. He and Marra watched me closely. I had to speak up. Every eye was upon me, every nose attuned to the truth of my words. I was terrified. But the truth was the only thing that might stop them from fighting.

I took a deep breath.

"Yes," I admitted, swallowing hard. "I rescued a human child from drowning in the river and have been spending time with her." I said nothing of Ázzuen or Marra. "That's how I know many humans don't hate us, they care for us. We can hunt with them," I said, thinking that if I showed the humans to be useful, my pack would like them more. "They are not unlike wolf."

There was a long silence. When Ruuqo spoke, his anger was quiet and controlled.

"I have seen a human child in our territories," he said. "More and more often of late."

"Gathering plants," Rissa added softly, "and carrying small prey."

"And did you take your packmates with you?" Ruuqo demanded.

I said nothing. I would not bring Ázzuen and Marra into my trouble.

"We went, too," Ázzuen said. "We have hunted together. That is how we were able to get so many rabbits and badgers. We caught a deer," he said proudly, "and hid it on Wolf Killer Hill. That is how we overheard the Stone Peaks."

Marra winced as he spoke, shoving him with her hip. He looked at her, surprised.

"So not only do you break the rules of the valley but you lead others into defiance," Ruuqo said. He raised his muzzle. "I can smell the human-scent on you." He shook himself, hard. "I knew I should have killed you when you were a pup. I should not have let the Greatwolves stop me. It is as the legends say. You bear the blood of human-lovers and I allowed you to live. This fight, this trouble, is the consequence of that."

"We just hunted with them."

"You *just* hunted with them? You broke the law of the valley and disturbed the Balance of the creatures here. If you had not, then the humans would not have grown so bold and we would not be in this war."

I turned to Rissa for help.

"We just hunted," I said again. "And only with their young. They're not dangerous. We didn't mean any harm."

"I'm sorry, Kaala," Rissa said, shaking her head. "The rules of the valley are clear." She turned to Ruuqo. "Need we lose all three pups? The others were following her lead. She influenced them."

Ázzuen opened his mouth to protest. I glared at him.

"Perhaps," Ruuqo said. He turned slowly to me. In his eyes I saw not only anger, but something like triumph. "You are no longer pack," he said. "Your familiarity with humans has brought calamity upon us. Leave Wood's Edge and the valley, and do not return to our lands again. We may have to fight the humans now that you have brought them so close to us."

"I won't!" I said, surprising myself. "I won't let you fight them. I'll tell the Greatwolves you are killing humans and they'll stop you." I was amazed at my words.

Ruuqo snarled. He slammed into me, pressing me into the ground, only letting me up when I whimpered.

"*I* am leader of this pack. The Greatwolves do not know what is happening. Perhaps their time is done." Rissa and Trevegg looked a little anxious at Ruuqo's blasphemy. "If I learn that you have gone to them I will track down your human and kill her. I will find her as she sleeps and I will tear the life from her throat."

My body reacted before my brain could catch up to it, and I leapt at Ruuqo. I heard Marra's and Ázzuen's surprised yelps and Rissa's anxious growl. If I had been thinking straight, I never would have challenged Ruuqo. He was stronger, more experienced, and angry. But he was surprised, and my initial attack bowled him over on his back.

Growling, snarling, we rolled over and over each other on the ground. This was nothing like the fights I'd had with Unnan and Borlla. There was a viciousness, a desperation, to this fight I had not experienced before. And no one was going to intervene to help me. I had challenged the rightful leader of the pack. Now I had to fight him on my own. I was not yet full grown and fought desperately, biting and pawing at Ruuqo with my front and back feet, using every scrap of strength I had just to keep him from crushing me. I tried to tell my legs to move more quickly, my head to snap around. But every time I tried to bite, Ruuqo evaded me and knocked his head against mine. When I tried to pin him down, I found myself tossed on my back. My muscles wouldn't respond quickly enough to what my brain wanted me to do. I'd thought I had grown strong but my strength was nothing compared to Ruuqo's. Every time I wanted to give in, I thought of his threat to TaLi, and I kept fighting. But it was over quickly. Ruuqo was so much stronger than I, and

I tired while he was still strong and full of energy. His sharp teeth ripped at my shoulder and I yelped and scrambled away. He did not let me run, but tackled me again. He held me down and his jaws closed on my throat.

"I could kill you," he said softly, "and no one would fault me."

I trembled, trying to find my voice, but all I could do was lie there looking up at Ruuqo, remembering the last time his jaws had been poised to kill me.

"Leave," he said, stepping off me. "Do not return to Swift River territory, or you will be killed. You are no longer Swift River. You are no longer pack."

The full impact of what I had done hit me, and I began to shake harder. I lowered my ears and tail, bent my head, and crept back to Ruuqo. He growled and bared his teeth. Remembering his sharp bites, I backed away. I made myself even smaller, coming forward again. I was not that far from being a pup. Surely he would let me stay. Again he chased me off.

"You are no longer pack," he said again.

I turned to Rissa, but she turned her head away. I looked at Werrna, growling angrily, at Unnan, who smiled smugly. I looked over at Ázzuen and Marra, whining anxiously, and at Trevegg's sad, sad face. None of them would, or could, help me. Yllin looked as if she wanted to intervene, but Ruuqo glared at her, and she stepped back.

I stood there, head down, until Ruuqo chased me once again.

"Go!" he growled and ran me down the path. I did not dare return again. I fled into the woods.

18

I did not see Ázzuen and Marra try to follow me. They were stopped only when Werrna and Minn pinned them to the ground. I didn't hear Trevegg arguing with Ruuqo, or Yllin speaking softly to Rissa. My head felt like it was stuffed with dried leaves and dirt; my tongue was thick in my mouth, making it hard to breathe. The sound of a thousand flies filled my ears and I didn't feel the earth beneath my feet or the dense bushes pressing against my fur when I left the path. I knew I should be thinking of some way to help TaLi, some way to get her to safety. And Ázzuen and Marra, too, if Ruuqo chose to fight. But it was all I could do to keep moving. I was so exhausted from the fight that I only made it as far as the river before my legs gave out and I collapsed into the mud.

I don't know how long I stayed there, listening to the river, feeling the cool, damp air reach deep into my fur and onto my skin. I knew that if Ruuqo found me still in the territory he would probably kill me. But I didn't care. I think if no one had come along, I might never have gotten up, but

instead stayed until the Balance welcomed me into the softness of the earth.

Only when I heard the heavy step of the Greatwolves and smelled their earthy scent did I raise my head.

"Come on, then," Jandru said.

I still couldn't bring myself to rise. I lay in the mud blinking up at them.

"You give up easily." I had hoped for sympathy, but Frandra's voice was contemptuous. "One fight and you lie here like dead prey. I thought you had more backbone."

I had nothing to say, so I kept silent, resting my head on my paws.

"What did you expect, when you challenged your leaderwolf?" Jandru demanded, his tone no kinder than Frandra's. "What did you think would happen?"

"He threatened TaLi." My voice sounded as if it came from far away. "He said he would kill her. I had to do something."

"So you did something." Jandru stretched his great shoulders. "Accept the consequences. You're no longer Swift River pack. So what are you? Why did you fight to live when you were a pup? Why did you bother to run now, when Ruuqo would have killed you?"

"I don't know what I am if I am not Swift River," I said, getting angry. "How can I?"

Frandra snorted. "Well, the surest way not to find out is to sit around feeling sorry for yourself. Let me know when you're done with that."

Stung, I got up to face her. She and Jandru turned and walked swiftly into the woods. My feet seemed to move of their own accord, and I followed them.

"Where are we going?" I asked.

They gave no answer. Their legs were so much longer than mine that I had to run to keep up, and was too breathless to ask again. It had been a long, long night and my body was tired. My head wasn't working right. It was like my thoughts were moving through thick mud. Frandra and Jandru didn't seem to notice that I was struggling, but at last they slowed a bit, allowing me to walk rather than scramble after them, and then stopped next to an abandoned fox den by several large boulders. I realized we were not far from the circle of stones where they had met the humans for the Speaking.

"We'll rest here, until nightfall," Jandru said, his eyes sweeping over me as I shook with exhaustion.

"I have to get TaLi," I said weakly. "I have to go back." I was so tired it was all I could do to talk, but I felt like I was leaving part of myself behind.

"We have to get out of the valley," Jandru said. "As soon as possible."

That made sense. Ruuqo had said he would kill me. Questions and worry buzzed in my head. I wanted to go back for TaLi. I wanted to know where the Greatwolves were taking me. But I had run from the Stone Peaks, and fought with Ruuqo and been banished from my pack. Exhaustion and despair overcame my will, and I was asleep before I knew I was lying on the ground.

When I opened my eyes, Frandra and Jandru were watching me anxiously.

"Good," Frandra said shortly. "Get up and get moving. We're leaving."

"And be quiet," Jandru added. "There are other Greatwolves around and if they find us, we'll all be in danger."

I forced myself the rest of the way awake. It was already past dusk. I'd slept through the daylight hours without noticing the passage of time.

I stood. The muscles in my haunches and shoulders protested as I tried to stretch. Even the creases between the pads of my feet hurt. But my long sleep and the cool evening air had revived my good sense, and concern for my friends had burned away my confusion. I felt like myself again. It was as if the wolf I had been the day before was a slow, stunned shadow of myself. Something less than me. I was angry with myself that I had let the Greatwolves take me away. That I had let a whole day pass without returning for TaLi, or finding out if Ruuqo was going to fight. It frightened me that I could so easily lose myself. That I had almost betrayed everyone and everything I cared about just because I was scared and tired. I shook myself hard.

Frandra and Jandru had already begun walking. When they noticed I wasn't following, they stopped and looked back.

"Hurry up," Jandru ordered.

"I'm not coming," I said. "I'm going to get TaLi."

Both Greatwolves stared at me for a moment, as if they couldn't believe I would defy them.

"No," Frandra said, and began to walk again.

I stayed where I was. Jandru growled and walked back to me. He prodded me with his muzzle. I dug my paws into the earth. I knew they could drag me if they wanted to. Well, let them, I thought grimly, because it was the only way they were going to get me to budge. Then I realized that the Greatwolves had been very quiet, as if they were hiding. And Jandru had said they were worried about being overheard by other Greatwolves. I stood my ground.

"I won't leave without my human. Or Ázzuen and Marra."

If Ruuqo joined the fight, I thought, they would need to leave the valley, too.

Jandru whuffed in annoyance.

"There is no time to argue with you," he snapped. "It is too late for them. They are all already as good as dead."

I felt as if someone had sucked the air from my lungs.

"What do you mean?" I demanded, forgetting to be quiet. The Greatwolves snarled at me. I lowered my ears in apology, but continued to meet Jandru's gaze.

"What do you mean they're already as good as dead?"

"We don't have time to discuss it now!" Frandra snarled. "We must leave the valley at once. If we are discovered by the other Greatwolves, we will be able to do nothing to help you."

"But why?" I demanded.

Jandru growled impatiently and took another step toward me, his teeth bared in a terrifying snarl. I was certain he was going to take me in his teeth and drag me away. I stepped back.

"*Wolflet!!*"

We all jumped at the sound. Tlitoo flew from the direction of Fallen Tree, barely visible above the treetops, wings beating hard. He flew straight down from high above, so quickly I thought he would crash into the ground. He pulled up at the last moment, landing at my feet with a thump.

"You should not have run off, wolflet," he said, his chest heaving. "It was hard to find you."

"Where have you been?"

"Away," he panted, "finding answers."

I was so glad to see him I almost howled. I knew that he was not really protection against the Greatwolves, but I didn't care. He had come to find me. I was not alone. I turned back to Frandra and Jandru.

"Why are they as good as dead?"

It was Tlitoo who answered.

"All wolves and all humans in the valley are to be killed if there is a fight, any fight," he said. He turned a beady glare on the Greatwolves. "You have not told all," he accused, flaring his wings. I realized that he was agitated as well as tired from a fast flight. "You have not told the smallwolves or the human krianans all. You don't care about the wolves here. It doesn't matter to you if they die." He turned to me. "There are other places, wolf."

"What do you mean?" I said, confused. "Of course there are other places."

"Other places like this!" he croaked impatiently. "With other wolves and other Bigwolves besides the ones here. I have flown outside the Wide Valley and beyond the grasslands past that. The old human told me to. The Bigwolves don't care if you live or die, wolflet. You must listen. They have other wolves in other valleys," he said again.

This seemed to be an important point but I couldn't figure out what he meant. "They will kill your family and your humans as if they were no better than prey and replace you with others." He raised his wings daringly at the Greatwolves. "It is true. I saw it. And spoke to my raven brothers and sisters from far away who told me of it."

I was still trying to sort out what Tlitoo meant and was startled by Jandru's voice.

"It is true," he acknowledged, looking coolly at Tlitoo. "What has been done here is an experiment to see if the humans and wolves of this valley can live together. And it is not the only place we have tried this. It's more than either of you can understand. There's a great paradox, of wolves and of humans, and if you don't understand the paradox you cannot understand what we do."

"The paradox is that humans and wolves must be together but can't be together," I interrupted, annoyed by his arrogance. Why did he think I was too stupid to understand? "Humans need us with them to keep them close to nature so they don't destroy everything. But they fear us too much to keep us near and then we fight with them. That's the paradox. That's why you meet with the human krianans each full moon. So you can be close to some of them without causing a war. The human krianan told us. And I saw you." I said nothing about the spirit-wolf. I figured if the Greatwolves had secrets, then so could I.

Frandra's eyes narrowed. "You were wrong to watch the Speaking," she said to me. "There are very good reasons we keep the secrets of the legends." For a brief, terrified moment, I thought she might attack me. Then she sighed.

"You do not understand as much as you think you do. Nor does that old human. What the paradox means is this: If we are not with the humans, the Ancients will kill us. If we are with the humans and fight with them, the Ancients will kill us. The only way we've found to avoid both is the Speakings. We Greatwolves have been struggling with the Speakings, the humans, and the paradox for longer than your soft puppy brain can possibly imagine."

Tlitoo raised his wings at her.

"But now your Speakings no longer work," he quorked. "Now the Bigwolves are dying."

"We may be," Jandru snarled, "or we may not be. But we need to have wolves to take over for us if we are no longer here. That is why you must leave the valley, Kaala. We have believed since your birth that *you* are the one meant to carry on the bloodline. The Greatwolf council disagrees. If you'd been accepted into your pack, like we told you to be, they might have accepted you. Now they will not. They prefer another."

I remembered what the old woman had said the day I first met her. "You want me to meet with the humans, like you do," I said, my voice barely a whisper, "with TaLi as my krianan." I looked around, half expecting them to have the girl hidden away somewhere.

Frandra and Jandru exchanged uncomfortable glances. Tlitoo stalked up to them and gave a strange hiss I had never heard from any raven.

"No," Jandru said. "It's too late for that. The girl's blood is tainted by the violence of her tribe. We cannot rescue her. We are not even supposed to rescue you. The Greatwolf council has determined that the wolves and humans of the Wide Valley have failed. If any humans or wolves fight one another, as it is clear they will, all in the valley must die. The council will kill them all. Otherwise, the war will spread, and wolfkind will be no more. You are too close to the humans, Kaala, to be a watcher yourself, but your children's children may be the ones to take over for us if need be. You must come with us now, or die as soon as any wolf attacks a human."

"What about my pack?" I demanded. "What about TaLi and her tribe?"

"What of them?" Frandra answered carelessly. "The future of wolfkind is more important than any wolf, than any wolf pack or human tribe. We will start again elsewhere."

I was stunned at the Greatwolves' callousness.

"I told you so, wolflet," Tlitoo said.

"I won't," I said. "I won't go with you."

"Then we will drag you by your tail," Jandru snapped, losing patience. He started toward me. I backed up, knowing I couldn't outrun him, but ready to try. Tlitoo flared his wings, preparing to take flight or to fight. I wasn't sure which.

"It isn't fair!" I cried, not bothering to be quiet. "You lied to me. You lied to all of us. You told us we are to stay away from the humans without telling us why. And without telling us we are really meant to be with them." The Greatwolves were looking at me furiously. I didn't care. "The legends say nothing of the paradox and it's the most important thing of all. Now you're going to kill all the wolves and humans in the valley when all we've done is follow the legends! All because the legends lie!"

"She's right," said an ancient voice, a voice of dry sticks and blowing dirt.

Frandra and Jandru swung their heads around. Zorindru, the Greatwolf leader who had presided over the Speaking, sat beside a large boulder. I didn't know how long he'd been there. Beside him, her hand resting upon his back, stood TaLi's grandmother.

"Did you really think," the ancient wolf said to Frandra and Jandru, "that she would just go with you? And did you really think that I would not find out what you are doing?" He spoke softly, and the fur on his back rose only the slightest bit, but it was enough to make Frandra and Jandru lower their ears. They looked so much like scolded pups, I found myself tempted to laugh.

I wanted to run to greet the old woman, but was too in awe of the old Greatwolf to move. Tlitoo had no such hesitation. He flew to the old woman and landed on her shoulder and then hopped down to land atop the ancient Greatwolf's back. From there, he hissed once more, and glared at Jandru and Frandra.

"NiaLi and I have been speaking," Zorindru said, nodding

to the old woman. "I think perhaps it is time to tell the smallwolves of the valley—and the humans—some of why we do what we do." He opened his huge jaws in a smile, and shook Tlitoo from his fur. The raven alighted on a nearby rock, still staring beadily at Frandra and Jandru.

"They are the secrets of the Greatwolves!" Frandra protested.

"And it is time you shared them!" the old woman snapped, fearless before the giant wolves. I remembered then that she could understand our normal speech as well as Oldspeak. "You have kept secrets from us for too long," she said. "Zorindru has told me that you plan to kill us all, and I demand to know why."

"It is not something humans, or smallwolves, can understand," Frandra said contemptuously. "We have taken on the burden of the covenant because you are too weak to do so. We need tell you nothing."

"I disagree," Zorindru said mildly.

Frandra opened her mouth to protest. Zorindru silenced her with the barest beginnings of a snarl. "I still lead the Greatwolf council," he said, "and if Kaala is to leave the valley, she has the right to know the real reason why. I will not tell you everything, youngwolf—there are secrets the Greatwolves still must keep—but I will tell you what I can."

I lowered my ears and tail to the ancient Greatwolf. The old woman held out her hand to me, and I walked over to let her lean against me as she lowered herself onto a flat rock. I sat next to her on the cool dirt. Zorindru settled his old body onto the ground next to us and began to speak in his crackling twigs voice.

"Your legends speak the truth in some ways," he said, "but

not in others. It's true that Indru and his pack changed the humans. It is also true that the Ancients nearly ended wolf- and humankind and that, to save them, Indru made a promise. But he did not promise to shun the humans. He promised that he and his descendants would watch over them, and would do so for all time."

I watched him silently for a moment. I believed the ancientwolf. Something in his manner made me trust him, and it made sense to me that Indru would want to watch over the humans, that doing so is what wolves must do. And if it were true, then everything Frandra and Jandru had said was true, too. "But it didn't work?" I asked at last.

"It did not. Wolves and humans fought and the wolves forsook their promise." Pain filled the ancientwolf's eyes. He shook himself hard and continued. "When the wolves broke their word, the Ancients sent a winter three years long, to end the lives of wolves and humans. Then a youngwolf named Lydda brought humans and wolves together again, and the long winter ended."

I knew by then that Lydda, the youngwolf he spoke of, was the spiritwolf who came to me. "Our legends say that she caused the winter by going to the humans," I said to the old Greatwolf.

"She did not. She ended the long winter when she brought humans and wolves together again. It's what convinced the Ancients to give us one more chance—a last chance—to be with humans without causing a war."

"But there was a war," I said, remembering what the spiritwolf had told me.

"There would have been," the ancientwolf said, "if we had not stopped it. Wolves and humans began to fight, and that is when the Greatwolf council came to be. We knew that if we allowed the fight to continue, the Ancients would send back the long winter. That's when we realized that if we were to watch humans, we must do so from afar. So we created the Speakings, to fulfill Indru's promise without risking war."

"What happened to Lydda?" I asked, a sick feeling swimming in my stomach. I wondered if Zorindru would lie to me.

"We had to send her away," the ancientwolf said, confirming what the spiritwolf had told me. "If she had stayed, she would have caused more trouble. She had not the strength to do what had to be done."

Tlitoo quorked what I knew had to be an insult. Zorindru must have seen the shock and disapproval on my face, for he lowered his nose to mine.

"Lydda thought only of her human and what was best for him," he said. "This was a decision for wiser wolves. We had no choice but to send her away. It was best for all wolfkind."

"And now the Bigwolves die," Tlitoo insisted.

Zorindru dipped his head. "For generation upon generation," the ancientwolf said, "we have been trying to find the wolves to take our place, selecting who may have pups and who may not. We have done so in many places—valleys, islands, and mountaintops. And in these places we have failed and failed again. Here in the Wide Valley we have come closest to success. You were a surprise, Kaala. Ordinarily when a pup is born without our permission, it must be killed, as were your littermates. But when Frandra and Jandru told us of your birth and saw the mark of the crescent moon on your chest, some of us thought you might be the one to give birth to those wolves who would be watchers. That is why you may be spared, and why we wish to take you from the valley."

"You know who my father is." I knew it then, as certainly as I knew the moon would rise each night.

"I will not tell you that," Zorindru said, and there was no yielding in his voice. "I will tell you that we believe that, in you, we have found what we have sought since the time of Lydda. The Greatwolf council disagrees. They believe that since you like humans so much, your children will as well."

Tlitoo's voice, when he spoke, was softer than I'd ever heard it.

You still lie. There's more.
The Bigwolves yet have secrets.
What now is to come?

I thought Zorindru would be furious. Frandra and Jandru certainly were. But the look the ancientwolf turned on the raven was thoughtful, and full of pain.

"Secrets they will remain, raven. There's not a roost anywhere in the world you could fly to that would protect you if I told you of the council's secrets."

"Kaala," Frandra said, doing her best to sound conciliatory, "you must trust us when we tell you it is best for all if you leave the valley with us now. We saved your life when you were a smallpup. We have only your best interests at heart."

I didn't meet her eyes. Lydda had left the valley. Lydda had done what she was told. I looked far up into the face of the ancient Greatwolf.

"I won't go with you," I said quietly. "If you make me go, I'll stop eating and I'll die. Maybe," I said, hoping I sounded as if I knew what I was talking about, "I can stop the fight."

I thought I saw a smile in the Greatwolf's eyes. It was gone too quickly for me to be sure.

"Then I will speak to the council of this," he said, surprising me.

I blinked at him. Jandru gave a small grunt of surprise.

"You'll ask them to stop the fight?" I asked. "To help my pack?"

"That I cannot do," the Greatwolf said. "As soon as teeth meet flesh, there will be nothing I can do. But perhaps they will spare the Wide Valley wolves and humans if there is no fight."

"It will be too late, then!" Frandra protested. "She must come away now, or everything we've worked for will be for nothing!"

"She has a right to make her own choice," TaLi's grandmother said sharply. "You cannot take that away from her."

Frandra and Jandru both growled and advanced upon her. She looked at them unflinchingly.

"No," Zorindru said, "we cannot take that away." He glared at the other Greatwolves, who flattened their ears and backed away from the old woman.

Zorindru bent his head to look into my eyes.

"But listen, youngwolf," he said gently. "I can make no guarantees. I am the leader of the Greatwolves, yet I cannot make the council do everything I say. They still may kill the Wide Valley wolves, even if there is no fight. What I can do is to take you from this valley. I will take your friends—Ázzuen and Marra—too, so you will not be alone. And I will take you to your mother," he said, watching me carefully. "I can find out where she is, and I will take you to her."

I looked at him in amazement and my heart beat fast in my chest. My mother. Not a day in my life had passed when I had not wondered where she was, when I had not thought about finding her. I had promised her I would do so. If Zorindru could take me to her, I wouldn't have to worry about Ruuqo or the Stone Peaks. I wouldn't have to worry about gaining romma or stopping the fight. I would be with my mother, and maybe even my father, and would never have to worry about being alone again.

And my packmates would die, even if they didn't fight. And TaLi would die. And BreLan and MikLan.

"No," I said. "I won't let my pack or our humans be killed. I'll get Ruuqo to stop the fight."

"Very well," he said. "I will speak to the council now," he said, and began to walk stiffly in the direction of the stone circle. He stopped before Frandra and Jandru. "You will come with me," he ordered. They looked as if they wanted to argue, and Frandra muttered under her breath, but they lowered their ears and followed him, glaring back at me over their shoulders.

I watched them go. Before their tails had fully disappeared, Tlitoo gave a great shriek.

"What do you wait for, wolflet? You are too fat for me to carry you!"

I paused for a moment, wondering if I should leave the old woman alone in the woods.

"Go, youngster," she said. "I have been taking care of myself in these woods from long before your great-grandmother's great-grandmother was born. I will join you when I can."

I let her lean on me again to help her rise from the rock. Then I began the long run back to our territory.

I had run for only a few minutes when soft footsteps on dry leaves made me stop. Ázzuen and Marra stepped out into my path.

"You didn't think we'd let you go alone, did you?" Ázzuen said.

⊡

At first I tried to get them to leave, to escape the valley and wait for me and our humans. I told them of Lydda and of the Greatwolves' plans. They wouldn't go.

"It's our future, too," Marra insisted. "We have the right to stay and try to stop the fight."

"And we won't leave BreLan and MikLan to be killed," Ázzuen added.

"We've made up our minds," Marra said, "so don't waste time arguing."

I took a deep breath to try to reason with them. Then I realized that I didn't want to argue. I rested my head on Ázzuen's back, and then placed a paw on Marra's shoulder. The last of my doubt left my heart.

"This way," Ázzuen said.

19

The night was half over before we reached the Tall Grass plain and crouched on the tree-hidden slope where we had watched our pack fight the bear so many moons before. The grass that gave the field its name was beginning to dry out, but stood tall after autumn's plentiful rains. The thick trees of the woods hid us from what was going on below. To our left, down on the plain, was our pack. Ruuqo, always cautious, was waiting and observing. To our right and farther out on the plain, in a bare spot cleared of grass, human females and children—TaLi among them—chanted and struck sticks against hollow logs in a complicated, captivating rhythm. Directly in front of us, half-way across the plain, about twenty human males stood in two circles around a cluster of elkryn. Six young ones, including MikLan, made up the inner circle, which was a scant six wolf-lengths away from the elkryn. Grown men made up the outer circle. BreLan was with them, as was the son of TaLi's tribe leader, the one she was supposed to mate with.

"We're too late," Marra whispered.

Behind the humans, hiding in the grass, were the Stone Peak wolves and a pack that—from their strong smell of pine—had to be the Tree Lines. They were stalking the humans as if they were prey.

The humans didn't seem to know the wolves were there. It was a ceremony, just as Torell had said. Eight of the men held hollowed-out gourds in their hands. They shook them back and forth and something inside of them rattled loudly, adding to the rhythm of the sticks upon logs. The pounding and rattling seemed to mesmerize the elkryn, keeping them in one place. I found myself being caught up in the sound, too, and had to shake myself awake.

"It's their test of adulthood," Ázzuen said. "Trevegg told us before we left."

"You asked Trevegg?" I said, alarmed that they might have given themselves away. I sighed. It was too late to worry about such things. "What do the elkryn have to do with it?" I realized there were only female elkryn in the circle, and wondered where the males were.

"The young humans have to show they're strong," Ázzuen answered. "It's like our first hunt. The young ones have to kill an elkryn on their own to prove they are ready to be adults. None leave the plain until all have killed an elkryn. That is why Torell chose this ceremony. They will be intent on the prey."

"They're intent all right," Marra said. "How can they not see the Stone Peaks? Or our pack?"

I was wondering the same thing. The tall grass of the field provided plenty of hiding places, but if the humans were paying attention, they would have noticed the movement of the grass as the wolves began to spread out, forming a semicircle just behind them. But they didn't.

The rattling of the gourds and the pounding of logs grew louder and I found myself drawn in once again.

"It's the rhythm of the gourds and sticks, I think," I said, hoping we'd be able to get to Ruuqo so he could stop Torell. "It catches their attention as much as the elkryns'." I looked over to TaLi. "Why aren't the females hunting?"

"Trevegg says that the humans don't want their females to hunt anymore," Marra snorted. "I don't see why they would want to cut their hunting force in half, but he says it's so. He's coming over here." She raised her nose toward our pack. "I think he knew we were going to run away, but he didn't say anything."

I tore my attention from the circle of humans and elkryn. I could just make out Trevegg's shape in the grass as he moved cautiously toward us. There was no way to know if he had told Ruuqo and the others we were here. We would have to act quickly.

"The first thing we have to do," I said, "is to get our humans away. Then we can try to get Ruuqo to stop the Stone Peaks from attacking."

"I don't see how we can get BreLan and MikLan to safety." Marra's voice was strained. "They're too close to the Stone Peaks. You could get your girl and leave," she said, watching me from the corner of her eye. "She's nearest to us."

"No," I said. "We save them all."

We had a good view of most of the plain from where we were. But not good enough. I couldn't tell for certain how many wolves were stalking the human males. I needed a better vantage point.

"I'm going up to that rock," I said, indicating a boulder overlooking the plain from a higher part of the woods.

"Be careful," Ázzuen said. "The Stone Peaks will be able to see you if you don't stay hidden. And hurry up. I don't think we have much time."

"I'll be careful." I rolled my eyes. Ázzuen was such a worrier.

The rock wasn't far, but I had to scramble forward on my belly under low bushes to get to it. I planned to climb just to the top of it and stay as low as I could. I didn't think anyone on the plain would be watching that closely. The top of the rock was flat, and I would be able to see over it easily.

I was almost atop the rock when the sky above me darkened and something grabbed me hard by the scruff. I was yanked off my feet and off the rock, then dumped in a pile of bark and dirt. I was so surprised I didn't even yelp.

A large paw came down on my muzzle.

"Be quiet," Frandra hissed. "Stand up and come with me."

I stayed where I was. Frandra grabbed my scruff again and began to drag me through the dirt, leaves, and rocks. I scrabbled my legs, trying to get away, but I had fallen awkwardly on my side, and the Greatwolf was much too strong for me to be able to break free. She stopped a few wolflengths away where Jandru was waiting, and let me go. I coughed dirt and leaves from my throat and stood. I glared at them. I couldn't stop my ears and tail from lowering. That didn't mean I had to be polite.

"Idiot pup," Jandru whispered angrily. "You should have just come with us. You may have ruined everything. Now follow us. And don't make a sound."

"I told you I won't go with you," I whispered back, shaking out my neck. "Zorindru said he would try to talk to the other Greatwolves."

"He is doing so," Jandru snapped. "But he doesn't know

whether or not they will agree to spare the wolves of the valley even if you can stop the fight. And it doesn't matter! The fight is about to begin and you can't stop it."

"The Greatwolf council is here," Frandra growled. "Even those from outside the valley. There are half a hundred of them surrounding the plain, and the moment the fight begins they will end the lives of every wolf and human here. Then they will find every wolf and human in the valley. There is no more time to waste."

"They haven't fought yet," I said stubbornly. "You can't know they will."

"It's obvious they will!" Jandru said, not even bothering to whisper. "You will come with us on your own paws or we will drag you. I don't much care which."

I felt my eyes narrow and my lips draw back. My ears lifted, pulling the skin of my face tight, and the fur along my back stood up tall. I growled at the Greatwolves.

They looked startled. Then Jandru laughed at me. "I will make sure the path is clear," he said to Frandra. "You bring *her.* Whether or not she wants to come."

He turned his tail on us and walked quickly and quietly away. I glared at Frandra, and growled again.

"Just come," she said tiredly. "I'd just as soon not drag you."

Black wings and sharp talons crashed down upon her head. Tlitoo grabbed on to the tender skin between the Greatwolf's ears. Frandra grunted in pain and shook her head, hard. A streak of gray shot out from the bushes, and Ázzuen leapt toward Frandra's left side. I moved at the same instant and we somehow managed to knock the Greatwolf off balance. It wasn't that different from hunting large prey.

"I told you to be careful," Ázzuen gasped, grinning at me as he leapt to his feet. I didn't know whether to growl at him or thank him.

"Get going, wolves!" Tlitoo shouted. "I will occupy the Blunderwolf."

Just then we heard Marra call to us.

"Kaala!" Her voice was frantic. "The Stone Peaks are attacking!"

Ázzuen and I dove into the deepest part of the undergrowth so that it would be difficult for Frandra to follow us. I heard frustrated growls and triumphant shrieks from behind us. Breathing hard, we dove into a crouch next to Marra. Trevegg was just reaching the top of the hill.

"The Stone Peaks and Tree Lines are about to attack," Marra said quickly. "We have to get our humans away."

"No," Trevegg said, lying flat beside us, "you can't. It's too dangerous. You must stay away from the fight. Ruuqo has yet to make his decision," he added. "What you said moved him, Kaala, even if he wouldn't admit it when you challenged his authority. I spoke to him after you left. Rissa doesn't want a fight, and Ruuqo will not go against her unless it's necessary. I came to tell you that Swift River will not fight today. Ruuqo may even allow you to return to the pack."

"It doesn't matter," Ázzuen said.

"Why?" the oldwolf demanded.

"Tell him, wolflet," Tlitoo said, landing beside me. I couldn't help but notice the tufts of fur still caught in his beak and his feet.

"Tell me what?"

"It doesn't matter if Swift River fights," Tlitoo said before I could speak. "Any wolf fights, all wolves die. The humans, too," he said as an afterthought.

"Raven, you speak nonsense," the oldwolf said, shocked. "And we do not have time for it."

"It isn't nonsense," I said, before Tlitoo could take offense and make a scene. "It's true."

"Your brain is like frozen mud, dodderwolf," Tlitoo snapped, and flew off.

"What the bird says is true?" Trevegg said.

"Yes," I said. I told him of the Greatwolf council, of the decisions they had made. I explained that the Greatwolves of the valley and beyond were there, watching us. I could see them now, surrounding the plain, trying to blend in with the trees. They were watching and waiting, poised as if for a hunt. I spoke quickly, glancing at the plain below us, where Torell and his pack were moving slowly toward their prey. Trevegg listened, his face growing grimmer and grimmer as he, too, saw the Greatwolves surrounding the plain, ready to attack.

"All wolves and humans in the valley," he said, squinting to count the Greatwolves. "Even those who do not fight?"

I dipped my head.

Trevegg rumbled in concern. "I'll go tell Ruuqo. We'll find a way to stop Torell." Before I could answer, Trevegg began to move slowly down the hill, crouching to keep out of sight.

"What now?" Marra asked. "I'm getting MikLan, no matter what else happens. And we can't just walk out to get to them. There's not enough cover."

"I don't know," I said, watching Trevegg slink to Ruuqo.

The Stone Peaks were moving in carefully, not wanting to give up the advantage of surprise. I kept waiting for Frandra and

Jandru to sneak up behind me and grab me again. I knew we had only moments.

"Maybe your girl can talk to the other humans," Marra said. "Maybe you could try talking to her in Oldspeak and she could get BreLan and MikLan away."

I didn't think it would work. Even if the humans were warned, they would just turn and fight.

"I have brought her," Tlitoo said. I hadn't paid attention to where he went while we were talking to Trevegg. He had flown to the human females, and returned followed by a breathless and bewildered TaLi.

"Wolf!" she said, throwing herself on top of me. I whoofed out air as she all but crushed my ribs. "The raven wouldn't leave me alone until I came with him. I ran all the way up the hill."

TaLi's usually sleek hair was mussed as if it had been repeatedly yanked. I had a pretty good idea how Tlitoo had gotten her to come.

"Look, human," Tlitoo said, nodding toward the field. TaLi, who did not understand him, sat in the dirt beside me.

"What is happening, Silvermoon?"

Tlitoo gave an impatient squawk and pulled TaLi's hair, forcing her head around to the field.

"Stop that!" I growled. "Leave her alone!"

"I am not hurting her, wolf. Not much. And she must see. Maybe she can talk to her people."

TaLi gasped. She had seen the wolves stalking the humans. The moon was bright and she could easily spot the dark shapes of Torell's pack from our hill.

"I have to go warn HuLin!" she said.

"You can't," I said, trying to communicate in Oldspeak, hoping TaLi might understand it. "It's too dangerous."

"We need you to get BreLan and MikLan," Ázzuen added, not bothering with Oldspeak. It didn't matter: TaLi was getting to her feet.

"She can't go!" Marra said. "What if she alerts the humans and it makes the wolves attack? It was stupid to bring her," she accused, glaring at Tlitoo, forgetting that she had suggested the very same solution.

The Stone Peak and Tree Line packs had completely surrounded the humans. The wolves were moving in, stalking the humans as they would stalk prey. The elkryn noticed them even if the humans did not, and they were growing restless. Panic rose in me. We had only moments before the wolves attacked. I knocked TaLi over and sat on her to keep her from running to her tribemates.

"We have to go to Ruuqo," Ázzuen said. "We have to help Trevegg stop the fight."

"We have to get our humans," Marra barked sharply. "We have to run to them and separate them as we would prey and bring them from the fight. We can do it. When the wolves attack we will run for our humans. Your girl will wait for us, Kaala, and you can help us get BreLan and MikLan." The recklessness in her voice made me nervous.

"What if they won't come?" Ázzuen demanded. "And what if the elkryn stampede?" He shivered, no doubt remembering the horse frenzy that had almost claimed our lives. "Then we'd really be in trouble. We have to get the pack to help."

"I am going down to be closer to MikLan," Marra said. "And I will force him to leave the valley with me. You two can do what you want." I saw a frantic gleam in her eye.

"Wait," I said. Marra and Ázzuen looked at me. Ázzuen had given me an idea.

"I won't leave MikLan and BreLan," I said. "We have hunted with them and therefore they are pack. But I won't leave the Swift River wolves, either. They fed us and taught us to be wolf. It's not worth saving ourselves and our humans if we do so at the cost of our pack and of the human tribe." I took a deep breath.

"The elkryn are already half crazed," I said. "What if they did stampede? The wolves couldn't attack the humans. There would be no fight and the Greatwolves would have no reason to kill."

"You can't mess with an elkryn frenzy," Ázzuen said, awe creeping into his voice.

Marra brightened. "It would give us some time."

"Better decide now," Tlitoo added.

Sure enough, just then Torell gave his command to attack. TaLi pushed me hard, toppling me off her. She stood and began to run down the hill to warn her tribe.

I didn't wait any longer. I howled. Ázzuen and Marra joined me. Torell's head snapped up, and even from afar I could see the snarl on his face. The circle of humans startled and looked around. One of them shouted and pointed to the wolves. The ones in the outer circle turned, aiming their sharpsticks at the wolves nearest them. I hoped that would be warning enough, that the wolves would back off. They didn't. The humans' actions seemed to anger them and they moved to attack.

"Now!" I shouted. Ázzuen, Marra, and I raced down the hill to the elkryn.

"You know you're crazy, don't you," Ázzuen gasped.

I grinned at him. It felt good to be taking action, even if it was going to get us killed. The closer we got the larger the elkryn looked. I felt fear rising up in me and swallowed it. Even if I did want to turn back, it was too late. Marra, fleet and fearless, dashed into the center of the elkryn cluster. Ázzuen and I followed, running past a startled pair of Tree Line yearlings and under the legs of an old human male. We ran straight into the herd of elkryn.

The elkryn scattered. Humans scattered, too, and wolves. For a moment I froze in terror, remembering the horse frenzy, and Reel's death. I shook myself hard. Since that day, I had hunted with the humans and brought down a deer. I had chased elkryn with my pack. I could do this.

"It's working!" Marra cried out as she ran past me. I wondered if she had any fear at all. "This way!"

Marra and Ázzuen spotted an opening in the running elkryn and darted through it. I dodged a hoof and ran to join them. Our momentum carried us clear of the running elkryn. We stopped, panting, to look at what we had done. Elkryn ran everywhere, and wolves and humans were too busy dodging them to attack one another. I couldn't believe it had actually worked.

"We're going for BreLan and MikLan," Marra said. "If the Stone Peaks still fight, we will meet you at the Tree Crossing and leave the valley."

Marra didn't wait for my answer, but bounded off to where MikLan last had stood. Ázzuen followed. I could see TaLi stumbling down the hill where I'd left her and began to run to her, making sure to keep an eye on the elkryn. Something about the way they were acting made me nervous. They were being chased by snarling wolves and humans with sharpsticks. They should have run away by now. But they hadn't. They were still swarming.

Then I heard a crashing of underbrush from far across the plain. Something was emerging from the woods almost directly behind where the Swift River pack had waited. I raised my head, expecting to see the Greatwolves coming to attack. But it wasn't them.

It's not possible, I thought. *It can't be. Bull elkryn don't travel together. Elkryn don't hunt.*

But that's exactly what they were doing. Seven of them, led by Ranor and his brother Yonor, ran like hunters from the trees, their heads lowered, and fury in their eyes. I heard their bellows and saw the anger in the way they ran. They must have been hiding there, stalking, waiting for the chance to attack those who threatened their mates. I watched in horror, and looked back to the female elkryn, realizing that I had misjudged the effect of the stampede. I had thought it would be like the horse frenzy, over almost as soon as it had begun. But the elkryn were still running, and when they saw the bull elkryn charging toward them, they turned to fight.

"They aren't acting like the horses did!" I said. "Why are they doing that?"

"They are elkryn," Tlitoo said, hovering above me. "They never act like normal prey." He landed and cocked his head left and right. "Looks like they've learned to hunt."

I heard Rissa's frantic bark of warning. Trevegg was in danger of being run down by two of the bull elkryn. The Swift River wolves had scattered when the elkryn charged toward them. Ruuqo barked a furious command and he, Yllin, and Minn took off after Ranor and the four elkryn he led toward the stampede. Werrna and Rissa remained behind to wait for Trevegg, who was on his way back from speaking to us, and who was directly in the path of two other elkryn. They had swerved as if purposely trying to run him down.

At Rissa's warning, Trevegg began to run. Then he tripped

in the dirt and came up limping. The two elkryn were upon him.

Werrna leapt for one of them. It was a young elkryn, smaller than the rest, and when attacked by such a large wolf, he bolted. But the other elkryn was Yonor, and he wasn't going anywhere. He lowered his head and charged Trevegg. There was no way the oldwolf was going to get out of the way in time. I began to run.

Rissa snarled and leapt directly at Yonor. It was a dangerous thing to do, for a single wolf to leap at a bull elkryn's head, but it was her only chance to distract him from Trevegg. Yonor bellowed triumphantly as Rissa jumped, and turned his head sharply, catching her with his huge antlers and tossing her to the ground. Rissa yelped in pain.

I ran as fast as I could make my legs go. Somewhere behind me I heard Ruuqo's frantic howl-bark. I could see Werrna rushing back to us, and I knew that the rest of the pack would be right behind her. They would be too late. I was closest. Yonor looked at me as I ran toward him and snorted, as if I were insignificant and certainly no threat to him. I could swear I saw him smile as he reared up on his back legs to crush Rissa. Fear closed my throat as I thought about how easily he had thrown her to the ground. I ignored it, trying to remember how I had hunted with TaLi—the timing of the jump, the angle of attack. With an opponent as large as Yonor, I had to use guile and strategy, not just strength. I didn't think I could slow him down enough if I grabbed his flank. I swallowed hard. I had only one chance. I forced myself to take a breath, bunched the muscles in my haunches, and leapt, seizing Yonor's nose in my teeth. He began to buck and kick, trying to throw me. I hung on. He swung me back and forth as if I were no heavier than a leaf, and I felt as if my neck would snap in two and my legs would tear free from my body. Nothing had ever hurt that much.

"Silvermoon!" TaLi's scream carried across the plain. I had forgotten her in my fear for Trevegg and Rissa. Even with my head snapping back and forth I could hear her feet slapping against the ground. *She must be wearing her foot coverings,* I thought. I was glad she wanted to help me, but there was no way she could get there in time.

Out of the corner of my eye, I could see Werrna, who had been closest, leap for Yonor's flank. I could see fleet Yllin almost upon us with Ruuqo right behind her. My grip was slipping and I knew I couldn't hang on much longer. Black wings beat at Yonor's head. Tlitoo was trying to help, confusing Yonor but also making it harder for me to hang on.

Suddenly Yonor choked and stumbled. It was all my pack needed. Werrna, Ruuqo, and Yllin pulled him down. He would have fallen on top of me, but I managed to roll out of the way just as he hit the ground. The pack killed him quickly.

I crawled clear and saw TaLi panting, standing a good ten wolflengths away. Her sharpstick was buried in Yonor's neck. She must have thrown it, and thrown it hard. It hadn't killed the giant beast, but it had startled him enough to allow the pack to bring him down. She clutched a stick thrower tightly in her hand and she had a hunter's gleam in her eye.

Trevegg was on his feet, but Rissa did not rise. Ruuqo reached us and began to lick Rissa's fur. She raised her head to him. She was gasping, as if she could not get enough air, and blood welled from a cut made by Yonor's antlers. Hesitantly, TaLi walked forward and knelt beside Rissa. Ruuqo's hackles rose.

"I want to help her, wolf," TaLi said softly, her voice shaking a little. "If she can't get air, she'll die. That's the sound my cousin made when his ribs were hurt, and I helped him breathe before grandmother came and fixed his bones."

"Let her," Trevegg said.

Ruuqo hesitated. Rissa wheezed, struggling to breathe. Finally, Ruuqo dipped his head and stepped aside.

TaLi lifted one of her sacks from her back and another from around her neck. She took plants from each, and mixed them in one of her hands. She took her water sack from across her shoulder and mixed the herbs into a paste that she held out to Rissa.

"You must eat this," TaLi said. "It will help open the paths of your breathing."

"It's all right," I said to Rissa, nudging TaLi's hand toward her. "She is pack."

Gently, TaLi placed the substance in Rissa's mouth, shaking a little as she touched Rissa's sharp teeth. I pressed against her. Rissa licked TaLi's hand clean. After a few moments, her breathing eased and she stopped choking.

"Her ribs are either bruised or broken," TaLi said. "I can do more when I get back to our home, but she will need to be careful." The girl spoke with authority, her eyes on Rissa.

TaLi looked up and caught Ruuqo's eye. They stared at each other. I don't think TaLi realized the danger she was in. Ruuqo began to pull his lips back in a snarl, then dipped his head and went to help Rissa up.

"Tell her thank you," Ruuqo said.

"Why did you start the stampede, Kaala?" Rissa said, standing shakily. "I saw you run among the elkryn."

"I had to stop the fight," I said. Quickly I told them of the Greatwolves' decree. Anger clouded Ruuqo's eyes.

"So the Greatwolves have been lying to us? And they would kill us all?"

"We must stop Torell from fighting," Trevegg said, licking his hurt foot. "He will try again as soon as the elkryn are quiet." The oldwolf looked at me and managed a laugh. "You started the stampede on purpose? Not a solution I would have thought of, but it has gained us some time."

"But that is all," Rissa said weakly. "Torell will not give up his fight." She looked toward the center of the field and gasped. "Nor will Ranor."

I looked up. Though the bull elkryn had attacked together, they did not have the discipline of a wolf pack. Their drive to compete with one another seemed to be greater than their anger with the humans and wolves, and whatever plan they might have started with, they had forgotten it. They ran from one place to another, trying to reclaim their mates. Some even fought with one another. Others were already leaving the plain with their females. Wolves and humans checked on their pack members to see who had been hurt, and seemed to forget about fighting with one another. It looked as if we had succeeded in stopping the fight, at least temporarily.

But when I followed Rissa's gaze, I saw that I was wrong.

Ranor stood, staring at his fallen brother, staring especially at TaLi's sharpstick, protruding from Yonor's neck. His eyes moved from the sharpstick to TaLi, watching as the girl felt Rissa's ribs and placed more plants on her bleeding cut. The great beast lowered his huge antlers, and a deep, rumbling gurgle issued from his throat, as if he were challenging another male. He called out to the other bull elkryn.

Come to me! he ordered.

Only two of the other elkryn males looked up. One of them

was the one Werrna had chased before, and both were young, low-ranking elkryn.

The human child has slain my brother, Ranor called. *Even half grown they are murderers. We will kill the young before they grow strong enough to kill us.* He hissed through his teeth and ran toward a group of small humans. They had gotten separated from the others and were hiding in an especially tall patch of grass. The two young elkryn followed, shaking their heads back and forth and bellowing.

TaLi gasped as she saw where Ranor and the others were headed. She took a few steps, and then looked back down at Rissa, who was walking slowly and breathing hard.

"I can't leave her," she murmured.

I touched the back of her hand with my nose and began to run toward the small humans. Or tried to. My back and neck hurt so much I could only move at a half lope. The elkryn would get to the young humans long before I could. I looked around, trying to think of what to do. Then I saw Ázzuen and Marra standing with BreLan and MikLan. They were close enough to reach the young humans, but their backs were to the charging elkryn, their eyes on Torell and his pack, who were pacing back and forth and arguing.

"Help them!" I called. But my voice wasn't strong enough and my breath came short. I was more hurt from my battle with Yonor than I had realized. My pack didn't hear me over the brays of the elkryn and the calls of humans and wolves. I looked for Tlitoo to carry my message, but couldn't find him.

"Pups in trouble!" Werrna's booming voice startled me so much I stumbled. She began to run. Ázzuen's head snapped around and he saw where Ranor and the other elkryn were charging. He shoved his head into BreLan's hip and BreLan, too, saw the charging elkryn. He called something out, and several humans began to run from across the plain to protect their young. They wouldn't make it in time, either.

We can fight them, Ranor shouted. *It is time for us to stop being afraid of hunters, time to take back the plains*. The two other elkryn ran faster. I heard rapid pawsteps as Yllin caught up to me.

"Tell me what to do," she said. "Tell me how to hunt with the humans."

"Open yourselves to them," I panted. "Find one that you can communicate with and hunt with it as you would with a packmate. Don't think of them as Other."

Yllin dipped her head and ran on, her legs a blur of fur and dust.

Werrna, too, was overtaking me. "I will hunt elkryn as I always have," she snorted, "with teeth and wits. But I will not allow them to harm pups. Not even human pups."

She put forth a burst of speed and followed on Yllin's heels.

I couldn't run any farther. I hurt too much. I kept moving at a limping walk. I could only watch and hope.

Marra and Ázzuen sped to engage the young elkryn who were charging to Ranor's aid. MikLan and BreLan were close behind them. I was too tired to call out to them, to tell them what to do, but they didn't need my help. The four of them moved like a wolf pack that has been together for years, like water flowing over river rocks. Ázzuen and Marra ran at the flanks of the two elkryn, driving them toward BreLan and MikLan, who shouted and waved their sharpsticks. The elkryn snorted and huffed and twisted aside. When they turned to attack again, the wolves and humans again drove them away. The elkryn lost their nerve and took off across the plain, Ázzuen and Marra following to make sure they stayed away.

That left Ranor. The huge elkryn roared in fury and ran faster toward the human pups. When he was but a leap away from the small humans, Werrna and Yllin rammed into him. Werrna yowled in triumph. At the same time, a human male, a human who must have been able to run almost as fast as a wolf to get there as fast as he did, threw his sharpstick. It grazed off Ranor's flank. The double assault startled Ranor, and he staggered aside. Then he lowered his head and charged again.

Werrna and Yllin were face to face with the young human. Werrna stared at him for a moment, then shook herself and turned away. But Yllin jutted her head forward and opened her mouth to inhale the scent of the human. She licked his hand. It happened so fast I wondered if I'd imagined it. Then the two of them ran together toward Ranor.

I had almost reached them when Ranor changed course sharply, dodging Werrna and Yllin. He stood still for a moment, and then looked over his shoulder.

Come to me, he called again to the two young elkryn. *Are you cowards? You will never win mates if you run so easily. Return to fight and I will share my mates with you.* They snorted and ran back to him. The three of them began to advance slowly toward the human young. Yllin and her human stood alone in their path. Werrna sprinted to join them. A moment later, Ázzuen, Marra, BreLan, and MikLan stood at their side. Humans held up their sharpsticks and hefted large stones. Wolves bared their teeth and growled. Tlitoo and three other ravens hovered above them. The young elkryn broke and ran.

Ranor hesitated for a moment, and then saw the large group of humans sprinting across the plain to save their young. He shook his head hard. *I will not forget this,* he hissed through his teeth. *I will not forget what you wolves have done.*

He shook his head once more and followed the other elkryn off the plain.

20

The Swift River wolves did not wait for the running humans to reach them, since anxious humans can be unpredictable. Werrna and Yllin trotted away quickly. Ázzuen pressed against BreLan's hip and Marra gently touched MikLan's hand with her nose, and then the two of them darted after the grown wolves. For a moment I thought the humans might chase after them, even though the wolves had rescued their young, but they just watched warily as the wolves loped away.

The fight, however, wasn't over yet.

Ruuqo and Minn had caught up with me, and the others gathered around us. I looked over my shoulder to see Rissa walking slowly in our direction with TaLi, Trevegg, and Unnan. Yllin's eyes did not leave the human she had stood with. Werrna stretched nonchalantly and yawned, looking pleased with herself. I couldn't believe how calm she was.

"It's a pity we can't go after Ranor and teach him not to hunt Swift River wolves," she said, watching the elkryn's retreating form. Tlitoo was following the elkryn, swooping down

to pull at his tail. "But I think Torell has something to say to us."

It was quite an understatement. Torell and six Stone Peaks pelted toward us, fury rising off them. The Tree Lines followed more slowly. I kept a nervous eye out for the humans in case they decided such a large group of wolves was a threat and decided to attack.

Torell and Ceela reached us at the same time, the rest of their pack behind them. I felt strangely disappointed that Pell was not with them.

"This is not over," Torell snarled. "Your pups have ruined our hunt, but we will have another. And you will not stop us again, or I swear, Ruuqo, I will kill every wolf in your pack."

"It's over," Ruuqo said. "It should never have begun. You will leave this plain and cause no more disruption. Or you will have your fight with Swift River."

Torell looked startled. I don't think he expected Ruuqo to accept his challenge.

"You have caused one of my best hunters to be injured. I don't know if he will run again."

I looked behind him to see Pell lying on the ground. My heart stopped for a moment. He was awake, and his head was up, but he did not stand.

"Your pride and stupidity cost you your hunter," Ruuqo said. "And nearly cost me my mate. I will not allow you to put my pack at risk. Leave the plain while you can, Torell. I have no patience for you today."

A growl rose around me as every Swift River wolf reinforced Ruuqo's command.

"If you do not leave," Werrna said, "you will have your fight."

"And you will fight Tree Line, too."

Sonnen, the leaderwolf of Tree Line, stepped forward. "We should not have listened to you, Torell. You have drawn us into trouble and put the lives of my pack at risk. If you fight Swift River, you fight us. Perhaps the valley would be better without the Stone Peak pack."

Torell growled in frustration. Ceela took a stride forward. Werrna panted and stepped to meet her. We all followed her, pressing the Stone Peaks back. The Tree Line wolves closed in on them from behind. For a moment I thought Torell and Ceela were crazy enough to fight against impossible odds. But they must have retained some sense. The Stone Peak wolves broke free and ran. My distaste for them increased when I saw that they had left Pell behind. Sonnen dipped his head to Ruuqo and led his pack to make sure Torell did not return to the plain.

As soon as the Stone Peaks were gone, TaLi's grandmother, who had reached the Tall Grass plain at last, strode confidently over to Pell. She gestured to TaLi, who walked rapidly to join her. They bent down and began to work with their plants to help the injured wolf. I looked up to see Greatwolves, hiding all around the plain, rising from their hunting postures, and stepping back silently into the woods. I felt my chest loosen in relief. My neck and back were stiffening up so much I didn't think I could stand much longer. I groaned just a little.

Ruuqo very gently placed his head on my shoulder. He didn't thank me or tell me he had been wrong not to listen to me—he just let his head rest on my back for a moment. Embarrassed, I ducked my head before licking his muzzle in thanks, and then watched as he returned to Rissa's side. Then, trying to ignore the aches in every part of my body, I set off toward a spot where the forest met the plain.

There was one more thing I needed to do.

⌑

I had seen Zorindru watching us as we sent the Stone Peaks away. He emerged from the woods before I could reach him. Frandra and Jandru were with him. They met me on a flat patch of dirt just beyond the trees, and the three of them watched me silently, waiting for me to speak. I knew that in spite of everything—in spite of the fact that we had stopped the battle and chased the Stone Peaks away—the Greatwolves still might decide to kill us. Tlitoo landed in front of me, standing between me and the Greatwolves, and pressed his head for just a moment against my chest. I took a deep breath, feeling every rib groan in protest. I lowered my head respectfully.

"They didn't fight," I said to Zorindru.

"And so?" The ancient Greatwolf's tone was unreadable.

"They didn't fight," I said again. "You said if they fought, the Greatwolves would kill them. Kill all of us. But they didn't." I looked up to meet his eyes. "They didn't fight, so you shouldn't kill any of the wolves or humans."

"They didn't fight because you caused a stampede," Frandra snorted. "How do we know they won't fight again the first chance they get?"

Tlitoo snapped up a spider and threw it at the Greatwolf.

I looked over my shoulder at the humans and wolves spread out across the plain. The old krianan had left Pell's side to walk toward us. TaLi stayed, doing something complex to the injured wolf's leg. A small boy squatted next to her, helping. Sonnen watched TaLi respectfully, and a female Tree Line wolf licked the top of the boy's head, making him laugh. All around the plain, wolves checked their packmates for injuries while the humans gathered up and cared for their young and their old with as much love and concern as any wolf would have.

"You never gave us a chance," I said. "You said the Greatwolves sent Lydda away. She never had a chance to try to stop the war. So you don't know whether or not she would have been able to." I raised my chin and lifted my tail just a little. "You should at least give us a chance."

All three Greatwolves regarded me silently. The old woman reached us then, and placed her hand upon my back.

"Well, Zorindru?" she said.

"The decision is not mine alone, NiaLi," he said. "You know that. The council believes there will still be a fight—that it's only a matter of time. But they have agreed to give me a year." He sighed. "They think that you'll fail, Kaala, but they will let you try, for a year, to keep peace in the valley." He looked at me hard, and for such a long time that I began to squirm. "My offer still stands, youngwolf. I will take you to your mother. And your packmates and your three humans could come as well. I think it is very important that you live."

"They always fight, Kaala," Jandru said softly. "No matter what you do, when wolves get too close to humans, they fight. You must come away with us. Your children will be watchers, and can save wolfkind."

"No," the old woman said suddenly. "You're wrong."

"What did you say to us?" Frandra snarled.

"She said you are wrong," Tlitoo said helpfully, looking for something else to throw at her.

"Look around you," the old woman said. She gestured to the field behind us. "I think you were wrong to keep a distance from the humans, to watch us the way you watch a creature you wish to hunt. You cannot be guardians if you hide yourselves away." She bent down to speak to me. "Listen to me, Silvermoon," she said urgently. "I think you have always known something the krianan wolves have never understood. That in order for wolves to truly watch over humans, they must not watch from afar and meet with a few of us in Speakings once a moon. They must stay very close to us, as you have done with TaLi. The two packs must become one."

"Then there will be a war!" Frandra burst out. "The humans will again learn too much from wolves. They will get even better at killing. Better at controlling things! As they did in the times of Indru and of Lydda!"

"Then wolves will have to get better at being with humans," Zorindru said slowly, gazing thoughtfully at the old woman. "It is worth a try. But if you do this, Kaala—if you choose to remain so close to your humans—you must find a way to be with them forever. They will learn so much from you that if you leave them, they will destroy the very world. No matter what you—and those who choose to follow you—must sacrifice, you cannot give up once you have begun. And you must convince others to follow you. Your pack's fate will be forever tied to that of these humans."

I began to shake. How could they ask this of me? I was not even a full year old. How could I make a decision for so many wolves? How could I give up finding my mother, perhaps forever?

"Well, youngwolf," he said to me, "what will it be?"

I looked out across the plain. I saw TaLi tending Pell's wounds as BreLan and Ázzuen stood next to them. I saw MikLan crouching beside Marra, stroking her fur and checking her over and over again for any injuries. As I watched, Yllin walked boldly over to the young human who had helped her drive Ranor away, and shoved her head into his belly, almost knocking him over. Trevegg, much more tentatively, crept toward an ancient female human, who reached into a pouch at her waist to give him firemeat. Two small humans began to wrestle with a yearling wolf from Tree Line as Sonnen looked on, laughing. They looked like any pack, relaxing together after a hunt or a fight. And a pack stays together, even when things are hard.

TaLi stood and helped Pell to his feet, and then looked over to where we stood watching. The old woman placed her hand once again upon my back.

"I will stay," I said. "We will stay with the humans."

"Very well," Zorindru said. "We will give the wolves of the Wide Valley another chance."

I licked him in thanks and bowed to all of the Greatwolves, and then to the old woman. I shook myself once and set off across the plain, where the wolves and humans of my pack awaited me.

Epilogue

Lydda stood at the tree line that marked the boundary between the spirit world and the world of life. She watched the young, moon-marked wolf, barely half grown, walk to the humans and wolves who stood together. There was still so much work to do, Lydda thought. She darted a glance over her shoulder, back toward the spirit world. She had only a few moments before she was missed, and she would likely be in trouble. Still, she watched a little longer. And as the sun rose in the sky and the creatures of the Wide Valley came together again, she felt a weight lift from her heart. And slowly, just a little, her tail began to wag.

ACKNOWLEDGMENTS

There are three women without whom this book would never have been written. My writing buddies, sages, and guides through the mist, Pamela Berkman, Harriet Rohmer, and my mother and mentor, Jean Hearst, were writing with me long before the wolves strode through the door. They helped me find my way as a writer, and to keep on going through the challenges of writing a first novel. My father, Joe Hearst, told me when I was young that the most important thing to do in your life is to find work you love, and has set an example of doing just that as a physicist, photographer, and Renaissance man. My parents also offered unending support and set a lifelong example of living with integrity and courage.

My brother, Ed, and my sister, Marti, have been my heroes since we were all puppies, my challengers and guides in adulthood, and have assumed all along that I would write a successful book. My grandparents are not here to meet the wolves, but their love helped make me the kind of person who could write books.

I have no idea how I got so lucky as to find my superagent, Mollie Glick. Her enthusiasm for the wolves, her thoughtful guidance, and her exceptional savvy and smarts have been a gift and a joy. I struck gold a second time when the wolves found their way to the wonderful Kerri Kolen at Simon & Schuster, whose insightful comments and wise advice took the book to the next level. Thank you to Victoria Meyer, Rebecca Davis, and Leah Wasielewski, S&S's savvy publicity and marketing team; to Marcella Berger and S&S's remarkable foreign rights team; to Stephen Llano and to Tom Pitoniak, for the insightful copyediting; and to Jessica Regel at Jean Naggar Agency, my guide through the world of audio rights.

If you are very fortunate, you get to work with a group of people who change your life and make you realize that you are put on the Earth to work toward something. To my partners in crime and dear friends, Paul Foster, David Greco, Xenia Lisanevich, and Johanna Vondeling, much love, and to the dream team—Jennifer Bendery, Colleen Brondou, Allison Brunner, Paul Cohen, Jessica Egbert, Lynn Honrado, Ocean Howell, Erin Jow, Tamara Keller, Bruce Lundquist, Deb Nasitka, Jennifer Ng, Mariana Raykov, Karen Warner, Jennifer Whitney, Jesse Wiley, Akemi Yamaguchi, Mary Zook—thank you for sharing the amazing journey. To everyone at the magical world of Jossey-Bass, thank you for creating a place of dreams and possibility.

Thank you to Bonnie Akimoto, Allison Brunner, and Cheryl Greenway for the wonderful friendship and support. I am unendingly grateful to the good friends who encouraged me—and reminded me to leave my apartment from time to time: Bruce Bellingham, Diane Bodiford, Laura Coen, Emily Felt, Diana Gordon, Rick Gutierrez, Nina Kreiden, Lesley Iura, Jane Levikow, Katie Levine, Donna Ryan, Mehran Saky, Carl Shapiro, Liane

Shayer, Starla Sireno, Kathe Sweeney, Tigris, Erik Thrasher, Bernadette Walter, Jeff Wyneken. And a special thank-you and much love to Allison, Bonnie, Cheryl, Johanna, Pam, and my family, who were there to catch me when I fell.

Thank you to Master Norman Lin, who taught me confidence, courage, and perseverance in the face of frustration. And to my fellow students and friends at San Francisco Tae Kwon Do. I could not have made it through the challenge of writing a first novel without everything I learned from all of you in this special place.

Thank you to Susan Holt for wonderful conversations on wolves and coevolution, for driving me across France to see ancient cave art, and for the loan of the huskies. And many thanks to Joan Irwin, for rescuing me from the huskies.

I had the good fortune to have wonderful mentors early in my career and great advice as I made my way through writing and publishing my first book. Thank you to Alan Shrader, Carol Brown, Debra Hunter, Frances Hesselbein, Lynn Luckow, Murray Dropkin, Debbie Notkin, Sheryl Fullerton, and Heather Florence.

I had the privilege of working with the great thinkers and authors in the social and public sectors, and I am grateful for the opportunity to have been a part of their work. Every book I worked on with all of you was an example of what is best in the world.

I was constantly amazed and humbled by the generosity of experts in the wolf, dog, and evolutionary science fields who graciously shared their time and knowledge. Wolf experts Norm Bishop, Luigi Boitani, and Amy Kay Kerber were kind enough to read an early manuscript and offer advice. Raymond Coppinger, Temple Grandin, Paul Tacon, and Elizabeth Marshall Thomas counseled me on the evolution of wolves, dogs, and people. Rick McIntyre, Doug Smith, Bob Landis, and Jess Edberg had wonderful wolf tales and advice. Connie Millar offered invaluable advice and great conversation on paleoecology and climate science. I also read about a million books in the course of writing *Promise of the Wolves,* and all of them influenced my writing. Especially helpful were the work of Luigi Boitani, Stephen Budianksy, Raymond and Lorna Coppinger, Jared Diamond, Temple Grandin, Bernd Heinrich, Barry Lopez, David Mech, Michael Pollan, Doug Smith, and Elizabeth Marshall Thomas, and the research of Robert Wayne and D. K. Belyaev. Thank you to the International Wolf Center, Defenders of Wildlife, the Yellowstone Association, Wolf Haven, Wolf Park, and the Wild Canid Survival and Research Center for great information and research about wolves. Thank you to Jean Clottes and to the wonderful people at Les Combarelles, Font-de-Gaume, and the museum at Les Eyzies. Thanks to James Hopkin and Bernadette Walter for helping me map out the Wide Valley.

Thanks to Sam Blake and Danielle Johansen at Never Cry Wolf Rescue, to Dante, Comanche, Lady Cheyenne, and Motzy for agreeing to pose with me, and to Lori Cheung for the magical wolf photos. Thanks to Jerry Bauer for the delightful photo shoot and terrific photos.

I can never quite believe that you are actually allowed to go into a library and read whatever book you want. I'm particularly grateful for these wonderful resources.

Much of this book was written in cafés in San Francisco and Berkeley. Thanks to Michael and everyone at It's a Grind on Polk, Alix and Golanz at Royal Ground, Phillip and the gang at the Crepe House. And a huge thank-you to all café owners who let writers sit for hours and peck away at their laptops. And for all of you who are also café writers: order stuff, share your table, and tip well.

I workshopped the first chapters of this book at the Squaw Valley Community of Writers, and the experience of being surrounded by other writers was transformational. I am especially grateful to the good advice I received from Sands Hall, James Houston, and Janet Fitch. Thank you also to Donna Levin and my fellow students at CWP.

And last but most certainly not least, thank you to all of the more or less domesticated wolves who helped me with my research: Emmi, Jude, Nike, Talisman (aka demonchild) and Ice, Kuma, Xöchi, Scooby, Rufus, Senga and Tess, Flash, Fee and Mingus, Shakespeare, Noni, Ginger and Caramel (thanks for the bit about grabbing your human by the wrist), and special mention to kitties Dominic and Blossom, all of whom taught me exactly who has domesticated whom.

Any resemblance between wolves in the book and people I know is coincidental. Kind of.